FROM THE
HALLS OF CUBA...

Published by Mindstir Media, LLC
45 Lafayette Rd | Suite 181| North Hampton, NH 03862 | USA
1.800.767.0531 | www.mindstirmedia.com

Printed in the United States of America
ISBN-13: 978-0-9998275-8-1
Library of Congress Control Number: 2018937615

FROM THE
HALLS OF CUBA…

By C. E. Porch

MINDSTIR MEDIA

INTRODUCTION

FROM THE HALLS OF CUBA...

A Novel
By: C.E. Porch

At the end of the 19th Century the United States had emerged as a nation finally united and taking full advantage of the industrial revolution. Theodore Roosevelt was stepping onto the world stage with America becoming a world power. Cuba was a lynch pin, a stage where the show begins.

I have used historical events and characters, some I knew personally and others extrapolated from real events in order to put some things into context and give the reader a little insight to history in the background. A few events which I thought that I had created were later in my research proved to have actually occurred, much to my surprise and continuing mystery.

This is a story of the Scott family which rode that wave into the 20th Century with all its wars, prosperities and depressions as reflected in the mirror of Cuba...until Fidel.

Obvious characters, like Teddy Roosevelt, were only mentioned to give context to the invasion, his immediate election three months later as governor of New York, then President and later the Panama Canal. General "Fighting Joe" Wheeler, the Confederate hero and at that time Chairman of the US House of Representatives Ways and Means Committee, was indeed selected for political reasons in the Deep South, then proceeded to show the Yankees how to fight a war.

While I was at the University of Miami working on my Master's Degree, one of my favorite professors was Dr. Eduardo Leriverend.

He had been a professor in the Havana Law School and the young lawyer who drafted the amendment to the Cuban Constitution which eliminated the United States' right to intervene in Cuban affairs via the Platt Amendment. He was, also, a former Supreme Court Justice, *appointed by Fidel Castro*. Castro had been a student of Dr. Leriverend, who he described to me as "…absolutely brilliant…but crazy." When I asked him why he left such a sinecure as a Justice, who had been handpicked by Castro, his soft and simple reply still rings in my mind and absolutely summarizes this period of Cuban history, ***"When there was no more LAW, I left".*** This distinguished man had lived through and participated in the most important times and events in modern Cuban history, and he was always glad to share with his students. He will be missed by those of us who took the time to know him.

In the chapter on Indochina in WW II, I knew Frank Tan as a friend in the last years of his life, and his story is backed up by any book on Ho Chi Minh or OSS operations in Indochina in WW II., including a BBC documentary, *Uncle Ho and Uncle Sam*. Only my Cuban book characters are fictional. Some facts about China towards the end of the war were related to me by my late uncle, Captain Thomas Hollin Scott, Jr., US Army Air Corps, China-Burma, who flew the last allied plane out of Peking while Mao Tse-tung's forces were shelling the airfield. The story was that he carried Chiang Kai-shek's *furniture*, for which he received a very big starburst medal from Chiang. At least when I was a kid, it seemed huge in my hand. Later he flew some places for the CIA as a civilian that he couldn't tell me about. All I knew was that big, shiny, brand new convertible sure was pretty.

Fidel Castro and Che Guevara at this time in history need no further introduction. I have tried to give some background and feel for Cuba and its stratification at the time and still remain true to the events as a whole. The Cuba I remember as a young man was a magical place, which turned into an inhospitable situation to many in the wrenching destruction of a whole society. Needless to say, my "yankee" father's business was one of the first to go. Many of my experiences and my Cuban friends are incorporated in this part.

Things about early Miami were related to me by my grandfather, who moved to Miami with my great-grandfather in 1919. I have tried to incorporate some of that fascinating history into the book. Many people have remarked to me about how many Cubans there are in Miami. My answer is simple and factual, "There have *always* been many Cubans in Miami. From the beginning they were a part of its fascinating fabric. History tells us that the "discoverer" of *Florida* (the Land of Flowers) was Juan Ponce de Leon, who sailed here from *Havana, Cuba*." Enough said.

Several years ago I had the honor and pleasure of having a personal conversation with Vernon Walters, Lieutenant General, US Army, Retired, who knew my late father-in-law, Colonel John Finn while the Colonel was serving on General Eisenhower's staff in North Africa. General Walters had one of the most extraordinary careers in Army history, stretching from a young lieutenant negotiating with German commanders in North Africa in WW II, Deputy Director of Central Intelligence Agency, advising and translating for four presidents in four different languages, assisting Henry Kissinger in the secret negotiations to end the Viet Nam war, and culminating in an appointment as Ambassador to the United Nations. I told him that I wanted to write a historical novel in which the main character was a combination of Vernon Walters and Audie Murphy. His response was, "Wow, that one I have to read".

Unfortunately, he died before I could finish. However, I always had him in mind while I was writing, and I read his books. I added a few twists which probably would have made him sit back and say "What the...?!", but I hope he would have enjoyed it.

I hope you enjoy what is coming **FROM THE HALLS OF CUBA...**

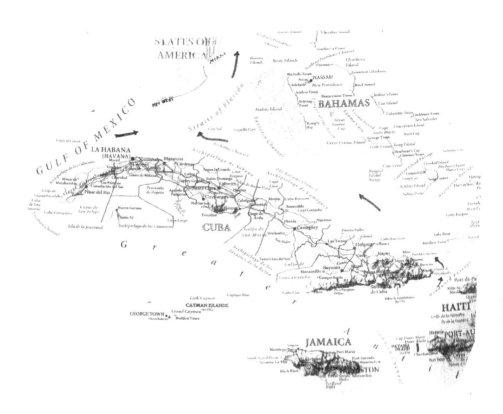

CHAPTER 1

CUBA 1897

The moon was waning, but still bright enough to work with necessary speed to unload cargo. Isolated clouds drifted by, creating swiftly moving shadows in the clear, shallow water. Small fish scattered as the line of men waded silently in the water to unload from the small boats supplies and arms that would sustain the revolution, and at last bring an end to the Spanish oppression of the Cuban people.

The small steamer of notorious "Dynamite Johnny" O'Brien had given the slip to revenue agents and Pinkerton men in Charleston. They had sailed to this small cove on the northeast coast of Cuba guided by a fifteen-year-old seaman from the Alabama farmlands, Thomas MacDougall Scott. Tom had been loaned to O'Brien by his uncle, Caleb Cameron MacDougall, because he knew this piece of Cuban coast well from hauling sugar cane and coconuts with his uncle. He also served as an interpreter, having picked up and studied enough Spanish to get his point across.

This wasn't the first time Caleb and Dynamite Johnny had collaborated in one way or another. There were just too many tempting dollars and pesos to be made by good sailormen to resist in these times of real or imagined independence throughout Latin America. This time, Caleb had too many legitimate business deals in Cuba to risk being recognized or one of his boats being seized. On the other hand, Johnny didn't care. Everybody knew what he was about. He looked at it as advertisement, but he needed some local knowledge he could trust. Thus, nephew Tom entered the picture, and the two old filibusters collaborated in gunrunning once again. Caleb knew Tom was smart, steady, and familiar with this section of coast, and it was about time for a little derring-do in his life. That is, if you don't count riding out a hurricane aboard a schooner in the Gulf of Mexico as enough excitement.

A section of reef jutted out from the shore forming the shape of a "J", with the long portion running for one half mile along the shore and abruptly ending in rocks. If you knew the shape of the land and trees, you could slip into the anchorage at night with ease. If not, you had a real problem, particularly if there was a strong northeast wind.

This night, General Maximo Gomez, the Supreme Commander of the revolutionary army, had personally come to see to the unloading of arms and fieldpieces, including several Hotchkiss guns, a 42mm wheeled, light mountain gun developed by the French Hotchkiss company. These heavier weapons were desperately needed.

With Tom interpreting, Gomez turned to O'Brien. "*Bien,* Johnny, I see you have once again slipped your authorities and the Spanish. We thank you. I am sure you are very well paid for these risks."

"Well enough, General. We'll keep coming as long as it takes." *And as long as you pay,* O'Brien thought to himself.

Turning to Tom, the general noticed for the first time how young his interpreter was. "*Oye, muchacho, cuantos años tiene?*" (How old are you?)

"*Diecisiete,*" (17) Tom lied. O'Brien explained that Tom was also their guide into the anchorage.

Gomez smiled, "I have many young boys fighting with me. Someday they will be free men and remember this beach and what you have done. I hope you will come back when the Spanish are gone. How do you know this beach so well?"

"My uncle, Caleb MacDougall, trades in Cuba and along this coast and sent me to guide Captain O'Brien."

"*Coño,* I know this man. You tell him hello, and I look forward to much trade when we run the Spanish *bastardos* out of Cuba."

A commotion suddenly erupted along the beach. A lookout was yelling from the top of a coconut palm. "*Un barco viene! Los españoles!*" He had sighted a patrol boat coming around a point of land approximately one half mile away. Its bow wave and wake clearly stirring up and exciting small organisms, which in turn created streams of bioluminescence in the water like thousands of tiny lanterns. They hadn't yet spotted the landing party in the shadows and reflections of the trees, but as their angle changed the steamer would stand out in the moonlight.

The sea was calm and the tide was high enough for the reef to be invisible at night. O'Brien hoped that the crew of the patrol boat was not completely familiar with this reef and in their excitement might actually run up on the reef.

"Get us out of here, Tom! Cut the anchor line! Leave the small boats! Throw everything else in the water! They can pick it up later. That boat is not going to come ashore looking for anything but us." Tom waited for the seamen to clamber aboard and leave their boats to whoever found them. He swung the bow to run for the opening in the reef. As soon as the propeller engaged, they threw up their own illuminating wake. A bright flash from the Spanish bow gun eliminated any hope that they wouldn't be seen.

The shot fell well short in the reef, giving Tom a brief thought that there would be some dead fish from that explosion, like when they had thrown dynamite to catch fish for a party. The next shot pushed that idea out of his head in a hurry as it screamed overhead into the palm trees, sending the shouting revolutionaries scattering out of the line of fire. He wished they still had that Hotchkiss gun on-board. At least they could shoot back, if anyone just knew how to operate the thing. Rifles and shotguns weren't going to help. Another shot threw up water close enough to feel spray.

"Tom, reverse course." Johnny shouted above the noise. Seeing Tom's confusion he shouted, "Damn it! Do it now!"

Tom was sufficiently unnerved to even argue that they were headed back into a dead-end of the little harbor. *Maybe*, he thought, *he's going to run aground, and we'll all run into the jungle to escape.*

"Dynamite Johnny" O'Brien had been in too many of these little chases to be giving up his boat that easy. He had run guns to every revolution in the Caribbean and eluded his own government and theirs. They were now steaming back parallel to the shore in the opposite direction and toward the patrol boat, making it appear that they were racing for a cut through the reef where there was none. The Spaniards took the bait. Tom slowed the boat to allow them to reach the imaginary point first. If only they didn't get a lucky shot.

One minute more, Tom could hear the bottom getting shallower as the propeller noise bounced off the bottom in an increasingly higher pitch.

"Now, go back!" Johnny again shouted. Tom spun the wheel 180 degrees for the second time.

This is going to work, he thought, as his mind raced along with the boat. He could almost feel the excitement aboard the patrol boat as they believed they had the steamer hemmed in. A loud, crunching, splintering of wood and screeching of the Spaniard's propeller as it came out of the water proved their miscalculation.

Tom hoped they couldn't still shoot. They had to be plenty mad. But a glance back showed the boat at an angle with the bow down and the stern out of the water some two hundred yards back. Scattered rifle fire could be heard as the rebels peppered the patrol boat.

Tom glanced at the captain who calmly looked back out to sea, puffing on his ever present Cuban cigar and thinking, *Just another day in the gunrunning business. Yessiree, filibustering is real satisfying to the soul and the pocketbook.* "Head'er for Key West, Tom."

"Aye, aye, sir." Tom turned his thoughts to the tricky entrance into Key West at night through sandbars and coral reefs. Tom had learned from Commodore Ralph Middleton Munroe in Coconut Grove that the tried and true directions, *Key West light under the North Star,* worked every time.

Tom came from a long line of Scottish farmers who left their bones and names on mountains, creeks, roads and towns, from the Carolinas all across the south after they settled in America before the Revolution. They had moved west as the Cherokees and Creeks were forced out. They had fought the British with Francis Marion, the Creeks with Andrew Jackson and the Yankees with Nathan Bedford Forrest and "Fighting Joe" Wheeler. Some of their names were still carried in the Cherokee nation, a reminder of their search for freedom in America and a shortage of white women in the 1700s.

Tom had already been to sea for two years on several of his uncle's freighters and had a high school diploma. He had started on a seventy foot schooner, carrying freight along the coast of the Gulf of Mexico from Mobile to Tampa, Key West, down to Havana, over to Vera Cruz, Mexico, up to Galveston and back to Mobile. His uncle Caleb had said learning the sea aboard a sailing vessel was the only way he would truly understand. After a year aboard, the confusing mass of lines, knots and sails had now become second nature to him, as well as winds and tides and storms and calms. On the clear nights at sea, the names and shapes of stars and constellations had become a never ending source for his imagination, blending magical sources of mythology and ancient civilizations with his coveted books on navigation, Columbus, Magellan, Cook, and all the great sea explorers.

His second year at sea had been aboard one of the steam powered freighters personally captained by his uncle, sailing to Cuba, Haiti and Jamaica, then farther down the Caribbean. There he spent more time in the wheelhouse being tutored in navigation, ship handling and the business end of freighting.

Tom officially had a high school diploma, even though he had dropped out at age thirteen, because he figured there was nothing else to learn in that one room schoolhouse. His ability to read and absorb advanced algebra had so astounded his teacher that she had promised to help him learn higher mathematics, guide him through the classics and give him a diploma, if he would stay for one more year and help her teach the other children.

He had convinced his uncle, Angus MacDougall, to hire him in the local general store, where he was taught how to keep the books and fill orders. So, in the mornings he walked five miles from the family farm to school to help the teacher and after school, he learned whatever else she could teach him. Then he would continue his walk into town to work at the store into the night. Occasionally, he rode one of the family mules if it wasn't needed for work that day. Later his uncle fixed a storage room with a bed so he didn't have to make the trek every day. He was officially off the farm. His brothers and sisters inherited his chores.

In addition to the books available in the store, Tom was allowed to read the letters sent from Uncle Caleb. Nothing could fire a boy's imagination more than real tales of life at sea, foreign ports, and the characters aboard ship. His prized possession was a frayed, old copy of the *American Practical Navigator* by Nathaniel Bowditch, the legendary 18th century New England merchant, lawyer, and sea captain. Here, he thought, was the perfect practical use of his math ability and so he pushed his teacher to help with the complicated math of celestial navigation.

Near the end of Tom's agreed year, Captain Caleb Cameron MacDougall, himself, had arrived on one his very infrequent visits to the farm he had abandoned for the sea so long ago. He had come to see his aging father one last time. As was his custom, he brought gifts for all from his travels. For Tom, he brought one very used and slightly battered, but functional, sextant, the perfect gift. Celestial navigation was about to become real for Tom.

He only knew of Tom from letters forwarded to him, but was curious to meet this young phenomenon with MacDougall blood. His first impression was amazement at Tom's height. MacDougalls and Scotts seldom reached the height of 5'9".Yet here was a lad already almost 6'. His next surprise was the depth of knowledge in navigation, winds, currents, and geography he had already grasped just from reading books. Long into the night the sea tales spun until no one was left to listen but Tom.

The next morning Angus was not in the least surprised to hear Tom asking permission to leave the store and go to sea. Angus knew his brother Caleb and the magic of the sea that he could cast about him. Tom's parents had long ago given him permission to seek his own way, secure in the knowledge that he was smart enough to handle life even then.

With the admonition that, "Books won't make you a sailor, lad, only the feel of a deck beneath you. I'll be back in Mobile in two months. If you want to go to sea, come to the docks and ask for

Captain Caleb." He returned to the sea, leaving his birthplace for the last time.

Two months gave Tom time to fulfill his promise to his teacher and receive a diploma. He caught a ride on a freight train hauling produce to Mobile, and the rest of his life began at age fourteen.

CHAPTER 2

A MESSAGE TO GARCIA

WASHINGTON, D. C.
April 8, 1898

With the sinking of the battleship *USS Maine* in Havana's harbor on February 15, 1898, relations with Spain continued to become strained. March 17, 1898 Senator Proctor of Vermont gave a damning report to Congress of his findings on the situation in Cuba. A failed secret attempt had been made to purchase Cuba in 1896. Now President McKinley had lost hope of any agreement with Spain as to Cuba, and he desperately needed information on the military status of the rebels.

Colonel Arthur Wagner, head of the Bureau of Military Intelligence, was called to the President's office. On entering the office of the President, he faced a worried President who immediately asked, "Where can I find a man who will carry a message to Garcia? We need information on Spanish troop strength and the rebels."

Wagner's prompt reply, "There is a young officer here in Washington; a lieutenant named Rowan, who will carry it."

The President's immediate response was, "Send him!"

Andrew Summers Rowan, West Point Class of 1881, was on a train for New York at 12:01 a.m. that night and on a boat to Jamaica by noon, April 9. He had established a competence in Latin American intelligence and even written a book on Cuba in 1896. Colonel Wagner had explained that his verbal instructions would be all Rowan would have, no written documents other than to the British in Jamaica, identifying him. He was reminded by the colonel about Nathan Hale of the Continental Army and Lieutenant Richey in the war with Mexico. They both carried written dispatches and were put to death when caught.

HAVANA, CUBA   April 9, 1898

Captain Caleb MacDougall received a hand delivered message at 0700 hours from the American Consul in Havana, Fitzhugh Lee, requesting his immediate presence. Caleb had been coming to Havana over thirty-five years on his freight ships. He had known all the Consuls since the end of the Civil War. He looked up at the American Consulate and was unimpressed. He had personally known this Consul since he was assigned there in 1896. Consul Lee was a part of the famous military Lee family of Virginia from the Revolutionary War to the Civil War, and had written a biography of his uncle Robert E. Lee. He had graduated from West Point in 1856 and was a Confederate Army major general by 1863, the Governor of Virginia by 1885, and now the Consul General in Havana. Caleb was shown into Lee's office.

"Mornin', General. I got a strange summons this mornin'. Am I in some kind of trouble?"

"Not at all, not at all, Caleb. Close the door and take a seat." Lee sat down and studied the top of his desk for a moment. "Caleb, as you know, we are close to war here, and we need some information."

MacDougall's eyes narrowed. "As usual, Fitz, you know I will do whatever I can."

Lee hesitated again for a second. "Caleb, I need you to get a US Army officer into the interior to take a message to the rebel general, Calixto García, from President McKinley, then get him out again with his information. He will be in Kingston, Jamaica by the 23rd. This came straight from Washington early this morning, and I suggested you."

MacDougall stared out of the window at the harbor for a long minute. "Fitz, I can get him in there and out, but my best man to do that is my nephew, Tom Scott. He speaks Spanish and knows that part of the island and the people from our tradin' there. However, he joined the damn Navy after the *Maine* blew up, just to get in on the action. Not much I could say, considering my time at age fifteen as a seaman with my uncles, running the Yankee blockade."

Lee gave a nostalgic laugh. "Those were the days, Caleb."

Caleb continued, "Now he's over in Key West on some shore duty in the Signals Section. Damn waste of a good seaman, if you ask me. If you can get him sent down here, we can get your man in and out."

Lee smiled, "I think I know the man who can do that. I'll send a cable now. Tom should be here by morning." He turned and scowled out at the harbor and the wreck of the *Maine* for a minute. "I told them not to send that damn battleship down here. However, as usual, this Yankee government appreciates your assistance." The two old Confederates laughed, and Caleb left to plan for Tom's arrival.

HAVANA   April 10, 0900 hours

US Navy Seaman Thomas Scott entered his uncle's house in Havana near the harbor. "What's happening, Uncle Caleb? I got orders last night to get on a freighter to Havana and to report to you. Here I am."

"Welcome back, Tom. By order of the President you are about to see action quicker than the rest of the Navy. Don't look so surprised. We've been doin' this for a while. This time it's just *official*." Then Caleb explained the problem. "Day after tomorrow I'm sending you on a freighter down to Santiago de Cuba. Officially, you will be a working crewman in the wheelhouse working on charts. Once you get there you will contact the men on *this* list. Two days later the same boat will carry cargo to Kingston where you will meet *this other list* of men, then wait for this Lieutenant Rowan to arrive and hustle him about eighty miles down the coast to catch a sailboat. It will be about one hundred miles back to Cuba. In Santiago someone will tell you where to find General García before you get to Jamaica. Then you'll know where to come ashore in Cuba. All the charts you will need will be on my freighter. The captain knows to give you whatever you need. You have met most of these men before on our trips. You're goin' to have a week or so to figure it out before Rowan arrives in Kingston on the *Adirondack* out of New York somewhere around April 23. Now, go get some sleep, *Seaman Scott.*"

Two days later, as the sun arose over the old stone fort at the entrance to Havana Bay, they slipped into the clear blue waters of the Straits of Florida and headed southeast along the coast of Cuba. The half-submerged remains of the *USS Maine* were still visible astern. The American flag fluttered at half-mast from the one mast remaining above water. It was over five hundred miles to the eastern tip of Cuba and the Windward Passage between Cuba and Haiti, then another one hundred miles back west to Santiago de Cuba. It would be a little more than a two day trip.

At midnight on the third morning, the freighter steamed into the beautiful harbor of Santiago de Cuba. Tom disembarked and headed directly to the waterfront *Palacio de Oro* restaurant, which also housed a well-known, but higher class, bawdy house in the rear of the restaurant. There was nothing suspicious about a sea-man right off the boat going into a brothel. However, this Madame was a *long-time friend* of Capt. Caleb MacDougall. Tom gave her the customary gifts from Caleb and was led into the back rooms beyond the bordello. There he found most of the men on Caleb's *list*. The gist of the conversation was that Gen. Garcia was near the town of Bayamo preparing to lay siege. Next was a conversation as to where to land in the shortest time to reach him, and the pro-posed place and day of landing back on Cuba. All this arranged, Tom decided to avail himself of the pleasures he knew existed in the other rooms.

Morning mist hung over the harbor and obscured the large stone fort guarding Santiago de Cuba when Caleb's steamer weaved its way down the channel to the open Caribbean Sea then straight to Jamaica. As they entered the open sea, the mist blew away and the magnificent Sierra Maestra Mountains seemed to rise with the sun. *El Turquino,* "The Tutor," at almost 8,000 feet, glistened in the distance with the morning dew evaporating like stars with the rising sun. Tom waved to the mountain, "Señor, wish us luck!"

Course was set for the eastern tip of Jamaica one hundred miles south. The water was green then rapidly turned dark blue as the bottom fell away to 2000 fathoms in the Cayman Trench.

As faint light came with the next morning, rain squalls obscured any sight of land. Only a glow through the clouds indicated the sun was rising. The wind picked up. The rain squalls blew to the west, and an emerald mountainside glistened with rain-washed trees glowing in a rising sun with the smell of fresh rain. Jamaica!

Kingston's waterfront was a mass of color and noise as merchant ships loaded and unloaded their cargo; sugar and coffee to England and America, manufactured goods coming in. The ever-present British warship was anchored in the harbor with its flag proudly fluttering from the mast and decorative signal flags waving on lines strung fore and aft from the tops of the masts. It sat like a mother hen protecting this most prosperous of colonies.

Tom was first off the boat and cleared customs quickly with his documents, then headed off to find the individuals on his *list*. He had one week to arrange the clandestine trip back to Cuba with a very important passenger. It was a busy week, meeting Cuban exiles and sympathetic Jamaicans, arranging transportation, food and a boat.

The *Adirondack* arrived in Kingston April 23, 1898 while Spain was communicating its intention of noncompliance with America's request. Now it was only a matter of hours before war was actually declared. It wasn't hard for Tom to pick out an Army officer, even in civilian clothing, as he departed in the crowd of passengers.

"Lt. Rowan, I'm Tom Scott, U.S. Navy. Please come this way. I'll get you cleared quickly." Special arrangements had already been made and the proper people paid. Rowan was hustled into a carriage, through the back streets of Kingston and down the coast as fast as the horses could pull. Several stops were made for food and changes of carriages during the night.

"Sir, don't try to talk to the drivers. They have been warned not to speak. They were only told to hurry." Tom continually peered out for any signs of danger. America was now probably at war with Spain, and they were violating Britain's neutrality.

Nine hours later they halted in a cane field and walked a mile to a small bay. Enough food and Jamaican rum had been provided along the way to keep them going. Another of the men on the *list* appeared, a Cuban exile named Sabio, who had a small fishing sailboat in the bay. Sabio moved silently and quickly to get them aboard. They rowed out of the bay to catch the wind and sailed toward Cuba with a fresh breeze from the ever-present Trade Winds out of the east, but one hundred miles is a long way in a small sailboat. Only brief alarms occurred during the day when Spanish patrol boats appeared on the horizon. The next day *Pico Turquino* appeared to arise out of the endless sea. By night they were lifted over the surrounding reef by a following wave and into a small hidden cove.

As if by magic small lights signaled them to come ashore, and the long trek through jungle and mountain ridges began. The *list* was working…so far. Occasionally, the jingle of horses' harnesses and the clatter of Spanish short sabers would alert them to hide until a patrol passed by. It was customary for rebels to roast sweet potatoes and leave some in the ashes for the next group who came by. Tom thought of the stories of his ancestors doing the same thing when they rode with Francis Marion in the American Revolution.

At the end of the third day's march a small group of ragged men appeared, claiming they had deserted from the Spanish army because of harsh treatment by their officers. Tom and Rowan had a quiet talk in the shadows, while Sabio quizzed the men.

Tom turned to Rowan. "Lieutenant, this doesn't smell right. You best stay out of sight, and I'll have a talk with Sabio. There's bound to be some Spanish spies in that bunch. The Spaniards would really like to know that an American officer was traveling to see General García."

That night Rowan slept in his hammock, and, unable to sleep, Tom watched from nearby. At midnight a sentry shouted and a shot was fired. Simultaneously, a shadow moved toward Rowan's hammock. Tom could see the dark form had a knife. Rowan, awakened by the shot, rolled out of his hammock just as Tom swung his machete down through the man's shoulder and into his lung.

Before the man died he confessed, with some added persuasion from Sabio, that the two of them planned to report Rowan to the Spanish or kill him if they could not escape. The other was killed by the sentry. This was becoming more than a hike through jungle and mountain ridges, which was to continue another four days. Now that war was officially declared, they were spies subject to immediate execution. The Spanish had increased patrols and covered all the shore and inlets.

The final day they descended the slopes looking down on Bayamo. Evidence of Spanish General Valeriano Weyler y Nicolau's theory of warfare was everywhere in the burned out haciendas and miles of once productive fields laid to waste as far as the eye could see. More than 500,000 inhabitants all over Cuba were herded into *reconcentrados* (concentration camps) where almost 300,000 died of starvation and disease. Tom had seen - and smelled - some these camps while he and Caleb were still trying to trade in the interior. Weyler had been nicknamed "the butcher." His theory was to deny the support of the population for the rebels. Ironically, his model was Civil War General William T. Sherman's march through Georgia. Rowan's group now walked through weeds higher than a man in what was once a rich agricultural landscape. Rowan exclaimed, "My God, it's a tropical garden gone to weeds."

They came out onto the Royal Road and followed it, which passed from *Manzanillo* on the coast to *Bayamo* in the interior, and paused at a river guarded by rebels. Burned Spanish blockhouses, which had guarded both sides of the river, were now just reminders of the rebel advance. They were escorted after a slight delay to a delighted General Calixto Garcia. Apparently, the translation of Rowan's credentials had been as a "confidence man" rather than properly as "a man of confidence," a significant difference. Tom stayed in the background. This was not his part, and Sabio was sent back to the coast for more assignments.

General Garcia considered the situation and the urgency. His response was to send three important officers to Washington with Rowan rather than rely on Rowan's memory to grasp all the important details of the return message. Additionally, he requested they leave the same day. *Ouch, no rest for the wicked,* thought Tom.

Tom had a planned route and people from his *list* waiting for his arrival, but the rebel officers said they knew the territory, and they would lead the way. Nothing he could say or do. He was just a low ranking sailor, but he knew he had his own instructions to see it through. Their route took them north of Tom's planned route and away from his contacts. The result was the officers were only able to secure a small sailboat, with 104 square feet of gunny sacks sewn together for a sail, and the area was patrolled by Spanish boats. Several members of their party were forced to return because of its size. Tom was left as the primary seaman, and he thought again about being in this situation before with "Dynamite Johnny" O'Brien. But then they had a steam propelled boat, not a tiny boat with inadequate sails to get them 150 miles north to Nassau, Bahamas.

In spite of some rough weather requiring constant bailing of water from the small boat, they were able to sail and ride the current in the eastern part of the Gulf Stream coming out of the Windward Passage to the bottom of Andros Island in the Bahamas. There they caught a ride on a sponge boat to Nassau, then a schooner headed for Key West. They sailed back down the inside of Andros Island on the abyssal *Tongue of the Ocean* to avoid the north flowing current of the Gulf Stream, and then across to Key West.

On May 12, 1898 US Navy Seaman Thomas MacDougall Scott was back where he started, on Navy shore duty in Key West. Rowan and the Cubans sailed to Tampa and took a train to Washington to deliver their message *from* García and add a new expression in military annals. However, as promised by Consul Lee, Tom received an assignment to a brand-new US Navy cruiser passing through Key West on its way to Tampa, Florida, to escort troop ships for the invasion of Cuba.

CHAPTER 3

Off To War

Cuba, June 1898

US Navy Seaman Thomas MacDougall Scott sat as far forward on the bow as he could climb, watching and listening to the deep blue water of the Straits of Florida part beneath the massive steel hull of the cruiser. He sensed it, not really seeing or hearing. A school of Atlantic porpoises rode the bow wave, darting in and out and over and under like pictures in a book he had seen on native Hawaiian surfers. He loved the sea and all the sights, sounds and smells of it. They blended into one sensation. Up here he could only feel a slight vibration of the mighty engines driving the steel mountain through the water, rather than the constant throb be-low decks in his sleeping area. This was the most peaceful part of the ship. He could sit undisturbed and think and dream between watches. It was a long way from Goodwater, a small farming town in east central Alabama.

Tom had enlisted in the Navy just before he was sixteen with the help of his uncle, who had lied about his age. He had already been to sea for two years on several of his uncle's freighters and had a high school diploma. He had started on a seventy-foot schooner, carrying freight along the coast of the Gulf of Mexico from Mobile to Tampa, Key West, down to Havana, over to Vera Cruz, Mexico, up to Galveston and back to Mobile. His uncle Caleb had said learning the sea aboard a sailing vessel was the only way he would truly understand. After a year aboard, the confusing mass of lines, knots and sails had now become second nature to him, as well as winds and tides and storms and calms. On the clear nights at sea, the names and shapes of stars and constellations had become a never-ending source for his imagination, blending magical sources of mythology and ancient civilizations with his coveted books on navigation, Columbus, Magellan, Cook, and all the great sea explorers.

His second year at sea had been aboard one of the steam powered freighters personally captained by his uncle sailing to Cuba, Haiti and Jamaica, then farther down the Caribbean. There he spent more time in the wheelhouse being tutored in navigation, ship handling and the business end of freighting. Consequently, by the time he got the itch to join the rush to war with Spain, he had more sea knowledge than any recent graduate of the United States Naval Academy. That, coupled with the fact that he was close to genius in mathematics and was already six feet tall, made the recruiters more than willing to accept his uncle's word and sign him up.

Uncle Caleb had spent his life at sea all over the world and escaped what he deemed as pure, endless drudgery on the farm. His life was the sea. He had no wife or children (at least not that he knew of) and looked upon Tom as his heir and successor. Obviously, he was not pleased by Tom's request to join the Navy, which he considered an unprofitable and unduly regimented use of a sailor's life. But he remembered his own excitement sailing with his uncles while running Yankee blockades, and tales of sea battles during the Civil War, or War Between the States as it was referred to in the Deep South. Considering a few of his adventures over the years, there was no way Uncle Caleb could deny it, provided Tom promised to return after his tour.

Now they were in the Straits of Florida on course to join the ships already blockading the Spanish squadron in Santiago and to land the invasion troops. The officers and crew were in a high state of excitement for what they believed would be a glorious engagement with the Spaniards, and the end of escorting slow troop ships. This would be their Trafalgar.

It was rumored that the newest battleship in the Navy, the *Oregon*, had left San Francisco to sail around the tip of South America to join the fight. The officers didn't think there would be much left for her to do by the time she arrived.

Tom's ship and several other smaller warships were escorting forty-eight troopships carrying sixteen thousand men, horses, wagons, supplies, weapons, and ammunition in three columns, including Teddy Roosevelt's Rough Riders, aboard the *Yucatan,* all loaded in Tampa for the land engagement. The ships made way at a disgusting six knots, forcing the sleek warships to slow to less than half speed and bob along in the swells. He could imagine what it must be like for soldiers in cramped troop ships in the southern heat. Unbearable and seasick were words that came to mind.

The fact that the Assistant Secretary of the Navy, Theodore Roosevelt, had resigned to become a Lieutenant Colonel in an Army unit had caused some amazement and questions about his sanity among the ship's crew. The Spanish expected an attack on or near Havana. It seemed natural, since that is where the somewhat disputed and alleged cowardly sinking of the *Maine* took place, but they were staying clear of the Cuban coast in order to slip around the north coast and join in the invasion on the other end of the island near Santiago. The main elements of the Spanish ships under Admiral Cervera were blockaded in the harbor by the Navy's Flying Squadron under Admiral Sampson. The Spanish were hopelessly overmatched by the modern American fleet, but the anticipation of battle was still glorious. At least, that is what the newspaper barrage of William Randolph Hearst had been trumpeting.

Tom's sea experience and knowledge had been brought to the attention of the executive officer by the chief boatswain's mate, and Tom had been made one of the quartermasters, or helmsmen, steering the big ship. His other duties were maintaining charts and records for the ship's log and more importantly, taking celestial observations, plotting courses, and assisting the navigator. Nothing could have pleased him more. In the wheelhouse he could listen to all the orders, as well as the conversation between the officers. Taking their lead from the executive officer, he was treated well by the officers. Lieutenant Commander L. M. Crosby, the XO, was a Mississippi shrimp boat captain's son with lineage back to the infant Navy of the American Revolution, who went on to graduate from Georgia Tech. The officers readily gave Tom advice about Navy life and descriptions of different ships and what the enemy ships would be like. All except one young lieutenant, who seemed to resent the attention given to this young farm boy with an atrocious, southern, country accent. No obvious knowledge of navigation, experience or seamanship could change his mind.

William Barnes Spalding, Lieutenant Junior Grade, USNR was a Yale graduate and son of an old New England banking family, dating back before 1700 and proud of it. He was bright and looked forward to a bright future, as soon as this war was over, in a new stock and bond venture started by the family in New York; Spalding, Whitman & Sterling. He would have added a little more glory to the family name. Or at least he could brag that he had done his share.

Upon hearing of Tom's sea experiences in Cuba, Lt. Cmdr. Crosby suggested the Captain invite the Chief Boatswain's Mate, accompanied by Tom, to the ward room or officers' mess to talk about Cuba, its coast and people. The confidential part of Tom's file regarding Lt. Rowan was kept quiet by the captain and the executive officer. Officially, the protocol was the Chief of the Ship to be the guest to talk about his prior experience in Cuban ports, and Tom was just his attendant. This satisfied everyone, even though they knew it was Tom's knowledge in which they were interested, and the Chief didn't care since he was the one who brought Tom to their attention in the first place.

The captain, the executive officer and most of the officers were present, with the exception of Lieutenant Junior Grade Spalding, whose name somehow turned up on the duty roster for Officer of the Deck on that watch. After formalities of salutes and reporting to the captain upon entering the ward room, Tom was brought forward from behind the chief and introduced. Fascinated by his firsthand accounts of actual dealings in Cuba, only places they had seen on charts or an occasional visit to a port, the officers' questions were lively. What was the attitude of the people? What kind of fortifications existed? What kinds of warships had he seen, and their conditions?

Tom's explanation that he had been a 2nd mate aboard a 170 foot freighter drew unconcealed doubt among the younger officers. This was quickly muffled when the XO and chief vouched for it. The XO explained that he too had been elevated to an important position aboard his father's shrimp boat, that of chief bilge-cleaner. He went on to explain that there could be nothing more important on a shrimper, in case they had never thought what the smell could be like without the *Chief Bilge Cleaner*. The room filled with laughter at the thought of the XO in the bilge, cleaning up rotten shrimp.

Tom quoted an entry he had memorized from the log of the *Santa Maria* written by Christopher Columbus upon first sighting Cuba: *"Everything is green as April in Andalusia. The singing of birds is such that it seems as if one would never desire to depart. There are flocks of parrots that obscure the sun. There are trees of a thousand species, each having its own fruit, and all of marvelous flavor."* These too had been Tom's first impressions. He fielded questions the best he could in that his experiences were as a merchantman. The types, shapes and depths of harbors, types of cargo hauled out and in, what the big merchants and landowners thought, he related as best he understood from listening at his uncle's side. What he picked up from the common seamen and small farmers were subjects he personally knew. Stories of gunrunning 'Dynamite Johnny' and contacts with the revolutionaries he carefully kept in the third person.

He discovered that the officers, particularly the young ones, in general, were ignorant of the real causes of the revolt against the Spanish and though this was not the first revolt, it had been going on for three years. After hundreds of years, the wealth and power was still enjoyed only by a few. The increased population of poor native-born Spanish, and former slaves were more and more unrepresented in a government controlled by the central government in Spain. The recent *reconcentrados* program of General Valeriano Weyler y Nicolau was his answer to the revolt. Entire populations of towns and villages were removed in areas where rebels were active and placed in secured compounds, and the land scorched. This was supposed to deprive the rebels of supplies and a friendly population from which to recruit. The Spanish ambassador to the

United States had justified it to the Secretary of State in a poor analogy to Sherman's march through Georgia in the Civil War. The result was thousands of men, women and children dying of hunger and disease in wretched and inhumane conditions. Tom had seen some of this misery for himself on trips inland to pick up cargo. This brought a somber note to the meeting.

Attention was turned to whether he had seen the *Maine* in Havana harbor, and what did he think. This brought a perceptible increase in attention from the senior officers. Everyone had read the official version, but no one had seen the wreck. Knowledge of coal burning ships and their hazards was well known by sailors. Each had his own private suspicions.

Tom was careful to explain that his knowledge of naval architecture and naval mines was far too little to give any opinion as to the twisted parts of the battleship he could see sticking out of the water, even at low tide.

Every officer knew of the interview given to the *Washington Evening Star* by Lieutenant Philip Alger, a mathematics professor at the Naval Academy. Alger was also the Navy's leading ordnance expert. He had stated that he knew of no submerged mine that could have caused the explosion, and he felt it was not necessary to look beyond the common hazard of coal bunker fires.

Tom knew the feeling among the young officers was that they desperately wanted it to be an act of war, not an accident. So, he said, from his limited experience at sea he did understand the dangers of spontaneous combustion from unstable coal and other fire hazards aboard a steamer. But now, based on his knowledge of Navy procedures, he doubted the crew could have been at fault. This caused a murmur of approval around the room. He noticed that the captain maintained a level, expressionless gaze, commanding him to continue with whatever he could add to this naval conundrum. From what he heard on the waterfront, one of the Navy divers had stepped into a large hole near the wreck, which could have been made by an underwater mine explosion, but other long-time locals who knew the harbor swore that there were no mines out there. On the other hand, one Cuban had noted that he had never seen the harbor master moor a warship in that exact location before. The explosion had appeared to be mid-ship. The forward part of the ship was completely destroyed, the forward superstructure was turned upside down by the blast, and steel frames were bent inward. Eyewitnesses had said that there were two explosions, the first a sharp, gun-like report and a second more massive, prolonged explosion. The first explosion appeared to lift the forward part of the ship. The keel had been strangely bent upward in the shape of an inverted 'V' fifty-nine feet back from the bow.

One local had described how he and other seamen from ships in the harbor rushed to the site, picking up living, dead and dying sailors from the water as ammunition exploded from the ship, sending bullets flying in every direction and cannon shells flying into the night sky like fireworks. He had told how Spanish warship sailors and officers took their lifeboats closer into the maelstrom, risking their own lives to save American sailors. Nods of admiration went around the room. More confirmation of The Code of the Sea, they were thinking. Two hundred sixty-eight men had died, and flags had been lowered to half-mast on the Spanish Governor General's palace, on ships in the harbor, and in the city.

In any event, the official Board of Inquiry had determined that the explosion was caused by a mine, not spontaneous combustion, but declined to blame the Spanish government itself. This left an opening for simple demands of reparations for negligence in not preventing unknown radicals from planting mines. But events overtook President McKinley's attempts to reach a peaceful settlement. The drums of war were beating louder, Americans wanted to flex their muscles. The age of isolation was about to end and a new world power was about to enter the stage. Hearst's papers increased the beat. Sentiment in congress turned with a speech by Senator Redfield Proctor of Vermont after his visit to Cuba. He was formerly an advocate for peace, but now he argued against the Spanish for their inhuman treatment of the Cubans and he reminded his colleagues that it wasn't just about the *Maine*. It was about freedom of people. Additionally, the Germans had been making moves indicating they were about to become a presence in the Caribbean. The Monroe Doctrine of America for the Americans was being challenged.

When asked if he knew Santiago de Cuba, Tom described the pretty city with its streets lined with blooming hibiscus and bougainvillea, coconut trees and stone walls winding their way down to the waterfront, the smell of night blooming jasmine, the picturesque deep water harbor and the looming stone fortress guarding the city and harbor. He might have added all the cute girls smiling from the doorways and pretending to be shy, but he kept that to himself. Yes, he knew Santiago de Cuba, from the sailors' haunts to the grand houses of the merchants and port officials. Uncle Caleb made sure he knew them all, with emphasis on the business side.

Tom had made quite an impression since he came aboard. His natural seamanship and curiosity about all shipboard things found him all over the ship. He had learned semaphore flags and code signals in Key West. Now he learned range finding from the gunners mate, which he found was another interesting use of his mathematics ability. The great triple expansion steam engines were a never-ending source of fascination with the instruction of the engineering officer. He made mental notes on how he could improve Uncle Caleb's little fleet when he got out. The Chief Boatswain's Mate remarked that, "one more cruise and he would probably be running the whole damned ship." He became such a remarkable and likeable character among the crew that no resentment existed when he was promoted to petty officer 3rd Class far ahead of the normal time. His part in *the message to García* was only known by the captain and executive Officer. There was some talk of recommending him for an appointment to the United States Naval Academy at Annapolis when this tour was over. There was considerable grumbling from a certain officer at this suggestion.

Now on the eastern end of the island, they had been "steaming close to the Cuban coast with its high barren-looking mountains rising abruptly from the shore," as Teddy Roosevelt was later to describe it. Six days after departure they rounded the eastern end of Cuba passing through the Windward Passage between Punta Negra, Cuba and Cap a Foux, Haiti. It was night and the Southern

Cross appeared low above the horizon, causing excited cries from young officers from northern latitudes to see both the Big Dipper and the Southern Cross in the same sky.

They passed Guantanamo Bay where 650 men of the 1ˢᵗ Marine Division had gone ashore six days before to eliminate any Spanish resistance guarding this natural harbor, and to establish a coaling station in the first land engagement of the war. In 1741 the British had landed a force of five thousand men in this ideal harbor and attempted to march on Santiago forty miles away. They had to abandon their attack sixteen miles short of Santiago. The Spanish hadn't fired a shot. The heat, the rain, the jungle and tropical fever had cost the British two thousand soldiers.

The commander of the American expeditionary force—portly, three hundred pound General W. Rufus Shafner, a veteran of the Civil War—had been reminded of the British experience. Mindful of his own suffering in the tropical heat, he was determined to find a landing area closer to Santiago. Santiago was obviously not an option with the Spanish squadron there and the harbor guarded by the large stone *Moro*. The Spanish seemed to call their stone fortresses a *Moro*. Between Guantanamo and Santiago three parallel rows of hills and mountains looked down on the Caribbean. These were overlooked six miles inland by the peaks of the Sierra Maestra range. The coast had no extended shallow shore, only a sharp drop-off into the sea, presenting no reasonable anchorage or landing beach. There were some docks extending into the water serving the iron ore extraction companies, and some smaller ones at Daiquiri. These would have to do.

The Cuban General Calixto García, had come on board Admiral Sampson's ship to report the status of the Spanish forces. He was a tall, elderly, distinguished gentleman who had been fighting the Spanish for four years and bore the scar in his forehead where he had unsuccessfully tried to shoot himself rather than be captured by the Spanish in the prior Ten Years War for independence. The problems he described were a few thousand troops and some artillery located in the heights commanding the landing area and the difficulty of attempting to locate and concentrate naval gunfire on concealed emplacements, some of which were on reverse slopes. The solution was to send a Navy gunnery officer ashore with the Cubans to signal down accurate range and bearing instructions to the ships.

Tom's ship was closest to shore and was signaled instructions to so proceed. There was no shortage of volunteers, but the captain selected LTJG Spalding who had excelled in gunnery. In addition to Spalding, two marines, simply referred to as Jones and O'Rourke, were sent for added protection and to send semaphore signals down from the heights. As an additional backup the XO assigned Tom, over Spalding's heated objection to his having to take this "bumpkin" as unnecessary baggage.

With a withering look the XO called Spalding to the side, out of the crew's hearing. "Listen you arrogant jackass. This landing could succeed or fail depending on what happens up there. There are going to be a lot of people shooting at you. Scott is the most uniquely qualified man on this ship for this assignment. He knows signals, range finding, speaks Spanish, has a level head and, not least important, he is an expert rifleman. Now if you want to share your moment of glory with another officer, maybe I will consider that, but if you fail because of inadequate backup it is all on your shoulders. Understand? Besides that, I'm ordering you. Now get your equipment and get your ass in gear!" There was no argument to this, only a quick, "Aye, aye, Sir."

The climb up the bluff was started in the dark and supposedly timed to arrive before daylight, and they would rest until it was light enough to see the enemy and signal the ships. Two raggedy Cuban scouts, carrying weapons that looked like they dated back to Columbus, led the way up the two hundred foot ridge over limestone outcroppings, cactus and chaparral scrub. Tom wondered how this side of the hills could be so dry and so much vegetation farther inland. He vaguely remembered that it had something to do with dry and salty trade winds on this side of the heights and rain not falling until it was on the other side after sweeping up to cooler air, or something like that. Right now they were struggling up in the dark. The cactus was pulling at his clothes and the coils of climbing rope draped over his shoulders.

The sun was coming up by the time they reached the edge of the plateau. Crouching in the chaparral, the scouts pointed to what appeared to be a clearing with rifles stacked in the middle approximately 200 yards to the left and down in a slight crease in the rock. A lookout was posted, but he was too intent on the sight of the armada below him to pay attention to the possibility that anyone had tried to climb up the face of the heights during the night. The day before he had excitedly reported the arrival of the troop ships and had counted one thousand ships below. Whether he could count to one thousand was in doubt, but there was no dispute that no one had ever seen this many ships before. The message that had finally arrived from the lookout on top of the Moro, the large stone fortress guarding the harbor, to Admiral Cervera on the *Maria Teresa* anchored at the top of the bay was that seventy ships were in sight, including seven modern battleships.

Spalding searched the terrain with his binoculars for something more significant than this small group of lookouts. He seemed to be a different person away from the ship and its company. He was calm, in command and focused on his mission. None of his petty animosity showed. Tom was impressed and determined to hold up his end, whatever it turned out to be.

Spalding stiffened. They could see but not hear him curse under his breath. He had located the main body of probably five hundred to six hundred soldiers three hundred yards farther down the back slope and slightly hidden by trees. Farther on, more entrenchments extended on the next ridge, a half mile away. Barely discernible in the trees were a dozen howitzers on wheels, ready to move to any location to fire or retreat under rock ledges. Naval gunfire would probably sail right over them, and they could fire from defilade positions. They would have to blast away the top of the hill down onto the enemy. For large naval guns this wouldn't be a problem. He just needed to place the fire correctly. He guessed that they also had mortars to lob shells onto the shore and something to roll down the slopes. Now he had to signal the ships the locations and not get himself and his men killed in the process. He motioned to the marines and Scott to come forward and take up positions from which they could suppress any fire coming at the signalman, namely himself. Then he turned his binoculars to his ship. The prearranged flag signals flew from the signal halyard, indicating that he was in their sight. Next he called Tom forward to bring maps and take notes on the direction and ranges to send. On board they had already calculated where he would be and just had to adjust fire from there to where he signaled. The problem was he had to silhouette himself against the skyline in order to give the ship a clear view of the signals, so as not to be blurred by the undergrowth and shadows. His marines could handle the flag signals, but he knew he could translate ranges faster, and he would need them to cover, should he be spotted by the soldiers.

Well, he thought, *you wanted to be a hero and here it is, if you live through it.*

He called Tom forward and gave him instructions as to what he needed to do if Tom had to take over. Then he looked at him and said, "I apologize for the way I have acted toward you. Scott, you're a good man, and I'll make it up to you if we live through this." Although surprised, Tom received and accepted it for what it was, men about to share a common fate who needed to depend on each other.

With a long sigh, the young lieutenant heaved himself upright against the skyline and began the rapid wig wag signals, not bothering to waste time acknowledging the ship signal flags. The instant communication was acknowledged by a visible movement of the forward gun turret and a following flash of explosives as the six inch shells left the muzzles. Five minutes later gunfire from all other warships designated for this bombardment commenced. Projectiles whined overhead, and Spalding coolly adjusted them onto troop emplacements as rapidly as the shells struck.

The concussions of the muzzle explosions against the side of the cliff caused rock slides and numbed the men directly in the path of the concussion while blowing their hair and clothes in one direction, then another. Tom thought, *This is truly hell on earth,* and could only imagine what it must be like where the shells were actually landing. Compounding the blast effect from the ships firing was the reverse concussion of the explosion on the ground several hundred yards away. Inevitably, a round would fall short, caused by defective manufacturing or being fired on a down roll of the ship, showering earth and rock on the shore party. Tom wanted to jump off the cliff or crawl deep into the earth to escape this ungodly storm, but he looked up and there stood Spalding clearly etched against the blue sky and calmly waving his little flags signaling ranges and directions. Tom felt a little ashamed of his own fears and the thoughts he had harbored against Spalding. Whoomp! Bam! Another short round and Spalding disappeared in the smoke and dust, only to reappear covered with dirt. The concussion had knocked him off his perch on a big rock.

The Spanish sentry had been intently peering over the edge of the ridge from under a bush, focusing on the nearest ship as her gun turrets began to move. Not knowing what would come next, he failed to see the man waving two small flags from atop a boulder two hundred yards away. At the first flash of gunfire and the shrill passage of projectiles overhead, he dove for whatever cover he could find. The ground-shaking thunder was equally terrifying to the Americans, who were not even the targets. As projectiles passed overhead the sentry realized that it was aimed away from him, and he began to look around. At that moment he saw the solitary figure on the rock with his flags, but not Tom and the marines lying prone in firing positions. He sensed that this must be the cause of all this horror and rose to fire. The marines who had been watching him simultaneously fired and knocked him off the cliff. The different sound of small arms fire alerted the small sentry group that more than ships were firing on them. They rushed out of their camp and marine marksmanship took its toll. More than half of the dozen men fell before they found cover. Tom used his rifle skills for the first time to shoot a man instead of a squirrel or a rabbit. He didn't have time to feel queasy at the thought. That would come later. He had already killed one man while protecting Lt. Rowan with his message to García. At this moment the Mauser rifle bullets were flying by in what he would later read as an accurate description in Stephen Crane's account of the war, *as if one string of a most delicate musical instrument had been touched by the wind into a long faint note.*"

Tom turned to see Spalding crumple to the ground, hit by three bullets at once. The Spanish normally fired too high but not high enough to miss the man standing on a rock. Simultaneously, he heard a wet thud next to him. O'Rourke had been shot in the forehead and was rolling down the small embankment, his eyes staring in surprise. For the first time, he noticed that the Cubans had disappeared.

On board the *Yucatan* the Rough Riders had excitedly watched the bombardment when they noticed the lone figure on the ridge wig wagging away. A sergeant turned to Roosevelt and said, "Colonel, look at that crazy fool standing up there in plain sight." Roosevelt turned his binoculars on the figure saying, "By God. He's one of ours, a sailor I believe." He could barely make out the small figures lying prone and firing at the enemy. Turning to the ship's captain he asked, "Commander, what are those men doing up there by themselves? It seems like suicide."

"Very close to it, Colonel. That's a navy shore party directing gunfire on the enemy. From very close up, I might add. I hope they make it back."

"Great Scott! What incredibly brave lads." A murmur of admiration went around the group of soldiers.

"Look, he's down," a soldier shouted. A groan went around. "Another guy's up there! No he's down too. He's up again, waving them damn flags."

"Bloody hell!" swore Roosevelt. "If we could only get ashore to help…"

"I don't think you want to be up there in the middle of that hell, Colonel," said the captain as they watched shells explode all over the ridge and the blurred figures of the enemy trying to close. The Navy had also noticed the enemy unit trying to move in on the shore party and shifted one of its four inch guns with deadly fire to rain on the Spanish unit.

Tom had tried to stop the blood flowing from Spalding's

wounds by stuffing pieces of cloth in the entry and exit holes in his shoulder and leg. The wrist was shattered and he could only try to stop the flow with a tourniquet. Spalding would never fully use that hand again. "At least it's his left hand," Tom thought. He had butchered many farm animals and helped repair many farm accidents to men and women and seen more than his share of blood and bones, but this was beyond imagination. The world was exploding all around him, people were trying to kill him and his companions were dying. He was numb now and trying to think. He had seen artillery being moved farther down a ravine and Spalding had been unable to get fire on it. The Navy had shifted fire closer in to break the enemy attack when a larger force threatened. He glanced at the remaining marine, who gave him a thumbs-up sign and continued to pick off soldiers as they stuck their heads up. Spalding moaned and looked up at Tom, mouthing what Tom took as a request to continue directing fire. After so many explosions, he couldn't even hear the ringing in his ears anymore.

"God, help me," he prayed, and grabbed the bloody flags still clutched in the lieutenant's hands. He paused a moment to get the flag positions back in his mind and jumped up into the music of war, bullets singing, canons thundering, and shouts of the men coming for him. He thought briefly of the *1812 Overture* he had once seen in an opera house in Mobile, with soft wind instruments, crashing cymbals and thunderous drums. It was all here, with death thrown in for free.

His mind was racing, but seemingly calm, calculating ranges and directions in his head. His teacher would never believe this use of arithmetic. His mind seemed to shut out the noise and concussions as though it had thrown a protective shield around him. He managed to direct fire on the artillery pieces and other units coming up from behind the second row of hills. He could see the carnage that effective naval gunfire had done to the original units camped nearby in an indescribable mass of human and animal remains in a landscape rendered to look like the surface of the moon. Never had he actually imagined what destructive power was carried on his ship.

Suddenly, his legs seem to spin and go out from under him. He was falling through air. The sudden jar of hitting the ground stunned him for a moment. He had been hit in the thigh, seemingly through the muscle, no bone damage. He was alive and it didn't hurt too much, just a lot of stinging. He turned to check Spalding, who was now very pale and quiet. He tightened the tourniquet and stuffed some cloth in his own wound. It didn't seem to be any worse than any torn muscle that he had suffered before. The remaining marine had blood streaming down his face, but he was still firing, using ammunition from the dead marine's pouch. Tom needed to get back up and finish directing fire.

Once again he heaved himself up on the rock, which was now slippery with blood. 'I should have thrown sand on it like an old man-of-war gun deck,' he thought. The rifle fire slackened as the shelling found its bearing and range on the attacking troops. Although occasional bullets whistled high or chipped rocks nearby, they were long shots, and he could concentrate on ranging on the second row of hills. He was now standing on one leg and sometimes propping himself up when a flag was in a lowered position. A few more salvos and any remaining units were in rapid retreat. As he signaled the results, the world turned suddenly and eerily quiet.

He turned his attention to Spalding, who was unconscious but breathing steadily. The marine, Jones, had suffered three wounds of his own, but they weren't life threatening and he was treating himself with a big grin on his face, "*Semper fi, sailor.*"

"*Semper fi*, marine." Tom grinned back.

"Now, how the hell do we get off this damn cliff?" Tom said to nobody in particular. He looked around and spotted the ropes he had so painfully carried up, now covered in his and Spalding's blood. "Well, going down has to be one hell of a lot easier than coming up," he said. Considering the numbness he felt all over, he wasn't sure whether he was actually speaking or imagining it.

The crew and captain of his ship had been watching through binoculars and telescopes as the drama on the heights unfolded. For the most part, from their angle they could only see and identify the men who stood up against the sky and fell down again. They could see the short rounds falling, and between salvos, faint rifle reports drifted down, leaving them to imagine what was happening. The marines could identify the sounds of their own Winchester-Lee rifles as sort of a "prut" and that of the Spanish Mausers' "pop" and sadly described the increasing numbers of Mausers joining the fight then fading into an ominous silence.

The captain could only whisper, "Incredible, incredible bravery." The XO stood silently beside the captain, unashamed of the tears that streaked his face.

On the top and out of sight of the ships, Tom had scooped sand onto the slippery ropes and tied a loop, using his best seaman's bowline knot, to lower the marine, fending off brush and cactus, to a ledge, who in turn would catch Spalding as he was lowered to that point, then Tom would lower himself and retrieve ropes for the next relay, and so on until they reached the bottom. It was a lot easier than trying to climb down with holes in his leg. The stinging had turned into real pain now that the adrenalin was wearing off. They were now covered all over with blood and sand, not even recognizable as the men who went up the cliff. As they were almost to the bottom, the two Cubans returned, riding horse-back down the narrow shoreline with Gen. Garcia and a company of rebels. A little late, but they carried the men to an aid station in Daiquiri, run by a sympathetic doctor, and retrieved the body of the dead Marine. The Spanish had now withdrawn from the coast in the face of the heavy naval bombardment, but increasingly rough seas had prevented evacuation to the ship or landing of troops.

On board the troop ship, the Rough Riders had watched anxiously to see what had happened. As Tom's figure appeared at the edge with ropes in hand, a loud cheer went up from the ships, the echoes of which were loud enough to drift up the cliff causing Tom to look up and wave. More cheering and shouts from Roosevelt of "Bully! Decorations for all of them!" A promise he subsequently pursued all the way to the Secretary of the Navy, his former boss.

Tom had stuffed the bloodstained semaphore flags in his shirt and now took them out and presented them to Spalding and Jones. The marine cut his in half and gave back a half to Tom with his usual big grin. The lieutenant could only give a weak smile. The marine would fully recover and lead more men in battle in the Philippines and the grisly trenches and frontal assaults of World War I. The lieutenant would lose most of the use of his left hand, but otherwise lead a long and healthy life, confident that he had done more than his share, and added a little more glory to the family tree. Tom had more complications than he thought. During the descent he had added damage to the tendons in his leg that would give him a slight limp the rest of his life and end any thoughts of attending the Naval Academy. His uncle would later kid him about Captain Ahab of Moby Dick fame doing better on one leg, even if he was fiction.

The next day six thousand men were ferried ashore to scramble up piers and docks from boats rising and falling with the waves. The water was later strewn with equipment and carcasses of horses and mules forced to swim for shore, because they could not be carried in small boats and landed on the docks and piers. Staying on land away from that mess was fine with Tom. They had been moved up to a clean little house farther up the hill with a perfect view of the landing, which seemed to be mass confusion. It was a cooler up there and had a wonderful salt air, sea breeze. His uncle had always said that nothing cured you better than salt air and water. Strong Cuban rum had been poured on their wounds to clean them and a little inside to cheer them. Aside from a bit of pain, this was a fine, fine, time. Spalding was in more pain with his wrist, but he was equally enjoying the site, and some morphine was being sent from the ship.

Dr. Edelmiro Gonzalez, a distant cousin of Garcia, had studied medicine in New Orleans and Madrid. He normally practiced in Santiago, but with his rebel sympathies had found it expedient to work on the outskirts and among the farmers and fishermen and away from the eyes and attention of the authorities.

The story of the shore party had spread through the ships, and the XO had found his way to the aid station with the help of General Garcia, accompanied by no less a personage than the former Assistant Secretary of the Navy, Lieutenant Colonel Theodore Roosevelt. Upon entering the house Roosevelt bellowed, "Bully! Is that you Spalding under all those bandages?"

"Aye, sir." he replied, feeling much, much better after a little morphine.

"A fine show, lad. I shall write immediately to your father and your uncle in New York to describe your heroic action, as well as the Secretary of the Navy and the President. Of course, as an endorsement to your commanding officer's report," he added in recognition of Lieutenant. Comander Crosby's presence. "And who is this fine lad?"

"The man who saved my life and completed the mission, sir, Petty Officer Third Class, Thomas MacDougal Scott," he indicated towards Tom with his good hand. He then explained the situation as it had unfolded and Tom's role as marksman, signalman, gunfire controller, doctor and mountain goat.

"Astonishing! My mother's family were Scots. Good blood. Well, lads, I still have a war to fight. I hope to see you again when this affair is over." With that he whirled around, mounted his horse and galloped into history.

"A truly astonishing man," Garcia noted. To Tom, he asked how he learned Spanish.

"I worked on my uncle Caleb MacDougall's freight ships in Cuba, read books and picked it up enough to translate for him."

"Ah, now I know you! You are the *muchacho* who translated for General Gomez and Captain O'Brien when he brought us the Hotchkiss guns, and you were with Lt. Rowan when he delivered the message to me from President McKinley!" Garcia exclaimed, with the sudden recognition of who he was talking to.

"*Si, General,*" Tom said, then realizing that he had forgotten Cmdr. Crosby was standing there he started to cover up his slip, "I…"

Crosby interrupted with a grin, "It's OK, Tom. I read your file, and I already figured that one out."

"I also have heard of your uncle's help. The revolution is grateful, and you will be rewarded for your service when the Republic of Cuba is finally established," Garcia added. A younger, handsome Cuban officer, who had been standing behind the general, was now introduced.

"This is my nephew and my aide, Major Rodrigo Garcia. He is another hero of the revolution." The major extended his hand to Spalding and then Tom, "*Con much gusto y mi admiracion, caballeros.*" He appeared to be about forty, tall for a Cuban, black hair combed back over his head, thick mustache and a bright smile, clenching the classic Cuban cigar. The most distinguishing characteristic were his eyes. They seemed to flash, taking everything in at a glance. They bordered on wild looking. Tom could only imagine what adventures and battles had been seen by those eyes, and by the way Juanita, the doctor's assistant, was gazing in awe, what women he must have known.

Spalding had been watching and listening to the exchanges in considerable awe himself, wondering what surprise was next. At that moment a commotion could be heard outside and a loud commanding voice shouted, "Where's that boy from Alabama?" and in walked General "Fighting Joe" Wheeler with saber rattling on his belt, snow white beard and looking very much ready for battle.

Gen. Joseph Wheeler, West Point class of 1859, Confederate Lieutenant General at the age of twenty-eight and currently Democratic Congressman from Alabama and Chairman of the powerful House Ways and Means Committee, was now in full charge of the room. It had become a political necessity for President McKinley to reappoint him once again as a U.S. Army officer thirty-three years after the Civil War. It was too soon after the Civil War to be sending an invasion force of sixteen thousand soldiers in federal uniforms into the Deep South, even for embarking in Tampa, without some conciliatory efforts of assistance from this legendary old confederate cavalry officer. Little did he suspect that wiry, old Wheeler would prove to be one of the hardiest and best generals in the field in the battles to come, even at the age of sixty-two.

"Morning General, here he is, Petty Officer 3rd class Tomas MacDougall Scott," said Crosby, indicating Tom.

Noticing Gen. Garcia, Wheeler turned and said, "My compliments, sir, for your fine campaigns."

"*Gracias.* At your service, General," replied Garcia.

Seeing all this, Spalding exclaimed to himself, "My God, what next!?"

"Boy, Alabama is damn proud of you. You saved one hell of a lot of lives with that mission on the hill." Turning to Crosby, he said, "You Navy boys better take good care of him when he is back to duty."

"Aye, aye, sir." Crosby acknowledged and turned away to avoid anyone seeing the concern on his face. Tom would never return to duty.

Realizing instantly his mistake, Wheeler added to Tom, "or whatever you choose to do when this little war is over." Changing the subject, he went on, "I had some MacDougalls in my regiment. Any kin? Damn fine cavalry men they were."

"Yes, sir, my uncles." Also, trying to change the subject and make light of it. "I'll be going back to Mobile and get back to sea with my uncle, if I can stand steady on the quarterdeck like Capt. Ahab." A laugh went around the room at the thought of that image.

"Well, I might run for the senate when this thing is over. Make sure you register to vote when you get back to Alabama, and vote for me. Ya heah?!"

"Aye, aye, sir."

With, "General, Gentlemen, I bid you adieu. I have one more fight to do," the old soldier turned on his heel, forgot the politicking and, with saber rattling, clattered out the door and into the fray.

Feeling he couldn't stand any more of this, Lieutenant Junior Grade Spalding closed his eyes and drifted off into the arms of Morpheus. A faint snoring could be heard from the next room where the marine had already taken a little too much medicinal "Cuban cane" and missed the excitement.

Troops and supplies continued to pour onto the shore for days, clogging piers and roads through the gaps in the hills. When it rained the roads turned to quagmires for wagons and rendered impassable spots which were only wide enough for one wagon. Gunfire rumbled back through the hills, and walking wounded streamed back on the congested roads. Dr. Gonzalez's aid station further down the hill had become a stop along the way, and additional supplies were provided by the Army in consideration of his help.

Tom, the marine and Spalding remained ashore in the house. There was no use getting in the way, and they were never going back to duty, anyway. Besides, the view was magnificent and they had a very pretty nurse.

Black-haired, brown-eyed Juanita Calderon was the daughter of a local fisherman and excelled so much in school that she was recommended to Dr. Gonzalez for nurse training. She was slender, with strong hands from helping her father with his fishing, because she had no brothers. It took a stern argument from her mother to convince her father to let her go. She took an instant liking to Tom, to whom she gave the special treatment. She even borrowed Dr. Gonzalez's little cart burro to give Tom a ride through back trails not used by the Army and to picturesque overlooks, and he taught her English. All of this was to the great amusement of Spalding, who called them Romeo and Juliette.

On those deserted overlooks, mutual attraction turned into stronger desire and the ultimate result, all in the middle of a war. One day they saw the Army's big observation balloon in the distance and scurried under bushes. Afraid of being seen, it didn't occur to them that the enemy was receiving the full attention of the balloon's occupants and the balloon receiving the attention of the enemy. Rifle fire had concentrated on it with the result that soldiers far back down the road were wounded from bullets dropping behind the balloon. This did not cause the soldiers any great affection for its crew, regardless of any observation intelligence gathered.

CHAPTER 4

BATTLE AT SEA

Sunday morning, July 3, 1898

The invasion had commenced on **June 22, 1898**. The Army had advanced in jerks and jumps across the tropical landscape, Teddy Roosevelt had led his Rough Riders up Kettle Hill in the San Juan Heights on **July 1**, and Gen Shafter had received news of substantial Spanish reinforcements on the way. He gave Spanish General Toral an ultimatum to surrender or have the city bombarded on **July 3**.

Spalding had recovered enough to go outside, substantially aided by pain killers supplied by a Navy doctor and the ample supply of local 'rum anesthetics' at hand if desired. Sea air did indeed cure everything. The sight of so many warships made him long for the glory of the sea battle to come that he would never be part of. 'As if I hadn't had enough,' he thought. Suddenly, he had a thought to go down the coast nearer to the harbor, but not near the battles occurring farther inland. He called for Juanita, and inquired through Tom as to whether there was some sort of wagon to which they could hitch the burro. It took her thirty minutes to come back with the burro and a two wheel cart. With Juanita walking and leading the burro, they set off down the narrow coast road toward the entrance of the channel leading into the harbor, hopefully to get a better view of the harbor and maybe the Spanish ships, and, with luck, not be shot again. Tom kept thinking that this stupid donkey and a two wheel cart were a poor substitute for a mule and a four wheel wagon with springs. This thing felt like you were being rolled on the rocks instead of the wheels, even though he and Spalding were sitting on a pile of cane husks and blankets. But it was better than walking, besides they had brought '*Cuban cane* anesthesia' along to numb the pain. The thought of going on a picnic with black beans and rice and Cuban rum in a donkey cart in the middle of a war did cause a round of laughter.

Juanita knew a farmer who had a house on a hill overlooking the channel entrance, but out of sight of the Moro. She urged the burro up the narrow, rutted path. The farmer's house was deserted but the well water was cool and they took time to relax and marvel at the view and ships below.

Meanwhile, aboard the Spanish flagship, *Infanta Maria Teresa,* Admiral Pasqual Cervera had received the senseless order to break out of the blockade via telegraph from Spain by superiors who knew nothing of the situation. Ever the brave old sailor, Cervera gave the order to run down the channel. They steamed past the sunken wreck of the *Merrimac* whose American sailors had tried to run under the Spanish ship's guns and those of the Moro to sink her in the narrowest part of the channel to block in the fleet. But her rudder had been blasted away before she could steer to the spot. Navy Lieutenant Richmond P. Hobson, who commanded the attempt, was later awarded the Medal of Honor for his "extraordinary courage." Now her sailors sat in a Moro dungeon.

Smoke from the Spanish ships firing up their boilers had been seen the day before and caused some speculation, but no concern among the Navy commanders. Today smoke seemed to be moving toward the entrance. A six-pounder thundered across the open water from the deck of the *New York,* fired by the officer of the deck, Lieutenant F. K. Hill. Signal flags went up the mast showing "250," meaning "Enemy ships are coming."

Spalding was reclining in the shade against the stone base of the well when he saw a cloud of gun-smoke burst from the *New York.* Seconds later the gun's boom rolled up the hill. He sat straight up, heart pounding and hardly noticing the pain in his shoulder. Flags sprouted all over the fleet like instant spring flowers among those dull grey shapes. Aboard the ships alarm gongs clanged, bugles sounded, watertight doors were secured, decks wet down and boilers fired up steam pressure.

The Spanish ships came out in a line at ten minute intervals and six hundred yards, with the *Maria Teresa* in the lead, followed by the other large cruisers and destroyers, then escorts. George Edward Graham of the Associated Press was to write from the deck of the *Brooklyn*:

"We saw what probably has not been witnessed since the days of the Armada, ships   coming out for deadly battle, but dressed as for a regal parade or a festal day. From their shining black hulls, with huge golden figureheads bearing the crest and coat of arms of Spain, to the tops of their mast where fluttered proudly the immense silken flags...to the brightly colored awnings over their decks, they bespoke luxury and chivalry, and proud defiance."

Aboard the *Maria Teresa,* Captain Concas was to later write:

"It was a solemn moment, capable of making the calmest heart beat faster...I asked leave of the admiral to open fire and that received, I gave the order. The bugle gave the signal for the commencement of the battle.

The sound of my bugles was the last echo of those which history tells us were sounded at the capture of Granada. It was the signal that the history of four centuries of grandeur was at an end and that Spain was becoming a nation of the fourth class."

As seen from the bridge of the *Iowa,* Captain Robley Evans later described the scene:

"As the leading ship, the flagship Maria Teresa, swung into the channel leading out of Punta Gorda, she presented a magnificent appearance with her splendid new battle flags and her polished brass work...

As she passed the Diamond Shoal at the entrance to the harbor she swung off to the westward and opened fire smartly with her port broadside and turret guns. From this moment the battle may be said to have been on, and the roaring of the guns became incessant...The speed I judged to be about eight knots as the ships came down the channel, which increased to thirteen or more as they kept away to the westward in the open sea. They came at us like mad bulls."

Prior to the movement of the Spanish, Admiral Sampson aboard his flagship, *New York,* had left the area to go ashore for a meeting with Gen. Shafter and was now steaming some seven miles away toward Siboney and out of sight of the *Brooklyn* with Commodore Schley, the second in command. Schley was now smiling at the prospect and relishing his own glory when one of his lieutenants shouted, "Commodore, they are coming right at us!"

"Go right for them!" was Schley's quick answer.

As ships from the squadron began closing from all directions on the Spanish, Spalding's temples were throbbing with excitement, as he was thinking, 'This is the battle in which I should have been engaged, not being shot up by a bunch of peasant soldiers.' He could imagine his replacement shouting orders and commanding the roaring guns in the middle of smoke and exulting as his shots struck the enemy ship. He continuously shifted and adjusted his binoculars from one ship to the other and back and forth from the enemy ships.

Tom was standing beside him, his mouth agape with the immensity of the scene and the horrendous firepower being displayed of ship on ship. The smell of smoke drifted up as the rumble of gunfire and the concussions began to bounce off the hills and echo into the harbor giving Tom cold chills at the thought of what must be happening on ships which were on the receiving end of these broadsides. The memory of the carnage he had seen close up was too fresh in his mind. He had faced death on the sea and now it had passed by his door in battle on land. But these were nature's own elements, water, rocks and sand. The thought of a violent impersonal death on the cold, hard plates of a steel deck or trapped below decks with fire and steam sent chills through him. These had been places of his fondest memories. Now he saw them as places of unnatural death. 'So this was the glory of naval battle,' he thought, 'God help us.'

"Look, there! The *Brooklyn* almost collided with the *Texas* trying to avoid the charge of the *Maria Teresa*. She's turning in the opposite direction of the other ships." Spalding was calling out the names and maneuvers of the ships, both friendly and enemy. "The *Iowa* is trying to ram the *Maria Teresa*, now he's swinging to fire a broadside. There, a hit! See the steam escaping! She's slowing!" Tom was trying to bring into the focus an old telescope he had picked up at the house, but gave up in lieu of taking in the whole scene without magnification. Now he could see everything at once and depend on Spalding to narrate.

The Spanish were now racing along the coast with the *Maria Teresa* in flames and losing steam. The *Iowa*, *Texas* and the *Brooklyn* were running parallel and trying to keep up. The *Iowa* swung one way and then the other, firing alternate broadsides as two of the Spanish cruisers began to pull ahead. As the *Cristobal Colon* passed she landed two shots on the *Iowa*, which the captain of the *Iowa* described as, "…two as beautiful shots as I ever saw made by any ship."

Now limping, the *Iowa* closed with the *Oquendo* coming from behind and under shelling by several navy ships. Shot holes appeared in her sides and shells were exploding inside, but she continued to steam past the *Iowa*. More hits and flames could be seen coming from below decks and more explosions. In a desperate situation with more explosions threatening in the torpedo room, the Spanish captain turned toward the beach in flames and lowered his flag in a final attempt to save the remainder of his crew by running aground. Ships moved through banks of smoke from guns and fires aboard damaged ships, firing as fast as the gunners could see and the guns could be brought to bear. As each Spanish ship exited the channel, a new set of engagements commenced as more Navy ships continued to converge on the entrance. Tom and Spalding watched mesmerized as the classic sea battle unfolded below them. Juanita stood frozen with hands over her ears as thunder rolled up the hill. The frightened burro jerked free and ran up the path braying loudly. The cart bounced wildly behind the animal for a hundred yards until it turned over, holding him in one spot. Now, he could only stand, trembling and braying pitifully.

The *Maria Teresa* was now burning badly and losing speed. Still under bombardment and in danger of a massive explosion of its ammunition, Admiral Cervera also struck his colors, turned his flagship to the beach and flooded all magazines.

The cruiser *Vizcaya* had been trading salvos with the *Brooklyn* amid dense clouds of smoke when the Spaniard turned abruptly, intending to ram the *Brooklyn*. Firing desperately from its eight-inch turret gun, the *Brooklyn* struck the *Vizcaya* a glancing shot on its bow igniting a torpedo. Spalding, who had been focused on the Spanish ship, yelled "My God, her whole bow blew up!"

"I'll be damned, the *Gloucester's* engaging that torpedo boat! I know that boat. It used to be J. P. Morgan's private yacht. I was aboard with my father, when she was named *Corsair*. The former XO of the *Maine* is the captain. Ah, she got her! I wonder what old J.P. would say about that?" Spalding was smiling now and thoroughly enjoying himself, and the rum was adding to the fun.

The assortment of Spanish torpedo destroyers was being chased down and sunk, but the *Cristobal Colon*, which had crippled the *Iowa*, was pulling away from the *Brooklyn*, *Texas*, and the *Vixen*, and out of range.

"Looks like she's going to get away,' said Tom.

Spalding swept the sea with his binoculars. "No! Look at this! It's the *Oregon*! After sixteen thousand miles of sailing around the 'Horn' she's going to get in the fight!" Thick black smoke poured from its stacks as all boilers pushed her through the water at slightly better speed than the *Colon*. Great white, foaming waves curled up the sides of her bow, giving her the appearance of what the sailors called "a bone in her teeth." A great cloud erupted from her massive thirteen-inch forward turret guns, hurling a half-ton of steel and high explosives toward the *Colon*. The range was closing and the Spanish captain finally struck his colors and turned onto the beach to save his crew from the inevitable end.

It had been one hundred minutes since the first ship had exited the harbor until they were all destroyed, and another hour to chase down the *Colon*. Tom and Spalding could only see her beached in the distance with the aid of Tom's long telescope. Tom took particular notice that *Colon* was beached very near the spot where he landed with Lt. Rowan and his *message to Garcia*. They sat for a long time staring at the scene below, indelibly imprinted in their minds, then rode silently back, each with his private thoughts.

CHAPTER 5

SURRENDER

On **July 17, 1898,** the Spanish surrendered Santiago, and on **July 25ᵗʰ,** the Americans invaded Puerto Rico.

August 12, 1898, the peace accord was signed. Unaware of this, Admiral Dewey destroyed the Spanish fleet in the Philippines and attacked Manila on **August 13, 1898.**

November 8, 1898, Theodore Roosevelt, the descendant of Dutch settlers of New York and a mother of Scots lineage and a Confederate family, was elected governor of New York State and became President **September 14, 1901.** He is the only man in history to receive both the military Medal of Honor for valor and the world's foremost prize for peace, The Nobel.

December 10, 1898, the Treaty of Paris was signed, officially ending the war. The United States was ceded Puerto Rico and Guam and paid Spain $20,000,000.00 for the Philippines. Cuba was granted independence.

February 4, 1899, The Philippine Insurrection breaks out and places a new American legend on the stage, a brand new 2ⁿᵈ Lieutenant from West Point, Douglas MacArthur, another Scotsman.

The active part of the campaign was over and units were returning to ships for the return voyage. The rainy season was coming with its deadly outbreaks of yellow fever. Tom had attempted to obtain his discharge while still in Cuba, but the Navy said regulations prohibited it until he was officially listed as medically able to leave in a state where no more could be done. Obviously, Tom thought that was right now, but he was still in the Navy.

After faithfully promising Juanita that he would soon return on his uncle's boat, it would be six months before U. S. Navy red tape and shipping schedules allowed it, and only then at the request of the Cuban military. Tom and Spalding had specifically been invited for ceremonies in Havana honoring heroes of the revolution. Spalding's father had even chartered a yacht for the trip, with Tom as a guest.

The Navy had recommended Tom and Spalding for the Medal of Honor, which originally had been restricted to enlisted men, but had now been expanded to include officers. Some prodding by Roosevelt and a few congressmen and senators had expedited the time frame. The medal had been authorized by President Lincoln in 1861 to recognize and promote efficiency in the Navy. Later it came to be the recognition of *conspicuous gallantry and intrepidity at the risk of life.*

For lack of other available and appropriate decorations, Tom and the young marine, Jones, had been awarded the Navy Good Conduct Medal. By some sleight of hand, the brass had rationalized and condensed the required three years' service or one year in wartime into this brief "war." The original time had been set when the medal was authorized in 1884 to recognize outstanding performance and conduct by enlisted men. No other medal for valor existed at the time, but the Navy exercised another prerogative for the marine by awarding him the Gold Lifesaving Medal, actually a Coast Guard medal, authorized in 1874 for heroic conduct at sea while risking his life to save another. It really didn't seem to be much of a stretch. However, he had already shipped out to serve in the rebellion now arising in the Philippines.

The Governor General's Palace was now the temporary headquarters of U.S. Army General John Rutter Brooke, who was in charge of the American occupation. As young Tom Scott stood on the balcony adjacent to the anteroom where he and Spalding were to receive special recognition, he could see the aft superstructure of the *Maine* still visible above the water with the American flag flying half way up the one remaining mast. After his experience on the bluff at Daiquiri and the subsequent naval battle below, the two hundred sixty-eight violent deaths in Havana's harbor were now more real, more poignant than he could have imagined. Realizing what Tom was looking at, Spalding came out on the balcony and stood silently, both with their own emotions.

The general's aide broke their reverie with the announcement of the general's entrance alongside Cuban General Maximo Gomez. His voice echoed softly from the marble floors, fresco covered walls, and twenty foot ceilings, which still whispered of the grandeur that once was Spain's.

General Gomez saw Scott on the balcony. "Ah, my young friend, we meet again. This time you are the hero." Gomez briefly explained their prior meeting to a surprised General Brooke.

After a brief ceremony with brave words of the new Cuba and a toast to its martyrs of independence, Tom and Spalding were awarded green silk sashes with a gold crest of Cuba engraved with the word "HEROE." They were to wear these at many receptions with great effect in the years to come. Also recognized were many American volunteers who had fought with the revolution. Not the least of which was "Dynamite Johnny" O'Brien, who would be appointed later as the Port of Havana's chief pilot, and guide the refloated *Maine* to its final resting place in the deep waters of the Straits of Florida. Even Uncle Caleb discreetly let it be known that he also had played a role.

The following reception would substantially affect the future of Cuba for the next fifty years. In addition to the requisite diplomats, businessmen, bankers, railroad men, and agricultural interests were represented and eager to profit in free Cuba. Old man Spalding worked the room like the professional banker he was with his hero son by his side. Not to be left behind, Caleb greeted his old merchant and planter friends with Tom, and met new business interests with banker Spalding.

The new brokerage firm of Spalding, Whitman and Sterling, announced its Havana branch office with former decorated hero and Navy lieutenant "BB" Spalding as its manager. Young Spalding was called "BB" from his first names William Barnes after his maternal uncle. Old Bill Barnes was a successful politician in New York and a confidant of Theodore Roosevelt, who was now governor of New York. Issuing new railroad bonds would be the first order of business and there were plenty of takers right there. Next would be stocks in new sugar mills, etc. Boom time was about to hit Cuba. The Cuban politicians, of course, would get their share.

Trying to absorb this overwhelming scene, Tom wondered if they had simply exchanged one form of colonialism for another.

In addition to accolades, Tom and BB were each granted adjacent 2,000 hectares. At 2.471+ acres per hectare that equaled almost 5,000 acres of land confiscated from absentee Spanish landholders in the richest part of Oriente Province. General Garcia and his aide and nephew, Rodrigo, were granted a similar amount of adjacent land. Tom hadn't noticed Rodrigo and his uncle at first, but he did notice a pretty young girl with flashing and expressive eyes. She turned out to be Rodrigo's young daughter. It was impossible for him to take his eyes off hers as he was introduced. Noticing the obvious stare and some discomfort, Rodrigo laughingly said, "Don't worry, she often has that effect on people. You will recover." His own captivating eyes made Tom wonder again how many women must have been seduced by them.

Fascination was equal with Graciela. She had heard the stories of this young American who had single-handed destroyed the Spanish army, or so the tale had expanded. Tom found himself stumbling with his Spanish when her eyes focused on him. He tried to think of Juanita or any other girl to break this spell and pull away from those eyes. Being on the other end of her gaze, he could readily imagine what it must have been like for women transfixed by her father's look. General Garcia broke the spell by pointing out a distinguished gentleman on the other side of the room. "That gentleman will be the first president of our new republic. Come, I will introduce you."

Scott was introduced. Estrada Palma appraised Tom with an experienced eye. "Young man, I hope you will remain in Cuba. We will need good men like you. You know, I was a school teacher in Orange County, New York for several years after the Spanish exiled me during the Ten Year War. Indeed, I am an American citizen. José Martí and I spent many weeks in Washington, D.C. talking to members of the government and members of congress on behalf of our cause in Cuba."

General Garcia noticed General Brooke walking by. "General, you have met my friend, Tomás Scott. Something you probably have not heard is that he is the one who helped guide Lieutenant Rowan to deliver the message to me from President McKinley."

General Brooke said, "Really? I had not heard that part. Young man, no one may ever know your name, but you are now part of military lore with the expression, *Get a message to Garcia.*"

Finally, he was rescued by Uncle Caleb in order to meet more new business associates, but he could still feel Graciela's eyes on his back as he walked away.

Caleb was in high spirits. He had made more contacts and deals in the last two hours than he had in the last two years, and he wanted Tom to be in the middle of it. He even obtained financing for two new ships from banker Spalding, and agreed to buy BB's land for a good price. Caleb had not liked to farm, but he knew the value of good farm land, and how to ship and market the products. This had created almost 10,000 acres of prime sugarcane land under his and Tom's control. Next, he rushed over to get a piece of the new sugar mill being arranged by, of course, Spalding, Whitman and Sterling. His island shipping company would never be the same. It was about to become a multifaceted international corporation.

Determined to make his promised return to Juanita Calderon, Tom prevailed upon his uncle for passage on one of his boats going to Santiago. When he arrived he rented a horse for the trip back to the coast. Occupation forces and signs of battle were still very obvious, giving him a queasy recollection of recent events that took place here. In Daiquiri, no one, including Dr. Gonzalez, knew Juanita's whereabouts. Her parents had died of yellow fever that year, and she and her sister had gone to Santiago or Havana or somewhere. Nobody seemed to know. For years afterward, he would imagine he saw her face in crowds all over Cuba, but she never materialized.

On the return trip to Havana his thoughts had turned back to another promise to return he had made when he had left Goodwater to sail with Uncle Caleb. Her name was Lilly, the granddaughter of a slave and a white farmer. Her own mother was half white and had become pregnant by a white traveling salesman. The result had been a strikingly attractive girl with very light skin, hazel eyes and long brown hair that hung in ringlets. Later her mother married a local black man who worked some of the land owned by Tom's father, and the two children grew up together on the land.

Lilly had been a very bright child but wasn't allowed to attend the better white school. By the fourth grade Tom's father had used his influence to get her a job as a helper to the teacher. This seemed to mollify the community sufficiently to allow her in the white school house. In the Post-Civil War South no one really cared if the Negro children went to school anyway. So, she stood unobtrusively in the corner, erased the blackboard, swept the floor, listened to the white children's lessons, and smiled at Tom. *And what a smile,* Tom remembered. She stayed after school to clean and do her own studying, with a little help from the teacher, while Tom worked on his advanced math. Then they walked home together. Tom's physical size kept any classmate kidding to a minimum. By the time they were teenagers, things got a little more serious.

One day Tom's father called him aside. "Son, I think you better slow down some with Lilly. This ain't goin' to work. You got to remember where you are. Lilly's a right pretty girl and smart and damned near white. 'Bout close as you can get, I reckon, but she's still a nigra as far as folks around here are concerned. That's how they're goin' to treat her. You got to turn loose for both of your sakes, and that's a fact. I like her, your mama likes her, but it ain't goin' to work. Just heartache. Think hard on it, son. You got a bright future ahead of you."

Tom did think on it, but the so-called race problem was not his main concern. He had already decided that his father had to be wrong. It was Uncle Caleb's promise to take him to sea that presented the dilemma. He decided to go to sea and come back to get her when he made his fortune, and that is what he had told her. It was such a romantic proposal that it captivated both of them, setting off a whole new set of dreams. Unfortunately, he didn't get back and his letters were never answered. His Uncle Angus had written that the family had moved to Chicago looking for work. Tom remembered the last time he had seen her. He was walking down the dirt road to town kicking up clouds of red dust with his bare feet when she rode by in a wagon with her stepfather. She waved, and her stepfather said something that made her look to the front. Then she slipped her head around and threw that great big smile at him, and what a wonderful smile it was! He hadn't even had time to say goodbye before he left for Mobile.

As the Cuban coastline slipped by, he thought, *Everything would have worked out here in Cuba. Colonial life in the islands would have paid little, if any, attention to slight variations of color. That was just part of life in the islands. He was even darker than she just from the sun, and in the city of Santiago the majority of the population was of mixed blood, even if Havana was more prejudiced. Now, here in Cuba it was once again too late.*

Life for a young entrepreneur in American investment-heavy Cuba was filled with opportunity, especially if you had some connections on both sides. And Tom really had them. His land was now cultivated in sugarcane in cooperation with his neighbor, Rodrigo Garcia, and processed by the new mill financed by Spalding, Whitman & Sterling. Strong bonds were being forged with the Spaldings and their wide spheres of influence. Caleb's fleet increased and Tom spent more of his time ashore making business deals. He discovered his ability with math had marvelous advantages beyond navigation. His Spanish had become more fluent, but even with his affected Cuban accent, his southern drawl, as it did in English, overlaid the language like soft cream.

CHAPTER 6

POST REVOLUTION CUBA

After the revolution, American investment was heavy, maybe too heavy. Economic interest equaled political pressure. There was still strong sentiment to make Cuba part of the United States, like Puerto Rico, but Cuba had not been ceded directly to the United States by treaty, as were Puerto Rico and Guam. This was a very substantial difference in international law. However, economic pressure being what it was, and the American 'security occupation' being what it was, and Cuban politicians being what they were, the grand constitution of the new republic contained the so-called Platt Amendment, which was derived from an Army appropriations bill named after U.S. Senator Orville Platt. The Platt Amendment provided that the United States would "leave the government" of Cuba to its own people but reserved the right to intervene in Cuban affairs if U.S interests or Cuban independence were threatened. There wasn't much alternative for Cuba, and the U.S. did intervene several times between 1906 and 1923, also in Nicaragua and Haiti under lesser pretenses. In both of those events Caleb MacDougal and "Dynamite Johnny" O'Brien got their share of the action, of course. However, Cuba had been proclaimed an independent republic on May 20, 1902, and Tomas Estrada Palma had been elected President in December 1901 and again in 1905. Theodore Roosevelt had been elected as Vice President with President McKinley in 1901, and became President after McKinley's assassination on September 14, 1901. In the same year a boy was born in the distant city of Banes on the eastern end of Cuba, who would come to shape Cuban politics for a whole generation, Fulgencio Batista. From Estrada's long time in New York, he was very familiar with Roosevelt. Now he had the ear of the President of the

United States and used it to request support.

WASHINGTON, D. C. April 1, 1903

On January 22, 1903 United States Secretary of State John M. Hay negotiated a treaty with the Republic of Columbia to build a canal across the Isthmus of Panama from the Caribbean Sea to the Pacific Ocean, but the Colombian Senate refused to ratify it after the United States Senate did. They wanted more money. Now the Secretary sat in the office of President Roosevelt to consider the next move. An agitated President scowled at his Secretary of State, "Hay, man has dreamed about connecting the Atlantic and Pacific since Balboa hacked his way through the jungle across the isthmus about four hundred years ago. When I was Assistant Secretary of the Navy, I dreamed of having a two ocean navy. Now, by God, we will have it in spite of those scoundrels in Colombia. That French fellow, Bunau-Varilla, who worked on the canal for the French, indicated that there is a portion of the population calling for independence from Colombia. Maybe we ought to make a deal with those fellows. Who do we know who is quietly trading down there?"

Hay smiled, "Well, Mr. President, *unofficially* I hear there are a few Americans still running guns into Central America to the various revolutionary groups. There is one you might know, Captain Caleb MacDougall, since you pushed for his nephew, Tom Scott, to receive the Medal of Honor in the invasion at Santiago de Cuba. I hear he is working out of Havana."

The President gave a big laugh, "Bully, Hay, you've done it again. That's perfect. President Estrada is even in favor of our navy protecting the Caribbean from overseas powers. He's not going to object to MacDougall sneaking into Panama from Havana to deal with the rebels. Telegraph, in code, to my minister in Havana and tell him what I want."

Hay smiled and turned to leave as Roosevelt slammed his fist on his desk. "Bully!"

The next morning Captain Caleb received a summons to report to the office of the new representative to Cuba, Herbert Goldsmith Squiers. He thought, *Uh-oh, what now?* He was ushered into the office of Minister Squiers. Herbert Squiers was a former army officer in the U. S. 7th Cavalry in the western campaigns. As a diplomat, he had served in Berlin and China. Squiers smiled and closed the door. This scene was looking familiar to Caleb. "Captain MacDougall, I received a cable from Washington, direct from the President, to contact you. It seems you have some contacts in Panama that could be useful to our government, unofficially that is." Caleb waited for the other shoe to drop.

Without waiting for a response Squiers continued, "As the owner of a fleet of trading vessels, you know we have been trying to negotiate a treaty to build a canal across the Isthmus of Panama. Now the Colombians have again rejected our negotiated treaty. All that being said, let me be blunt. We wish to use your connections with the revolutionaries in Panama to assure them of our support in the event they actually revolt against Colombia. Of course, any commercial transactions you may arrange with them are not our concern." He let Caleb absorb that bombshell before he continued.

Caleb was actually smiling to himself, *Here we go again.* He doubted that this minister was aware of all the past connections and unofficial *favors* he had done. This time it looked like he could really make some good money while doing this *favor,* disguised as his patriotic duty. *So, negotiate it out, don't seem too eager,* even though he knew there was no saying NO. "Mr. Minister, may I have until tomorrow to check some things?"

"Certainly. Just remember where this request came from."

Caleb left while jingling the coins in his pocket.

At age twenty-three Tom had become captain of one of Caleb's small freighters, just the right size to slip into small coves with his "cargo." When Caleb explained his assignment, Tom smiled at the memory of "Dynamite Johnny" and that night along Cuba's coast.

ISTHMUS OF PANAMA
San Blas Islands

The San Blas Islands off the northeast coast of the isthmus were inhabited by the Kuna Indians, who were never kindly disposed towards the Spanish in Colombia. They made their living fishing, selling coconuts, and a little smuggling, a perfect place for Caleb's *business.* This trip, Tom's little freighter carried the usual amount of trade goods for the Kuna, covering a load of weapons for the rebels on the mainland, plus a special message from the U. S. Government on official letterhead. The Minister in Havana gave his endorsement of Caleb and Tom, and indicated that the United States would not object to a revolution. Of course, the document had to be destroyed as soon as it was read.

The Kuna were experts at slipping in and out of the mainland while avoiding Colombian patrol boats. Tom always paid them a *bonus price* for the coconut cargo he would carry on his return trip. Tom could never remember the Kuna names. So, he just called all of them *jefe* or boss. They seemed to like it. The San Blas Islands consisted of forty-nine inhabited islands and over three hundred small islands. Smuggling and trading with pirates since the 16th Century was in their blood. The islands had been a natural haven for pirates preying on the rich Spanish treasure fleets from South America. Tom's freighter was anchored behind one of the closest islands and his *cargo* was loaded into small native sailboats which slipped into the mainland at night where other Kunas had villages. This night Tom delivered his cargo to the chief of the local revolutionary group and one of the main financial supporters, Manuel Velazco. Financing was not a problem. Many people looked forward to the profits to be made from the canal under a treaty with Panama, not Colombia.

Small lanterns reflected off the waves and the beach as the rebels unloaded cargo. Tom thought of the many times he had done this up and down the Central American and Cuban coasts, starting with his first run with 'Dynamite Johnny.' "*Buenas noches, Manuel.* I have a little surprise for you this time," Tom said as he waded ashore.

"A good one I hope, Captain Tom."

"Better than you can imagine. Let's go into a hut with light." They stepped into the closest hut, and Tom pulled out his official letter.

"*Increible*! There will be much celebration when I show this."

"Sorry, Manuel, I have to burn this now." A look of dread spread across Manuel's face. "No one will believe me. Wait, wait. The Frenchman is nearby. He wanted to see that we were receiving the weapons. He must see this."

Tom had been told that he might find Phillipe Bunau-Varilla somewhere near the action but in the background. Actually, he was standing in the shadows two huts away. "Phillipe, Phillipe, you must see this," Manuel said in a frantic whisper barely loud enough to be heard.

The Frenchman appeared out of the shadows and introduced himself. Tom showed him the letter which simply indicated that the United States would not intervene against a rebellion by the people in the Isthmus of Panama against the Republic of Colombia. The dim candlelight flickered across his face and broad smile. "*C'est magnifique!*"

Tom took back the letter, held it into the flame of the same candle and ground the ashes into the dirt. Still smiling, Bunau-Varilla asked, "Now tell me what it really means."

"Well, sir, I am not the President, but what the Minister explained to me was our government assumes that Colombian troops can't get here through the narrow Darien Gap by land with that dense jungle. So, our navy will send ships to blockade both sides of the isthmus to prevent Colombia from bringing in troops and supplies. I understand some U. S. Marines will be landed in Panama City just to protect the American interest, and that is all I know. I'll keep bringing weapons as long as you need them and somebody can pay."

"Young man, we will pay double your price for bringing us this news!"

Back to Havana with coconuts... and money, and many more

trips in the months to come.

November 2, 1903, American warships blocked sea lanes in both oceans with no less than ten ships, preventing Colombian reinforcements. Panama declared independence November 3 with a bloodless revolution, and the United States quickly recognized the new republic. November 6, Bunau-Varilla, as foreign minister of the new Republic of Panama, signed the treaty granting the United States the right to build the Panama Canal on essentially the same terms that Colombia's Senate had rejected in the negotiated Hay-Herran Treaty. Roosevelt later denied that he created a revolution by stating, "I simply lifted my foot off it." In a later Cabinet meeting, Secretary of War Elihu Root joked to the laughter of the Cabinet, "Mr. President you were accused of seduction...and proved that you were guilty of rape." However, nothing diminished Roosevelt's popularity at home and abroad.

HAVANA

After Estrada's December 1905 re-election in Cuba, a revolution was threatened by the opposition party led by Miguel Gomez, who had 15,000 men under arms opposing the small Rural Guard left from the American occupation under Gen. Leonard Wood. President Estrada requested American aid; then he and his supporters in the legislature resigned September 28, 1906. The next day two thousand U. S. Marines landed in Havana to restore order. During the occupation a standing army was formed, election reforms were accomplished and a system of guaranteed jobs to pacify the *elite* of Cuban society was instituted. By 1908 the Liberal Party under Miguel Gomez finally came to power with the U.S. government looking over his shoulder. Corruption continued to increase, resulting in political 'musical chairs'.

The ebb and flow of Caribbean politics only served to enhance Caleb and Tom as persons who had their feet firmly planted in both sides because of their history in the revolution, ties to the Garcia family, the Spalding banking connections, and the Roosevelt administration. By 1906 Tom had mostly left the sea and

ships to concentrate on the business end. He had married Graciela Garcia, the daughter of Rodrigo Garcia, his neighbor. She was
now a beautiful young woman of twenty with three years of private
school in Paris. Her eyes still mesmerized Tom. On the walls of his
office hung photographs of General Gomez signed, '*A mi amigo y
heroe de la revolution,*' of General Garcia saying simply, '*Bienvenido
a Cuba y gracias por todo.*' and of Teddy Roosevelt, and of course,
"Fighting Joe" Wheeler, along with the citations for his Navy and
Cuban decorations and a small box containing his Medal of Honor
with an accompanying letter from the President.

Scott was reading in his office when Graciela came in with the
housemaid and a little boy. "Tomas, this beautiful little boy is Maria's nephew from Banes. He is so smart. I want you to meet him."

Scott put his papers aside and smiled at his beautiful wife and
the little boy. "*Bien, muchacho.* What is your name?"

"I am Fulgencio Batista Zaldivar, Señor Scott," was the boy's
quick reply. Scott noticed his bright eyes and handsome face. He
was obviously of mixed blood, a mulatto, and probably the son of
poor plantation workers, but there was something else. There were
still people in the Banes area with Taino Indian blood. He figured
that must be it, a very nice combination.

Before Scott could say anything else, Graciela said, "*Querido,*
this boy is so smart, I would like to send him to private Quaker
School in Banes, *con tu permiso.*"

Scott could see she had made up her mind. He smiled, nodded his head and said, "I am happy to agree with you, *mi amor.*"
She gave him a hug and left happily chatting with Maria and the
boy. Scott returned to his papers. Twenty years later he would be
reminded of that meeting with *El Mulatto Lindo.*

World War I turned out to be a boom time for sugar in Cuba,
because the beet sugar industry in Europe was destroyed. It also
helped insulate them from the 1929 stock market crash and the
following depression. The Spaldings had foreseen the market dif-
ficulties and managed to get their favorite clients and friends out
early in order to pick up the pieces later. Obviously, that included
Caleb and Tom. However, the unanticipated passage of the Eigh-

teenth Amendment to the United States Constitution in 1918, prohibiting the sale of intoxicating liquors, came with both problems and opportunities in Cuba, and Caleb's fleet was ready. The world famous Cuban rum business had a problem next door in its biggest market, even with the increase in "alcohol tourism" in Cuba.

Caleb and Tom sat on the wide front porch of Caleb's Havana house, drinking Cuban rum, watching ships in the harbor, and discussing prohibition. "Tom, that fellow, Santo Trafficante, came to see me with a lucrative offer to use some of our ships to sneak rum into Tampa hidden under our sugar. He's supposed to be a big deal in Tampa with the Sicilian and the big Cuban communities and local politicians. He seems to have a lot of connections to sell rum all over the east coast. He's also known to be some kind of gangster, but he seems to be a gentleman. From what I hear he is not like most of the American gangsters trying to beat prohibition. I told him that we would have nothing to do with that character from Chicago, Alfonse Capone, or that same kind from New York, just in case he was thinking of dealing with them. And no drugs. What do you think?"

"Well, Uncle Caleb, we've always had very good "back door connections" with Washington. We could spoil it if we get caught violating American law, even if it's a stupid one. We can still sell sugar. Our investments in rum aren't that big."

"That's what I was thinking. I want you to go up to Tampa on our next sugar boat and look around, more like snoop around. See what the story is on Trafficante. You know all the people on the waterfront. Hopefully, that beautiful wife will turn you loose for a few days."

Tom smiled, "I'll work on it. Our baby is not due for four more months."

A week later Tom was back in Havana. "Uncle Caleb, Trafficante, *is* a big deal in the city. He controls the *bolita* games and in most other illegal activities he gets a piece. He seems to have pretty good connections with the politicians too, but we're dealing with the Feds here. This prohibition doesn't seem to have had much effect on drinking in the city, especially in Ybor City where the Sicilians and Cubans are heavy. On the waterfront they say there is very little enforcement, and the agents are usually on the take. That's for Trafficante to take care of. I think I could take a boat in there and unload in broad daylight, if the price is right."

Trafficante did make the price right, and they sent a lot of sugar covering barrels of rum for six months until a very quiet warning came from the backdoor of the U. S. Ambassador's office. Caleb was quick to react. "Tom, I just got that warning we've been watching for. I informed Trafficante that we would look for another way that did not involve our boats in U. S. waters, but he seems to want to work with some of the other characters still going into Tampa, Louisiana and Texas. We've been makin' a ton of money in this. Let the gangsters have *Havana Club* rum and any other nearby distilleries. They are probably going to water it down anyway, and they are too busy enjoying Havana to have any wish to travel to the other end of the island. Our connections have always been in Santiago de Cuba with the old premium rums, *Bacardi* and *Matusalem*. They've been around makin' good, smooth rum since the middle of the 1800s. Most of the rest of that crap tastes like moonshine. So, I want you to go to Nassau and see what's happening on Bay Street. I hear they are looking for good rum, and the British are laughing at this *no whiskey law.* I read where that English fellow, Winston Churchill, who used to be the First Lord of the Admiralty, even said, '*It is an affront to the whole history of mankind.*' Now that's funny. I guess he takes it personal since his mother is American. Hell, old man Bacardi is even advertising in New York for tourists to come down and bathe in Bacardi rum. Let's go sell rum to the British."

"Well, Uncle Caleb, you know we just had the baby while you were sending things to Tampa. Let me talk to Graciela since I won't be doing anything dangerous, and she does have relatives in the rum business in Santiago."

"Good, or as our late friend used to say, *BULLY!* How is my great nephew, Thomas Rodrigo Scott, doin'?"

"He's doin', as our late friend also used to say, "SPLENDID.""

Really sad that he didn't live to see the first time our Pacific Fleet passed through the Panama Canal. That was his dream for the Navy. At least he got to see it open in 1914 and the impact on the world, and we got on the inside with The Founders. I'll always appreciate his inviting us to the White House and the fact that he recognized me after all those years."

Caleb nodded his head then laughed. "Indeed, a remarkable man, but let's face it, Tom. You are becoming a legend in your own time." They both laughed at that.

NASSAU, BAHAMAS

During the "Roaring Twenties," Nassau was indeed roaring. *Rum-running,* the term applied to smuggling alcohol by water into the United States, was the thing of the day. The row of shacks along Bay Street, called "booze avenue," were doing a thriving business with representatives of companies selling Cognac, Champagne, Canadian, Irish and Scotch whiskey. They busily filled orders for the smugglers. A good smuggler could make $100,000.00 on one trip, up to 700% profit. This was the big party of the world's adventurers and scoundrels into which Tom Scott landed. Good Cuban rum was his product and he need to find a "runner." He was just going to sell rum, not violate American waters. On the water front, he was told to go to the old Lucerne Hotel on Frederick Street owned by the Lightbourn family, which seemed to be an unofficial bootleggers' headquarters. The front veranda was filled with an assortment of all types and nationalities mixed with reporters and writers gathering first hand material to weave their stories, both truth and fiction.

Tom went to the front desk and signed in as a representative of the "Good Cuban Rum Company." That did draw attention. His problem now was to sort the "good" smugglers from the "bad" smugglers. "Good" was defined as those who paid promptly. To Tom it seemed like a never ending drunk, sometimes orgy.

The first day he took the advice of the manager, an American nurse named Dorothy Donnelle, who previously worked at

an insane asylum, to just sit and listen. The second day she pointed out a big American drinking coffee. "That's Bill McCoy, a former boat-builder from near Daytona Beach and a gentleman. He
doesn't even drink. He just comes here to meet suppliers. They say
he doesn't cut his whiskey with water either. So, folks have taken to
calling his stuff ' *The Real McCoy*."

Tom smiled and said, "That's the man I need to meet. Please
introduce me."

Dorothy guided him across the loud room. "Bill, this is Captain Thomas MacDougall Scott from Cuba. He would like to talk
to you." Then she walked away, allowing them to talk.

McCoy waved Scott to a seat. "Cuba, eh? Fun place."

Tom took a seat. "Actually, Alabama, but my uncle, Caleb
MacDougall, and I have been working out of Havana since the
revolution. We have a dozen freighters trading all over the islands
down to South America and up the Gulf of Mexico. We represent the best distilleries in Cuba and other islands, but we are not
rum-runners. I understand you do not water down your cargo, nor
buy from anyone who does, nor deal with gangsters and crooked
politicians. Our customers will like that. They are proud of their
brands."

"That sounds interesting, young man. Dorothy already told me
about you. I understand you are already a captain of a ship in the
harbor."

"Yes, sir. Along with the sugar and tobacco, she also has half a
cargo of rum ready for your inspection."

"I like that, no screwing around and getting drunk. Let's go to
a quiet restaurant and talk." On the way out he slipped a $50 bill
to Dorothy. The restaurant was a small, open, wood building two
blocks off Bay Street named *Scott's Corner*. It served lobster, various species of fish, conch chowder, pigeon peas, rice with peppers,
cilantro and onions, and not much else, but it was quiet. Papayas
were for dessert and good digestion.

Tom smiled, "It smells like home. Great name."

"I thought you might like it. It's more of a native restaurant
away from Bay Street and the docks, too quiet for the restless souls

at the Lucerne. And the owner *is* named Scott. He's a native black man, and the food is good native food."

Tom laughed, "He's bound to be a cousin. We even have Scotts in the Cherokee Indian tribe."

McCoy laughed, "There are a lot of Scot names left here over the last 400 years by seamen and pirates. Now we have Scotsmen here representing the Scotch whiskey distilleries. In fact one is even named MacDougall, probably another relative of yours. He is tough but honest."

"Probably is another relative. All MacDougalls claim they are related. I see on the Bahamas coat of arms, *Expulsis Piratis Restituta Commercia.* Nowadays it looks like they have both pirates and commerce."

McCoy laughed again, "Right you are, but let me tell you how I operate. Bimini Island is just fifty miles due east of Miami. I used to sail right into Government Cut in Miami and unload, but the Feds closed that easy route. I just stay outside the three mile limit in international waters and let the smugglers come to me. Now everybody is doing it. It's called Rum Row, and it does get crowded and nasty out there. I mounted a machine gun on the bow just to keep those characters in line. You can see Rum Row all the way up the east coast. Tomorrow I will let my taster try your rum. Don't worry. This man is a devout Methodist. He doesn't even drink, and he spits it out after he tastes it. But he really knows taste."

With a dubious look Scott said, "This I have to see. Have you been at sea very long, Bill?"

"Well, my family has been to sea for generations. My brother and I used to build boats in Florida. We built some for Andrew Carnegie and the Vanderbilts. I served on the *Olivette.* She was in Havana when the *Maine* blew up. My father was in the Union Navy during the Civil War serving in the blockade of the South."

With the last statement Scott broke out in uncontrollable laughter. To McCoy's confused look he explained, "Wait until I tell my uncle! He was a fifteen-year-old-kid sailing with his uncles, running the Yankee blockade down to Cuba and Jamaica. I guess your father never caught him." More laughter from both of them.

"I look forward to taking a run out there with you when I come back with a full load." Tom related his brief history, including filibustering, *a message to Garcia,* the invasion at Santiago, the Panama Canal, and that he married Gen. Garcia's niece.

McCoy sat and looked at him for a minute. "No wonder you are a captain already. That is more than one lifetime of experience."

A rain squall blew in off the ocean and Tom stared at the rain in silence. "It does seem like another lifetime passed… but we're here to deal with you now. I guess we will find out if

"what's past is prologue." We've had enough of trying to deal with gangsters and revolutionaries in the Caribbean, and you can introduce me to this MacDougall kin. Also, I need to find another hotel away from that insane asylum at the Lucerne."

"Shakespeare's *The Tempest,* Act 2, Scene 1, '*what's past is prologue,*'" smiled McCoy.

Scott nodded. "I see you didn't waste all your time aboard ship."

McCoy smiled. "Tom, at the end of Bay Street is the old Colonial Hotel with 300 rooms. Henry Flagler spent some of his oil and railroad money to build it back in 1901. You will find it much quieter. I do."

Scott met Alastair MacDougall, who confirmed that they must be relatives. Then he sailed back to Cuba with a boatload of money from satisfied customers and a backup agent in MacDougall.

Two weeks later Tom was back with a full cargo of prime Cuban rum …and his uncle Caleb, who wanted to see this piece of history for himself.

Back at *Scott's Corner,* Caleb met Bill McCoy and Alastair MacDougall. "Aye, Caleb, I'm glad this Irishmen has led me to meet a long lost MacDougall."

Caleb smiled, "The pleasure would be all mine after two hundred years, Alastair, and I look forward to taking some good Scotch whiskey back to Cuba with me."

"And that pleasure would be all mine but only for a wee discount in the price." That sent laughs around the table. "Meanwhile, Nassau does have its distractions, which I would be delighted to show a MacDougall kinsman while these laddies do a bit of derring-do."

Tom was laughing and thinking, 'A *real* Scotsman, a WEE discount, indeed.'

The next day Tom sailed off to the Bimini Islands, approximately 105 nautical miles west, with McCoy and a boatload of prime Cuban rum. And Caleb went to enjoy "the distractions of Nassau" with his very distant relative.

A northeast wind blew down the deep *Northeast Providence Channel* past Nassau and across the *Tongue of the Ocean* until it ran into the shallower *Great Bahama Banks* north of Andros Island. On the edge of *The Banks* large waves built up as the deep blue water waves tried to enter the shallow green water of *The Banks*. It was only a few minutes of water over the bow until they crossed over onto the waters of *The Banks,* heading East Northeast to the Bimini Islands, about seventy nautical miles. They passed through the deep channel between Cat Cay and Gun Cay at the bottom of the Bimini chain, then out into the Gulf Stream and on to the *Rum Row* off Miami, but outside the three mile limit. Tom noted to McCoy, "You know, Bill, I can probably cut a lot of time off this trip if I just ride the Gulf Stream up to Bimini when I leave Santiago and enter the *Windward Passage* instead of going all the way over to Nassau. I can probably save both of us a lot of fuel too."

"Damn, Tom, nobody else has suggested that. You are absolutely right. The other whiskey is coming from Europe and has to go through Nassau. Have another cup of coffee and give me another suggestion."

The moon was bright reflecting off the deep water. The surface shattered as flying fish took flight across the surface when the boat's bow wave frightened them. Schools of Tuna could be seen migrating north like rivers in the flowing Gulf Stream. Tom thought about how much he missed this silent, wonderful world, but Graciela and his son were back in Cuba. He would have to make do with these occasional trips.

Before sunrise the lights of Miami Beach appeared in the distance. By exact calculation McCoy hove to at three miles offshore and a flock of small, fast boats appeared to unload the cargo. Two of McCoy's men manned the machine gun on the bow, just in case. Tom stood off to the side to see how the money was actually collected and how fast they could do it. A shout came from a crewman, "Boat coming fast astern!" The bow machinegun swiveled astern as bullets banged into the schooner. Tom ducked, wondering how crazy could these men be, or how desperate. The crew seemed to be well-trained for this. Several brought out rifles as the machine gun blasted away at the boat. It managed to get within fifty yards of the schooner. He could hear McCoy hollering, "Goddamned lunatics!" Tom could hear laughter on the other side of the boat from smugglers tied up for loading. Above his head he could see wooden rail blasted away by the 'lunatics.' "You OK, Scott? We can't lose you now."

"OK. Does that happen often?"

"Nah, just some characters who don't know better. They picked on the wrong boat. They won't do it again." Tom looked over the rail at the fast sinking small boat. No signs of life were visible.

The trip back to Nassau was uneventful, and Tom figured that he had seen enough. Three days later Tom and Caleb were back in Santiago to pick up more rum, and Caleb made his pilgrimage to the *Palacio de Oro,* satisfied that another no risk money-making scheme was in progress. Tom went back to the plantation.

The old wooden Colonial Hotel burned down in 1922, and McCoy was finally caught by the US Coast Guard, but in international waters, November 23, 1923. He received a six months sentence and retired to enjoy his wealth. Meanwhile, Alastair MacDougall continued to broker their rum in Nassau until prohibition ended in 1933. It was a very, very profitable time.

While Scott and his uncle Caleb were insulated from the economic and political problems by their ships and *business* in Nassau, things were changing in Cuba. The back and forth of volatile politics had caused several "incidents" where U.S. battleships and marines intervened to restore order and protect American interests. Riding the sugar boom, Alfredo Zayas was elected President, with subsequent rampant corruption. Resistance to Zayas' regime brought a former cattle thief, Gerardo Machado, to power, with the support of Zayas. Machado was reelected with attendant election fraud, and student and labor unrest increasing. In 1933 President Franklin D. Roosevelt sent his representative to mediate, with a little background from Uncle Caleb and Tom, who continued to be in the background as *unofficial* information sources. Things started turning against Machado, and he left with seven bags of gold to Nassau.

In the years following the 1929 crash and depression, Caleb and Tom picked up a lot of property in the Miami area at bargain prices to complement their shipping business. This included a home in Coral Gables where Tom and Graciela could escape the politics of Cuba, establish a residence, and put Thomas Rodrigo in high school. They were now really in both worlds, and Tom became active in the Democratic Party. Their always open "back door" swung wider.

ORIENTE PROVINCE

At the far eastern end of the island among the waving fields of sugarcane and far away from the turmoil in Havana, the Scott plantation continued to grow and sell, through ups and downs in the price of sugar. In fact, in some of the downs Tom had been able to buy more land. The Cuban overseer managed the operation when the Scotts were in Coral Gables.

One day, a field worker rushed up to the main house to announce that an airplane had landed on the Scott's small dirt landing strip. Tom and Graciela went to the front door in time to see two men in Cuban Army uniform approaching, and their housemaid, Maria, following them. Tom muttered, "What the hell is this about?"

Graciela suddenly recognized one of the men. "Tomás, it is Maria's nephew, Fulgencio Batista."

They had received letters occasionally thanking them for his better education and kindness, and informing them about his position as a stenographer for a colonel and his increases in rank, but they had not seen him since he was eight years old. They knew Maria had gone to Banes for her sister's funeral.

"Señora Graciela, it is my nephew Fulgencio. He is all grown up and an important man in the Army. He was at his mother's funeral and let me fly home in the airplane." Her eyes were still wide with amazement.

Graciela rushed out to give him a big Cuban *abrazo*. "*Bienvenido, bienvenido!* Please come in."

Tom walked out smiling to shake his hand and be introduced to his pilot. "Well, this is a surprise. Do come in and tell us what is happening to our country. My uncle Caleb tries to stay at sea and away from Havana these days. We only get half stories from newspapers in Santiago and Miami."

Batista smiled his handsome smile. He appeared to have developed into a very good-looking man of thirty-two years, deserving the label of *El Mulato Lindo*. "Don Tomás, it has been too long. Many things are happening, but I am happy to be back in this quiet world with wonderful people away from Havana and politics." Upon seeing Tom's fourteen-year-old son in the background, he said, "Who is this magnificent young man? I bet it is Thomas Rodrigo Scott by the descriptions in my aunt's letters. *Mucho gusto, muchacho.*"

Young Scott managed to respond politely, "*Es mi placer, Señor.*"

Over a pleasant country Cuban meal and premium rum, Batista began to reveal the events in Havana, again thanking them for giving him a head start from his humble beginnings. "As you know I was able to become secretary to a colonel as a sergeant. In that assignment I was able to sit in on top level meetings. What you learn being quiet in the background as a stenographer is very amazing. I was even able to study a little law. When Machado left for Havana with his bags of gold, Manuel Cespede became president with support of the *elite* white officer corps, if you will pardon me, who decided to protect themselves by prohibiting sergeants from becoming junior officers unless they graduated from the Military Academy. As a former enlisted man, I am sure you can understand how we sergeants accepted that. So, because I had much experience at the high levels of the Army, the other sergeants followed me in what they now call "*the sergeants revolt*" with the workers and student support. We supported Carlos Mendieta, the U.S. favorite. Then President Roosevelt eliminated the Platt Amendment, but not their economic influence. So, that is where we are. Nothing is settled and these politicians are crazy. However, Señora, this meal was wonderful. I would love to stay here in this quiet end of Cuba and away from Havana, but I am now a colonel and head of the Army. I have to go protect the interest of my men and the people of Cuba. Please permit me to escape here again sometime." With that *El Mulato Lindo* flew back into the boiling cauldron of Cuban politics.

After a five-man ruling group dissolved, Batista met with students and other groups and used the influence of the Army to form a new government with a former member of the group of five as president, Professor Ramón Grau San Martín. His "leftist" actions were not supported by the United States, who refused to recognize the government. This led to installing Carlos Mendieta, the U.S. favorite. After a succession of politicians, and with Batista and the Army doing a lot of good public works in the background, a new constitution was written and a now popular Fulgencio Batista was elected president in a free election in 1940. His military support of the Allies during WW II increased Batista's backing by the U.S. until he retired to Daytona Beach, Florida, in 1945...for the next eight years.

CHAPTER 7

INDOCHINA 1944

Frank Tan sat near the open door of the U. S. Army C-47 (Dakota) transport aircraft, watching the green jungle slide beneath him and marveling at the depth of color and the extraordinary blue of the sky. This was such a contrast to the smoky, crowed streets of Shanghai and Kunming. It all looked so peaceful down there, but he knew that Japanese eyes somewhere had to be turned up watching for the direction of his flight. They had been flying for three hours now and changed direction three times to confuse those eyes. The droning, sometimes throbbing, sound of the twin 1,200 hp. 14 cylinder, radial, Pratt & Whitney engines alternately lulled him to sleep and alarmed him. The C-47 had a wide wing span of 95 feet on 64 feet of fuselage, giving the appearance of a large bird simply gliding high on air currents. With a range of 2,125 miles carrying 6,000 lbs. of cargo at a maximum 234 mph, it and the C-46 had been the workhorses of the China-Burma-India Air Force, hauling supplies over the Himalaya "hump" into China when the Japanese closed the land route. It had dropped the American 82nd and 101st and British 6th Airborne Divisions over Normandy and was considered the most dependable cargo plane in the world.

Frank's parachute harness was beginning to chafe and his limbs were becoming numb from lack of circulation, causing him to stand up in the plane and stretch. He hated that. It always created a feeling of dread that he might fall out of the airplane before he hooked his parachute static line to the cable inside. He looked around at all the bundles to be kicked out with him, mostly radio communications gear for his mission with guerilla groups to report on Japanese movements and weather. He hoped none of it would land on him.

Frank was a young Chinese American from Boston whose father had sent him to China for the university education made difficult for young Chinese in America. Then the Japanese had come and eliminated any chance to complete it there. He had been recruited by the Office of Strategic Services, which would become the forerunner of both the Central Intelligence Agency and the Army's Special Forces. The OSS had been created in 1942 as an intelligence gathering arm of the U. S. military, which also served as a behind the enemy lines cadre for indigenous resistance groups in all theaters of war. Although he didn't speak any of the many languages spoken in the large area designated as Indochina, he was oriental and many of the guerillas spoke Mandarin Chinese. That was enough to get by in the areas not tightly controlled by the Japanese. He would soon master Vietnamese.

As light was beginning to fade the plane made its final turn and the green light next to the door blinked on, indicating "go." There was no hesitating. The jump master already had his foot firmly planted against Frank's backside and now gave an 'assist.' For a moment he hung in midair with the roar of the big piston engines in his ears, then the wind snatched him sideways and the tail wing of the plane seemed to part his hair as it swept by. The proximity of the door to the tail wing always gave the jumper the feeling that he was going to be decapitated as he exited the plane. The hazard was real enough that the Army added length to the static line in order to open the 'chute a little later. 'Damn, I'll never get used to that feeling,' he thought. He looked up as his 'chute popped open, and he could see other 'chutes beginning to deploy with his equipment.

They had dropped him at 500 feet to minimize detection and exposure, rendering his reserve 'chute a useless impediment. At this altitude by the time you realized the main wasn't open, it was too late for the reserve. The light was fading and the triple canopy rainforest below appeared dark.

The trees came up fast and suddenly he was tumbling through branches until his 'chute finally snagged on a large limb, leaving him dangling fifteen feet above the ground. "So now is the time I'm supposed to pop my reserve and climb down it," he mumbled to himself, "Damn, what am I doing here?" For the moment he was content to just hang there and recover what was left of his senses, at least no one was shooting at him. Or were they? He could see movement in the undergrowth about thirty yards away where a small wiry figure with a goatee was emerging. He walked to a spot under Frank, looked up and said in perfect English, "Ah, Mister Tan, we have been expecting you. My name is Ho Chi Minh." And so began Frank Tan's war effort for his country.

Ho's efforts had come to the attention of American officers after his little group had safely delivered a downed American pilot back to China. Ho was in need of help for his own struggle against the Japanese, and he calculated that the Americans looked like the best place to get it. They were big and had no colonial aspirations like the British and the French. In addition, France had already surrendered to the Nazis and the French Vichy government had been cooperating with the occupying Japanese to the extent that they had run the country as before, except now for the benefit of the Japanese instead of France. The native Vietnamese still had no say.

In spite of the Vichy collaboration, French loyalists had been providing valuable intelligence to the allies. This had prompted the Japanese to crack down on the resident French by launching a *coup d'etat* and ending over a century of French rule to the extent that intelligence sources were drying up. In Ho's words, *"Thus, the French imperialist wolf was finally devoured by the Japanese fascist hyena."* The Allies badly needed new intelligence sources, and this was the opportune time in which Ho arrived on the scene offering his help.

Knowledge of Ho's communist leaning was known, but Russia was also an ally against the Axis powers and those philosophical differences would have to wait until this common fight was over. Even Mao Zedong's Red Army was receiving aid from the OSS to fight the Japanese. Intelligence was needed and assistance for any pilots lost over the area. The same was already being done in Europe against the Nazis, by British and OSS operatives. Consequently, Frank Tan and many others were recruited for these dangerous and secret missions behind enemy lines.

At this moment Frank was being pushed to his physical limits in their race to get out of the area and put distance between themselves and any Japanese who had seen the American plane. Frank wondered how the skinny old man called Ho could keep up the pace that seemed to be killing him. But Ho kept pushing and encouraging Frank to exceed to the point where he thought he could go no more. The OSS hadn't prepared him for this. 'I'm just a radio operator, not a Ranger,' he thought. But his mission was to offer more military assistance, if Ho proved valuable, and that is what he ultimately did as the intelligence poured in to Headquarters. More support in the form of supplies, arms and military advisors arrived.

Once in camp with the guerillas, Frank had time to observe this motley group of peasant farmers and intellectuals. Here was Ho Chi Minh, a true believer in his cause, serving as the intellectual and spiritual leader of promised Vietnamese independence.

Ho was born in 1890 as Nguyen Sinh Cung, the son of a Confucian scholar, teacher and civil servant in the Vietnamese Imperial Palace. He received a French style education and went on to teach school. He was fluent in Vietnamese, French, English and several dialects of Chinese. He was also known to speak Thai, German, Spanish and Russian. He had lived in the United States in Boston and New York, where he was employed in menial jobs in 1912-1913, and again in 1915. He later worked in and around London for several years. But his real activist life started in France where he joined the Communist Party in its early stages and changed his name to Ho Chi Minh. Roughly translated it means, "The one who enlightens." He moved back and forth between Russia and China making himself known as "the man" in Asia, and lecturing on revolutionary movements in Indochina until returning to Vietnam to lead the independence movement in 1941. Now he was battling the Japanese before he could get back to independence.

And there was the neatly dressed school teacher, Vo Nguyen Giap, who would later become Vietnam's most famous general, learning his new trade as he fought first the French, then the Japanese, then the French again, and finally the Americans. Vo Nguyen Giap was born circa 1912 in a province near where Ho Chi Minh had been born, and attended the same French school. He obtained a bachelor's degree in political economy and a law degree from the University of Hanoi. In the 1930s he taught history, worked as a journalist and founded a French language newspaper, *La Travail,* espousing communism and independence. He escaped into exile when France outlawed communism, but the French captured, tortured and executed his wife, father and sister-in-law. Now he was back in Vietnam to fight for independence with his idol, Ho.

Much of this background had been provided by the OSS, but the one who raised Frank's curiosity the most was a young boy they called François. He looked much more European than oriental. It turned out that he was the son of a second generation French planter from near Saigon. His mother was half Vietnamese and half Chinese.

François de Rousseau had the obligatory French education and visits with relatives in France, but had taken a different turn and gone to a university in Spain instead of France. This break in tradition had obviously caused some family dispute, but he prevailed and a little different perspective was added. Spain was still in the throes of its long smoldering and underlying socialist resentment of the fascist regime of General Francisco Franco. Of course, the usual university intrigues existed for students to imagine reforming the world. He was only eighteen when war in Europe erupted, and to escape being in the middle of it he returned to Vietnam. The Indochina planter's world seemed so remote and untouchable by the insanity of Nazism. Although Japan was already invading China, they hoped that Vietnam would somehow escape.

When war did come, the French had already surrendered. Now with the French Vichy government collaborating with the Japanese, the colonialist clung to the hope that life would go on. François, still inflamed by his antifascist feelings, refused to stay on the plantation and left with some of his idealistic friends to join resistance groups in the hills and jungles. The leap from socialism to Ho's nationalist brand of communism was an irresistible siren's call, preached by a master.

François related his mixed ancestry in a tale of commercial

family connections. His grandmother had come from Hainan Island in China across the Gulf of Tonkin as a young girl with her father, Fong, to establish trading connections in Vietnam. The most amazing part of the story was her cousin "Charlie" Soong was taken to America by missionaries to study in a missionary school, which later would become Duke University. He was later to return to China to become a very wealthy man printing bibles. He fathered three boys and three girls. All were educated in American universities; daughters E-ling and Ching-ling at Wesleyan in Macon, Georgia, May-ling at Wellesley in the Boston area and the oldest brother, T.K., at Harvard. Frank had taken notice of that fact. All Boston Chinese had known that Madame Chiang had gone to school at nearby Wellesley. The real surprise was that Ching-ling had married Sun Yet Sen, the Chinese hero of independence, who had cooperated with Mao Tse-dung and the Communist party until his death in 1925. May-ling became the wife of Chiang Kai-shek, then the current leader of Nationalist China. The oldest daughter, Ai-ling, was the manager of the Soong fortune and married to the former Treasurer of China. T.K. was now Treasurer and happened to be the Chinese official responsible for funding the American Volunteer Group (AVG) while they were known as The Flying Tigers and part of the Chinese Air Force. This incredible connection to the sources of power in China had led some scholars to sarcastically refer to them as "The Soong Dynasty." While Frank knew the strong emphasis Chinese placed on family connections, this was the ultimate in relations. 'But here is François associated with Communist leaning rebels known to be friends with Mao Tse-dung and the Chinese Red Army, implacable enemies of the Nationalist Chinese. A puzzle we won't have to worry about until the Japs are gone,' Frank thought to himself. The Chinese puzzle was compounded more by Ching-ling taking sides with Mao, upon the death of Sun Yat Sen, against her sister and Chang Kai-shek's Nationalist Party.

Over the many jungle nights, the long tortured history of Indochina was related to Frank by these men who would become significant parts of its history.

Vietnam had been dominated or ruled by its giant neighbor, China, for more than two thousand years and its population derived, according to anthropologists, from the original Chinese 20,000 years before.

Taking advantage of a weak and divided Chinese government, the French had claimed it along with Cambodia and Laos as an associated colony by driving out the Chinese in the mid 1800's. It had been in this colonial status since, but the Japanese now controlled it. There always seemed to be someone suppressing independence. The French took on a facade of teaching their little brothers civilization while preparing them to rule themselves, of course, within the French sphere of influence. Meanwhile they ruled with an iron hand, and all the wealth of Indochina flowed out of the colony for the benefit of France.

Ho's small group had now expanded its influence among other guerilla groups, thanks to the added assistance given Ho by the Americans. Ho related his famous story of receiving an autographed photograph and a dozen Colt 45 pistols from the legendary General Claire Chenault of the 'Flying Tigers,' which gave an enormous boost to his prestige. He had distributed those pistols to other guerrilla leaders to increase their prestige through him. He was controlling the flow of arms into the guerillas and became the undisputed leader of the scattered resistance groups.

Rescue of pilots continued to be a source of goodwill for the Americans. Fighter planes, transports and observation planes crashed all over Vietnam, and Ho's group was able to coordinate the rescue of many who survived the crash.

The OSS had now provided a medic for assistance to the group. Ho had been very ill for a long time and the medic had been trying to nurse him back to health. He had said to Frank, "This guy has every disease known to man. He's already had tuberculosis, now he has dysentery and several types of fever. I don't even know what all he has. All I can do is keep dosing him with antibiotics and Sulphur and hope. He's one tough old bird." And sure enough, Ho recovered again.

The medic also treated the downed flyers brought in, including one transport pilot from the China-Burma group flying from Burma in the airlift known as "the Hump." He had been carried in on a litter with a nasty cut on the head and some fever thrown in for good measure. He was babbling in what seemed to be Spanish. The words had been too fast for Ho to catch, so he called in François.

The pilot turned out to be a twenty-five year old, half Cuban, American named Thomas Rodrigo Scott, Captain, U. S. Army Air Corps. His C-46 had been chased by enemy planes and forced off course, then caught in a storm before he ran out of gas. He was a long way from where he was heading. The American medic was now becoming an expert with fevers, using penicillin, sulphur and magic local remedies. With the fever subsiding, Scott reverted to his native English.

Fascinated with this American pilot speaking Spanish, François spent many hours practicing the language he hadn't used for the last few years and listening to tales of Florida and Cuba. TR, as he was called, lamely tried the French his mother made him learn and his wife insisted he practice, but his "R's" always came off the end of his tongue, as in Spanish, not the back of his throat, as in French. François handled both equally well, and also spoke Vietnamese. Pronunciation notwithstanding, they had a good time remembering their own exploits in Paris and Madrid.

Scott's first name, Thomas, was from his father and his middle name from his Cuban grandfather. He explained that his Cuban mother really wanted to name him Tomas, not Thomas, but his father objected. They settled for a Cuban middle name, Rodrigo, her father. His father called him TR by his initials and from his admiration of Teddy Roosevelt, but his mother called him Tomasito. It seems in time of stress and illness, and intoxication, Spanish seemed to take over. François had thought this a strange phenomenon but assumed somehow his mother's side exercised the strongest influence on his psyche. Another oddity was that Scott appeared to sense when enemy action was about to occur, though not exactly where.

Scott had been carried up trails on the Laos border where Japanese penetration was not likely and into the base camp. The glorified paths would later be known as the Ho Chi Minh Trail in the Second Indochina War against the Americans and South Vietnamese. Scott was now well enough to travel up to China, but he started to get that strange feeling of enemy action about to happen. Ho had acknowledged that he had seen this sort of sixth sense thing with men in war and took special interest. This time he also felt that they had been safe too long with too many radio messages being transmitted. He sent extra lookouts higher up in the hills.

Apparently, the Japanese had been triangulating on the radio signals from different directions and had narrowed the search area but not the exact spot of the camp. Runners came with news that a force of maybe one hundred had crossed the small river five miles away. Ho had called Giap and his OSS advisor to organize an ambush. The enemy would probably send out scouts and then attack at night. It was unfortunate to lose the camp, but they would make the enemy pay dearly. The plan would be to get as much equipment out as possible and leave small fires burning and the appearance of an occupied camp. Unfortunately, one radio operator would have to stay and continuously send signals for them to detect. One of the men who had no knowledge of radio had been selected to just tap out meaningless signals. The Japanese would just think it was some kind of code. Some rifles would have to be stacked in plain view and straw men built to resemble sleeping sentries, thus giving the appearance of complete surprise on an unsuspecting camp. The operator was given one hope in the form of a deep hole to dive in when the attack started and wait it out. Scott was issued a rifle and assigned a place from which to fire. Mortars were taken to locations where they had previously been sighted with dummy non-exploding rounds in the event the Japanese attacked. Excitement was building among the men, and the hill tribesmen among the group were counting what ghastly trophies they would take.

The guerrillas withdrew as darkness fell. Sentries melted into the jungle gloom and would never be seen by the enemy. These were tribal men of these mountains, who were part of the landscape themselves. Night or day made no difference to them. They would send signals by imitating sounds of the night, birds and insects.

Scott crouched behind a large boulder with François in the darkness watching the fires die down in the camp. His hands had made his rifle slippery with sweat. He had been in combat before, but it was almost impersonal even when he could occasionally see the opponent's face from his cockpit. Being on the ground with no airspeed or space in which to turn or roll was not an advantageous place to be, as far as he was concerned. Still, the thrill of close combat caused that familiar faster beat of his heart and the aviator's calmness so necessary to fly a plane in combat.

He remembered his father's stories of bullets whistling by and the death surrounding him with canon shells bursting and the numbness and then the pain. The Cuban revolution had seemed so real as he had listened, but this *was* real. Could he fight on the ground like in the air was the question. He hadn't been able to fight back while flying those slow transports, just trying to evade the fire aimed at his aircraft.

But he had had his dogfights in the Philippines with overmatched old fighters against the newer, more agile Japanese Zeros. The Japanese had been coming in overwhelming strength and MacArthur was trying to hold out with no support from Washington. Europe was the area of most importance to them. Scott had been on patrol when he saw four Jap Zeros attack a Navy torpedo boat that didn't have a chance with its light armament. He was high enough that they couldn't see him. So, he timed his dive onto the line they formed as they began to strafe the boat. They never saw him coming and he knocked down two on the first pass and a third one as he banked away. Unfortunately, the forth was on him before he could twist away, damaging his engine and filling his fuselage with holes. The sudden slowing of engine speed and Scott's "throwing on the brakes" with his flaps caused the Zero to overshoot just enough for him to loose a final string of shells with enough hits to cause the pilot to lose interest and leave the scene. The resulting splash down felt a little better. The PT boat guys were very, very happy to take him aboard. At the Navy's insistence he was awarded the Silver Star. They had demanded the Medal of Honor, but the Army objected. They called it a stupidly brave thing to do, and it lost a valuable and irreplaceable plane at that point in the war. What the Army was thinking was it lost a plane to save a stupid wooden speedboat for the Navy. Scott was promptly grounded as an excess pilot without a plane to fly. As the Philippines fell to the Japanese, he was sent to China to fly transports. His commanding officer had put an angry notation in his file to keep him out of fighters the rest of the war, in spite of his obvious ability in combat.

Scott now started to get that sensation somewhere in his brain that something was about to happen. It wasn't a visceral feeling, nor a shot of adrenalin to his system, just some sort of clarity and alertness that he could not focus into a vision. Now, the man next to him noticeably stiffened. He had heard something different that Scott couldn't differentiate from the jungle noise, probably a signal. It was past two in the morning and even from his spot he had heard the radio operator start sending signals again with continuous *dit dah dit*, sounds clearly audible in the night air. A flash of gunfire, then a continuous fusillade of fire enveloped the camp. The radio shed collapsed and signals halted. "Poor guy" he thought out loud.

With unintelligible screams the enemy rushed into the camp, firing, waving swords and bayonets, confident that they had caught the ignorant peasants asleep. As the first officer cut off the head of a straw sentry, his realization was too late. A barrage of mortar shells was in the air zeroed in on his sword. The officer in turn was beheaded by shrapnel, which flew in all directions causing the guerillas to duck for cover even at a distance. Scott was transfixed by the scene and had to be shoved on by François when the attack on the enemy commenced. He ran screaming with the rest into the smoke and fire, pulling the trigger as fast as he could eject shells from the old bolt action rifle he had been given, but only pointing, not aiming, in the direction of any figure that popped up in front of him. The thought crossed his mind that this was not the way he had been taught to shoot, but the sheer volume of fire seemed to cut the enemy down, and bullets did sing and buzz by him. Some Japanese appeared to surrender but were immediately cut down with machete-like knives. Obviously, no prisoners were to be taken. Some tribesmen could be seen in the firelight cutting off ears of the dead or whatever trophy they deemed appropriate.

Suddenly, there was that eerie quiet while his ears were still ringing and his feeling numbed. The smell of smoke and gunpowder and death overwhelmed his senses. "Jesus, this is what Papa was trying to describe," he thought to himself. He collapsed onto a log, having lost all strength in his knees, hardly noticing that the end of the log was still burning. François just stood by and smiled at his friend's condition, reminding him that the log was on fire.

Some comic relief occurred when the ruins of the radio hut began to shake. With all guns trained on the shaking palm thatch, out popped the head of the radio operator with a big grin of crooked teeth, causing a great deal of laughter all around. When the first firing started he had dived for his hole and kicked out the hut center pole to collapse the shack on top of him and been lucky enough that no mortar rounds fell too close.

The next few days were spent moving deeper into the mountains for a secure camp, but the Japanese seemed to have lost their appetite for any more deep incursions into guerrilla territory. Consequently, the guerrillas moved closer to them to keep up accurate intelligence reports. Scott took part in several more skirmishes before he was escorted back up the long jungle trails to China. He said his goodbyes in Spanish to François and hoped he would see him again after the war. The two friends gave each other a good Cuban *abrazo* and the traditional French kiss on both cheeks. "*Hasta luego, mi amigo,*" from TR, and "*Bon voyage et bonne chance, mon ami,*" from François. To Ho, Giap, and the OSS team, he gave his eternal thanks for his rescue. He promised to have his father contact Frank's father through the Spalding's Boston connections to convey that he was fine and doing a most honorable service for his country.

Frank Tan stayed with Ho and his group as they sent intelligence and harassed the Japanese until they abandoned Vietnam. In the power vacuum following the surrender and before President Truman succumbed to French pressure, Ho organized a provisional government and took charge. He forced the Japanese supported puppet, Emperor Bao Dai, to recognize his government. He even modeled his inauguration speech after the Declaration of Independence, of which he had demonstrated an amazing prior knowledge to the OSS team.

Ever the spellbinder, in Ho's "Appeal to the people" he said in part:

> "The decisive hour in the destiny of our people has struck. Let us stand up with all our strength to liberate ourselves!
>
> Many oppressed peoples the world over are vying with each other in the march to win back their independence. We cannot allow ourselves to lag behind. Forward! Forward! Under the banner of the Vietminh Front, move forward courageously!" and for the last time in history signed his name Nguyen Ai Quoc.

Unfortunately for Ho and his followers, units of the Nationalist Chinese Army under Chang Kai-shek arrived, ostensibly to accept the Japanese surrender. Now they once again faced the prospect of being occupied by their historical nemesis, the Chinese. Truman, unlike Roosevelt, was more interested in assuaging Charles de Gaul and the French than assisting independence movements in the backwaters of Asia. Roosevelt had once said that the "French have milked Indochina for one hundred years and that is enough." But beset with huge postwar problems, Truman needed the French more, and acquiesced to their reoccupation of Indochina in spite of pleas from Americans on the ground there.

The trek through the mountains and rain forest had lasted five days before Scott reached the Chinese border and was escorted on to Kunming by members of the OSS network. Kunming, China was now the Headquarters of the U.S. 14th Air Force, with Claire Chenault in charge as a Major General. Chenault's famed American Volunteer Group of the Chinese Air Force, known as the 'Flying Tigers' had now been absorbed into the 14th as the 23rd Fighter Group, and their Walt Disney designed insignia of a tiger with wings flying through a "V" was adopted by the 14th as its own.

General Chenault had made it a point to greet each pilot returned from Indochina by Ho's group and send his note of appreciation. After some scrubbing and new clothes Scott reported to the general.

"Well, Scott, you're not looking much worse for wear. How's my old friend Ho?"

"Still giving the Japanese hell, general. He certainly has my everlasting thanks."

"Lots of downed pilots feel that way. Hope everything turns out for him, but the damned French will probably come back in after we've saved their asses in Europe. That colonial mentality just seems to never go away."

"No, sir. Most of the men and boys in the groups I met all had horror stories of torture and death in their family by the French, but that's not to say they don't do a lot themselves. It's pretty primitive out there. I saw some gruesome stuff with the Japanese and the Vietnamese," Scott said with his head down while remembering some of the things he had seen.

"Well, this war is almost over. The Japs are on the run and the supply lines are opening up for us. It looks like you won't have to fly "the Hump" anymore. What do you think you want to do now? I've read your file. Looks like you were a pretty good fighter pilot before you got assigned to transports. Anybody who could knock down three zeros and smoke a fourth by himself could have flown with my "Tigers" any time. But it looks like you really pissed off your CO by the notes I see here, in spite of what the Navy said."

Scott related the Philippines story, and the general thought for a minute. "I know how he felt, actually. In our early days with the American Volunteer Group in the Chinese Air Force, we had precious few planes to fight the Japs with, and they were hard to come by. The Brits were getting everything Washington could produce before Pearl Harbor. We had the old versions of the P-40 like you had in the Philippines and a bunch of crazy pilots like you who would jump on anything. Of course, having a $500 bounty per Jap plane did give them some excessive incentive," the general explained, with a very large grin on his face.

Then with great relish he went on to explain how he had taught his men out of the Japanese flying and staff manuals, emphasizing acrobatics, and that the kill ratio for the AVG was 14 to 1, while the British pilots accustomed to fighting the Germans in Europe were lucky to get a 1 to 4 against the Japanese, even flying the superior Spitfires. No one ever described Chenault as a modest person.

"Tell you what, Scott. We got a couple of new P-51Ds in. They're tearin' up the Germans over Europe, and we're tryin' to get some pilots to fly 'em. Want to take a crack at it?"

Scott was struck by lightning. Here was the chance he thought was forever lost. He could only stammer, "I...I..."

Chenault didn't give him a chance to finish, "I thought you might. Report to Major Dickinson in the 23rd hanger. Dismissed!" With that he returned to his paperwork and didn't look up again.

My god, I have died and gone to heaven, thought Scott as he walked across the runways leading to the famed Fighter Squadron 23, formerly the AVG Flying Tigers.

The North American P-51 Mustang was considered as the most effective, famous and beautiful fighter aircraft of WW II, and designed to fulfill British requirements in the early days of the war. Unfortunately, the British found the performance lacking in that power decreased dramatically above 12,000 feet, which was a significant problem in air-to-air combat. The solution was to replace the engine with a 12 cylinder Rolls Royce Merlin engine with 1,430 horse power mounting six 12.77 mm machine guns in the wings and a 360-degree-view bubble canopy. The new model P-51D had an even more powerful 1,695-HP Packard Merlin which could fly at 437 mph and reach an altitude of 41,900 feet with a range of 1,300 miles. It carried two 1,000 lb. bombs or six 127mm rockets. Now, here was an incomparable fighter plane.

On the way he passed a squadron of P-38s, the twin engine, twin fuselage fighter which laid claim to one of its squadrons having shot down Japan's most famous admiral, Isoroku Yamamoto, the mastermind of the attack on Pearl Harbor. He shuddered looking at them. Even if they were fast and rugged and had more firepower and carried more bombs, anything that you had to turn upside down when it was crippled in order to bail out he wanted no part of. He remembered the stories that the Japanese actually preferred to fight the P-38 squadrons which had come from fighting the Germans and Italians.

He walked past rows of bombers and his old C-46 transports, which could carry more cargo than the more famous C-47, to the squadron awarded the honor of the first hanger in line, the 23rd Fighter Squadron, the old American Volunteer Group (AVG) better known as the "Flying Tigers." As he approached he could see one of the new P-51s being rolled out of the hanger. Love at first sight! Guiding the movements was a short muscular man with jet black hair and tech sergeant stripes on his sleeve. Scott thought for a moment that he may be Puerto Rican, *until he spoke*. "Cuban to the core," he exclaimed. "*Oye, sargento, como estas!*" he yelled out using the more familiar second person tense common for Cubans regardless of how long they have known you.

The sergeant turned abruptly at the sound of a Cuban voice way out here in China. He squinted at the fast approaching figure until he could see the twin silver bars of a captain on the collar of the shirt. He instinctively came to attention and saluted while wondering how some Cuban had become an officer in the Army. "Bien, Capitan, Sargento Juan Echeverria a su servicio," he replied automatically in Spanish before he caught himself. "Pardon me, sir, I don't hear much Spanish out here, especially a Cuban accent. You got me by surprise."

Technical Sergeant Echeverria had been a mechanic in what constituted the very small Cuban air force in 1943 and been able to join the U. S. Army Air Corps based on his knowledge of airplanes. He was good and the Army had sent him to school for the new P-51s. Somehow they thought his Spanish would be helpful in the Philippines, but he ended up in China with the new fighters. He was from Havana and had worked in his father's car repair shop as a teenager before joining the Cuban Air Force.

Scott explained his Cuban heritage, and the son of a mechanic and the son of a wealthy landowner, businessman, and banker made each other alternately happy then homesick talking about places they knew and family left behind, starting an unlikely friendship in the most unlikely place in the world that would last for the rest of their lives.

Major Dickinson was an old AVG pilot who wasn't thrilled about turning over this new fighter to a former transport pilot, regardless of what the boss said. But the boss was now the commanding general, and he knew when Chenault said something, he meant it. So he would see what this guy could do. Thus commenced the re-education of Thomas Rodrigo Scott as a fighter pilot.

It seemed like yesterday that he was soaring over the Philippines, but this plane had power and speed and maneuverability and gun sights and instruments that he never even dreamed of, so much so, that he had to hold himself back lest it get away from him in the beginning. By the end of a week's training on the ground and in mock dogfights in the air, the major confessed to Chenault, "OK. I admit. The guy is one of the most natural stick and rudder men I've ever seen. Let's put him out there."

"Thought so," the general grunted.

With Sgt. Echeverria as his crew chief, Capt. T. R. Scott was back in the fight. There were now five P-51s and they flew together in a nontraditional formation protecting bombers flying over the remaining areas occupied by Japan. After some initial skirmishes, the Japanese preferred not to fight this new plane with its pilots schooled in Japanese tactics by Chenault.

It was now into the Spring of 1945, and enemy planes were fewer as Japan's sphere of influence continued to shrink. It was rumored that Germany would surrender any day, and more materiel and supplies were being shifted to the Pacific Theater. But Scott could still "smell" Japs when they were around. At least that was what the other pilots called his uncanny ability to sense enemy action. Unfortunately, it hadn't helped him score more than one kill. This day as they returned from a patrol, Scott's premonition kept drawing him to his right, so much so that he asked permission to fly out of formation in that direction, but still in sight. It had been a boring patrol and the Major decided, "Why not?" Everybody had accepted that he may really have a nose for it.

On the edge of visual contact, he could feel it stronger. Down low to his right he could make out shapes moving above the ground. He transmitted one word back, "Contact." Nothing else was needed.

He had come across a flight of five enemy bombers trying to sneak in an attack on allied supply depots. They were escorted on top by six Zeros.

With the high flying P-51s, they were far above the enemy flight and angling to come out of the sun. Major Dickinson smiled to himself and spoke into his mike. "OK, Scott. You're the only hotshot here who hasn't gotten to be an Ace. You want first crack at 'em?"

"If it pleases your highness, I would be most honored to send some sons of Nippon to hell," Scott retorted.

"Screw you! Go get 'em! Flight, Scott's in the lead. Follow him. Cover your wingman."

Scott rolled into his dive and took aim at the rear bomber knowing that the Zeros would soon see them coming out of the sun and scatter to take up the fight with their tight turns back onto the flight. The following P-51s spread out of the line to protect any quick Zero attacks from the side or behind while the two lead planes concentrated on the bombers.

Scott's heart began to race as the adrenalin started to pump into his system. "Steady, calm, watch," he told himself. Memories of that day in the Philippines rushed back. He could hear Dickinson's calm voice, "Try to knock down a Zero before they break, then rake your fire from the back bomber toward the front. Don't chase the nips 'til you finish your run, then bank right fast and cover the planes behind you. I'll be on your left doing the same thing."

As the Mustangs screamed out of the sun in their powerful dives with all 12 cylinders maxing out that 1,600+ HP, Scott was thinking, "What a difference this plane is from those old P-40s in the Philippines and what the AVG had. This is one magnificent machine. Just don't overshoot. Just line the turkeys up like before." And he did.

POST WORLD WAR II

The Germans surrendered unconditionally on May 7, 1945 in Rheims, France. Now the heat was on the Japanese, who were forced in desperation to turn to suicide "kamikaze" attacks with the few pilots left. Things were quieting down in China and the atomic bombs in Hiroshima and Nagasaki that August 7th and 9th ended the war before invasion of the main islands was necessary. MacArthur and the Navy got the glory of that surrender onboard the battleship *USS Missouri* and the 14th Air Force prepared to go home.

Enough senior officers had convinced Scott that there would be too many pilots after the war for any future in the military, and his father was insistent that he come home and help with the businesses. So, he figured, "My days of glory are at an end. Back to the farm or the bank or shipping or stock brokerage or real estate. Oh, hell, I think I'll go to law school."

And to law school he went at the University of Miami, right down the street from where he attended high school. He had wanted to go back to the University of Florida, where he had played halfback on the football team, joined ROTC and had a hell of a good time, but his father insisted that he stay closer to home in Miami where he could also work part time and watch out for the family interests there. He also had a wife, Margaret, who he met while visiting Florida State College for Women later known as Florida State University in Tallahassee. Margaret Futrell had been a debutante from Jacksonville's Riverside part of town, studying education and French, and, of course, immediately blended into Coral Gables society. She had absolutely captivated him with her looks and manners, so different from the wilder Cuban girls he preferred and the overly protected ones he admired from a distance. They were married when he graduated and within a year had a son, Thomas MacDougall Scott II. However, WWII storm clouds had been gathering, and his ROTC commission had obligations. Besides that, he had some pretty strong military heritage to live up to between his father and grandfather Rodrigo Garcia.

The concessions he wrangled from Old Tom were the purchase of two new crop dusting planes, a six passenger twin engine Beechcraft and hiring his old crew chief, Juan Echeverria, to maintain and fly them. After all, there were over 2,000 acres in south Dade County that they had purchased for farming before the war, and they had to fly back and forth from Cuba. It was a legitimate expense, and it would help to keep TR's more rambunctious side occupied, at least when he wasn't back in Cuba enjoying the night clubs: Tropicana, San Souci or the Luna Azul. Old Tom had already decided that it wouldn't be a bad idea to have a lawyer in the family; considering all the blood money he had to pay lawyers to keep all the operations functioning and out of trouble. Another compromise was that TR should be both a Florida and a Cuban lawyer. This obviously required taking courses at the Havana Law School also. Nothing could have pleased TR more.

Remembering the demand for sugar and vegetables in Cuba during World War I, and as storm clouds gathered over Europe in 1939, Tom had bought a few thousand acres of farm land in Homestead, a small farming town south of Miami. True to history, this proved an extremely profitable venture and continued to be so after the war. However, the two Art Deco hotels in south Miami Beach he had purchased in the 1930s were taken over by the military during World War II and were only now beginning to recover. The land he bought along the river in downtown Miami was becoming very valuable, and, as Commodore Ralph Munroe had predicted, Coconut Grove on the other side of the river was a dream area for homes, so close to downtown yet far enough. The vast and varied Scott enterprises were becoming a management problem, even with TR as a lawyer in Cuba and Florida, and Tom's younger brother managing things in Miami. Compounding the problem, unrest was spreading against Fulgencio Batista's regime, both in the countryside and mountains, as well as in the cities. While these were separate groups with different aspirations, they were spreading Batista's incompetent and corrupt army very thin, and creating confusion. The possibility existed that one group may be able to unite or subjugate the others into one force. Which is not exactly what happened, but the result was the same.

With the backdrop of these storm clouds in Cuba, TR had continued to enjoy the insulated existence of the very wealthy in Cuba and fly back and forth from Coral Gables society to Havana's country clubs and back streets. After all, Cuba had always had revolutions and the "presidents" always took their portions and let business continue as usual. He had even managed to buy two scrapped P-51s and spare parts from the military airplane 'graveyard' in Arizona. It seems Sergeant Echeverria had served with the manager of the facility, and with an ample supply of good Cuban rum had been able to pick the best of the lot, including weapons. Their mock dogfights over the tomato fields in Homestead became legendary.

In the summer of 1958, the world of the Scott family was about to turn on its side, if not upside down.

CHAPTER 8

CUBA 1958

Havana twitched with excitement, fear and anticipation in the spring of 1958. Walls all over the city were painted in scrawling letters of "*no mas,*" "*vaya Batista,*" and "*basta bombardes,*" usually splashed in bright red paint. Signs of random explosions from homemade bombs could be seen, and trash blew down the streets. But Havana being Havana, casinos were thriving. The Tropicana and Sans Souci night clubs and mob controlled casinos were in full swing and the pretty young girls still leaned from the doorways speaking in low husky tones, "*pssst, Americano, venga por aca.* I show you good time."

The corrupt and disorganized regime of Fulgencio Batista was falling apart from the inside. Guerilla groups were in the mountains far from Havana, but an assortment of unconnected revolutionary groups, including the Communist Party, were always just below the city's surface, using even the slightest opportunity to disrupt the regime in any manner possible. Diverse, far outnumbered and scattered armed paramilitary groups mostly, but not all, under the leadership of a former exile, Fidel Castro, were causing the poorly disciplined Batista army to chase all over the countryside after them. The army set up ineffective, nuisance roadblocks manned by ill trained and unmotivated soldiers who preferred to extort money from passing motorists simply by waving guns and wearing ill-fitting uniforms.

That all this had happened before in the musical chairs of Cuban politics was the general feeling in the air. Business would go on as usual, and the government officials would get their piece. And so it seemed to Thomas MacDougal Scott II, now called Tommy, and his young Cuban friends and visiting college classmates. Cuba was still paradise and Havana the center of the world.

Tommy's father, Thomas Rodrigo Scott, now called TR, (pronounced Teh Erre in Spanish) was in his favorite clubs drinking with entertainers, movie stars, lawyers, politicians, business associates, judges and sometimes American gangsters; dancing with the girls; playing his trumpet along with the band in the wild and expressive manner needed in Cuban music (the perfect outlet for his Cuban soul), and enjoying the lifestyle of the very upper class. His wife had learned to stay in Coral Gables most of the time when TR was in Havana. This was Cuba and would always be so, at least for the rich. After all, the United States had always backed Batista.

Tommy had split his time between Coral Gables and Cuba all his life, except for a year of prep school in Paris. At the time, his mother was a high school French teacher at Coral Gables High, and his grandmother had spent several years in college in Paris, and she loved her French. So, off to France he went to be totally immersed in French and play soccer. In Cuba he was close to native, but not like his father with the mesmerizing Garcia eyes.

He had taken his friends from Miami and the University of Florida to Cuba many times before. He had even obtained a pilot's license for the smaller plane the company owned, making the trip from Miami to Havana in a little more than two hours.

Tommy had been, like his father, a track and football star at Coral Gables High when they won the State Championship, and with a little 'pull' had received a scholarship to Florida, like his father. Needless to say, Old Tom was a substantial "booster" of the university. But an injury to Tommy's shoulder canceled his football career. So, he ran track, *very fast*, and joined his father's fraternity and ROTC, where he excelled. The Army ROTC faculty had him scheduled for top leadership in the cadet regiment. ROTC was required of all male freshmen and sophomores under the Morrill Land Grant Act. However, the last two years were optional. If elected, there was a mandatory military obligation, and Tommy had so elected, just like TR.

TR had joined the Florida National Guard (FNG) after WW II and was now a Lt. Col. and on the list for Colonel. With substantial family political connections and with his WW II experience and multiple decorations he had been able to become the pilot for the FNG commanding general. As a result, Tommy had joined "The Guard" to gain time in service before he was on active duty as a "last lieutenant" from ROTC. The difference in pay from "less than two years" and "over four years" service was almost double. TR regarded this as a little advance planning. Tommy was able to enter the FNG several months before graduation from high school.

The weekly meetings of the FNG were sometimes "credited" as ROTC participation, and the annual two weeks of summer camp were not a scheduling problem. FNG basic training at Camp Blanding, FL, for three weeks had qualified him as "trained." With a 'little influence' he was even allowed to attend airborne school at Ft. Benning, GA. Even though no airborne units were authorized in the FNG at that time, he was allowed to wear his parachutist wings.

On this trip to Cuba, Tommy had brought with him Jacob Stern, a high school and college friend, along with three Cuban classmates: Enrique Gonzalez, Eduardo and Carlos Hernandez; and two fraternity brothers. Jacob's father was a Jewish doctor who had escaped the Nazis during WW II and made it to the United States. However, his uncle Abraham, also a doctor, had only managed to be smuggled later into Cuba from the Bahamas. Other parts of the family had ended up in Bolivia, a world away from the lifestyle of Havana. This was the first time Jacob was able to visit his uncle in Cuba. Abraham Stern was now a successful doctor living in the well-to-do Vedado section of Havana near the Scott's Havana townhome. The families were only slightly acquainted, and solely because of Dr. Stern's excellent reputation as a doctor.

After having worn out the usual Havana amusements of the nights at casinos, night clubs, dance halls for 25 cents a dance (until after midnight) and girls on the streets; and in the day beaches, sight-seeing and the *cervecerias* (beer breweries) all accomplished in TR's white '58 Cadillac convertible at 70 kilometers per hour down the Malecon along Havana Bay, the little group was now ready to hit the road. Their destination was Tommy's grandparents' plantation in Oriente on the east end of the island, much to the objections and pleadings of the Stern family to stay longer and avoid the long trip through a very unsettled countryside.

Eduardo and Carlos were the sons of a tobacco grower in Pinar del Rio on the west end of Cuba, whose uncle was also a doctor in Vedado. He was gratefully utilized for precautionary medicine by all the boys after too much night-time activity on the streets of Havana, even though the large hypodermic needle wielded with a flourish by the grinning, mustachioed uncle was not a pleasant experience.

Enrique was the son of a sugar merchant who dealt with Don Tomas, the honorary title given to Old Tom, the *Heroe* of the Cuban Revolution. All of them were students and friends at the University of Florida. It was the summer break before their junior year at the university, and the world was wonderful.

In the morning the boys started the long trip eastward along narrow two lane roads alongside small mountains and between fields of tall sugar cane and cattle farms. But Enrique knew some very good hostels along the way with good food, rum and pretty girls. He drove a family car which was kept in Havana, with Tommy and Jacob as passengers. Eduardo drove one of his uncle's cars, with his brother Carlos and the two fraternity brothers.

Graciela Garcia Scott had not lost her mystery and spirit in spite of now being a grandmother. Villagers whispered *bruja* (witch) when her name was mentioned, but very softly. It was more a feeling of awe and uneasiness in very superstitious Cuba. Some were even afraid to look into her eyes for fear she could look into their soul. But her husband and her family were true heroes of the Revolution, and they treated their workers well. United Fruit, which acquired almost 300,000 acres surrounding the family land grants after the Revolution in 1899, allowed their workers to squander money on cockfights and rum and shift for themselves in the hard times after planting and harvesting of the sugar crop. Old Tom would not allow those activities on his land. He even set aside 200 acres to be farmed by his workers for food in the off seasons and required small savings to be withheld in banks for difficult times.

He also leased an additional 5,000 acres from United Fruit for a total of 30,000 acres in the rich soil of Oriente Province, including the land Graciela had inherited from her own family.

TR had definitely inherited those piercing eyes from his mother and grandfather Rodrigo, and tendencies to feel things others could not. But this was seemingly lost in Havana's nights and the release of his Cuban soul, then covered up in polite Coral Gables society.

All these elements were mixed into Tommy and blended with the simple genius of a down-to-earth, yet worldly, Alabama farm boy grandfather. The complexity of these elements always caused a conflict of emotions and directions for him. However, this night, Tommy and his friends had found, with Enrique's instructions, a great roadside hostel just east of Camaguey, which had all they ever wanted for a night.

El Paraiso was a plain one story stucco building painted in white with gold trim and the typical hand-made Cuban red barrel tile roof. The paint and the hand painted sign in front proclaiming *"Bienvenidos a Paraiso"* were the only things distinguishing it from the assorted farm buildings and houses set back from the road along the way. When customers pulled up, they were indeed greeted to paradise by the large welcoming grin of the owner/proprietor, Alejandro, with a matching enormous girth and a large, black, bushy moustache.

The inside was brightly lighted by kerosene lamps, well vented by adjacent open windows, because there was no electricity on this stretch of road. The brightness showed evidence that the owner kept his place clean. Wooden tables and chairs, which must have been hand-made in some nearby farm house, were scattered around the room in no particular arrangement. The bar was made from large split timbers and polished shiny with coconut oil. This gave a pleasant, sweet smell, while serving to also create a somewhat waterproof surface to spilled drinks.

If the lamps didn't shine bright enough, the smiles of young country girls at the bar seemed to make the place feel like a full moon was inside the room. They were dressed in loose prints of various patterns. This made Tommy think of the brightly colored flour sack material his grandmother always gave to her workers, and it probably was. The dresses were loosely fitting yet still revealed firm young curves. Their long, black, hair hung well-combed, down their bare backs, natural and clean, not like the girls in Havana trying to imitate the latest hair fashions.

The effect of the scene even had Tommy gaping along with his friends. Enrique stood to one side smiling broadly and thoroughly enjoying his coup. "Enough, *caballeros y senoritas,* I am hungry and thirsty," he laughingly exclaimed in breaking the spell lingering over the boys. "Alejandro, *lechon, frijoles negros con arroz blanco, y platanos maduros y mucha Hatuey* (young pig, black beans with white rice, ripe plantains in cane sugar syrup, and a lot of beer.)

Hatuey beer was named after a Taino Indian *Cacique* or chief who was acclaimed as the first leader of the rebellion against the Spanish. He became a legend for telling the Spanish priest that he did not want to go the heaven, because there were Spaniards there. They promptly burned Hatuey at the stake and into legend in 1512.

As rounds of *Hatuey* continued to come, steaming mounds of *lechon* appeared on large wooden platters with all the side dishes and Cuban style bread that was mashed flat on the grill and smothered with butter and fresh garlic.

At some point during all this, a guitar-playing singer had appeared at the corner of the bar and began to sing **Guantanamera,** the song that had come to symbolize Cuba. It still brings a sense of melancholy and longing for Cuba. Credited to a radio announcer, Joseito Fernandez, circa 1929 and written about a country girl from the Guantanamo area of Cuba with words adopted from *Los Versos Sencillos* (Simple Versos) by poet and independence hero José Martí. The simple tune easily lends itself to verses made up by local musicians who want to tell a story. The original verses are usually picked up by those interested in words instead of feeling, but the haunting chorus of **Guantanamera...guajira Guantanamera,... gujira Guantanamera** is always picked up by everyone in the room and continues in their brain over and over for hours or days after.

This night, true to form, everyone joined in the chorus loudly or softly as the guitarist picked up or slowed down the beat and the verses. But Enrique insisted that tonight everyone learn at least the first original Martí verse:

Guantanamera, guajira Guantanamera...
Yo soy un hombre sincero
De donde crece la palma
Y antes de morirme quiero
Echar mis versos del alma.
Guantanamera, guajira Guantanamera...

For the non-Spanish speaking friends he translated:
Guantanamera, (*girl of Guantanamo*)
guajira Guantanamera (*country girl of Guantanamo*)
I am a sincere man
From where the Palm grows
And before I die, I want
To emit verses from the soul.
... Guantanamera, guajira Guantanmera

The term *guajira* was generally used to denote a country person, deriving from a term used to name a remote peninsula of land.

Tommy sat taking in the happy scene, too full of Hatuey and fresh country cooking to even want to move. One of the girls had "chosen" him and now relaxed with her head on his shoulder. Her long hair hung almost to his wrist with the fresh, country smell of her hair enhancing his senses. Gradually, he became aware of a sensation or vision that he could not see, but he could hear his grandmother Graciela. "I must be really *boracho* (drunk) to hear my grandmother in here. I need to go out in the night air," he thought to himself.

He mumbled something to the effect that he needed to see the *bano* (bathroom) and headed for the door. No one bothered to even look up as he left. Outside he found the hand water pump and water-trough, reminders that people still passed by in wagons and on horses the same as they had for centuries. He splashed water over his face and stared at an incredibly clear sky, so full of stars that he almost felt among them. Nowhere in Miami could you find a sky this clear and peaceful except halfway to the Bahamas on a sailboat, always looking east.

"That's better," he said aloud to no one. But the voice came back, He shook his head and pumped more water over it, but the vision only became more clear. "Que pasa?" he said to the sky. "*Abuelita,* (little grandmother) you cannot be here." A voice softly came back, "But I am here for only a moment. I want you to enjoy yourself and take care of danger ahead." The vision faded, leaving him to wonder what it could be.

"It's only the Hatuey." he reasoned to himself and dismissed it as that. "We have to switch to good Cuban rum."

TR, in anticipation of what was going to occur, had given Tommy $300 and a bottle of premium *Matusalem* rum with a wink and told him to make sure his friends had a good time. *Matusalem* was a classic rum of Cuba distilled in Santiago since 1862 by the Alvarez family, whose younger members were long-time friends of TR, and business associates of Old Tom. It was made by the Spanish system used to make brandy. The larger and slightly older rum distiller, *Barcardi,* was also in Santiago, but TR had a few disagreements with members of that family. So, *Matusalem* it was around the Scott household.

Upon reentering the *Paraiso,* Tommy produced with great fanfare the bottle of the top of the line *Matusalem,* while holding it high and shouting in French "*La piece de resistanc*e," meaning in this situation the final and best part of the meal. It was just enough for one shot for everyone, including the inn keeper and guitar player. After which, all retired to rooms in the back of the bar with the nice cold showers provided by the windmill in the yard, plain but clean and room enough for two. *Buenas noches*!

Morning dawned with a cooling rain and gave everyone an excuse to stay in bed another hour, in spite of the racket of crowing roosters and cackling hens in the yard. Fresh eggs, fried *lechon,* black beans, fried plantains and fresh Cuban coffee made a whole new world.

It was more than 170 miles to the old colonial city of Santiago where Enrique's parents lived. Tommy had been there many times to relive the American invasion with his grandfather and climbed the cliffs overlooking the troops' landing site in 1898. He wanted to show this and tell the story of his grandfather's medal again to his friends. Mayarí, the town where his grandparents lived, would be a short drive north through more sugarcane land.

They had left the large cattle ranches of Camaguey behind and drove into more rolling land and trees. They could see mountains off to the right and the towering Sierra Maestra Mountains farther to the east. They passed through Bayamo, the town which had been part of Fidel Castro's disastrous plan to attack the Army's Moncada barracks in Santiago five years previously. It cost most of his men their lives and put him and his brother in prison, then exile to Mexico.

As their cars rounded a bend in the road, a soldier stepped to the edge of the road signaling them to stop. They could see a small camp set back into a clearing with probably five soldiers lounging about, a 2 1/2 ton army truck, obviously US Army surplus, and a small house with a radio antenna.

Enrique muttered a curse under his breath, "*Coño, los hijos de putas,*" and slid his hand under the seat and around a pistol hidden there.

It was one of the Batista army roadblocks. They were looking for young revolutionaries, and that is exactly what this group looked like.

The soldier approached the car cautiously with his M1 Garand .30 cal. rifle, another part of US assistance, pointing at Enrique. Things happened very fast after that.

The soldier demanded to know who they were, where they were going and proof. He continued to approach the driver's window until he could see inside. Enrique started to move his pistol hand, causing Tommy to say, "No, Enrique!" The soldier caught sight of the pistol and raised his rifle to Enrique's face in the car. In one quick motion Enrique shoved the rifle up into the roof of the car, fired directly into the face of the soldier and jerked the rifle out of his hands. The rifle had discharged into the car and out of its roof just over Tommy's head. The discharge of a .30 caliber round that close inside a car caused immediate shock and loss of hearing to Tommy. Shock was hardly the word to describe the reaction of Jacob in the back seat, who sat unable to move or even to emotionally react.

Enrique was already out of the car and firing at the next soldier running toward the car. Over his shoulder, he was shouting to Tommy to pick up the rifle and shoot. Tommy's ears were ringing, the explosion had numbed his senses and no sound seemed to be coming from Enrique's mouth. It only took another moment for Tommy to see the obvious. There was not going to be a good ending to this, if he didn't do something quickly.

He threw himself out the door and behind the engine compartment of the car. No one had to tell him what to do with an M1 rifle. For two years in ROTC and the Florida National Guard he had been marching with it, cleaning it and firing it. His automatic reaction surprised him, but did not cause any hesitation. He aimed at a third soldier, shot him, then a fourth.

Enrique had grabbed a rifle from the second soldier he shot and dashed behind trees continuing to fire at soldiers who were now coming from the building. There were definitely more than five here.

Tommy looked in the back seat. Jacob had somewhat recovered and was lying on the floor. He shouted at him to take the rifle and fire while he dashed to recover another from the first soldier he shot. Jacob was also in ROTC and the M1 felt comforting in his hands. It seemed to bring him out of shock and into the fight.

On seeing and hearing the events in front of him, Eduardo had thrown the car into rapid reverse back down the road. He assumed everyone would be killed by all the soldiers and headed, shaking, back to somewhere, anywhere, hoping no soldiers had paid attention to the second car, which had not yet reached the roadblock.

Enrique continued firing from the trees and Jacob kept firing from behind the car. Tommy had run across the clearing to the left side, picked up two more rifles and was now firing from that side. The road block soldiers were now convinced that they were under full attack by a large group of guerillas from the mountains. Seven soldiers were now on the ground and two were running for the trees in the back of the clearing.

Tommy ran into the building, but all the soldiers had run outside and fallen except the two running for the woods. More shots came from Enrique and Jacob and one of the soldiers fell. Tommy yelled in Spanish to stop firing.

Enrique ran up shouting "Why didn't you shoot the last one."

Starting to calm down, Tommy's reply was, "Let him go. He's just going to say a whole guerilla army ambushed them. He'll never know what happened. He's not going to stop running for an hour, and sure won't admit three young guys did all this." Saying that, he fired three quick shots into the trees just to keep him running.

No longer able to hold his rifle up and out of bullets, Jacob had collapsed on the ground behind the car in nervous exhaustion. He managed to shout that he was OK.

It seemed strange to Tommy, but he was calm and already discussing what to do next. Someone must have heard the firing and reported it, but everything was very, very quiet now. They went in the building and found an old US Army radio. The soldier in the woods had run so quickly that he had not even turned it on.

The boys returned to the car only to find it full of holes and inoperable. The other car was nowhere in sight, and they guessed it must be halfway back to Havana with the other boys thinking they were all dead. Only one thing to do, they decided. Take off the license plate, take the truck and get out of there. Enrique knew some back roads and farmers about ten miles further down the road. There were canned food supplies, water and one heck of a lot of US Army C-Rations, some dating back to the Korean War, but edible.

Enrique had been quiet for a few minutes. He began in a firm voice, "Fidel can use all this ammo and supplies, and even the radio. We need to get it to him."

"What's this 'we' business," piped up Jacob. "We're not guerillas. We need to get the hell out of here before anyone comes."

With that, Enrique launched into his patriotic revolutionary speech. They had heard it before, but only considered it bluster and vicarious wishing. This was different, and he was adamant.

"Whatever, we have to get out of here. If carrying supplies to anybody, even farmers, will help us get to where we need to go, fine. Let's go." was the only answer Tommy could think of to get everyone moving.

It was now afternoon. The brief gun battle had only taken ten minutes, but it seemed like hours to them. It had taken another hour to load as much food, weapons (including .45 cal. pistols, M1 rifles and a .30 cal. light machine gun), ammunition, rations, radio and whatever they could find, into the truck. The bodies had to be hidden in the trees and dirt thrown over blood stains. The bullet riddled car was pushed off the road and down a dirt track behind the building. On a casual glance it looked like an abandoned roadblock. No passersby would be interested in inspecting an army roadblock for fear they might return.

They had been lucky no one had been on the road. They hoped the possibility that the sound of shots, if heard this far out in the countryside, were taken as another waste of ammunition by Batista's drunken soldiers.

Tommy was still amazed at how easily he had shot these men, and all were kill shots. He felt it should not have been that easy mentally, but it was shoot or die.

"Did anybody find a key to the truck?" Enrique suddenly thought to ask.

"The army $2^{1/2}$ ton REO truck doesn't have a key, just an off/on switch. I've driven lots of them in the National Guard. No problem, but we need some uniforms to pass for soldiers driving on the road." Tommy assured them.

"Oh, God! This is getting worse." Jacob moaned, thinking of the bloodstained uniforms on the soldiers they had dragged into the trees. He was still not sure whether he had actually killed someone. He had hoped not, but his subconscious kept assuring him that he did well in a do-or-die situation.

"Good idea! There are some clean ones in the building," Enrique agreed. Jacob's stomach got a little less queasy.

The truck had fortunately come equipped with a standard olive drab canvas top and curtain across the back causing the entire cargo bed to be concealed. Tommy drove and Enrique rode in the front seat in order to speak with anyone who stopped the truck. Jacob was hidden in the back, gripping an M1 and sweating profusely, both from fear and the tropical heat.

They continued on that way for ten miles with only an occasional civilian car passing them. Tommy waved and smiled at the passing cars. No problem. The land was relatively flat and slightly rolling. They were still in sugarcane fields, but the towering *Sierra Maestra* Mountains were looming closer. They seemed to jump up from the land, unlike the Smoky Mountains, where his family had a summer home in North Carolina, which gradually rose to 6,684 feet. Tommy mused on the geography of how there were no lines of rolling hills before the mountains. From his geography class at the university he remembered it to be called the *fall line*. However, Cuba had been formed by the violent fusion of three large islands in a more recent geologic time. The result was a primarily flat island with three mountain ranges from the *Sierra del Escrambray* in the south-central region, the *Sierra Maestra* running eastward across the southeast region with its highest peak (Pico Turquino) at 6,580 feet, tapering off to join the *Sierra Cristal* rising from the coast on the eastern tip of the island to 4,300 feet. The appearance of these mountain ranges from a long narrow island in the middle of a deep blue sea was dramatic. These same mountains that now harbored Fidel Castro's guerrilla bands had for centuries concealed uprisings, all the way back to *Hatuey*. On the extreme western end of the island, a lower and different chain, the *Cordillera de Guaniguanico,* had been formed by a collapsing limestone dome, which created fantastic caves previously inhabited by ancient Indian peoples.

Tommy's thought was broken by Enrique's shout, "Alla! Turn on that dirt road *a la derecha* (to the right)." His conversation was becoming more mixed in Spanish the more excited he became.

They continued down the dirt road kicking up a cloud of red dust through cane fields, passing small houses of peasant farmers, and into a valley entering the mountains. Coffee fields began to appear as the elevation increased and occasionally a farmer was seen working the fields. Tommy suspected there were more who preferred to be unseen by this army truck driving fast through the countryside.

"OK, stop. I need to walk from here. This truck will frighten my friends. We need to take off these uniforms." Enrique was half out of the truck before he finished.

Jacob asked what was happening through the canvas, and Tommy told him to take off the uniform and come out. "Thank God." was the reply.

The two boys stood by the truck looking down the road shaded by trees on either side. Light was beginning to fade now and no Enrique. He had disappeared 200 yards down the road and around a bend. They began to consider whether to go back down the road and abandon the truck with hopes of getting a ride from a passing car or farmer in a truck. Every possibility seemed as bad as the previous one. They decided to take two rifles and hide in the trees to see what would happen. Just as they were moving to the side of the road, they could hear faint voices carried by the wind and saw movement down the road.

Enrique shouted to let them know who it was. "This is my friend, Aurelio. He can help us to find Fidel and hide the truck." No one had stopped to think of what to do with a 2-1/2 ton army truck full of supplies and weapons. No one knew how far they could or had to go into the mountains.

Supper with Aurelio was a hot bowl of chicken soup with beans and fresh coffee from his fields prepared by his wife and cans of fruit cocktail from the C-Ration boxes. Tommy showed them how to use the small folded metal opener in the package, familiarly referred to by American soldiers as a "P 38." Small children sat in dark corners eating the sweet fruit cocktail treat as fast as they could and giggling at the sight of these strange men in their house.

Aurelio showed them a place farther down the road, away from his small house. It was more of a trail which they crashed through with the big truck to a small clearing overhung by trees and relatively invisible from the road and the air. A cool light rain had started to fall reminding the boys that they had come up to a higher altitude. The canvas truck top and sleeping bags, more US Army surplus, were very welcome items.

Aurelio promised to get word to any guerillas in the area and left on his horse. Unknown to the boys he had already sent his oldest son to advise a nearby guerilla camp. Exhaustion and sleep took hold, and it never occurred to them to post a guard, if they even cared.

They were now over 1,000 feet elevation and morning streamed cool and damp through the corners of the back canvas, a surprise from the steaming heat on the flat land. An assortment of bird calls and fluttering wings seemed to welcome them to a new life. Suddenly they stopped.

Tommy immediately sat up listening intently and trying to look through cracks in the canvas. No doubt something had just happened. Jacob hadn't stirred and Enrique turned over and opened one eye, vaguely aware that Tommy was alert and peering outside. Tommy held a finger to his lips to signal quiet. Both boys moved quietly to pick up their rifles and lay flat behind the steel tailgate. Obviously, someone was out there. The question was whether the army had found them or the guerillas thought they were an army patrol. Neither possibility was a pleasant thought with good consequences.

The silence seemed to last forever. Finally, there was no alternative but to yell, "Quien es?" (who are you?) Another long silence passed. Jacob was now awake with his eyes wide, sickening at the thought of another firefight coming. Finally, a voice in Spanish came back from somewhere, but the direction was obscured by the trees. "Come out without your guns and hold up your hands, or we will start to shoot."

There definitely didn't seem to be any alternative, whoever they were. Very slowly they pulled aside the canvas with their hands clearly showing no guns. The rising sun now poured through the trees, temporarily blinding them as they climbed down the back of the truck. Extreme anxiety was now setting in.

Shadows began to move and ragged looking men with beards emerged from all sides. Tommy's first thought was they may be just bandits. They did not look like any organized guerilla force. Fortunately, he thought, he wasn't wearing the army uniform he had used on the road.

One of the men appeared to be the leader and asked, "Who is Enrique, the friend of Aurelio?" The boys' relief was immediate, but left Tommy wondering, "What the hell happens now?"

What happened now was they were accepted as fellow revolutionaries when Aurelio confirmed the story.

They had to move deeper and higher into the *Sierra Mardre* quickly. The cargo had been roughly inventoried to the amazement of the guerillas. They decided to drive the truck as high as the narrow roads would allow, and then hide it. Local peasants could use carts and horses at night to carry the cargo to various sites. Ammunition was the most important, then food. Weapons were last, because most were already in the hands of the guerillas from operatives in the cities and captures from the army. By this time Castro even had five captured machine guns, but maintenance was a problem. Tommy's National Guard experience was going to be very valuable. Castro had also captured a jeep in a raid of a local garrison, which he drove rapidly all over the mountains coordinating his units.

The boys were corrected to say *guerilleros,* meaning the men and women who fight and the term 'guerilla' meaning the 'little war' itself.

It was June 1958 and Castro's band of *guerilleros* had grown to almost three hundred with recruits from the countryside coming in. His problems were now other revolutionary groups acting separately in the cities and trying to become established in the *Escambry* Mountains closer to Havana. One failed assassination had been attempted on Batista in his palace, which practically destroyed one group in Havana. The Cuban communist organization was staying clear of armed revolution and would not back Fidel or his methods. They still considered him just another opportunist with no convictions. However, his brother Raul had been a member of the communist party for several years, and Che was a true believer. They did receive support and recruits from the communists in their separate units.

Additionally, Batista had decided to crush Castro, once and for all. Until now he had considered Castro as a minor irritation in the mountains at the far end of the island. However, newspaper articles in the *New York Times* written by a reporter smuggled up to meet Fidel had created a Robin Hood image, much to the aggravation and embarrassment of Batista, who had already boasted that Fidel was dead. This summer he was sending ten thousand soldiers to finish the nuisance. This was the time Tommy and his two friends arrived deep in the *Sierra Maestre,* before the army push had started.

Two days later, Fidel arrived back at his headquarters and discovered the three boys and the supplies. "*Coño,* these three *muchacos* have captured more supplies at one time than all my units," he exclaimed with a little exaggeration. He had heard of the fire fight at the road block, but until now didn't understand who or what had happened. He was relieved to know it was not a rival revolutionary movement.

"Now, *muchachos,* you must tell me everything. Who are you? How did you attack the road block? I have done many foolish things, but that seems a little crazy for civilians to do, even to *me.*"

For a man with so much going on, Fidel seemed to have an endless capacity to listen, as well as his proverbial ability to talk for hours. Enrique started the explanations of the action, but when he mentioned that Tommy had National Guard training and both he and Jacob were in ROTC and their family connections in Cuba, he raised his eyes and turned his piercing gaze on the two *Americanos.* "I know of both your families. Don Tomas Scott is one of our Cuban heroes and Dr. Stern is a very reputable physician. They must be concerned as to your fate. I want to know more of your military training."

Enrique explained that Aurelio had sent someone to Santiago to tell their parents they were safe in the mountains.

"SAFE?" Fidel's voice boomed, "You see these ragged men

and poor conditions? We are bombed and strafed by Batista's air force every day with planes, bombs and bullets provided by the Americans. We can see them. We have photographs of them being transferred in the U. S. Navy base in Guantanamo. Now, they are surrounding us with thousands of soldiers, but that is nothing to us. We have the high ground and the conviction of right!" This gave him another excuse to launch into an impromptu revolutionary speech. Over the next couple of months innumerable versions would be heard. Almost beneath the surface, his plans for land reform and social restructure of Cuba's entire society began to emerge. That had been a primary source of loyalty among the peasant population. This loyalty provided food, intelligence and recruits for the revolution.

It was a mesmerizing moment for the boys, who were now renamed as Quique, (pronounced *Kee kay* and diminutive for Enrique), Tomas (Spanish for Thomas) and Chake (Spanish has no sound for 'J' only the 'ch' as in 'change'), or for short, *Los Tres Amigos*. Fidel's reputation did not do justice to his spontaneous and spellbinding oratory. He was now all of thirty-one years old and seemingly indefatigable.

The boys were kept in the headquarters area, rapidly moving as it was, until some use could be determined based on their capabilities. They were now completely immersed in the guerilla mindset. Everything appeared crude and temporary, like the ragged men themselves. At these elevations, temperatures were close to freezing at night. That, and frequent rain, made it extraordinary that these men had survived these conditions for two years and were still fighting. The *tres amigos* were very, very glad to have their captured water-proof ponchos and sleeping bags from the roadblock. For this, they were thankful for American aid to Batista.

Fidel had returned from an inspection of several nearby camps. His brother Raul was further east in the *Sierra Cristal,* and Che Guevara more west in the *Sierra Maestra.*

Che, the young doctor from Argentina turned *guerillero* and espousing pure Marxism, arrived with two men after a two-day march. His first reaction on seeing the boys was hostility at having these sons of the *bourgeoisie,* especially Yankees, in the camp. Fidel stated it was his wish to do so and explained the *Tres Amigos* role at the roadblock. Che somewhat adjusted to the idea, but was very interested to know the Stern family's medical background and that "Chake" was studying premed. This he could definitely use in his aid stations scattered among the mountains. He had no use for Tomas, the son of rich landowners.

Raul arrived next with several men. Among them was a tall, good looking man speaking Spanish with a slight French accent and faint oriental features. 'Definitely not Cuban', Tomas thought to himself. Che greeted him warmly calling him *Comrade François.* Tommy, now known as Tomas, sat at the edge of the clearing, watching and listening to this fascinating event until they went inside the hut to discuss strategy. This experience was becoming more intriguing every day.

A short while later the man embraced by Che as Comrade François came outside to sit by the small fire while the other leaders discussed their operational areas. Tomas' curiosity could wait no longer. He approached the man with the best French accent he could "*Pardon mois, monsieur, etes vous Français?*"

With some surprise, François looked up at this bearded young man speaking to him in a very pleasant French. The only French he had heard since arriving was the somewhat butchered version spoken by Che. Spanish had served him better. "*Oui* and you are *amercaine, non?*" he asked without really needing the answer. "How do you come to speak French so well?"

"My mother is a French teacher and my grandmother went to school in Paris. They insist that I do not forget the language and often speak to me in French only. I also went to school in Paris for a year."

"*Incroyable* that I should find such an educated young man looking like, how do you say a ragamuffin, in these terrible mountains in the middle of a revolution. What is your name?"

"Thomas Scott, my grandfather lives in Cuba and my father was born here."

"*Sacre blieu!* You are the son of Thomas Rodrigo Scott, *non?*"

His French was coming faster with some excitement and Tomas had to listen carefully. "I know your father from the war in Indochina. I am François de Rousseau."

Now it was Tommy's turn to be dumbfounded. Of course, he knew of François de Rousseau and his amazing background. His father had spent many hours relating his war experiences in what is now North Vietnam. Now he was here in Cuba. Why?

Reading Tommy's mind he said "But of course, now I am here to lend my experience to this peoples' revolution at the request of your Cuban leaders." Then he told his story of Ho Chi Minh after the war, the betrayal of Truman in his support of De Gaul to reclaim Indochina for the French, and how he had been sent to Moscow and Beijing as Ho's representative to ask for support.

"But do not be confused by the term 'communist' as you Americans use it. In Vietnam we are communist only in the sense of nationalistic goals for our people, not worldwide domination such as preached in Moscow and Beijing. We have great fear and resistance to China and its methods. They have dominated us for two thousand years and would wish to do it again with the slightest opportunity. Ho once said during the war, '*Thus, the French imperialist wolf was finally devoured by the Japanese fascist hyena.*' Now we have added, '*The suffocating Chinese red tide of ignorance threatens to roll over the hopes of the people of Southeast Asia.*' When you leave these mountains, as you surely will, you must give your father my warm regards and hope that we will meet again in free Cuba."

Che had come out of the meeting to find Comrade François in conversation with the yankee boy, and in French. Upon seeing Che, François shouted in Spanish, "Do you know who this boy is?"

"Si, he is the yankee son of *bourgeoisie* who oppress the people and mistreat the peasants who work for them."

"*Non, non,* maybe *bourgeoisie,* but I fought side by side with his father and Ho Chi Minh in Indochina."

This took Che aback for a moment until he recovered enough to replace the half scowl on his face. He had never heard this story, but it only slightly modified his attitude.

François left this time with Che, and Raul went back to his end of the island.

From other *guerilleros* the boys heard the real story of Castro's "invasion" from Mexico aboard the leaky, converted yacht, *Granma* which grounded on a mud bank off the western peninsula of Oriente Province and at the foot of the *Sierra Maestre* on December 2, 1956. The "invasion force" of eighty-two men had to struggle through a huge mangrove swamp in order to reach dry land. Then they were ambushed by the Rural Guard which almost killed the "revolution" before it began by killing many and splitting the group in all directions. Only sixteen survived to regroup and fight later in the mountains. Castro and two companions were able to hide under sugarcane for several days without food or water before the army left the area, with Fidel whispering day and night how and when they would regroup and fight in the mountains. Che was later to remark, "This wasn't a landing. It was a shipwreck."

Batista had bragged and publicized that Castro was dead. This misinformation had proved an embarrassment and added more impetus to this all-out push.

Tomas remembered mangrove swamps from trying to duck hunt around the edges. The thought of trying to carry weapons and supplies for almost a mile through massive tangled air roots, hanging vines, knee-deep sucking mud, cutting barnacles, and clouds of mosquitoes brought a cold sweat and chills to him.

At the conclusion of the leaders' strategy meeting, Fidel announced that Chake would go with Che to inspect aid stations and assist in handling the wounded. Out of fear of leaving his friends, Chake gave a feeble protest that he was not a doctor or trained medic.

"Then, you will learn… quickly." Che said in a matter of fact manner in his broken English.

Tomas was to be used in a makeshift armory repairing weapons and teaching these civilians turned revolutionaries, *guerilleros,* basic maintenance and repair.

Quique was pleased to hear that he would be used as a front line combatant in recognition of his aggressive initiative at the roadblock. It didn't occur to him that he was being told he was only useful in that manner.

Tomas was sent to a nearby village of coffee growers high in the mountains where a weapons cache had been established. There he met Marisol, a villager's young daughter whose task was to prepare food for the *guerilleros*. If he thought the girls at the *El Paraiso* were a refreshing change from the girls of Havana, or any on his grandfather's plantation, here he thought was the perfectly named girl. Marisol literally translated means *'sea and sun.'* In her plain dress, with bare feet, strong legs, long thin nose, high cheek bones, and a smile that did seem like the sun rising over the ocean, she was the girl of his dreams. Needless to say, the sight of this handsome young *Americano* smiling at her was a bit overwhelming right in the middle of the continuing struggle in the mountains.

Activity began to heat up as Batista pressed his generals to end it quickly. Air attacks increased, infantry stormed the mountains and Tomas was frequently called to defensive positions where Fidel would beat back attacks when they penetrated the interior of the mountains. Tomas wondered, as he was firing down on soldiers trying to climb steep slopes, "Why can't these people even coordinate air attacks when they assault?" He assumed the dense forest and poor joint training of infantry and air power was to blame. A lesson he was to remember years later.

After each attack across the mountains, more repairs were needed by Tomas and more aid to the wounded by Chake, who also was called upon to act as a rifleman at times. Tomas remembered his friends who had joined the marines telling him, "Everybody is a rifleman first and always." Here it was a necessity with so few fighters and so many soldiers.

Air raids had become so intense in Raul Castro's sector in the *Sierra Cristal Mountains* that he had taken it on his own initiative to kidnap forty-five Americans, including a bus load of Marines, much to Fidel's alarm. However, it had the desired effect of causing the American government to pressure Batista not to bomb for fear of harming the hostages. They were ultimately released with Fidel's intervention and a little bargaining, but it had given Raul time to recover and resupply. It seems Batista was very sensitive to American pressure

During this brief lull, Tomas spent more time with Marisol. Together they found a hideaway, where amid all of the chaos, they could be together in the solitude of the mountains. Tomas never ceased to be amazed at how sparsely settled and unspoiled these mountains were and how peaceful when there was no action by the army. Unlike the Smoky Mountains, where resorts and developments seemed to spring up like mushrooms after a rain and roads dissected the mountains, here the people lived like they had for hundreds of years, never needing or seeking modern conveniences. Their only disruptions were demands and maltreatment from overseers and managers employed by large landowners. But Fidel promised them he would end all that. In fact, he had executed many when he caught them and their abuses had been proven.

Cuba was a bird watchers paradise, particularly in these remote mountains. The number and bright colors of the island birds were far more than found in the Smoky Mountains. The blue, white and red Cuban Trogon, Cuba's national bird, the colors of the Cuban flag, sometimes called the *tocroro* like the sound of its song, was a frequent sighting. But the tiny Bee Humming bird, the smallest bird in the world at 2 inches, was their own special bird and native symbol of love. Somehow it seemed to have found this exact spot. Sometimes in the distance a pink cloud of Flamingos could be seen on their way to feed along the mangroves. For a brief moment Tomas thought of his mother and her Audubon Society members back in Coral Gables and how they had helped him get his Boy Scout Bird Study merit badge. He thought to himself, 'Boy, they would never believe this, beautiful birds and bullets too.'

In the bright lights and crowded streets of Havana it was easy to forget how beautiful the rest of the island was. With 3,746 miles of coastline surrounded by 4,000 islands and cays and countless coral reefs, the contrasts and diversity of the sea and mountains and rolling fields of sugarcane and tobacco were a magnificent sight when seen from vantage points high in the mountains.

Meanwhile, it was late August and the tide was turning. It dawned on Tomas and Chake that classes had started at the university and their families must be frantic. Little time had been spent by the boys on that subject, far from the rest of the world, with the only contact being bullets and bombs.

Their families had not been idle. The American Embassy had been besieged with political pressure to get them out. Old Tom had leaned hard on his contacts in the Batista government. The response had been weak because of the possible tie-in with the rebels.

TR had been working his former teammate and fraternity brother, who was now a U. S. Senator from Florida. The State Department and CIA were getting an earful from everyone, including the Spalding family. One of the grandsons of B.B., Jonathan,

happened to be a brand new assistant to the Vice Consul in Santiago, who was actually the CIA station chief with some limited connections to the 26th of July Movement. The station chief had been trying to arrange a meeting with Castro to discuss some of the aid the Agency was secretly and indirectly providing as a hedge to their bets on Batista.

Jonathan Spalding was a young Yale graduate, like his father, grandfather and great-grandfather, who had been recruited directly out of college. He knew the stories about the Spanish-American War and had seen his grandfather's medals, but he had never been to Cuba or met the Scott family. His father and older brothers handled what was left of the Cuban business. Somehow in the Agency's own convoluted sense of logic and association it had decided that he would be the ideal person to negotiate with Fidel, and collaterally, assure the Scott family that it was indeed   dealing with the rebels on the matter of the boys. So, off into the mountains he was sent to deal with a man no one had been able to reach, while wondering to himself how he was supposed to handle this. He recalled an Agency and military expression, __W__*hisky* __T__*ango* __F__*oxtrot,* (**W**hat The **F**uck), which adequately expressed his feelings on the subject.

Fidel was in his headquarters camp when word came that a CIA agent was on his way into the mountains with a guide from his own movement and no advance permission; not the sort of thing to engender a welcome or allay suspicions. If he was inclined to appear less eloquent, he would have expressed the same *Whisky*

Tango Foxtrot aloud.

As was Fidel's usual manner in meeting visitors, he left word that he was inspecting his other units throughout the mountains and would arrive as soon as possible. This was, obviously, designed to create the illusion of a much larger force and give the visitor a little taste of the living and fighting conditions which the *guerilleros* could overcome.

Jonathan was taken to a small clearing on the side of *Pico Turquino* at approximately 3,000 feet. It was only half way to the peak. A soft drizzle of rain began to fall and the temperature dropped. Ragged men with unkempt beards began to appear from the shadows in the heavy surrounding woods. They sat on rocks along the edges of the clearing speaking quietly in their rapid Cuban Spanish. This position offered the men a rapid escape in the event of attack, either by land or air. It had become automatic and second nature to these survivors.

Jonathan's Agency-schooled Spanish in no way had prepared him to understand their conversation, especially when they chose not to let him. He had taken notice on the way up that the mountain was cut with sharp ravines, deep river valleys and impassable areas of sinkholes and caves formed by water and referred to as *karst* by geologists, ideal for guerilla operations. As light faded, he could see this spot commanded a view of most of the eastern slopes with the nearest projection of land approximately 1,000 yards across a deep ravine, *Certainly a well-chosen spot,* he thought.

He was given a small bowl of black beans, a poncho, a blanket and left to find a protected spot among the rocks and trees until morning. A nearby stream provided a source of sweet mountain water.

The *Tres Amigos* sat among the other men watching this young man who had been sent by himself to deal with the *Robin Hood of the Sierra.* They were by now indistinguishable from the others. Chake had expanded his high school Spanish to a reasonable level of comprehension, but he kept quiet. No one spoke to the Agency man. That was the job of the *Comandante.*

Daylight had begun to dawn, but the sun had not crept over

the lower crest to the east. Jonathan had only slept in fitful naps, curled up in his blanket and poncho. Fortunately, he had been warned to bring a heavy coat, even though the temperature in Santiago when he left was tropical. Half asleep in the predawn twilight and shadows, he could sense something happening. Fidel had arrived. Jonathan couldn't know, but Fidel had only been three hundred yards away around a bend and out of sight and hearing.

Fidel surveyed the scene and determined that the intended impression had been made. He ordered one of the men to go into the woods and build a small fire where it could not be seen nor the smoke observed. A thankful Jonathan was escorted to finally meet Fidel, and get a little warmth and drink fresh coffee. Of course, Fidel had to launch into one of his speeches before he got around to asking what the hell Jonathan was doing there. Conciliatory diplomatic speak was the tone of this opening round, then possible relations between the two countries.

Fidel sat looking at this young man and wondering why the mighty CIA had sent such an inexperienced person. Then it occurred to him that he, himself, was only thirty-one and most of his men were younger than this one. Suddenly he said, "Spalding!? Are you related to B.B. Spalding?"

"He is my grandfather."

Ah, of course, Fidel thought to himself. *They would be clever to send a grandson of the Hero of the Revolution. A magnificent move!* To Jonathan he said, "Yes, I am a great admirer of your grandfather. What can I do for you and what can you do for me to rid the Cuban people of this monster, Batista?" He was careful not to mention his plans for a social revolution and land reform, to say nothing of the bloodsucking Yankee corporations.

Spalding reminded Fidel that substantial aid had been clandestinely sent to him, most of which Fidel had not realized. *Of course,* Fidel reasoned to himself, *they want to hedge their bets, now that I am winning.*

Spalding was looking into the incredibly intense eyes of Fidel and listening to the different tones and modulation of his voice. He tried to understand what he was seeing and hearing. It was impossible. Fidel was too deep, too intent and too far ahead in his thinking. All this added up to danger. *I better get to asking about the boys,* he thought.

Upon the mention of the American boys, Fidel stood up and motioned him to follow while thinking to himself, *So this must be the real reason. I shall bargain hard for them.*

When they reached the clearing, he waived his arms expansively and said loudly, "Do you see any *Americanos* here? I see only my brave *barbudos,* true sons of Cuba."

Spalding had looked at these men all night and had to admit to himself that these suntanned, bearded, weather-worn and ragged men did not look like any American college boys. "Perhaps, they are in other groups in the mountains," he said lamely.

The sun was now over the eastern slopes and pouring into the clearing with a welcome warming for the *barbudos.*

Tomás and Chake sat with the others feeling quite like they belonged and amused by this secret agent's confusion.

Quique sat with his back against a tree enjoying the warmth of the sun with his eyes closed and caring less about this American agent that Fidel was toying with.

Tomás began to fidget. Something was happening to him. There it was again. His grandmother was there, but she wasn't there. This time more urgent. "Tomasito, leave quickly! You are in great danger!" she pleaded. He could only hear and see a slight haze around him. "Chake can you hear that?" he whispered to his friend. "Hear what?" Chake answered, "I only hear Quique snoring."

"No, no something is happening," he said louder in Spanish. At this the others looked up. They had learned that Tomás seemed to have some sixth sense.

Fidel picked up on the tension and looked in the distance as though he could see forever.

Spalding could tell something wasn't right, but had no idea in this strange setting.

Suddenly a deep whistling rush of air passed through, immediately followed by a loud and distinctive BAMM and successive BAMM...BAMM...BAMM...BAMM. Only a U.S. made

Browning .50 caliber heavy machine gun made that sound. It fired 40 rounds per minute in five round bursts. With a maximum range of 7,440 yards and effective at 2,000 yards, it was an easy shot from 1,000 yards across the ravine.

As the first round passed by, Tomás shouted in English for Spalding to get down. Jonathan had never heard a .50 caliber in his brief combat training at the Agency, but he damn sure knew to get down and behind big boulders of rock. The *barbudos* scattered into the woods.

Tomas looked for Quique. The tree he was sitting against had been cut down with the first round and fell into the woods behind. Quique sat with his eyes wide with surprise, then fear, then realization. The armor piercing round had passed through his chest and the tree before burying into the mountain. No sound could come from his mouth as he slid sideways from the bloody tree stump, but his mouth moved in what Tomas clearly saw were the soundless words of "Mama, Mama…"

Fidel stood in his typical arrogant pose shouting *"Hijo de la gran puta y comemierda!"* and shaking his fist in the direction of the firing until two of his men pulled him to the ground.

Chake had crawled to Quique, then turned to Tomás and shook his head. There was nothing he could do. He crawled on, treating others who had been wounded by rock fragments as successive rounds had crashed through the clearing.

Fidel had now recovered and ordered everyone higher up the mountain to plan a counterattack. Apparently, the army had somehow reached the ridge across the ravine and spotted the group in the clearing. With binoculars they may even have recognized Fidel. This meant that any minute an airstrike would be coming.

Tomas' duty was at the 'armory' bunker in the village to assure weapons and ammunition were available. He ran the half mile to the village in what he thought must be an Olympic record, but not fast enough. He could hear planes coming overhead. He continued to run and shout to Marisol as he neared the village. Her family's small cottage was at the near end of the village. He caught sight of her in the doorway waving. Planes roared overhead. Explosions knocked him down and into semi-consciousness.

When he recovered, he could only see a large smoking hole in the ground where the cottage had been, no sign of life. Another plane was coming in to strafe what was left of the village with its machine guns. He could not move, only sit and watch in horror. He had killed and seen his fellow *guerilleros* killed, even other villages destroyed, but this double tragedy was too personal, too much.

Chake was the first to reach Tomas, carrying his aid kit, and sat with his arm around his friend's shoulder, trying on some level to reach understanding and comfort. The two boys sat still for a long time, while other *guerilleros* kept their distance.

Spalding sat on a rock nearby, silently trying to understand what he could not. However, in that moment of terror in the clearing he had clearly determined who the American boys were. 'Now,' he thought, 'I have to figure out how to deal with this Castro character. Aid has to be the way, considering this near miss and new incursion by the army.'

Meanwhile Fidel had organized countermeasures to cut off the army unit, with his men in areas behind the army. His men knew every rock and the army did not. There had to be some informant to allow this to happen. It couldn't be the CIA man, or maybe? No, they were too soft to risk their man and the boys. Now one boy was gone, a Cuban. These *Americanos,* in spite of their skills would be more useful for trade. It was decided.

Spalding's near death episode seemed to give him more assurance in dealing with Fidel. He had now shared an experience and seen the war up close, as brief as it was. He had given aid to the wounded and helped carry them up the mountain. Perhaps, Fidel felt a little less hostile.

It only took a few hours to negotiate a safe passage for the boys to Santiago and to promise cash aid from the coffers of the CIA. Fidel had seemed more distracted and didn't avail himself of the opportunity to launch into a speech. Things were moving fast now.

Jonathan hoped he could deliver, but at least he had the boys.

Their original suitcases with clothes had been taken from the disabled car at the road block and stored in the mountains. They were dressed in their own clothes and shaved, but there was no mistaking the pale beard patterns on their bare faces when the rest of their bodies were deeply tanned and weathered. Some more personal items were taken for Enrique's parents, and his grave was marked. Their names were now back to Tommy and Jacob, but their lives had been changed. Even Spalding felt changed and was not looking forward to the debriefing they were going to face in the Consulate in Santiago. He was sure by now someone would have been sent from Washington. The boys had no idea that they would not be allowed to go home immediately.

Exactly as Jonathan suspected, the "Washington people" kept the boys sequestered in spite of pressure from the family, except for ten minutes of reunion. TR had flown Tommy's mother and the Stern family directly from Miami to Santiago.

After one and one half days of intense questioning and pledges of silence, the boys were allowed to leave. The twin engine Beechcraft with TR at the controls landed on the dirt landing strip on the Scott plantation to a reception committee that appeared to be everyone employed on the plantation. Women and men who had known Tommy since birth waved and cried. Tommy tried to greet them all through the hugs of women and *abrazos* of the men.

Jacob's mother was still crying and refused to release him from her arms. The family's Nazi nightmare was replaying itself. His father was now taking on a more determined look. Later he delivered a stern lecture, mixing family history with expectations that Jacob must respect.

Tommy's mother was only slightly less emotional. She had lived this before with TR in World War II.

As a courtesy to the Scott family and in recognition of family ties, Jonathan had been allowed to fly with the family to the plantation for the night.

Supper had been a happier occasion. Afterward, the men were allowed to retire to Old Tom's study for some frank discussions on what probably was ahead for Cuba.

The atmosphere and sheer history of the room always created a respectful silence from those entering for the first time and never failed to bring chills to Tommy. He suspected it had the same effect on his father, even many years earlier. Over the stone fireplace hung a box frame containing the Medal of Honor and a separate frame with the Cuban *Heroe* Sash. Around the room were fading letters and autographed photos of Theodore Roosevelt, General Gomez, General Garcia, General "Fighting Joe" Wheeler, and pictures of battle scenes from 1898. The room felt warm, comfortable and confidential, with the leather furniture, hand-made on the plantation, and hand-woven rugs of bright colors covering polished stone floors. Another wall was covered with pictures of TR playing football in college and flying planes in WW II. Part of a wall was just taking on the story of young Tommy. The smell of rich Cuban tobacco clung to the room and blended into the rich dark paneling, even though Tom had ceased to smoke years before.

In this room Tom was once again Thomas MacDougall Scott, patriarch, remembered as Tom. TR was Thomas and the third generation was Tommy. No names created by outsiders and no nicknames were spoken here.

The effect was not lost on Jonathan Spalding, especially when he noticed the photo of his grandfather and Old Tom together on a hill somewhere as young men with a warm letter to his 'friend and comrade in arms.' The depth of feeling in this room brought a new meaning to this special land and his own family ties to it.

Tom closed the heavy wooden double doors and waved everyone to take a seat and help themselves to the top of line *Matusalem* rum served in silver goblets brought from China by TR after the war.

His limp had worsened with age, and as he sat, he leaned his silver-handled cane into the corner with an assortment of plain and ornately carved hiking sticks, gifts from friends and workers on his plantation.

"Well," Tom began in his still rich southern accent, "I believe we have rehashed all the exciting events of the last few months and it begs the question, *What now?*" He swept the room with his still alert eyes, now covered with bushy gray brows at age 74, inviting anyone to venture their opinion.

Understanding the reluctance of strangers to break the momentary spell, he spoke first.

"Jonathan, when your grandfather and I stood on that hill in the middle of a hell, neither of us could imagine, and in fact doubted, that we would live through it. There was little time to think about our future in Cuba. But we did live, and we did become part of this country's future, and we did make a lot of money here. We saw and lived with the corrupt politics, unwise US government policies, and gangsters. Now I am old, and I feel something different. Maybe I am just an Alabama farm boy after all, but I need to hear some opinions. Jonathan, you are supposed to represent the government's intelligence. *Dime que piensas.*" (Tell me what you think.)

Jonathan paused to think, 'How much could he say in his official capacity? How much would the agency expect him not to say to this family and to his own?' Tom could see him wrestling with his official responsibility versus the duty to family, both his and this family. They all had substantial history together in this country, as well as assets.

Finally he spoke, "Mr. Scott, in the privacy of this room and considering our family histories together, I feel obligated to give you my unofficial opinion of what I saw and believe. From my brief experience under extreme circumstances and extraordinary stress, I would make the observation that Mr. Castro is a very clever, very intelligent man who needs to control all things as he sees fit, and he will use every means and artifice to accomplish that. He is a relatively patient man when necessary and violent when he deems it effective. He is a master of theatrics and expediency. I think he will take everything we will give him and say, up to a point, what we want him to say. He is not in control of other revolutionary groups, who do not trust him, but he is getting the headlines, thanks to some in the misguided American Press. That is most important at this point. The people in the countryside will ultimately influence the decision, not the splintered groups in the cities. Listening to him, I do not believe he will be another Batista or Machado. It is the power and the illusion of reform that drives him. He sees this not as a coup in traditional Latin American attitude of a dictator bent on enriching himself, but as a true revolution. He thinks of himself as a savior and a man of destiny. This is what he perpetuates. His bravado reaches the point of recklessness...or insanity. Beyond these brief observations I would not be permitted to discuss Agency plans or determinations. There are too many economic and political interests at play, which you know better than I. I will apprise my own family of these same things in the same vein of privacy. One thing in which I will express my own opinion strongly is that the American press is very naïve."

Tom stared into his rum as if mesmerized by the amber liquor reflecting off the Chinese silver cups.

From the corner of the room came the soft, almost frightened, voice of Dr. Stern, "*Mien Gott*, it is Adolph Hitler all over!"

Tommy and Jacob looked at each other, both wondering how Jonathan had learned so much in forty-eight hours.

TR stood up, obviously aggravated and intending to speak, but Tom raised his hand to silence him. "Son, before you speak, I want to hear from the boys." TR sat back down.

Dr. Stern murmured his apologies that he must leave to comfort his wife.

"I understand completely, Dr. Stern. Jacob, do you wish to leave?" Tom said while never looking up from his rum.

Jacob stared at the floor avoiding his father's eyes and said, "No, Mr. Scott, I have some things to add." Tom raised his eyes, first at Jacob, then at Tommy.

"Granpa, I think I should speak first. I believe Jacob and I agree with Jonathan. What he says is basically what we think. How we ended up in the mountains now seems inevitable from what we have seen and heard over the last three months."

Dr. Stern quietly left the room and closed the large wooden doors behind him.

"We have seen and listened to the poor farmers and how Fidel feeds on their hopes. His own brutality matches anything the overseers and plantation managers have done to the *campesinos*, but he does it for effect, not conviction. He magnifies his own successes at this far end of the island while Batista is occupied with the internal struggles in Havana and other cities, but those groups are fragmented, and he can physically overcome them when Batista finally is convinced to take his money and leave. We have seen his houses and land in Miami. We know he is ready. Jacob and I really believe, without Jonathan's confirmation, that the U. S. Government will give Batista an out at the last minute."

"We have heard Fidel already discussing the free-for-all the other groups and politicians will start, but they do not have the stomach for what Fidel is prepared to do. They do not have the open warfare mentality of Fidel. He gives many spontaneous speeches and bluster, but there is a frightening cunning barely below the surface. My time was mostly spent at the headquarters in the armory, and Jacob in the scattered medical aid stations with a lot of contact with Che. He has some very definite impressions." Tommy paused and looked at Jacob.

Jacob waited for a sign to speak while Tom was digesting and filtering what he just heard from his grandson. Finally, a tilt of his head indicated that Jacob should speak.

"Mr. Scott, there is no question of the influence and intent of Ernesto 'Che' Guevara to reform an entire society on the communist model. He quotes Lenin and Marx to poor peasants who can't even read. Even though he hates 'yankees' and capitalism, my family medical background, even though I am only a premed student or maybe even because I am Jewish, and my usefulness in his aid stations softened his attitude. He allowed me to listen to his conversations, and he spoke to me about his dreams for society. It was not like Fidel's hypnotic bragging and scheming. It was almost like being back in my humanities class reading about communism versus capitalism. He is not Cuban, but his attitudes and beliefs are infectious. His men believe in his cause. Sometimes, he has severe asthma attacks and drugs have to be smuggled in from Santiago, but the light never goes out of his eyes. I don't agree with him, but I will never forget him."

Tom thought for a minute and nodded to his son.

"*Papi*, I understand these boy's university student impressions and even Jonathan's brief stressful exposure, but this guy Castro is just a loudmouthed bully. When I watched him play basketball at Belen High School in Havana, he was the same, the largest and loudest kid on the court, always shoving and yelling at the smaller kids. Now he has guns and kills people and brags that he is a hero, a savior. He is only a *comemierda* (shit eater)! I say let Batista take care of him. If there is a revolution there are many capable people to take over. Most are friends of mine. And, NO, I am not a revolutionary. We don't have anything to worry about."

Tom stared at his son for a long time. No one spoke. This was obviously going to be a decisive moment in this family's history. Jonathan and Jacob began to shift in their chairs as their unease increased at being present in this family affair. Tom motioned to them with his palms down indicating that they should stay.

Finally, Tom spoke, "Our family has been a part of this country for over half a century and your mother's family for hundreds of years. Much history has flowed through our blood and into the soil of Cuba. What I am about to say, I do not say without a great deal of thought. I have listened to all of you; I have listened to my business associates and my longtime friends; and importantly I have listened to the people who live on and work our land. They feel and speak with a passion from the heart that I have not heard before. They care for us, as we care for them, but a different feeling is in the land. It is felt here in the far end of this island paradise, not just in the bright lights of Havana where politicians come and go in various corrupt changes of government in order to line their pockets. We have known Batista since he was a little boy. The last twenty years have changed him. I can't talk to him anymore. He will take all his money and run soon." He hesitated for a moment and continued, "I have been talking to United Fruit. They still think they control the world and this is just another banana republic to be bought."

Tom let this sink in for a minute, while he watched the ebb and flow of emotions around the room.

Jacob was beginning to feel the fear his parents were reliving, but he couldn't move.

Jonathan began to realize the depth of his own family's involvement in this country's history. These were feelings and connections that had only been stories and financial statements handled by his father and brothers. The insulation of the Agency and his government was suddenly wearing very thin. It was as though all Cuban history was being foretold, if not decided in this room by these participants.

Tommy suddenly felt that it was decided, and he no longer had to worry or even think. It seemed to lift a burden, create a calm, and clarify the future.

TR was now becoming frightened and angry. He knew United Fruit had been trying to buy them out for years. No, his family, his country could not be ending. He suddenly stood up and shouted, "NO, NO, I forbid it!"

Tommy had never seen his father in this state before and began to fear what he might do. He had to do, say something quickly.

"Papa, I didn't tell you, but François de Rousseau was there in the mountains sent by the Chinese. He said to tell you, '*Bon voyage et bonne chance, mon ami.*'"

TR stood for a moment absorbing what Tommy said; then his knees weakened and he groped for a chair.

Tom stood up in alarm, "What's that about?"

Jonathan's heart skipped a beat. Nothing had been said in the debriefing about any Frenchman or Chinese. Tommy had been holding back. 'What was the connection?' he thought, while trying not to act like an Agency person and intervene.

TR recovered some composure and quietly said, "He was in the mountains with Ho Chi Minh during the war when they rescued me. He was my friend, and those were the last words he said to me when I left for China. He had told me that if the Americans abandoned them to the French again they would have to turn to China and Russia."

Jonathan's mind was racing now. Ho Chi Minh and China meant communist. Fidel said he was not a communist. This meant

Chinese involvement. 'Oh shit,' he said to himself, 'How do I report this without getting Tommy in a mess, or putting the whole family under suspicion? Those words must have brought back incidents and significance beyond a rebel in the mountains fighting a corrupt dictator.'

Tom recognized the reality of the presence of de Rousseau. He knew the whole story of his son's involvement with the guerrilla band under Ho Chi Minh and President Truman's failure to support Ho after the war in favor of the French again. He also knew this had forced Ho to turn to Russia and China for support. There was no question now where Fidel was turning. He looked at his son and felt a great sadness at what he must do and say to his son and his wife. No Coral Gables life, no University of Florida, and no French finishing school, could change the fact that they were both heart and soul Cuban.

Now Tom spoke, as if to get things moving as rapidly as possible, "United Fruit has made me a very generous offer to buy all our land. Revolutions do not bother them, and they don't think this is any different than Central America. I'm going to up the ante a little and keep the house with 100 acres for your mother and 1,000 acres for our farm people to keep. I doubt any revolutionary preaching land reform will take land from the working people. I know Fidel Castro has already burned the fields of his own late father. Very sad, Don Angel Castro came to Cuba from Spain as a poor young man and worked very hard to accumulate his wealth, just so his sons could destroy it."

Tom turned to Jonathan, "I'm going to return the favor your grandfather did for us in 1929 when he liquidated our stocks before the crash. Let him and your father know that I will quietly arrange to liquidate their holdings before this gets worse. If I am wrong, at least we will get a very good price since the rest of the world seems convinced this revolution will be a good thing. I tell you this as a family friend, not a government agent. I assume liquidation of private holdings in a foreign country is not of significance to the United States Government?"

Jonathan smiled, "Absolutely not." He had already decided how he could "discover" by other means that a Frenchman had been in the mountains. Based on certain powerful politicians' views, they would probably consider it of little importance anyway. His brain was now in high gear.

Tom continued, "Jacob, of all people, I am sure your family in Cuba will know what to do. Quietly. Do you understand?" Jacob nodded.

"Tommy, both of you just need to get back to school. Your father and I will call whoever we need to call to get you in one month late. Everyone try to get some sleep. We have this under control." Turning to TR he said, "Son, stay with me a minute." There was no question. Old Tom had this situation under control.

The next morning the rain came, then the tropic sun shone brightly, the roosters crowed and the chickens cackled as they laid fresh eggs for breakfast, prepared Cuban style, scrambled with ham, olives and pimentos served with strong, sweet Cuban coffee. Tommy preferred his coffee as *cortadito*, (cut) mixed with boiled milk. Breakfast was quiet, but calm. Afterward TR' with Echeverria as copilot, left to fly the Sterns to Havana to plan with the rest of the Stern family.

Tommy spoke quietly to his grandmother in the hallway as they left breakfast, "*Abuelita,* I need to talk to you, *por favor.*"

"I know, *querido,* let us walk among the palms, and they will whisper to us," she replied.

Tommy knew that it was whispered among the local people that she could communicate with spirits and did listen to the palm trees as breezes blew through the fronds, but he always considered it superstitions of the poor and simple people of the land. Throughout history they seemed to need their beliefs to give meaning and purpose to things they could not understand, but now he needed to understand.

Tom retired to his study where he could relax and think for a few minutes before he started making calls. He had given TR instructions last night on things to do and people to see. All should be in motion by the time he landed in Havana.

He sank down in his favorite hand carved wood and leather

chair, which now was fitted with colorful cushions made by his wife and house maid to make his aging joints more comfortable. The wound to his leg from so long ago was now becoming more painful. He looked around the room at his walls of memories, as he had done so many times before. Now it was different. This would not be the beloved place where he would draw his last breath. So many years, so much history, and so much love seemed to float around the room. He turned toward the window.

He could see the well-tended green lawn, with bursts of colors from varying shades of hibiscus, bougainvillea, and the orchids hanging from mango and avocado trees. Pink and yellow tabebuia trees blocked his view to the left along with the *flamboyan* or royal poinciana, which literally seemed to explode in bright orange flowers. The house garden was just beyond, and he could see the old gardener tending his assortment of vegetables. In this tropic climate and rich soil everything seemed eager to show life. The people said this old man spoke to his plants and trees, and they spoke back to him. They told him what they needed. He gave it to them, and they responded with incredible and continuous fruit, vegetables and flowers. Over the years many people had tried to hire him away, but he would never leave this place of his birth and his friends in nature. Tom thought it all must be true. The old man had always been here, and everything responded to him. No one knew how old he was. He had just always been there. 'What would this poor man do if the revolution took it all away?' Tom wondered. The answer seemed too obvious, and too painful. He looked further out to see the thousands of rolling acres of sugarcane, which seemed to dance in waves as the trade winds blew in from the Caribbean, past the mountains and over the island. A field of tobacco grew nearer to the house. Although Tom did not smoke anymore, this would not be Cuba if there was no tobacco, and he still loved the smell of drying leaves. He smiled to himself and thought he would probably have his own local revolt if he didn't provide his people with tobacco.

His thoughts were interrupted by the sound of TR revving the Beechcraft engines before takeoff. Then the little plane suddenly rose beyond the trees and banked towards Havana. He watched the sun glint off the wings until it was only a dot in the distance. He sighed and thought what a perfect metaphor for this end of an era.

The driveway of polished stone circled the house and was lined with towering royal palms always in perfect trim and even height, now at thirty feet. The old gardener made sure of that. He too was convinced Tom's wife could speak to them and hear them. He had no doubts.

Now, Tom could see his wife and grandson walking slowly, and talking, among those palms. The breeze seemed to pick up and the palms waved as she walked by. Whenever he saw that happen, he always had goosebumps, but not chills. It seemed so natural with her.

Tommy was walking with his head down and watching the paving stones pass under his feet. He couldn't bring himself to look up at the waving palms… not yet. "*Abuelita*, was it really you speaking to me on the road and in the mountains?" he was finally able to ask.

A small silence ensued as she looked up at the palms, as if waiting for advice to come. "*Si*, it was a part of me." Another pause before she continued, "Since I was a young girl in Paris, I have come to understand many things about our family. Things that had always confused me, things I could feel but not see, things my father would say, but he could not understand. Sometimes my dreams were so real. At first, I went to confession. I was afraid that I may be possessed by some demon. Then I dreamed that I could see the inside of the priest chambers and other houses on the street. The priest said he could find no sin in my dreams and instructed me to say ten *Hail Marys* and two *Our Fathers*.

"Two days later I met the same priest and the monsignor in the church court yard and explained I was still having strange dream experiences. They looked at each other in an odd manner and assured me that the devil had no part in my dreams, but requested that I talk with one of the nuns who served the church. Now I was becoming frightened for my sanity.

"Sister Angela was a middle aged nun, who in other circumstances would be a very attractive woman. She had warm, understanding eyes that seemed to wrap themselves around you in peace and comfort. She looked into my eyes and said, 'Those of us who live more solitary lives have much time to read and reflect. There are many places between here and heaven and many dimensions unexplored, because our mind wishes simplicity in our fear of the unknown. Unfortunately, our western religions have not been able to absorb or accept these unknown spaces. That is why the priests sent you to me. They quietly recognize their unease and inability to communicate with a young girl about these things or even discuss other religions.'

"She stopped for a minute and looked gently into my eyes and said, 'What you have experienced is something I have tried to control but could not. Holy men in many Eastern religions have long claimed to reach a state where they can leave their physical body to achieve indescribable mystical insights and experiences. Have faith. God will protect you and those you love. You must learn to control your experiences for the good. You are truly blessed.'"

Graciela looked into Tommy's eyes and continued, "Since that meeting, Sister Angela and I had many conversations about my dreams and visitations. She called them experiences that I should take meaning from for the good of those involved. She died many years ago, but I remember her comforting manner. I have met many people of many religions since that time who have experienced this and more. All have convinced me that it is not the work of the devil or a form of evil, only the ability to experience our existence on another plane and sometimes see things before they happen. There are very few times I have been able to communicate with a person. You are one of those people. I know your father and my father had such abilities, but their minds were not open and their priorities were only in the present with their ideas of what they wanted and enjoyed. You will now be able to reach out and come to understand the benefit of this gift."

Tommy was becoming more and more uneasy. He kept looking up at the royal palms. They did seem to whisper and wave as they walked by…or maybe it was only his excited imagination. He tried to think if he had ever experienced this when he thought it was just a very real dream. He had seen things immediately before they happened and other people had told him of similar experiences. A chill ran through his body, and he tried to think of something else.

As they walked a Cuban trogon, commonly called a *tocororo*, flew to a nearby hibiscus, turned its head to one side to see them and sang its namesake song. His grandmother looked and listened. A tear came to her eye.

My God, Tommy thought, *is this Cuban national bird actually singing Good-bye to us?*

Graciela nodded at the bird, and it fluttered away still singing, "*tocororo, tocororo.*" The breeze seemed to stop in the palms. They stood silently for a long time.

Finally, Graciela spoke, "*Mi nieto,* please consider this a gift from your ancestors. You will learn to control your experience, because you are now aware you will meet many others with similar gifts. Very few speak openly, because so few will or can understand. Now I am happy. For many years I have wished for someone to receive me. Your grandfather has tried to understand through his love, but his mind is so strong and tied to what he sees and understands. You have inherited his strong, intelligent mind, but you have unconsciously allowed the Garcia side to reach you."

She paused for a moment, looking back at the family house and the window where she knew her husband would be sitting and watching. "I know your grandfather understands without needing to say so. He listens patiently and lovingly to me as I tell him what I see and what we should do. We both saw this sad end of the life we knew, he through his experience and I through my spirit. I know he is feeling pain now with having to tell me it is all true and that he has put things in motion."

"*Abuelita,* how did you see and how do you experience this out of body travel? How did you know Quique would be killed that morning on the mountain or that we might be in danger at the roadblock?"

More silence before she spoke, "I could only see from above the soldiers preparing to shoot. I was only concerned for you. I did not see poor Quique. How did I arrive there? I have learned to relax and focus my mind in a direction. Sometimes I feel vibrations, sometimes a ringing and then a lifting, as if something is gently pulling me up and away from my physical body. Then I think about where I should go, and I fly there while looking down. I have learned through many years that these are more than dreams. As Sister Angela told me there are more levels to existence than we are taught."

They had completed their walk among the palms and the breeze had again picked up. Tommy wondered if he would ever understand their whispers, and whether he would be able to sleep tonight. Tomorrow he would fly the single engine, high wing Cessna 172 back to Miami with his mother as a passenger. His father had installed the more powerful engine with a cruising speed of 140 mph and a range of more than 600 miles. The 350 mile flight to Miami was easy flying. There would be plenty of time to think, besides he was already late for university classes, and he had missed the two weeks of National Guard summer active duty. He was done with Fidel, Che and Raul.

Another trogon flew overhead trilling his call, *tocororo, tocororo.* His grandmother smiled and waved as the bird landed among the blooms of a royal poinciana, creating a kaleidoscope of color. He thought how ironic that the bird's colors of red, white and blue were the national colors of both Cuba *and* the United States.

The flight to Miami was smooth and uneventful. He and his mother had only talked about finishing school. Through considerable pull and political manipulation by his grandfather and father, he and Jacob were readmitted one and one-half months late. The course load had been slightly reduced, which affected ultimate graduation dates, but doable. ROTC was not a problem because of TR's National Guard influence.

Jacob's father had unequivocally declared his military adventures at an end, and no more ROTC, just premed studies from now on.

The academic year of '58 - '59 seemed to flow past in a vacuum. He was elevated to company first sergeant in ROTC, attended fraternity parties, ran track, had his share of sorority girls and tried to forget Fidel and the fanfare created by his successful entry into Havana in January. His grades reflected the neglect.

ROTC six weeks summer camp was in June and July, conducted by junior officers who had never seen nor heard incoming rifle or canon fire, and it felt like a poor imitation of the National Guard. The song *Mickey Mouse* kept going through his head. His evaluation also reflected his uninspired attitude, except on the rifle range where he was consistently rated *EXPERT.* The result was that he was only made platoon leader instead of the expected battalion or regimental rank.

Back in school he was assigned an ROTC advisor, Captain Sean McCauley. The Captain was a West Point graduate who had been awarded the Medal of Honor as a seventeen year old infantry private in the closing days of WW II, which had earned him the appointment to the United States Military Academy at West Point. Although superior officers had to salute him because of the medal, he was still a captain after ten years. He had a Combat Infantryman Badge with a star on top and a couple of Purple Heart medals signifying that he had been in the thickest part of battle in two wars. This was an unspoken mystery known only by the commanding officer of ROTC.

McCauley had read Tommy's file and in their first meeting directly asked the question, "What happened?"

There was no need to explain the question. They simply looked each other in the eyes for a minute. Tommy finally took a deep breath and said, "If I tell you, will you tell me?"

Without shifting his gaze, the captain said, "Yes." An understanding seemed to pass between these two men. Tommy could no longer be called a boy.

He started his story with his grandfather's own Medal of Honor and the family history in Cuba. McCauley knew very well TR's history and influence at the university, but the Castro story he did not, nor did anyone else in ROTC. He suspected this was not something the CIA had allowed Tommy to tell anyone. Now he understood the "mickey mouse" attitude, and he was about to explain how very much he understood.

McCauley thought to himself for a moment, *You don't kill and see your friends killed only to be told not to say anything without some effect. This young man deserves to know my own story.*

It was the captain's turn to take a deep breath. "What I am about to tell you, you must keep to yourself, as I will keep your story."

What unfolded were events Tommy could never have imagined. McCauley was an infantry company commander as a 1st lieutenant in Gen. MacArthur's surprise amphibious landing at Inchon, where the North Koreans were cut off and chased all the way back to the Yalu River bordering China. While MacArthur argued with President Truman about the Chinese danger, the Chinese took matters into their own hands. From hidden places in valleys and mountainsides thousands of Chinese infantry emerged, blowing bugles and firing their "burp" guns, pouring down on unsuspecting American and South Korean troops. MacArthur and his intelligence officers were caught totally by surprise by an estimated 30,000 or more Chinese.

In a panic the regimental commander had ordered a retreat into an area perfectly set for a Chinese trap. McCauley's company had been assigned as rear guard for the retreat. From his hilltop position he recognized the closing pincers of the trap. His frantic and continuous radio warnings to headquarters were ignored by the regimental commander himself, who adamantly refused to believe his plan was wrong.

As the trap was starting to close, McCauley ordered his small company to attack one side of the Chinese advance. Although outnumbered 20 to 1, the ferocity of his unexpected attack completely upset the Chinese timing in order to defend it. The result was he lost 75% of his company and the rest wounded, but it gave the regiment time to deploy and maneuver out of the onslaught. In effect, he had sacrificed himself and his men to save the regimental commander's hide, and his regiment.

However, the embarrassed colonel maintained that his plan had been correct and McCauley had used bad judgment, and foolishly and needlessly sacrificed his company. When McCauley and the few survivors managed to get back though the lines, he was placed under guard for disobeying orders. Even though everyone in a responsible position knew he had saved the entire regiment, no one spoke up. It seemed that the colonel had very good political and military family connections and was determined not to let his bad judgment become part of his record. Career oriented officers were not going to risk his wrath. He did, indeed, become Army Chief of Staff as silence continued. Enough said.

McCauley was awarded another Purple Heart and a Bronze Star for personal bravery as a token. But, by order of the colonel, a personal notation was made in his personnel file to the effect that he should never be given another combat command. The only thing that had allowed him to stay in the Army was his Medal of Honor and West Point graduation.

Now the captain and the cadet were even, and each understood. His lackluster ROTC performance continued. Only he and McCauley knew why.

The year dragged by with some interesting classes and others not, some good parties and others not, some interesting girls and others not. He ended his senior year two classes short for graduation. Without graduation there was no 2nd lieutenant commission from ROTC, or the Army would take him as a Private First Class for all his efforts in ROTC, but go he must.

Time was getting short to apply for summer school. Tommy thought for a long time before he decided, *Heck with summer. I'll go to National Guard camp then sign on as crew on one of grandfather's ships working the Caribbean.* It wasn't a cruise ship but it would get him away from everything. Of course his mother strenuously objected, but his father was too involved with some counterrevolutionary group referred to as the *Frente,* to care.

The National Guard camp was the usual 'run around' in the woods, firing blank ammunition, and practice with a map and compass.

The freighter he signed on made the circle around the Caribbean from Miami east to the Dominican Republic and Puerto Rico, and down the Lesser Antilles islands to Venezuela, over to Colombia to Panama, and back up Central America. There always seemed to be interesting tourist girls on the popular tourist islands.

His grandfather always had special connections in the Canal Zone, dating back to its beginning and his relationship with Teddy Roosevelt. He managed to fly down when Tommy docked in Panama to meet with old friends from the early days of the Panama Canal, and introduce his grandson to the "gentry." It happily reminded old Tom of how his uncle Caleb used to take him to meet merchants and sea captains and enjoy the pleasures of the ports in his own youth.

"Tommy, how would you like to go to Paris with me and your grandmother for a week? I have some business there, and you know how your grandmother loves it. Leaving Cuba has been very hard on her, and Coral Gables is a poor substitute. We still have the apartment in Paris just sitting unused. Don't worry about the ship. I have a strong feeling the captain will not object. Anyway, he can easily pick up a seaman here in Panama, if he needs one. You want your mother to come and exercise her French?"

Seeing a little hesitation in Tommy, he said, "No problem. I understand you don't need to be nagged about school. I am sure you will find something interesting to do."

This was a great surprise, Tommy thought, *This is one time I don't feel guilty about being the owner's grandson.* His mind wandered off to his old classmates from his time in private school there, and all the *interesting things* they could get into. "Absolutely. Thank you very much," he remembered to say.

He did find some very *interesting things* in the cafes along the nearby Avenue des Champs-Elysees, *la plus belle avenue du monde* (the most beautiful avenue in the world) where he and his old friends found great pleasure in explaining Parisian history and taking tourist girls' photographs in front of the *Arc de Triomphe* and Eiffel Tower. On occasion his grandparents would encounter them while having dinner on the Avenue. A wink from Tommy would send them both into hilarious laughter. And, of course, his grandmother would come to their table and engage Tommy in French, just to show off in front of any American girls. She was having as much fun as the boys, and his grandfather loved it.

When it was time to leave, he had no problem convincing his grandparents to allow him to stay in the apartment for another week...or two. This stretched into a month.

In the final week, out of curiosity and a little boredom he took a travel agent tour bus of all the places he knew, just to sit and listen to someone else tell the history, or their own version. He actually found it interesting, as well as amusing. He only had to sit and watch this beautiful city pass by and think of what he should do... until they arrived at Napoleon's Tomb.

As they walked under the great church dome and beside Napoleon's sarcophagus they were joined by another group to listen to the guide. A ray of sunshine streamed through a window. As he followed its path, it seemed to burst into a brilliant glow of long yellow hair. *Uh, oh. My grandmother is playing tricks on me,* was his first thought.

He edged his way around the crowd to where the light ended on a young girl's hair. His next thought was that it was the end of the rainbow not just a ray of sunshine. This was one very gorgeous girl, who turned out to be an American university exchange student studying in France. She was from the small Midwestern farm town of Douds, Iowa. Denise Johansson was the daughter of an old Swedish immigrant family on her father's side, and French trapper/traders on her mother's side, a real piece of history of the early days of Iowa and the Midwest. She was having some trouble asking questions about her guide book.

Tommy saw his opportunity and asked in French, "May I help you, *mademoiselle.*" Startled, she looked at him and only saw another French boy trying to pick her up. "*Non, non,* go away."

Taken by surprise at this reaction, he recovered in obvious American English, "Whoa, let's start again, lady. I am just trying to help you."

Now it was her turn to be surprised, "Oh, oh. I am sorry. I just can't understand where I go next according to this book."

"Well, permit me to introduce myself. Thomas MacDougall

145

Scott II at your service. I am American, but I did go to school here."

The ice was broken and Tommy decided to stay another week as a personal guide. Dinner on the Champs-Elysees was much better, and so was the show at the Moulin Rouge and the Lido, even for the hundredth time. She even enjoyed the beautiful, multiple colored, symmetrical dancing girls at the Crazy Horse Cabaret. For once, Tommy hardly noticed the girls in his all-time favorite night club. 'This girl is really a delight, so different from the typical tourist,' were his only thoughts.

The week ended quickly and Denise went back to Nantes University where she was studying, and he flew back to Miami. A few letters were exchanged, but it was not a rendezvous to be forgotten.

He was already late to register for school, but it had been worth it. A letter from the Army ROTC was waiting. He was being reminded that he had signed an obligation. If he did not graduate, he would be inducted as an enlisted man. He really had not been thinking about the Army. *Oh, what the hell. I've been a common seaman. I can be a common soldier. If I want a degree, I can get it later,* were his only thoughts. Then he thought, *Oh, shit. My mother is going to be mad, very mad.*

She was indeed very mad…for a short while. She realized Tommy was twenty–two now, and he had experienced some traumatic times. TR was a big enough problem at the moment, running off to conspire with some counterrevolutionary group. She needed to let Tommy go.

CHAPTER 9

BAHIA DE COCHINOS, CUBA

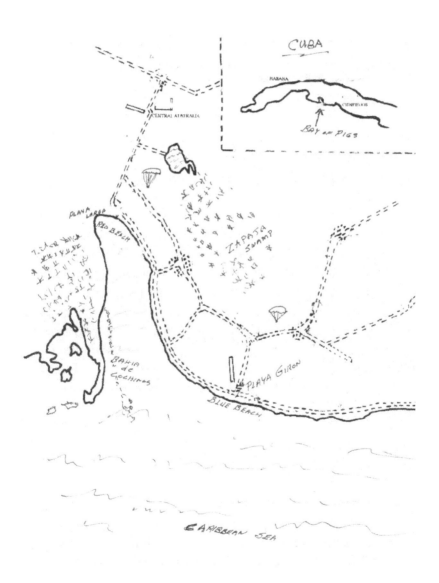

Castro's triumphant sweep into power in 1959 was greeted by relief and exhilaration unknown in Cuba since the liberation from Spain. The hoped for joining of the various revolutionary groups soon turned to dismay and despair as the true intentions of the Maximum Leader's vision began to take shape.

During the two years of "revolution," eight hundred sixty-seven lives were lost on both sides. In the following two years of Castro's regime, five thousand executions were effected. In spite of the enormous disparity, many in the highest levels of the U. S. government and the American press pleaded for patience until Castro could cleanse the society for a new democratic beginning.

The mass exodus of professional and business classes soon became a flight of the disillusioned, which included former comrades-in-arms. More than eight hundred thousand Cubans fled the country. Even old members of the Communist party soon discovered the Maximum Leader had his own vision, and they were not welcome.

This fractured and somewhat dysfunctional group came together in Miami as the *Frente Revolucionario Democratico*, known as FDR or *Frente* (Front). However, each group seemed to have its own idea of a post Fidel Cuba and its own aspiring leaders. Some groups consisting of former disillusioned members of Castro's revolution were not trusted, and excluded. They all came together, then split apart, then reluctantly came together again in the common cause of eliminating Fidel. Much of this was with the coaxing and prodding of the CIA, under the direct orders of the Eisenhower administration. The *Frente* was to be the basis of a government in exile.

Meanwhile, a plan had been set in motion by the CIA for a paramilitary operation. All this was in the middle of the 1960 presidential campaign, with Kennedy taunting Nixon, "If you can't handle Castro, how are you going to handle the Russians?" Of course, Nixon could not reply as to what was happening behind the scenes, and, based on the public opinion surveys and vote counts, this may have cost Nixon the election. John F. Kennedy had previously described Castro as "part of the legacy of Simon Bolivar, the Liberator of South America." The winds of politics swirl in strange directions.

With his father's instructions and guidance in the fall of 1958, T.R. Scott had been very effective in liquidating the Scott and Spalding family holdings in Cuba. But T.R.'s anti-Castro fervor had not diminished. Back in Miami with friends, associates and former competitors, he joined and schemed in the "common cause." Unlike some leading State Department officials, the CIA had come to realize the true threat early in the revolution. Its operatives were active in attempts to organize resistance groups. The early warnings had earned Jonathan Spalding a prominent role in these agency activities. Of course, he turned to the Scott family for influence and assistance. Old Tom said he had already fought one war for Cuban independence, and he was too old for another. Some financial assistance and influence was all he could contribute. However, he had given somewhat of his blessing to T.R.'s participation in some form.

T.R. had little taste for the petty bickering of political groups vying for advantage. Direct military action was his preference. Spalding talked him out of volunteering for the groups now being infiltrated back into Cuba as guerillas. "T.R., have a little patience. We're working on a plan which will involve direct action by land, air and sea. You will be much more valuable to us in this."

TR had heard rumors and whispers about this group being formed separate from the politicians. Now he was really interested. "What kind of air support are you talking about?"

Jonathan looked at him for a moment before speaking, "Do you remember our conversation in your father's study after we got Tommy out of the mountains?"

"Of course. You were right and the boys were right. Papa made the smart decision at the moment. Now we need to get it all back." T.R.'s blood was starting to rise at the thought of what this might mean.

"You also remember how I held all that in confidence among the family until you accomplished what you needed to do?" He watched T.R. carefully.

"Yes."

"All right. You will hold this in the same confidential way. No conversation until I get you cleared into the plan. Right?"

"Roger that." This is what he had been looking for. He ignored the fact that he had not been brought in sooner.

"I'll be back to you in two days."

True to his word, Jonathan set up a meeting with T.R. two days later in the penthouse restaurant of the old Everglades Hotel on Biscayne Boulevard. They sat in an isolated corner facing Biscayne Bay. As they looked down, the bay was calm and the shallow water shone green and clear from the white sand bottom. The peaceful scene belied the turmoil and excitement beneath the Cuban community.

"T.R., we need you to help the air portion. We will have a squadron of B-26s, six C-46s for parachute drops and cargo, a couple of C-54s for cargo and an old Catalina amphibious patrol plane. I know you put a lot of hours in a C-46, as well as C-47s, flying the "Hump" from India. We need your expertise. The Alabama Air National Guard was the last unit to fly the B-26, and we have some of their pilots as instructors. They are being flown because they are the same type of plane Castro has, and we will have trained Cuban pilots with Cuban markings on the planes. This should create confusion and give the illusion of pilots deserting to our side, or I should say the *liberating forces*. We already have a first class practice airfield in Retalhuleu, Guatemala on the Pacific side, compliments of a rich rancher and agency money."

'Damn,' T.R. was thinking, 'I know those guys in Alabama and nobody said anything.' To Jonathan he said, "Actually, I'm a pretty good fighter pilot."

"We know your record, T.R., but we need help with the transports." He could see by the reaction he needed to throw in a little hope, and he knew about T.R.'s little air force in Miami. "I tell you what. Somoza has agreed to "loan" us his four F-51s if we can get long range fuel tanks that will get to Cuba, fight a while and get back to Nicaragua. Maybe, just maybe we can use some help there."

T.R. could feel his hair stand on end. "Can I take Escheveria with me?"

"Already done." Jonathan smiled. "Want to hear the rest of the plan? And remember this is you and me. I don't think you are cleared beyond a *need to know* basis."

"Absolutamente, Jefe!"

"The landing site will be near the town of Trinidad on the south coast over two hundred miles from Havana with no military base and sufficient distance to make reinforcement by Castro difficult. It has a defensible beachhead and an airfield. The plan is to seize and hold the beachhead and airfield while the brigade's B-26s wiped out Castro's air force, and attack his army and supply depots in successive waves. Once the holding force has established itself for a couple of weeks and continued to reinforce itself, it is believed the majority of Cubans will join in the effort. In any event, the nearby *Sierra de Escambry Mountains* are an escape route to ontinue a guerilla operation there. Additionally, a very noisy electronic illusion of a landing will be created on the far western end of the island to draw away Castro's reinforcements.

"The ground force will consist of six infantry battalions, a heavy weapons battalion, an armored truck battalion and a tank company. Experienced and trained former army officers will be selected as leaders, some from Batista's army and some from Fidel's. These battalions are really more company size than regular army battalions. The tank company will have five new M-41 tanks. With its new 76 mm high velocity gun it can outshoot the famous old German 88 mm Tiger Tank, but the heavy Stalin tanks Castro has have to be outmaneuvered for flank shots. The crews were trained at the U.S. Army Armor School, Ft. Knox, Kentucky. All of these units are designed to increase in size as the force picks up support, both in Cuba and in the U.S.

"The maritime unit at the moment consists of six cargo ships, four LCVPs (Landing Craft Vehicle and Personnel), and three LCUs (Landing Craft Utility). Obviously, the old landing craft are WW II vintage and the old cargo ships are donations from the Cuban Garcia Line, and…one by the Scott Line, compliments of your father." Jonathan laughed at T.R.'s expression on this revelation. "However, you can be sure that Spalding lawyers have worked out a tax deduction for him through some *charitable organization.*"

"Jesus, it's sounding like a mini Normandy invasion. What about Navy support?" T.R. exclaimed, as he wondered what else his father had not told him.

"That is being worked on. This presidential election is causing some confusion in the middle of planning. With Eisenhower we knew where we stood, and he certainly understood the problems. With the "New Frontier" coming in, we are a little up in the air."

"How about the air plan? Fidel sure doesn't have much of an air force. It sounds like you have more combat planes than he does, except for a few of the T-33 jets. I assume you are going to knock out all that stuff before you land."

"That is the plan, but we need you in Retalhuleu *tout suite.*"

"*Oui, Oui, mon general!*"

T. R. flew from Miami to Guatemala City, then caught a private plane operated by the Agency to shuttle appropriate parties to Retalhuleu. It was at approximately 800 feet above sea level on the western plateau of Guatemala overlooking the Pacific Ocean. Mountains towered to the east and north. Smoking volcanoes could still be seen in the distance. Spalding had been right about this nice facility being created from scratch, temporary but comfortable. Obviously, the CIA had been planning this for a while. A few Guatemalan Air Force planes were practicing landings and takeoffs and Guatemalan soldiers stood guard. To a casual observer it would appear as a government base. A closer look showed the planes Spalding had talked about, except no F-51 (the post WW II designation as F (Fighter) instead of P (Pursuit). Then he remembered they were Nicaraguan planes not Guatemalan. They were actually down at Puerto Cabezas, Nicaragua, on the Caribbean Sea, where everything and everyone would eventually be sent. The maritime group was already assembling there for departure to Cuba.

The adjacent mountains contained the training facilities for the ground units. It was a much cruder facility and colder, but plainclothes U.S. Special Forces personnel had created an excellent training environment. However, for warm climate Cubans it was not pleasant. The brigade had now increased from 400 to 1,500 men. A training accident caused the first death of a soldier by a fall from a mountain cliff. **Carlos Rafael Santana.** His serial number was 2506, and the brigade called itself, *Brigade 2506,* in his honor.

T.R. was very happy to be at the air base, not in the mountains. He could not even imagine what his son had gone through with Castro in the high mountains of the *Sierra Maestra.* His mountain experience in Indo China was at a warmer climate. His job was to train these pilots to safely fly and drop their loads on target while twisting and turning through the mountains with a C-46, whose wings spread to 108 feet and a fuselage of 76 feet. That, and dropping paratroopers of the 1st Battalion into the combat zone. These were improved versions of the "flying coffin" he had flown over the India-Burma-China "hump" in WW II. More powerful engines and improved electrical systems were very comforting. Still, he watched with considerable envy as the B-26 pilots did their strafing runs and bombing practice. The B-26 was a twin engine fighter/bomber used in WW II and Korea, and later turned over to reserve units. They had eight .50-caliber machine guns in the nose and eight 5-inch rockets. It was a very effective fighting machine, but with an air speed of 355 miles per hour, not a match for jet aircraft. The Trinidad plan with twenty-two B-26s should effectively neutralize Castro's air force on the ground, if executed properly. Looming in the background was the intelligence report that Castro would have his shipment of Russian MIG fighters ready to fly by May 1.

After the Trinidad plan was formally presented on January 28, 1961, the new Kennedy administration finally got around to a meeting to approve the plan on March 11, one day after the invasion date in the plan. The Joint Chiefs of Staff had previously reported that the plan had a "fair" chance of success. The "New Frontier" was apparently in no hurry to approve it. At the formal meeting the Department of State objected that it looked too much like a WW II invasion, and there might be civilian casualties in the town of Trinidad. Public opinion seemed to dominate their thought process. In the end the president allowed the bureaucrats to prevail over the entities and personnel who knew what they were doing. Months of intense planning, preparation, and training went down the drain.

Later that evening, the White House called for a new plan. In the very early hours of the morning a new site was selected as the only one having the necessary requirements, Bahia de Cochinos (**Bay of Pigs**) and the nearby airstrip at Playa Giron. The Joint Chiefs filed written memoranda stating that they preferred the Trinidad plan. The "New Frontier" said no. The new landing was 120 miles closer to Castro reinforcements from Havana (a critical time frame,) spread the landing force over a larger area, had no escape route into the mountains, swamps on both sides of the roads and no deep-water port to offload, only coral and little sand. Landing craft would have to be used to wind their way through coral reefs. The most important piece involving a mass air strike of twenty-two B-26s on Castro's airfields was canceled for "political" reasons, and replaced with five raids of smaller size, which were to start two days before the landing. Then three days before the invasion scheduled for April 17, 1961, and one day before the scheduled air raids, The State Department persuaded the president to cancel critical air strikes and reduce the size of the one remaining strike to six planes and no napalm, again for political reasons. All this was done without consulting the JCS, or the CIA.

This was the situation in which T.R., "civilian" advisors, and the Brigade 2506 found themselves. The air support section knew more than anyone what would happen to their planes if sufficient air strikes were not allowed to effectively eliminate Castro's air force. The "turkey shoot" would belong to Castro. All units, land, air, and maritime, were now concentrated in Puerto Cabezas, Nicaragua, awaiting their time of departure.

April 14, 1961, the small fleet slipped out of Puerto Cabezas. Each ship took a different course in order to avoid detection of a large group. They converged the night of April 16, 1961 at a point twenty-seven miles southeast of Bahia de Cochinos, with the LCI *Blagar* as the command ship with another LCI, *Barbara J.*

As the ships entered Cochinos Bay, the *Blagar* and two freight ships turned east for the village of Playa Giron and landing sites designated **Blue Beach** and **Green Beach**. At three miles out, close to **2330 hours,** the Blagar launched its team of UDT frogmen. With a CIA officer, a retired Special Forces Captain, Grayston Lynch, went ashore, scouted the beach and marked the landing sites with lights aimed towards the ships. The *Barbara J,* followed by two freight ships, and the *Houston,* carrying the 2nd and 5th Infantry Battalions with a supporting heavy weapons battalion, continued sixteen miles north to the top of the bay. The ill-fated *Rio Escondido,* carrying the 4th Battalion, tons of supplies, ammunition, and 55 gallon fuel drums followed up the bay five miles in the rear to the landing site at **Red Beach**, but was redirected to **Blue Beach,** back at the mouth of the bay.

Meanwhile on **Blue Beach** the frogmen were discovered by the local militia at Playa Giron by accident and a fire fight started. The first shots fired in the Bay of Pigs were by the retired U. S. Army Green Beret, Grayson Lynch, from his BAR (Browning Automatic Rifle .30 cal.) The militia patrol was eliminated and everything went quiet.

At **0215 hours** the **Red Beach** UDT team supervised by William "Rip" Robertson, another retired U. S. Army officer, swam ashore and faced small arms fire from the village of Playa Larga, when they turned on their lights. The .50 cal. and .30 cal. machine gun fire from the UDT launch and the *Barbara J* silenced the village quickly. The *Houston* offloaded the 2nd Battalion using the UDT launches because some of the outboard motors on the landing craft would not start. For his own reasons, the 5th Battalion commander refused to disembark his unit to support the 2nd already ashore in spite of Rip Robertson yelling at him. It was now becoming daylight and a company of the highly trained 1st Battalion was parachuting from C-46s to block the road beyond the village. One thousand Castro soldiers were stationed up that road at a large sugar mill complex called Central Australia. The problem arose when a Castro B-26 showed up, another result of the cancelled air strikes by the "New Frontier" in Washington. The transport and cargo planes took what proved to be unwarranted evasive action, thereby losing their bearings and scattering the paratroopers and supplies off target. Things were getting to be a mess on the **Red Beach** end. The paratroopers ended up without their supplies and additional ammunition and were scattered all over, many in the swamps. Only a handful reached the dug-in positions of the 2nd Battalion, who were waiting to ambush the Castro troops now on the road from the Central Australia complex. Using their 75 mm and 57 mm recoilless rifles, 3.5 rocket launchers and machine guns they eliminated the advance column in less than two minutes. The enemy hesitated two and a half hours before trying again.

At **1430 hours**, scouts reported a large column of troops followed by many trucks loaded with more troops. By now the 2nd had received additional troops from the 4th Battalion sent up the road from **Blue Beach** at Playa Giron, and two M-41 tanks. Castro's men were walking into the center of the bulls'-eye. Within two hundred yards, all weapons, heavy and light, opened fire.

The M-41 tanks and recoilless rifles opened up on the truck column. The Cubans later referred to this as the "Slaughter of the Lost Battalion." It became greater when two brigade B-26s showed up. Only a very few of the 968 men were able to crawl off into the mangrove swamp. But things were about to go bad. One of Castro's T-33 jets swooped in on the B-26s. One was shot down in front of the troops and the other crashed at sea. All pilots were lost. Things remained quiet for some time, until two ambulances and a Red Cross truck appeared. The brigade held their fire, but scouts reported they were not picking up wounded. They were actually unloading troops and more trucks were behind them unloading troops and mortars. Again the 2nd Battalion eliminated everything in sight. They received good news from the brigade commander, Jose' (Pepe) San Ramon: At Blue Beach the remainder of 4th Battalion and one company of the 6th Battalion with a platoon of mortars and another M-41 tank, were on their way with more ammunition.

Meanwhile, the Castro B-26 that had spooked the troop carriers had eyes on the *Barbara J* and *Houston*. It was shot down by the UDT team's machine guns. However, the delay caused by the

5ᵗʰ Battalion commander's refusal to disembark the *Houston* necessitated its return to **Blue Beach** for better anti-aircraft protection. They had rushed six miles down the bay from **Red Beach** before a second attack from two Cuban planes, a B-26s and a British made Sea Fury fighter, swooped in. The *Barbara J* opened up with its fourteen .50-caliber machine guns. The planes swerved away to concentrate on the *Houston,* which had much less firepower. They raked it stem to stern and fired their rockets. Only one rocket hit the ship, but it blew a large hole in the stern and jammed the rudder. The captain was only able to turn the ship by using his alternating engines but was able to ram the sinking ship full speed up on the sandy bottom to save what he could. The *Barbara J* could not reach the *Houston* in the shallow water. The 5ᵗʰ Battalion commander now *had* to leave the ship. Now the two enemy planes appeared coming in low over the mangrove swamp and raked the men in small boats and those in the water trying to reach the mangroves.

The planes saved their bombs for the *Barbara J.* There were no direct hits but near misses caused hull plates to spring leaks, and the bilge pumps could not keep up with the incoming water. Communication was not possible with the *Houston's* communication gear shot out. The *Barbara J* was ordered to turn and run for assistance down at **Blue Beach** where she could be pumped out and repaired. The Houston was now on fire, but had rigged long lines to the beach enabling the rest of the soldiers to get ashore. Most supplies and ammunition were lost.

Continued attempts to relieve the 5ᵗʰ Battalion commanding officer of his command were thwarted by his simply turning off his radio and saying nothing to his staff. The 5ᵗʰ Battalion marched up the beach but was stopped by an enemy machine gun crew of six men in a small building. Instead of simply maneuvering around the emplacement through the swamp to join the fight further forward, the same commander retreated to the site of the burning *Houston.*

Down the bay at **Blue Beach,** the first Castro plane had arrived at sunrise in the middle of unloading on the beach. It avoided the well-armed ships and destroyed an empty landing craft on the beach, then flew off. Another alarm was sounded as two planes came in low. They turned out to be friendly, a B-26 escorting a C-46 carrying the second airborne assault to block the other road into Playa Giron. Friendly planes had blue stripes painted on them to differentiate them from Castro B-26s, but looking head-on no one could see any stripes. So, a few holes were put in the planes and only two paratroopers were slightly wounded, but the parachute drop was on target with all troopers.

Amazingly, at **Blue Beach** all troops and vehicles were unloaded even while under constant air attacks. In the middle of these attacks a message came in from Washington, "**Castro's air force 100% destroyed. Do not fire on our planes.**" The angry and well deserved reply was formulated then discarded. No one up there seemed to want to understand anything anyway. Fifty percent of supplies and ammunition were lost.

The last ship, *Rio Escondido,* had managed to get the 6th Battalion ashore and was in the process of unloading 55 gallon drums of fuel and ammunition when a Sea Fury came out of the sun firing its rockets. All rockets splashed into the sea, except the last one. It struck the forward deck in the middle of the gasoline drums. Fire spread across the ship, down the sides and into the hold full of ammunition. Small boats from all the ships frantically raced to pick up crew members now jumping over the side. Miraculously, all crew were rescued before the first explosion occurred. This was followed by a gigantic explosion with a huge mushroom-shaped fireball. The mushroom spread into a cloud one mile wide and several thousand feet high. As it lifted off the water, the stern of the *Rio Escondido* was seen slipping below the surface. The cloud continued to rise with a long mushroom stem.

"Rip" Williams felt and saw the explosion sixteen miles away on **Red Beach.** He put in a frantic call to the *Blagar* to confirm that Castro did not have an atomic bomb. The sinking had prompted Washington to immediately order the remaining ships back out to sea to save what was left, but left open the hope of U.S. Navy protection beyond the 12-mile limit, and then to return after dark with cargo transferred to smaller LCUs and LSVTs to unload on the beach. Attacks continued all the way to the 12-mile limit, but the Navy had now been informed to avoid engagement. Unfortunately, the faster cargo ships were leaving quickly and had no intention of following the *Rio Escondido* to the bottom. Castro's planes followed them with constant strafing, but no serious damage except to convince the civilian merchant seaman that they wanted no more of this. The still shell-shocked surviving crew of the *Rio Escondido* was trying to convince the crew of the LCVT *Blagar* to mutiny rather than go back to the beach. That was stamped out, and Navy destroyers rounded up the fleeing cargo ships one hundred miles away by firing shots across their bows.

At 1800 hours on **Red Beach** the reinforcements arrived and were told to dig in deep. At 1930 hours Castro's artillery opened fire with 122 mm howitzers in a slow rolling barrage. By 2330 hours the barrage had moved past with rounds falling into the bay. More than twelve hundred rounds had been fired. Two hours were spent under thunderous explosions, but only nine killed and few wounded, because they had dug in very deep to avoid exploding artillery shrapnel. The forward company reported a force with tanks was approaching at 0030 hours. It was beaten back and the tanks destroyed. Tank-infantry attacks came one after another for an hour. At 0330 strong infantry attacks continued for two hours, but were beaten off with Castro's troops taking heavy casualties. At 0545 the ground shaking rumble and metallic clanking of many tanks was heard. Then they stopped and withdrew for some unknown reason.

From a captured Castro soldier, the **Red Beach** commander, Erneido Oliva, learned he had faced a force of two thousand troops and twenty-two tanks on which the small brigade forces had inflicted 70% casualties and a loss of half its tanks. The soldier had previously served with Oliva in the Cuban army and knew him well. He warned that a much larger force was on its way. Now short of ammunition and his troops having fought for twenty-four continuous hours, the decision was made by headquarters to pull them back from Playa Larga to within three miles of **Blue Beach** for better support and supply.

At **Blue Beach** the brigade had secured the airfield at Playa

Giron, but Castro's planes had prevented its planned use except for some air drops from brigade transport planes, many of which went into the woods or water. The UDT teams were kept busy retrieving these water drops.

Meanwhile, the flight crews of the aircraft carriers *Essex* and *Boxer* had their planes on deck with pilots aching to get at Castro's planes, but no orders from Washington.

All of this was reported back to Puerto Cabezas by returning planes and relays from Washington via U. S. Navy ships, including the two aircraft carriers with planes on deck standing by with their hands tied by the "New Frontier." T.R. and the other instructors could only sit and sweat it out as surviving planes straggled in after the three and a half hour flight back from Cuba. The pilots were working hard now, back and forth from Nicaragua under the guns of Castro's planes, which could have been destroyed in the cancelled 'for political considerations' air strikes. The original plan called for refueling and rearming on the nearby airstrip at Playa Giron in Cuba, which had been captured and supplied by the Brigade Monday (D-Day), but Castro's planes had prevented landings there. The Brigade's planes were fewer after each long mission. By **Tuesday** April 18 (**D-Day +1**) they were down to six B-26s and exhausted pilots. That afternoon word finally came from Washington that the American 'instructor pilots' were allowed to fly missions. Six B- 26s returned to Cuba, three flown by Alabama NG pilots. They managed to catch Castro's forces moving south to **Blue Beach** from **Playa Larga** at sunset. Long columns of trucks, tanks and troops were bunched up, two and three vehicles abreast along the sixteen mile Cochinos Bay road. They turned the column into rubble before running out of ammunition and starting the long flight back to Nicaragua.

Four B-26s set out before dawn **Wednesday (D-Day +2)** with two manned by Alabama National Guard 'instructors' and two by some of the brigade's indefatigable pilots. One Cuban manned plane had to return for mechanical problems. The American pilots would never return. They gave their lives for something they believed in, but their government did not: **Riley W. Shamburger,**

Wade C. Gray, Leo F. Baker and Thomas W. Ray

Meanwhile, General Anastasio Somoza, commander of all armed forces in Nicaragua, had returned to Puerto Cabezas. He was a graduate of the United States Military Academy at West Point, and he felt that he needed to "feel" the action. He had been there previously to watch the little fleet depart with his words of encouragement, "Bring me some hairs from Castro's beard!" He also knew the Scott family from the "family businesses" in Nicaragua, which meant that Somoza had a finger in every significant business in Nicaragua. T.R. had wasted no time talking to him about the F-51s still sitting on the runway, which he had "offered" to let the brigade use. "*Commandante*, nice to see you again. Quite a show the boys are putting on, but that *comemierda* Fidel still has some fighters giving us fits."

"Ah, T.R. nice to see you again too. *Si*, that *hijo de puta* needs to be taught a lesson. It is too bad my extra fuel tanks did not arrive in time. You know I am a fighting man and a pilot also. But, *que lastima*, my responsibilities do not permit me to indulge myself in such personal satisfactions."

T.R. knew the ego he was dealing with and decided to work on it. He wanted those F-51s. "General, you know about the two P-51s I have in Miami. This is my comrade in arms from WW II in China and now my wingman and best friend, Juan Escheverria."

"*Mucho gusto, General!*" was Juan's response while he waited to see what T.R. was up to.

"Ah, thank you, Juan. Nice to meet another hero of the famous 'Flying Tigers.'"

"*Gracias, General.*" Juan was still watching T.R. out of the corner of his eye to see what would come next.

T.R. continued, "*Commandante*, we know your reputation as a top flight fighter pilot and a very brave warrior. Because you have offered these beautiful planes, Juan and I would like you to join us in a sortie to Cuba to show that *hijo de puta* what real fighting men look like." He waited for the flattered, but afraid, answer. He knew the answer, but hoped the offer would be enough to shame the "commandante of all armed forces" into allowing them to fly. T.R.

was sure Washington could not object to them as those 'instructor pilots permitted to fly'. Nobody had to tell the 'officials' which planes they were flying. Juan was smiling to himself as he watched this unfold.

"You flatter me, Tomasito, and you know how much my spirit wants to go. But you cannot return, and I will lose my planes, even if they do not shoot you down."

T.R. could see he had him backing up and even using his familiar name. "*Commandante*, I know you value the glory more than the planes. However, I will replace them with my own P-51s in Miami. Juan has kept them in first class fighting condition. If we have to ditch from no fuel after we have blasted Fidel's planes from the sky, my father has a ship out there where we can splash next to. I assure you Juan and I are excellent fighter pilots and wingmen for you."

For a moment Somoza was tempted by the flattery. Then reality set in. "Ah, Tomasito, how I want to go, but you know the Commanding General of Nicaragua cannot be involved in combat with another country, even if he is a *comemierda*. But I tell you what. If you can replace my planes, I will look the other way when you take off. But… you know I will be watching you and cheering on my brave companions." Now he felt like a hero himself for his part in this adventure.

'Coño,' thought Juan in amazement, 'T.R. actually made the general feel good, like he was a part of the crew.'

True to his word, Somoza ordered the planes prepared and turned over to T.R. and Juan. He was standing in the dark before dawn watching as the small group of B-26s and F-51s took off for Cuba on Wednesday, D-Day +2.

T.R. wrote his final letter to his wife and parents expressing his love and requesting release of the P-51s to Somoza. To his son, he wrote of his love and pride as a father. He closed each letter with, "I'll see you all after I take a little swim in the Caribbean."

The little air group arrived at dawn. Washington had promised Navy air cover, but through someone's confusion none arrived. As the B-26s crossed the beachhead, Cuban jets appeared, firing on them. T.R. and Juan were high and off to the side trying to fly cover. They jerked their F-51s into tight turns and climbed for altitude to dive in on the jets. The jets were in and out before they could turn. They had left the two B-26s flown by the Americans trailing smoke.

T.R. frantically called the other pilots, "Riley, Wade, how bad is it? Can you fly?"

"Scott, this is Riley. Its looks like we are going down, both of us. I'm going to try for that little strip at the sugar mill. See if you can keep 'em off me. It looks like Gonzalo is OK."

"Roger that. Wade, can you make it out to the ships for a splash down?"

"We'll make it out over the water, but we're going to bail out. We're on fire. Get the bastards for me."

"*Absalutamente, amigos. Buena suerte.* Juan, let's show these *comenierdas* some flying. You go left and I am right. See if we can catch them coming down after Gonzalo's B-26. When you see him coming just let go a stream of fire. He'll run into it."

The F-51s could make tighter turns and maneuver quicker but they were no match for the jet speed. The first jet came back out of the sun and flew right into a stream of tracers fired by both F-51s then straight into the ground. But the second jet had come around the side and caught T.R. banking into a turn. Its rounds tore into T.R.'s engine. By this time T.R. could see the crippled B-26 crashed in a field and Castro's troops closing in on the downed plane. One American crawled out of the plane firing his .45 cal. pistol at the troops before they killed him. T.R. could only turn his plane into a glide and fire as many rounds into the soldiers as he could before he crash landed.

Juan managed to make some hits in the tail of the second jet as it turned on T.R. The jet seemed to have had enough and turned for easier targets on the ground. Juan could see T.R. now out of his plane and firing his pistol at more troops rushing in for the kill. He banked his plane into a dive firing into the troops as machine gun tracers from a tank zeroed in on him. He could see T.R. go down, get up and go down again, still firing his pistol. He could hear the sound of hits on his plane. He felt the bullets hit his chest and legs. It didn't matter anymore. As he crashed directly into the tank, he looked one last time at T.R.'s body on the ground. "*Vaya con dios, mi amigo.*"

While the tank was burning in the background, a Cuban officer stood looking down at T.R's body. "Does anybody know this one?"

A soldier stepped forward, "*Si, capitan.* I know him. It is Thomas Rodrigo Scott, the son of Tom Scott, the *Heroe* of the revolution. I was born on their plantation in Oriente. They were always good to my family. He was a good man. I am sorry. My family will be sad."

Another soldier stepped forward, "I also knew him. I am sad, also."

"Well, they all died like men. Let us bury them and mark the grave so they can be found when this is over." The captain indicated to them to carry the bodies from the field, and turned back to the war at hand.

The American pilots in the other B-26 bailed out over the water and were picked up by the Cubans. Later photographs taken by Castro's men showed their bodies with life vests inflated, boots off and small caliber bullet holes in their foreheads. There was no doubt what had happened.

The indestructible Gonzalo Herrera in the third B-26 was able to deliver his strike on Castro's troops closing in on **Blue Beach.** He limped his plane all the way back to Nicaragua with thirty-eight bullet holes and one engine out. He had flown every strike since Saturday's pre-invasion strike. Now he was the last man standing on the last flight.

After 1400 hours Wednesday D-Day +2 the brigade had been driven back to the beaches at Playa Giron with Castro's tanks closing in. The brigade commander's last messages were, "Tanks closing on **Blue Beach** from north and east. Fighting on the beach. Send all available aircraft." Then, "In water, out of ammunition. Enemy closing in." Finally, "I can't wait any longer. I am destroying radio." Then silence.

Troops slipped into woods and swamps in small groups. Mysteriously, Castro's troops withdrew because they feared a trap. Their information led them to believe the brigade had 10,000 troops just waiting to suck them into a trap.

U.S. Navy destroyers, code named *Tampico* and *Santiago,* were sent racing into the bay to look for survivors with their guns trained on the shore, but never fired a shot. Castro's tanks and artillery fired on the destroyers, but failed to hit them.

All day Thursday and Friday the *Blagar* and the *Barbara J* cruised along the shore picking up ragged survivors off the beaches along the bay. The bay was now full of ships that could have been used earlier. Castro chose not to push his luck.

Chapter 10

US ARMY: FT. JACKSON –
FT. BENNING- FT. BRAGG

While TR was training Cubans in Guatemala, Tommy report-ed to Ft. Jackson, South Carolina. It had with 52,000 acres north of Columbia, and was midway between New York and Miami. It functioned as one of the main basic training centers for the Army.

Tommy watched out of the Army bus with the other inductees as they passed through the main gate, and long rows of old, frame, two story, WWII buildings with asbestos siding. There was a gener-al feeling among the recruits that it felt like going to prison, guards at the gate and no escape. Tommy was thinking, *Well, it doesn't look much different from the old National Guard Camp Blanding in Florida or the Harmony Church area of Ft. Benning, Georgia, where I spent the six weeks of ROTC summer camp.*

They passed by a group of soldiers marching in formation chanting to the lead of their drill sergeant, "You're in the Army now, you're in the Army now, you'll never get out, you'll never get out, you're in the Army now, LEFT, RIGHT, LEFT, RIGHT..." They could hear the group's drill sergeant's fading voice as they rode down the street, "You had a good home but you LEFT," "You're RIGHT," was the group response. "You had a good girl but you LEFT." You're RIGHT"... They would learn many versions of these cadence chants, and make up a few of their own, designed to keep them in step with the proper foot, instill obedience, good order...and keep their attention focused.

The bus stopped in front of a row of buildings that would be their home for the next eight weeks where a group of sergeants awaited. Then the shouting started, "Move, move, line up and have your paperwork in your hand!"

Next they were assigned barracks and marched for haircuts and issue of Army nondescript fatigue uniforms. They would not see their civilian clothes for eight weeks. Individual groups were divided into platoons with cadre noncommissioned officers (NCOs) explaining the rules. There was always the classic, and often forgotten, rule to not call Drill Sergeants "sir." This would evoke loud shouting that they were not "commissioned officers" and it better be remembered. Bunks were assigned and personal records were reviewed by the sergeants.

When Tommy's turn came the sergeant growled, "How the hell are you a Private First Class?"

"ROTC, Drill Sergeant."

"I see some bullshit here about National Guard too, PFC Scott."

"Yes, Drill Sergeant."

"Am I going to have a problem with you, college boy?" the sergeant growled in as menacing a manner as he could.

"No, Drill Sergeant."

"What the fuck? This says you completed Airborne School."

"Yes, Drill Sergeant."

"Shit. Get out of here. This ain't the National Guard." He continued to grumble to himself, "Fucking National Guard."

"Yes, Drill Sergeant."

The next day he was called into the company commander's office, who reviewed his records again and wanted to know why he didn't accept his commission. Tommy went through the story again. Captain William Jameson looked down at the papers in front of him and silently shook his head.

"This also says you went to basic training in the National Guard and were promoted to corporal. And you have a civilian pilot's license?"

"Yes, sir, but the Army decided that since basic was a special training for National Guard members it wouldn't count, and the rank wouldn't stand either. For those of us who already had been in for one year and had all the basics, the uniform, marksmanship, drill, etc., the Guard created a short version. My six weeks ROTC didn't count either, but the PFC is a permanent grade. The Army said my eyesight was not quite what they required to fly, good enough for civilians, but not the Army, sir."

The captain shook his head again, "Jesus, looks like the Army is wasting a lot of money training you all over again, but it appears they can't take your airborne qualification away from you. How did you ever get that in the Guard?"

"I volunteered, and I was lucky there was an open slot, sir." He could see the captain was wearing his own jump wings, but most of the cadre did not. He definitely did not want to explain the pull his father had to use to get him in that slot.

"Well, Scott you are the most unusual recruit I have ever seen and probably in this whole training center. You're dismissed. And don't forget to sew on your PFC stripe. They can't take that away from you either, and we're probably going to need your help in this cycle."

"Yes, sir."

As Tommy left, the captain was thinking he needed to do a little more checking on this recruit. *Damn, already airborne, ROTC and four years in the Guard, which makes a difference in pay, and a pilot.*

That night in the barracks, the pecking order started to develop. Tommy's first encounter came over his name. A very large light skinned, pale blue-eyed, black recruit with brown wavy hair from Chicago took exception to the name Thomas Scott, because his name was also Thomas Scott. He had already established that he was "the man" in the barracks and now turned on Tommy.

Tommy was thinking, *What am I going to do with this guy without getting both of us in trouble?*

The recruit lunged at Tommy saying, "You ain't gonna use my name."

Tommy's immediate thought was, *No time to talk.* His reaction was equally immediate. Using his opponent's own momentum, he grabbed his arm and flipped him completely upside down onto the floor with a loud thump. When he jumped up, Tommy gave him a short open handed jab to his solar plexus from six inches away, which again sent him rapidly back to the floor gasping for breath with another loud thud. All of the action was accompanied loud shouts of the recruits.

A voice shouted from the end of the hall, "What the hell is going on?" The assistant platoon NCO came out of his room ready to put someone on punishment duty.

"Sorry, drill sergeant, I was just showing the men some *tai chi* moves they could use."

"Well, cut out the horseshit. Lights out. You got a very active day to use that energy tomorrow."

"Yes, drill sergeant."

The other Scott was still on the floor looking very puzzled. "How the fuck did you do that? You usin' some kind of magic shit?"

"No magic. I'll show you tomorrow". It was something else he had not told the Army. Master Chen in Havana had schooled him for four years. Another family connection. Old Tom owned part of a Chinese restaurant and Chen was part of that family. In 1958, five percent of the Cuban population was Chinese. Tommy laughed to himself and thought most of them had fled to Miami and owned about all the Chinese restaurants there, and most of the martial arts studios.

Everything was defused for the moment.

Their platoon sergeant was Sergeant First Class E-7 Mario Tartaglia from the Bronx, NY. He delighted in correcting recruits who dared to pronounce the "g" in his name and he was not partial to 'ignorant red necks.' Of course, everyone with a southern accent was a 'red neck' to him. He was a private in the Korean 'Conflict,' and had received a Combat Infantry Badge, purple heart for his wounds, and a Bronze Star for bravery. Now he was saddled with the onerous job of shaping up this group before he could receive his promotion to First Sergeant E-8. He took any screw-ups personally as holding up his promotion.

The assistant platoon sergeant was a black Sergeant E-5, a three-stripe "buck sergeant," William Jones, from Cleveland, Ohio, with no combat experience and now trying to prove himself at the expense of the recruits.

'Oh happy days' were about to start.

The eight weeks of basic of training consisted of:

Week 1: Issue of clothing, medicals (with multiple shots all in the same day), daily physical exercise (PT), General Orders, unarmed basic movements, marching, drill commands and generally learning about the Army and what is expected of a soldier, all to the loud chorus of drill sergeants' voices.

Week 2: Unarmed combat training, map reading and compass work, first aid, introduction to tear gas and use of gas mask and without mask while having to recite the General Orders *"#1. I will guard everything within the limits of my post and quit my post only when properly relieved. #2. I will obey my special orders and perform all my duties in a military manner. #3. I will report violations of my special orders, emergencies, and anything not covered in my instructions to the commander of the relief."* And always more PT, and more drill, and more drill sergeant shouting.

Week 3: Introduction to the M-14 rifle with the 7.62 NATO round (newly replacing the World War II M-1 .30 cal. rifle) with disassembly, and marksmanship training, and more drill with rifles, and more PT, and more drill sergeant shouting.

Week 4: Actual firing on the rifle range, familiarization with grenade launchers, machine guns and anti-tank weapons, and more drill with rifles, and more PT, and more drill sergeant shouting.

Week 5, 6: More training proficiency in day and night operations and introduction to field exercises, and more drill with rifles, and more PT, and more drill sergeant shouting.

Week 7: Final special tactical field training exercise with recruits taking responsibility for command positions, squad leaders and platoon leader.

Week 8: Cleaning barracks and equipment for the next group, and more PT, while preparing for graduation parade with rifles and ceremony.

After the first night, Tommy's experience was becoming obvious to his fellow recruits, to say nothing of his throwing big Chicago Tom around the room. They looked to him for calm explanations instead of the fearful shouts from the NCOs. There were even a couple of Cajun boys in the platoon who spoke French, of a sort.

Even the platoon sergeant was noticing that Tommy was actually a help. Additionally, he had been impressed that Tommy knew about the soft Italian "g" and even spoke a little Italian, which, of course, was easy considering his Spanish and French…and a few Italian tourist girls in Paris.

After it became obvious that Tommy was already EXPERT with a rifle, the sergeants used him as an additional instructor. His hand to hand combat was a little more intimidating than they expected.

The first bivouac found them walking up a hill in a thunder storm, because they were trying to make up time in the exercise. Tommy tried to say something to Sergeant Jones, but was told to shut up and get back in line.

Damn, thought Tommy. He had seen this scenario before at Ft. Benning and the cadet had died from the lightning strike.

No sooner had the thought crossed his mind, two incredibly loud, flashing explosions hit the ground near Sergeant Jones, throwing him into the air and knocking Tommy and several recruits off their feet. The second bolt hit near S Sergeant Tartaglia, knocking him down and leaving him momentarily stunned.

Tommy shouted for everyone to lie down and ran over to Sgt. Jones who was not breathing and his heart had stopped. Old lifeguard training took over, and he started administering CPR, alternating mouth-to-mouth resuscitation with rhythmic pounding on his chest. He was yelling, "Come on, drill sergeant, come back!" over and over between breaths. Sergeant Tartaglia was still dazed, but he had now crawled back to where Tommy was working on

Jones. Tommy looked at him and shouted, "Get a medevac helicopter here quick!"

Jones eyes began to open. He could gasp for breath, but he couldn't speak or move. His clothes were still smoking where heat from the lightning had seared them.

Medics and the company commander arrived on the scene before the helicopter. "You alright, Tartaglia? Looks like Scott just saved Jones' life. You want to call it a day?"

"Yeah, yeah, I'm OK. It just jolted me off my feet." He thought for a minute, "Captain, let us finish this exercise. Scott can take Jones' place."

The captain looked at him and Scott, then looked over the rest of the platoon. They seemed alright. "OK, see you back by 1800 hours."

Two days later Sgt. Tartaglia was called in for his report. Captain Jameson looked up, "Mario, Sergeant Jones will be OK in a few months. The doctors are hopeful that he fully regains use of his limbs. He was one very lucky man that Scott knew what to do. I want to recommend him for a Commendation Medal. Do you have any objections?"

"Absolutely no objections, sir. The damned thing had me so stunned at the moment I was useless."

"Now for the bad news. Training command says they cannot replace him until the next cycle."

Tartaglia cleared his throat, "Sir, may I make a suggestion?"

"Of course." The captain thought he already knew what was coming.

"PFC Scott already knows all the shit we are covering. I would like to use him. The men respect him and do what he says."

The captain looked at him with an amused grin, "I thought you would never ask. I pushed it back up the channels with my recommendation and your reports. The Army has reconsidered and reinstated his corporal E-4 rank. I think this episode pushed them over the edge. He's yours for the duration."

"Thank you, sir. Uh, there is one other thing, sir."

"Yes, sergeant?"

"There is something about Scott. It's the way he reacts in the woods, the way he is always looking around, the way he sits, the positions he takes. It's like he has been there. Is there anything else I need to know, sir?"

The captain tapped his pencil on the desk, looking at the papers there for a long time.

"Mario, what I am going to tell you is classified. I am not even supposed to know this. You cannot say anything." He took a deep breath. "I called his tactical officer at the university asking what you are wondering. It seems our PFC Scott fought with Castro's guerillas in the mountains of Cuba under extreme combat conditions. After that he lost a little enthusiasm about being an ROTC officer."

"I knew it, I knew it. He's been in the shit. I could smell it on him, and Jones couldn't."

The captain's look became very serious, "Remember, Mario, you cannot say anything to him or anyone…or *we* will be in deep shit. Do I make myself understood?"

"Not to worry, sir."

Sergeant Tartaglia left with a whole new perspective. He would really put Corporal Scott to work immediately. The rest of the platoon already considered him part of the cadre and credited him with whatever success they were having.

Tommy and Chicago Tom had reached an agreement. Tommy would be "MacD," derived from MacDougall and Chicago would be Tom, who had *no middle initial.* Consequently, the Army labeled all his documents <u>Thomas NMI Scott</u> and "MacD" <u>as Thomas MacD. Scott.</u> A bond had been growing between these two. "MacD" considered "NMI" the leader of the platoon for the final exercise. He had been the recruit leader anyway since "MacD" was made an NCO cadre.

The last week of preparation for the final exercise with recruits in command positions consisted of a full tactical field exercise of several overnight bivouacs. This night heavy rain had been falling causing saturated ground and fast running creeks. Miserable conditions, but war does not stop for miserable weather.

The platoon was returning from a relatively successful operation. The last obstacle was crossing a narrow wooden bridge where the creek had swollen to twice its size and the current was running very rapidly. Tartaglia went out on the bridge to test its strength in this current. It had almost lifted off its anchoring because of the high water. Without warning an uprooted tree crashed into the bridge, violently throwing him into the railing and over the side. He disappeared under the water as the platoon stood shocked into inaction. "MacD" was the first to react by running down the creek bank trying to get in front of where the sergeant might be. When he saw a head and hand come out of the water he dived in. The current was even stronger than he thought as it swept him underwater.

Oh shit, he thought, *this may be a bad idea and drown both of us.* He was now being twirled around in the swirling water and banged against underwater things he could not see. Suddenly he felt his legs hit the sergeant's body. He was able to pull Tartaglia up onto another tree trunk which had banged into him. Now he was swallowing water and gasping for breath, but still hanging on to the sergeant. He had him over the tree trunk now shoving down in an attempt at artificial respiration. The sergeant was not moving. "MacD" could see his leg was broken and moving awkwardly in the water and his head had a bad cut from hitting something.

The men in the platoon had run parallel to the bank and formed a human chain trying to reach them. The log hit something underwater making it swing toward shore, close enough for the strong arms of Big Tom Scott to grab them and pull both to shore. MacD was almost exhausted but started CPR. He had squeezed a lot of water out over the log. Now he needed to get him breathing. No one knew if the sergeant was dead or could be revived, but MacD and other members continued to alternately and together give CPR. Finally, the sergeant began to moan and vomited into Big Tom's mouth as he gave mouth to mouth resuscitation. "Fuck you, you sonofabitch," Tom yelled as he spat out a very unpleasant fluid, much to the amusement and relieved laughter of the rest of the platoon. As the medics arrived to take over, MacD lay back completely spent, but glad he was alive.

MacD took over the platoon the rest of the week and the following week's preparation for the graduation parade and ceremony. He used Big Tom as his assistant with Tartaglia's recommendation and the captain's approval. And more PT. And more drills with rifles. MacD had to admit they did look good, and spirit was high. They knew they had done well through some pretty unusual circumstances. Thanks to additional instruction by MacD, along with the two sergeants, the platoon had qualified everyone on the rifle range. Their average scores were the highest in the training cycle.

Sergeant Tartaglia had returned the last couple of days on crutches to proudly tell them that they had been selected as the most outstanding platoon and would lead the graduation parade. He just grinned at Corporal Scott. He had already said thanks from his hospital bed, as had Sgt. Jones.

Graduation day came and Corporal Scott led his platoon to the place of honor in front of the reviewing stand in front of the Commanding General of the Post and the Colonel Commanding the Recruit Training Command. Beside them stood Captain Jameson as the commanding officer of the company of which the platoon was part. Standard speeches about upholding the standards of the Army and protecting the country were made and Corporal Scott was given the award for his platoon.

The Captain gave a short speech with some real surprises. For his life saving effort at the risk of his own life Corporal Scott was awarded the Soldier's Medal. And for his outstanding leadership under extraordinary circumstances, he was awarded another Commendation Medal. And considering all of the aforesaid things, he was promoted to Sergeant E-5. The captain looked at him and shouted, "Airborne, All The Way." Tommy saw the General and the Colonel both grinning and noticed they were also wearing their jump wings. Captain Jameson stepped aside and now Sergeant First Class E-7 Tartaglia hobbled forward on crutches to pin on the Soldier's Medal. The commanding general himself handed him his new sergeant stripes with the remark that he doubted that he would ever see this again. In the background behind him he could hear his troops shouting "Airborne."

Then, the biggest surprise. From behind the colonel stepped his grandfather to pin on his Commendation Medal. He was wearing the Medal of Honor replica in his lapel and being saluted by the grinning Commanding General and all officers and men on the reviewing stand.

That is the way the U. S. Army career of Thomas MacDougall Scott II started.

At the following reception, he found his grandfather talking to the general, Captain Jameson and Tartaglia. "Tommy, you have your young captain here to blame for instigating all of this. He is the one who alerted me as to what was happening. Obviously, I am very proud of you. This was better than Paris, eh?"

"No comment, sir," was all he could think to say. Everyone laughed at his embarrassment.

The general shook his hand, "Sergeant Scott, I do thank Captain Jameson for this unexpected pleasure of meeting your grandfather. My own father served in the Spanish American War. Now I have to go work at being a general. Good day, gentlemen."

"I need to go back to work also. Maybe if I have a few more days like this, they will send me back to the real Army," and the captain excused himself, taking Tartaglia with him.

Old Tom gave his grandson a big Cuban *abrazo*.

"Ah, granpa, I have someone I want you to meet," and he waved at Big Tom to come over. "This is my friend, Thomas Scott from Chicago,"

"Nice to meet you, young man. Fine name you have there." He stood looking at this tall, well-built, young, black man, with fine features and light skin. He turned to look at Tommy, "I take it he is in your unit?"

"Yes, sir. He was raised by his grandmother, Lilly. She was from Alabama, too,"

Chicago, Lilly, Alabama? Old Tom's mind was whirling now. *It can't be,* he thought.

He looked at Tommy, a questioning and stern look in his eyes which said, even without words, "Are you trying to tell me something, young man?"

"I don't know, granpa."

Big Tom was watching and wondering what was happening. He had no idea what was passing between these two.

Tommy turned to his friend and said, "Tom, please tell my grandfather your family's story."

Now completely puzzled, he said, "Naw, this ain't something he would be interested in. It ain't all that pretty or interesting."

"Tell him, Tom, it's an interesting story. He's from Alabama. He understands." Tommy was watching his grandfather's face. He was worried about the outcome, but felt it had to be played out. Big Tom had no idea what was happening. Tommy had just been thinking and trying to put the pieces together for weeks since he heard the story.

Chicago Tom started his story with his grandmother, who was already very white, from Goodwater, Alabama, being pregnant by another white man before she moved to Chicago. He was apologetic saying he meant no disrespect. He went on, that his mother was so white everyone thought she was, but the men she dated knew different and treated her like a "nigger." She finally died from a drug overdose, but not before she was pregnant by a black man. Big Tom stopped there and said, "That's the end of the story," still wondering why Tommy had insisted on telling the story.

Old Tom turned to Tommy with a look that said, *So? And the rest of the story is?*

"Granpa, his front teeth are lapped left to right." He saw a slight twitch in his grandfather's face. The lapped tooth was a genetic trait of the Scott family.

Turning to Big Tom, his grandfather said, "That is an interesting story. I do know similar stories. What is your grandmother's phone number? I may know some of her relatives. Boys, I have some business calls to make tonight. How about I see you for breakfast tomorrow? I'm staying in the base guest house, thanks to your general."

Still puzzled, Big Tom turned to Tommy, "He didn't write down her phone number."

"Tom, I guarantee he does not forget numbers."

The next day they had to clear the barracks before noon. There was just enough time for breakfast at an annex to the guest house. Tommy's grandfather was waiting for them to sit down. He had made that phone call and more than sixty years had come flooding back. Now he was trying to compose himself, as the boys sat down. "Tom, I do know your grandmother. I talked to her last night. She was a dear friend of mine when we were children. I lost track of her when I went to sea." Tommy could see this was going to be emotionally hard for him.

He cleared his throat. Tommy could see tears starting to form in his eyes. Even though he had suspected this was true, and he had wrestled with it for weeks, it was gut-wrenching to see it play out. Old Tom turned to Tommy and said, "Thank you, son, for finding him."

Big Tom was frozen in place, not able to comprehend the emotions passing between the two.

The old man turned his gaze to Big Tom with tears now running down his cheeks, "Tom, I am your grandfather. She was the true love of my life, and I lost her when they went to Chicago while I was at sea."

Seeing this big man completely speechless and unable to even move, he reached over and took his hand. Tommy took his other hand. "I was sure it was true, but I wanted grandfather to know and that he should tell you."

It was Big Tom's turn to cry as all the unknown years of loss and love from his grandmother came pouring back. They all cried. The moment passed, and Old Tom started laughing, "Now what in the hell do we call each other since we are all Thomas Scott?"

"Easy. I'm MacD, and he is Tom. We settled that in the barracks when I threw his ass around the room like your old friend, Master Chen, taught me. Now I guess I have to call him 'CUZ.'"

"It's true, sir. He whipped my ass," the newest grandson laughed.

"DON'T CALL ME SIR. I AM NOT A COMMISSIONED OFFICER," barked the old man.

Everyone had a good laugh at that bit of truth. "OK, granpa." Today his world had done an 'about, face,' 'right flank, march,' 'forward, march,' 'to the rear, march,' and 'column left, march,' all at the same time for Chicago Tom.

Tommy spent his permitted leave time back in Miami with his mother. His father was out of the country training in some secret location with the Cuban exile group.

Tom went back to Chicago for a long talk with his grandmother, then to Ft. Benning for his Advanced Individual Training (AIT) in infantry.

Old Tom took his wife back to Paris to try to explain his new situation. With no Cuba to return to, Paris was where she was most at home and at peace.

The Army had also decided that Tommy did not need to go to AIT in Infantry, because of his record, airborne qualifications and experience. Permission was granted to report to the Ranger School at Ft. Benning, GA.

The U.S. Army Ranger School was then part of the Army's Infantry School. It consisted basically of advanced patrolling and ambush training under extreme physical and weather conditions for 59 days. The first phase was in Ft. Benning; the second phase was mountain training in Dahlonega, Georgia at Camp Merrill; the final phase was waterborne and swamp exercises at Auxillary Field #6 Eglin Air Force Base in west Florida. Tommy's lasting impression was one of extreme lack of sleep, hunger, cold, harassment by cadre and still being able to function in leadership positions. More flashbacks from Cuba gave him confidence that he could do this. As a lower ranking NCO he seemed to receive less harassment from the cadre than the officers, especially the West Point graduates. The school cadre seemed to take a particular delight in making their lives miserable. It was much more brutal conditions than basic training, but he ended up as the Enlisted Honor Graduate. He was still thinking, 'I've been here before.'

He knew Big Tom was somewhere at Ft. Benning in Advanced Individual Training (AIT), and finally caught up with him before Big Tom reported to Airborne School, also at Ft. Benning.

Next stop was a brief time in NCO school which earned him another sergeant stripe to Staff Sergeant E-6. Then on to the famed 82nd Airborne Division at Ft. Bragg, North Carolina, where he was made a Squad Leader and was back on "jump pay," earning another $54.00 per month, just for jumping out of a "perfectly good airplane." At that time the 82nd was part of the Army rapid deployment plan with parts of the division always on alert and ready to fly anywhere in the world. Tommy's battalion did fly to some unusual places as practice, but most of the world was peaceful, at least on a large military scale. The first thing he had noticed on entering Ft. Bragg was that everyone on the street was doing double time or the "Airborne Shuffle." Nobody walked except the "leg" support troops and Air Force personnel, and some of them were shamed into jogging.

April 17, 1961 reports of an airborne assault and amphibious landing in Cuba by Cuban exiles began to filter into Ft. Bragg. The airborne assault obviously caught the attention of Headquarters. To Tommy Scott it had a whole different meaning. He knew something had been in the works, and he knew his father would be in the middle of it. After two days even newspapers had the story, and it became clear that the landing would be a failure. Casualty reports were very slow to come in because of the secrecy surrounding the operation. Tommy's constant calls to Miami had not been informative, but on April 18 he knew his father had died. His grandmother knew the instant he died. Tommy could feel it through her all the way to North Carolina. A month later it was confirmed. She went into a long depression and her health started to decline. Tommy's emergency leave to Miami could do little to relieve it, or to comfort his mother. He had a brief conversation with his grandfather to let him know that Big Tom was going to be assigned to the 82nd also. In Paris his grandmother had handled the news of his existence with considerable understanding and even a little pleasure that another member had been added to the family. She was Cuban. She understood, but now was not the time to talk about it.

After standing down from a long alert, sitting at Pope Air Force Base on the Ft. Bragg reservation, he read an announcement requesting volunteers who spoke Spanish to interview for Special Forces over on Smoke Bomb Hill. Their area was on the other side of Ft. Bragg. He only knew that they were referred to as "snake eaters" and "sneaky Petes," had some guerilla warfare mission, and 'may have' been involved in Cuba and other parts of the world. But just being on alerts, sitting in combat readiness alert at Pope Air Force Base and jumping out of an airplane once in a while at field exercises was getting monotonous after nine months. He had already gone to Jumpmaster School and Pathfinder School (the first men on the ground whose assignment was to set up beacons to guide the incoming airborne assault). He had even been able to take the Infantry Officer Basic Course by correspondence based on his ROTC eligibility, just in case he ever decided to accept his commission, and a couple of courses toward his college degree. Only one course remained to graduate.

So, let's check out Smoke Bomb Hill, he figured. He requested his personnel file be forwarded for review, but not without some loud, fruitless griping by his company First Sergeant. However, the announcement had the signature approval of the Post Commander and the Commanding General of the division. No arguments. He left, hoping he did not have to come back and face the wrath of the First Sergeant, who was thinking of the nuisance to get an experienced replacement. But he did have to face Big Tom who said, "Shit, man, I just got here, and now your ass is leaving. Who are these jokers, anyway?"

"I'll tell you when I get there. By the way, are you up to going to Miami, yet? Granpa said anytime you are ready." Big Tom still wasn't sure he could handle it.

Those "jokers" turned out to be a whole new ball game.

CHAPTER 11

US ARMY SPECIAL FORCES

Headquarters 7th Special Forces Group (Airborne)
Ft. Bragg, North Carolina

"Unconventional Warfare consists of the interrelated fields of guerrilla warfare, evasion and escape, and subversion against hostile states (resistance.) Unconventional warfare operations are conducted in enemy or enemy controlled territory by predominately indigenous personnel usually supported and directed in varying degrees by an external source. Within certain designated geographic areas - called guerrilla warfare operational areas - the United States Army is responsible for the conduct of all three interrelated fields of activity as they affect guerrilla warfare operations."
Department of the Army Field Manual **FM 31-21**
Guerrilla Warfare and Special Forces Operations

Major Guillermo Lazaro Rodriguez looked around the group of officers and NCOs, "Gentlemen, FM 31-21 will be your bible for the next couple of months and in the future. The normal rules of warfare and engagement will not apply. Special Forces are specialists in warfare at its most primitive; the knife, the noose, explosives. You have some extra reading provided, compliments of Mao Tse-tung and Che Guevara. I know all of you know who they are." He shifted his gaze to Scott and another Cuban NCO. "Some of you may even have had first-hand experience."

"In addition, we will be emphasizing Counterinsurgency Operations. That is where the action is in the world today. We have units operating in all areas of the world at this moment. As you know your group was selected for your Spanish language capability. You have been told you will probably be in Panama to cover all of Latin America where needed. Currently, Company D of the 7th SF Group is there, but we are forming a new concept and a new 8th Group there which will be a Special Action Force and include two line Special Forces companies, a military intelligence detachment, a medical detachment, a military police detachment, an Army Security Agency detachment and a Psychological operations battalion. The 8th Group organization will be two C-Teams. Each has operational control of three B-Teams, each controlling five A-Teams, the basic operational unit. Each A-Team, as you will learn, has twelve men which include two officers, a captain and 1st lieutenant. There are *no 2nd lieutenants* in our Table of Organization and Equipment (TOE). I am sure you NCOs will appreciate that." A knowing laugh went around the room. "In each A-Team there are ten NCOs, including the Team Sergeant. All of which are specialists in one of the areas of Operations, Intelligence, Heavy Weapons, Light Weapons, (2) Medical, (2) Demolitions, and (2) Radio. Each NCO is responsible for cross training the other members of his A-Team, including the officers. If you are not proficient in any of these areas, you will be before you leave here.

"Now Sergeant Major Hanley will give you a briefing on what you will be expected to learn and unlearn. Sergeants Scott and Avila, see me after the briefing."

Sergeant Major (E-9) Hanley was a career SF man, who had already served in areas of the world the new volunteers had never heard about. He would herd them through a very grueling course in very unconventional warfare.

Scott and Avila reported to Major Rodriguez's office, and were told to close the door behind them. "Gentlemen, as you suspect, I have read your files, including the classified stuff. I, too, was in Cuba during the *revolution,* but I was assigned there with the CIA. You will learn both SF and CIA come from the old Office of Strategic Services (OSS) in WW II. We frequently work together in different operations. I was in the Escambry Mountains closer to Havana with a group not controlled by Fidel. I know how the other groups distrusted him, but I didn't know of either of you until you turned up here."

"Primarily, our Spanish speaking soldiers in your class are Mexican or Puerto Rican with no experience or understanding of other Latin American countries, much less guerilla warfare. Some of the officers only have some Spanish language proficiency from college studies."

"We will not be dealing with Cuba or Castro, except for a scattering of groups he or Che are trying to influence or finance. Your experience will be valuable to us as we try to counter the same things you were doing in Cuba."

Scott was thinking that he was glad none of Batista's soldiers had been trained by Special Forces. His thoughts were interrupted as the major continued.

"If you are as much help as I think, I will personally see that you are promoted to Sergeant First Class (SFC E-7.) That's all, gentlemen, I just want to make sure we understand each other. Oh yeah, don't think Sergeant Major Hanley hasn't been in the mix. His name is Irish, but his mother is Polish. His Slavic language skills have made him very effective in certain unnamed parts of the world. Enough said."

They *were* helpful over the months of training, and they *were* made SFCs, and they *were* assigned to Panama.

US Army 8th Special Forces Group (ABN), Ft. Gulick, Panama

Scott was assigned to an A-Team as Light Weapons Specialist and, as guaranteed, had been cross trained in the other specialties. A certain proficiency in each was required in order to obtain the coveted "Flash" or patch on the Green Beret worn by Special Forces personnel and the suffix "3" added to their Military Occupational Specialty (MOS) number, which indicated the additional qualification of *Special Forces*. The "flash" of the 8th was half yellow and half light blue on diagonals. Officers received a "3" prefix on their MOS. The word *counter*-insurgency was the prevailing operational emphasis in Latin America. There were always some types of antigovernment groups operating in the countryside of most countries. If assistance was requested, or offered in some cases where U.S. interests were being affected, a mobile training team was sent in. In some cases operational A-Teams were sent clandestinely by themselves.

The 8th SF Gp. had the additional mission of supporting the Army's School of the Americas and Jungle Warfare School to train Latin American army personnel.

The *School of the Americas* was tasked in training Latin America military personnel in "anticommunist" counterinsurgency. Later so called "civil rights" groups referred to it as 'the school of assassins', because so many dictators and cadre were trained there.

The *Jungle Warfare School* trained U.S. personnel and Latin American military in jungle operations. An airborne training school was also operated there for foreign troops.

Scott was getting used to the country and the routine. It wasn't Cuba by a long shot and certainly not the long, undersupplied months of guerrilla warfare in the mountains, but he was comfortable there. This highly trained and cross trained A-Team was a close group that he really liked being a part of. Ft. Gulick, adjacent to the city of Colon and a leftover from WW II, had everything you could need on an Army post. On the other side of the isthmus at Rio Hato on an abandoned airstrip, A-13 was a special HALO team (high altitude low opening) prepared to covertly free fall from altitudes of 30,000 feet to avoid detection. They had conducted the first HALO school outside of Ft. Bragg.

Some connections through his grandfather made it better, but it was also better not to discuss them with the Army.

Scott and another Sergeant had been sent over to coordinate an exercise at the Canal Zone administrative office. Dealing with the civilians running the Canal Zone could get a little difficult for some of the Group's operations with the School of the Americas.

As they entered the building, they could hear an argument across the hall with a female voice rising higher every second. Both sergeants peered into the room. What they saw was the very shapely back of a young girl with short blonde hair yelling at a chubby little clerk.

Tommy exclaimed, "Things are looking up, Fred!"

"Forget it. She's a school teacher who was warned very specifically not to have anything to do with SF guys, and she won't. Damned rude about it, too. She teaches French in the Canal Zone. Rumor has it the colonel himself warned her off."

"French, huh? Interesting."

"Don't do it Scott. I'm telling you…"

By that time he had walked up behind the girl and spoken in French, "*Mademoiselle,* may I be of some assistance to you in this matter."

Without turning she replied in French, "*Oui,* this idiot will not order the supplies I need in my classroom." Still glaring at the clerk she turned to see who was speaking.

Suddenly Tommy Scott and Denise Johanson were staring into each other's eyes…again.

Tommy was the first to recover, "You cut your hair." was all he could think to say.

She stammered, "You changed your style of dress."

"You are as gorgeous as ever."

"And you, sir, are still Prince Charming coming to the aid of the *mademoiselle* in distress." Both started laughing, still speaking in French.

The other sergeant stood staring, barely able to keep his mouth from hanging open. There was nothing he could say, and he could not understand a word they were saying.

Tommy winked at Denise and said, still in French, "Don't tell him you know me."

"*Absolument non,*" (absolutely not) she replied, still laughing.

Turning to the clerk he asked in Spanish, "Is there something for which you need permission? I am just on my way to a meeting with the Chief Administrator. Perhaps I could help explain your problem with this young lady."

Looking up at two very large sergeants and the mention of the Chief Administrator had completely unnerved the clerk. He could only agree that he could be of service, and the Administrator need not be bothered with this minor thing.

Denise said in French, "What did you say to him?"

"I only said I was certain that he was very competent and would solve the problem."

"Yeah, right." was her sarcastic answer in English, which made Fred feel that he was correct about her after all.

In English, Tommy asked her if she had a ride home, and that his sergeant would be happy to give a ride while they sat in the luxurious back seat of the jeep discussing the beautiful countryside.

"That would be very kind of you, thank you." she replied. Fred was thinking that this was getting out of hand now.

After two months of dating, Tom casually asked, "How would you like to go the Annual Ball of the Association of Founders of the Canal? This year it's in the Grand Ballroom of the Presidential Palace."

Denise had been in the Canal Zone long enough to know that this was a big deal, and in a very skeptical and sarcastic manner asked, "How does a US Army sergeant get to go to this event? Are you pulling my chain, because you only take me to the NCO club, then hurry me back to my apartment? Paris, this is not. All of this before you mysteriously disappear into the jungle for weeks at a time?"

"*Au contraire, ma chérie,* my limited and lowly status in life does not preclude me from occasionally rising above my station to please and impress my true love when the opportunity presents itself."

Denise stared at him. She knew him well enough to know he was up to something. This was an entirely new side of her sergeant, not seen before. "OK, before I call you a liar, explain."

"Well, my grandfather happens to be a founder of this organization, and he cannot attend this year. So he asked me to represent him, since I am already here. It should be fun."

Denise stared some more and tried to keep her mouth from hanging open. She remembered his grandparents had the apartment in Paris, but this was something very different. "Are you really kidding me?"

"*Non.* Do you have a formal gown? If not, we shall find one courtesy of Scott Enterprises, Inc. This should be fun also."

She was now completely speechless.

"Let's drink on it," with that, he pulled out the bottle of Dom Perignon champagne he had been hiding.

In spite of her shock and misgivings, the champagne made the rest of the night go well.

The ball was to be held in three weeks, time enough for him to run an exercise down on the Colombian border and be back. He allowed her to go pick out a gown on the proviso that the company would pay and assurances that it was not a big deal.

Two and a half weeks later Tom showed up at the door for a preview. The effect of the girl and the new gown were stunning, and he said so.

Standing in the reception line, the pretty young girl in a beautiful gown and the handsome young man in a tuxedo were a striking contrast to the rest of the association of older gentlemen and chubby wives, including the President of the Republic of Panama.

"I cannot believe we are doing this," Denise whispered. The French Ambassador had just passed by and exchanged his greetings in French to both of them. She felt Tom stiffen. When she looked up, the colonel commanding the 8th Special Forces Group in formal dress uniform with medals shining was standing in front of them with his hand extended.

Tom was kicking himself for not realizing his commanding officer would naturally be here. Now he just hoped he was not recognized out of uniform. He had received a three day pass from his A-Team CO, but nobody knew he was here. He and Denise had taken the train from Colon to Panama City.

The Colonel spoke first. He had looked ahead when he heard the conversation in French. "Well hello, Denise, fancy meeting you here. You look beautiful. Our daughter tells us how much she enjoys your French class. I see you both know the French Ambassador. And who is this handsome young man?"

Denise glanced at the Colonel's wife standing beside him and caught her starting to laugh. Unable to control herself, she started to giggle.

The colonel turned a puzzled look to his wife, "Obviously, I am missing something here, Mary?"

"I'm sorry, John. I know who this young man is." Tom felt his stomach tighten and sweat began to run down the back of his neck at the thought of what might come next.

"Well?" The colonel's eyebrows had now raised in anticipation.

"He is one of your sergeants, John."

The colonel's face went blank with a moment of confusion, and Tom felt his heart drop to the floor.

The colonel quickly recovered and looked at Tom's name tag. "Mr. Scott, since I have to assume you are not crashing this event and standing in the reception line by accident with the President of the Republic of Panama, please do satisfy my curiosity." Now Denise was getting nervous as she felt a quiver go through Tom.

Tom cleared his throat, "Sir, my grandfather was a founder, and he could not be here as he normally would. So, he requested that I stand in for him."

"Are you an officer in his company also?" The colonel was now finding this mystery a little more interesting.

"I'm on the Board of Directors, Sir." He replied not knowing how this was going to play out.

"Really? You are a little young for that aren't you?"

"I don't think so, Sir. My father was killed at the Bay of Pigs, and I'm next in line." Damn, he thought. He had not meant to say that. "Sorry, Sir, I had not intended to let that out."

"I understand. I had some SF friends in that mess." Suddenly, recognition struck his face. "Ah! Now I remember. Thomas Mac-Dougall Scott. I have read this young man's file. Very interesting. Some parts very classified. He has turned down an officer's commission two times."

Mary quickly intervened, "John, stop interrogating him. You are holding up the line."

Realizing she was correct, he mumbled, "Of course, but I look forward to the rest of the story."

"Yes, Sir." Scott said as turned to the next guest in line. Denise was just starting to get strength back in her knees.

As the representative of the sole surviving founder, Tom sat at the head table and had been asked to give a short speech. Tom always enjoyed relating his grandfather's story, but now he had the commanding officer of the entire 8th Group sitting in front of him, and the President of the Republic at the same table. This was going to be an *interesting* experience. But he thought to himself no one is shooting at him, and that's good.

The President of the Association was now making his remarks on the state of the Canal and its future. Tom looked around the famous *Salon Amarillo,* where most formal events took place in the *Palacio de las Garsas* (Palace of the Herons) named for the Herons that wandered free in the courtyard, and marveled at the history of this spot where a palace was rebuilt after the pirate Henry Morgan sacked the city in 1673. He loved this old Spanish history of which his grandmother's family was so much a part.

He heard his name being introduced and took his place at the lectern, giving Denise a friendly squeeze on the shoulder as he stood up. She hoped she had not turned as many shades of red as she felt at this noticeable bit of affection.

Tom looked over the room with so many significant people for a moment, while trying not to make eye contact with the colonel.

With a slight clearing of his throat, he began recognizing in fluent Spanish the dignitaries from the cheat sheet in front of him. "Senor Presidente de la Republica de Panama, Roberto Francisco Chiari," and so on until he reached the French Ambassador where he switched to French, then back to Spanish and finally to "Coronel Bergeron, Commandante del U. S. Army Groupo 8th Fuersas Especial." There he had done it. It was no more difficult than speaking in front of the university students at orientation. Now he could tell his favorite story.

Colonel Bergeron turned and whispered to his wife, "That was very impressive."

"I know," she replied with a smile.

"With everyone's permission, I would like to give you greetings from my grandfather in English. I believe most of you know him and his involvement here, but I always enjoy telling his story, which is so much a part of this place and the maritime trade. When he first came here as a fifteen-year-old seaman working for my great-great uncle there was no canal. There were only the old French plans, some ditches and a stifled dream cut short by disease. I hope I can tell you a few things not commonly known about him and repeat those I enjoy telling the most."

Tommy went on to tell the story of the battle in Santiago de Cuba where old Tom was awarded the Medal of Honor and first met Teddy Roosevelt, and how his uncle had involved him in the organization of the maritime interest which resulted in this organization. He mentioned that he had been here as a common seaman on his grandfather's ships, and threw in a few anecdotes about sailors in port, which drew a knowing laugh from his audience.

"Whenever I think of the sea and how this country has linked two great oceans of the world, I like to remember an appropriate quote from President Kennedy's writings:

'I really don't know why it is that all of us are so committed to the sea, except I think it is because we all came from the sea. And it is an interesting biological fact that all of us have, in our veins, the exact same percentage of salt in blood that exist in the ocean, and, therefore, we have salt in our blood, in our sweat, in our tears. We are tied to the ocean. And when we go back to the sea, whether it is to sail or to watch it we are going back from whence we came.'"

He ended his remarks by telling the story of his grandfather going to the White House the first time with his uncle and associates to discuss the canal. Of course, President Roosevelt knew very well who Old Tom was, because of their meeting during the invasion, and remarked that he was glad to see Tom had recovered from his wound. He had also been the most important person pushing for Tom to receive the Medal of Honor. As the meeting ended, the President asked Tom if he liked apple pie. Without waiting for an answer, he ordered Tom and his uncle to follow him to the White House kitchen. Whereupon, he ordered the Chief Chef to bring out a huge apple pie and a large knife. Shoving the pie in front of Tom, Roosevelt commanded him to carve the isthmus of Panama and scoop out the proposed canal and the two oceans, then fill the connecting spaces with ice cream. This accomplished, the young seaman and the youngest President of the United States started at opposite oceans and consumed ice cream and apple pie until their faces were covered with it. All was to the hilarious laughter of the kitchen staff and Old Tom's uncle.

And that, ladies and gentleman, is the true story of how the Panama Canal was made! Thank you." Tommy took his seat to loud applause and laughter.

The colonel and his lady joined in the laughter and applause, with the colonel shaking his head in amazement.

President Chiari stood up, still clapping and laughing, and said to the audience, "I must confess. I never knew the true origin of the canal."

As the meal ended, the orchestra began to play. Tommy turned to Denise, "Time to dance, *ma chérie*."

"*Avec plaisir, mon cher.*" she quickly replied.

But there was no way the participants were going to let them pass without greetings of appreciation for Tommy's talk.

Finally, the *coronel* worked his way into the circle. Tommy had that sick feeling in his stomach again. "Well, Mr. Scott you are full of surprises. Relax. That was very well done. I think I should send some of my staff over to take lessons."

"Thank you, sir. My grandfather just happens to be my favorite subject. So, it was very easy."

Before the colonel could say anything else, President Chiari walked up to them.

"Ah, *coronel*, I see you know my young friend. Good evening, ladies. He was very good, *no?*"

"Yes, Mr. President. We… met in the reception line, and he was very good. I am quite fascinated by his connection to Panama." Tommy could not imagine what was going to happen next. He had only intended to be here as part of the Association.

"Oh, yes. His grandfather has been a good friend of our family for many years, and this young man has been a guest in our house with his grandfather. You know, *coronel*, my family is in the sugar business. For many years his grandfather was our competitor with his Cuban sugar. But his ships still carried much of our sugar, and he was our friend. But I am happy to say he is now our agent in Washington, all his ships are registered in Panama, and Castro has to barter his sugar to the Russians. Senor Tom was a very smart man to sell his land and move his ships before Fidel stole everything. You know, Senor Tom even knew my father when he was the President in 1925. Well, it is nice to see you, *coronel*, ladies, Tommy. Now I have to go act like the President and talk to the politicians. *Pardonme, por favor.*" As he walked away he spoke to another distinguished gentleman, who turned to greet Scott.

"Ah, Tommy, nice to see you again. I enjoyed your speech. I am sorry your grandfather could not be here, but I wanted to say hello."

"Colonel and Mrs. Bergeron, Denise, this is the Minister of Shipping, Carlos Mendez. His law firm has represented my grandfather for many years before he became the Minister."

"A pleasure, *coronel* and your lovely wife. And this is the beautiful girl I saw you with in the reception line. I already know she teaches French. *Enchanté, mademoiselle.* Tommy, I hope to see you later, but the President wants me for something. *Asi,* you will excuse me, *por favor.*"

The colonel watched the President stroll through the crowd, now quickly followed by the Minister, and thought that if this gets any more surprising, he will have to take four aspirin and call his S-2 Intelligence Officer to explain why he was so in the dark.

"Excuse me, Sir. I did promise to dance with Denise before the end of the evening."

"Yes, yes, of course. Excuse me for keeping him, Denise. Mr. Scott, I am sure I will see you around somewhere. Maybe, I will even learn what else I don't know." Denise and the colonel's wife had been standing silently, alternately amazed at the story and amused at the colonel's most unusual state of confusion.

"Sergeant, I think I need a drink and a dance quickly. Drink first," was the first thing Denise could say as the colonel and his wife walked away.

"*Mi coronel,* I could use a drink and you look like you need one," whispered his wife.

"Roger that!"

Over the next month, duty at Fort Gulick continued with a few uneventful exercises with the Panama National Guard, and short boring assignments to assist the Jungle Warfare School in field exercises at Fort Sherman on the north side of the canal. Tommy was beginning to feel better about the possible effects of his encounter with the colonel, but a sudden command to report to his A-Team's commanding officer started it all over.

He found his captain studying a piece of official looking paper. He looked up as Tommy saluted. "Scott, I have an order for you to immediately report to Colonel Bergeron. I have no idea why, but you better shine your boots and get over there quickly. Let me know what happens."

"Yes, sir" he said as he saluted and did an about face. *Oh shit,* was his only thought as he walked out the door.

He found the Group Sergeant Major waiting in the outer office at Group Headquarters. "Take a seat, Scott, we're waiting on Capt. Thibodaux from A-36. The colonel wants to see both of you."

Five minutes later the captain arrived. He was a West Point graduate from the Louisiana bayou country. Tommy was beginning to see a connection. He knew this captain was Cajun and spoke French. Normally, USMA graduates did not make a career in Special Forces. It limited their possibilities for advancement because of force size and being unconventional. Additionally, it was not a designated Army branch at the moment. However, this kind of unit fit Thibodaux's style. It made him feel more like he was back home in the bayou.

The sergeant major showed them into the colonel's office, and stood off to the side as they saluted and waited for the colonel to speak.

After returning the salute, the colonel waived some papers at them. "Gentlemen, I have an unusual request here. General Anastasio Somoza, the commanding general of the Nicaraguan military forces, has sent an official request for some assistance from our

Group. It's even endorsed by our Department of State through the Ambassador. I graduated from West Point with Somoza. I know him to be an arrogant, spoiled son of a very corrupt and ruthless dictator, who somehow thinks he is a military genius by education alone. His brother is now the President, and he probably will be, in time. He also fancies himself to be a 'Renaissance Man.' As an initial token of counterinsurgency assistance, I am to send a captain and senior NCO, not an entire A-Team, to assist in a 'training exercise' against some guerillas, who have been causing him some embarrassment."

The colonel let that soak in for a moment and continued, "All that being said, I am sure you are wondering what this has to do with you specifically. Number 1, you both have excellent records; Number 2 you are both fluent in French. What does Number 2 have to do with anything in Nicaragua? As I said, he thinks he is a 'Renaissance Man' and feels flattered to be spoken to in French. Get the picture now?"

He waited for them to digest that also, "I am sure his French is lousy, but you will do the best you can." Turning his gaze to Tommy, "It will probably help also that the President of Panama is a friend of Sergeant Scott's family and will send along his endorsement."

The Sergeant Major didn't blink, but the captain's eyebrows went up a little.

Uh, oh, thought Tommy, *so there it is. The colonel has figured out a way to get even.*

"Sergeant Major, give them copies of their orders, and have my S-2 brief them. That's all, gentlemen. Your plane for Managua leaves in the morning. Do us proud."

At 0600 they were wheels up in the colonel's own plane for the two hour flight to Managua. They were met by military escort, rushed to General Somoza's headquarters and presented to the general.

After returning their salutes in his best West Point manner, the general greeted them with, "*Bien,* gentlemen, It is always a pleasure to meet fellow soldiers. I am a graduate of West Point myself,

Captain Thibodaux. And, Sergeant Scott, I see a letter from my friend President Chiari. My old classmate Colonel Bergeron did not let me down by sending you two. I understand you both speak French?"

"*Oui, general,*" Thibodaux answered for both of them.

"*Magnifique!*" exclaimed Somoza. The conversation switched to French, leaving the general's aide to stand uncomfortably to the side. "*Capitaine,* I wished to meet you both personally, because I have a direct interest in this little operation. My nephew, Captain Alfonso Debayle, will be in charge of this unit, and I do not want it to have any embarrassing problems. You do understand my situation, *non?*"

"*Certainement, general.* We will exercise the greatest discretion," replied Thibodaux without hesitation. Scott was thinking *Oh no, a babysitting job,* but kept quiet.

A flicker of recognition crossed the general's face, turning to Scott, "Are you the son of T.R. Scott?"

"*Oui, general.*"

"He was a very brave man. I was saddened at his death, sergeant. Your grandfather also does business with us."

"*Merci, general.*"

Captain Thibodaux made a mental note to ask the rest of the story. He was beginning to feel like the colonel, 'What next with this sergeant?'

"*Bien*, gentlemen I knew I could rely upon you." Switching to Spanish, he spoke to his aide, "Major, make sure these men have everything and *anything* they need *or desire.*"

Of course, the major understood what that meant, and the meeting was ended. Later that evening the major complied with his orders at the finest restaurant in Managua and afterwards.

The mission was a simple 'search and destroy' in the mountains northeast of Managua. This group of guerillas was poorly armed and equipped, but they knew the people and the countryside. Somoza had always deluded himself that the people actually loved the Somoza family. US Army intelligence had advised Thibodaux and Scott otherwise. The problem they now faced was that Captain

Debayle and his unit were already deep in the mountains, and they had to parachute into the area. However, on the chance this might happen they had brought their own parachutes packed by the 8th Group's own parachute riggers. Each carried an M-2 .30 caliber carbine with the longer ammunition clips. It was light, easy to use in close terrain, and could fire at a rate of 750 rounds per minute when switched to full automatic fire.

The jump from an old C-47 was uneventful. Scott was thinking about his father flying one of these during WW II with Japanese shooting at him. They landed in a clearing, not trees, for which they were thankful. They were met by Debayle who immediately reflected the condescending attitude of the Somoza family of considering everyone to be theirs for their own personal use.

Oh shit. Let's see how Thibodaux handles this character, Scott thought. *A soldier he is not. A spoiled brat he is.*

Very smoothly in fluent Spanish Thibodaux greeted him with the proper deference and requested a briefing. Satisfied that he was in charge, Dabayle waved to his company sergeant to take care of this bit of detail while he spoke to some of the young girls in the village to 'gather intelligence.' He had already ordered the used parachutes to be brought to him. He gave the girls the light billowing nylon, telling them it was silk and a gift from him.

Sargento Gutierrez looked out of the corner of his eye at the Americans as if to say, *I know, I know* and laid out a map of the mountain they were on and explained the pattern of attacks by the guerillas on Somoza units.

Thibodaux and Scott listened very carefully. To them this did not appear to be a very sophisticated guerilla movement and Thibodaux said so. The sergeant agreed and shrugged his shoulders. They all exchanged looks of concern. This was obviously Somoza's attempt to show off and have the Special Forces assure his nephew of success.

"Muy bien, sargento. Entendemos. Vamos a ver que pasa cuando el capitan termina de impresiendo las muchachas." (Very well, sergeant. We understand. Let's go see what will happen whenever the good captain finishes impressing the girls.)

"Sí capitan. Gracias."

It was now midday and Debayle decided they should not leave until the next day. The Americans and the *sargento* just looked at each other. They knew the obvious reason he wanted to spend the night. Daylight came the next day with Thibodaux diplomatically shaming him to move.

Debayle selected a route up the mountain through a banana grove that had been harvested, and the stalks were now rotting on the ground. It didn't seem entirely unreasonable, considering that someone in the village had probably notified the guerillas anyway and there was little growth to conceal an ambush.

At this altitude it was still hot, and steam was beginning to rise from the moist ground and rotting banana plants. Scott was having flash backs to his months with Castro and their ambushes of the Batista soldiers. His senses were starting to send signals that a problem was arising. He waved to Thibodaux who nodded back he understood and pointed to his own eyes signaling Scott to watch out. Gutierrez caught the meaning and tried to caution Debayle. The young captain spoke to him in an irritated voice to keep moving.

Scott could see a slight mound ahead and turned again to signal Thibodaux. The point man was passing the mound with Scott twenty steps behind and abreast of two soldiers. Suddenly machine gun fire erupted from the mound and swept the column of soldiers. Out of the ground from under banana plants guerrillas appeared pouring rifle fire on the company. The man next to Scott was killed and the same bullet passed through him and hit Scott in the shoulder. Scott threw himself down and immediately cursed himself. He knew very well the first thing in an ambush was to return heavy fire and charge into the ambushers as your best chance of survival. The stink of rotting banana plants and fresh blood of the dead soldier who had fallen on top of him made a sickening smell. Vomit choked his throat, and fear he had never suspected gripped him.

He looked back down the column and could see a dozen soldiers on the ground. Farther back he could see Thibodaux had been wounded and Debayle was whimpering that he was wounded.

Thibodaux yelled back that his thigh bone had been broken

and that Debayle just had a flesh wound. Guerilla fire continued to rake the company, drowning the cries of the wounded. He could see Gutierrez scowling at Debayle, who was now crying from fright, rather than any pain from his wound, and pleading that he was so badly wounded that he could not command his unit.

Scott could clearly hear Thibodaux screaming over the gunfire. "Goddamn it, Scott, do something or this sonofabitch will get us all killed."

Scott looked at his shoulder. He could see that most of the velocity of the bullet had been spent passing through the soldier and had not reached anything vital.

Now is the time, he thought. "*Sargento, sigueme con sus soldados, rapidamente!*" (Sergeant, follow me with your soldiers, quickly!) he shouted to Gutierrez, and put his carbine on full automatic.

Firing as fast as his carbine would fire, he ran towards the now visible machine gun, tossing the two grenades he had, with the sergeant running behind him and urging his men to follow. The sudden change of events completely confused the undisciplined guerillas, who ran, leaving their gun behind. Seeing the machine gunners run created a panic in the remaining guerillas, who ran across the open banana grove with soldiers yelling in pursuit.

"Damn!" Scott shouted out loud to no one, "That actually worked." In all his time with Fidel no Batista soldier ever charged their ambush. Lesson learned.

He ran back to Thibodaux, now in considerable pain, but being attended by the company medic. Debayle was shouting at the soldier to aid him first, because he was the commander. He turned to Scott, "I told my uncle you would only get us into trouble. This ambush was all your fault. Without me you all would have died."

Scott could not believe what he was hearing. Then he saw Thibodeaux reach up and drag Debayle to the ground. "You worthless piece of shit. I ought to kill you now and save the rest of your soldiers' lives." The pain proved too much and Thibodaux lost consciousness before Scott could get between them. Debayle scampered away in obvious fear, again whimpering about his terrible wound.

The after action report was filed by Debayle as an outstanding victory lead by him. Part of the report had indicated the Americans had been only a hindrance. Now he stood before his immediate superior Major Antonio Gomez, a tough old soldier with the scars to prove it. He had been a sergeant for many years before Gen. Somoza had personally made him an officer. He had saved the general's life during an assassination attempt by taking the bullet himself. Now he sat looking at this nephew thinking about what to do with him. He knew the true story from Sergeant Gutierrez and other witnesses, *But this pavo real (peacock) still wants to pretend he is the hero.* he said to himself, *What do I do with him?*

Debayle started to speak, but Gomez cut him off, "Shut up you *comemierda!* I know what happened out there."

"You can't talk to me like that," protested Debayle. "My uncle is your commanding general…"

"I said shut up, you coward. Gen. Somoza already knows the truth. I told him myself." Debayle began to turn pale. "The general told me to handle this without completely shaming the family. Your options are very, very limited, if you understand me." The remaining color drained from the captain's face. He knew very well what his uncle was capable of doing.

"Here is what you will do. You will acknowledge that the Americans acted bravely and were invaluable; especially the sergeant who saved your whole company by his actions, and you will recommend your own sergeant for promotion to lieutenant. Next, you will resign because of your 'terrible wounds.' You will never speak of this again. In return I will give you a medal for bravery and recommend a medical discharge. Understood?"

The captain could only stammer, "Yes, yes, of course."

"You are dismissed, but I assure you I will hear if you do not keep this agreement."

The two Americans were treated and evacuated to Ft. Gulick hospital where Colonel Bergeron now stood looking down at them. "Gentlemen, you did us proud. General Somoza himself called me to thank you. He said to assure you he took care of things, and he was giving you both the Nicaraguan medal for valor. It looks like you both got your first purple heart. And, Scott, the captain here has recommended you for a Silver Star. I'll make sure you get it and a Bronze Star for the captain. The general also mentioned how sorry he was about your father and to express again his thanks to your grandfather for replacing his two F-51s." This last part had been another surprise for the colonel, and left him wondering how much more he did not know about this family.

"Oh, Scott, I also need to send someone to help out in the Jungle Warfare School over at Ft. Sherman. Since you like to talk, and you are 'walking wounded,' and I would like to keep all able bodied men here, you are selected." The colonel turned and walked out, trying not to laugh.

What the fuck? Scott said to himself, thinking of giving lectures to students about eating iguanas, monkeys and kinkajous. He turned to look at Thibodaux.

The captain broke out laughing and said, "No rest for the wicked, sergeant."

"*Oui, c'est l'armée,*" Scott mumbled, "*Plus ça change, plus c'est la mêm chose.*" (the more things change, the more they remain the same) and to himself, *The colonel is still getting even.*

The U. S. Army Jungle Warfare School at Ft. Sherman on the opposite side of the canal had been initiated to train United States military personnel and selected Latin American units, in the basics of jungle warfare.

Ft. Sherman was originally developed as the primary infantry base to protect the Atlantic side of the Panama Canal after its construction. It contains 23,000 acres of single and double canopy jungle with steep, rolling hills and many tributaries into the river and sea. It is bounded on the north and north-west by the Caribbean Sea, on the south and south-west by the Chagres River and on the east by Limon Bay and the Gatun Locks.

The school was designed for a three week course with the first week for jungle survival, camouflage, booby-traps, and plants and animals. The second consisted of small unit patrolling, attack and ambush techniques, followed by a week of field exercises.

This cycle was filled with a Bolivian Army battalion training to operate along the edge of the Brazilian rain forest and up the east side of the Andes Mountains. Continual Indian and mine workers' unrest in that area had necessitated different training for troops accustomed to the high *altiplano* regions of Bolivia.

So, Sergeant First Class Thomas MacDougall Scott II, with his arm still in a sling, packed his duffle bag, and headed across the canal for 'light duty.' He had gone through this course himself and been living it for the last year. He took some humor from the thought of a Bolivian soldier's first reaction to being told to eat an iguana lizard. Maybe this would not be so boring after all. He could teach everything that did not require him to go into the jungle with his bad shoulder. The lesson plans were already made up and he could just teach in Spanish with Panamanian assistants handling any lifting.

Lt. Col. Alfredo Suarez was the school commandant. He was a former Green Beret who had served in Colombia with the teams assigned to assist the Colombian Army in counterinsurgency there. He was Puerto Rican and had also served as a plain clothes SF advisor in the training of the 2506 Brigade before the Bay of Pigs fiasco. He had not known Scott's father but knew the story of the F-51 and Tommy's own story. There was an immediate kinship.

Commander of the Bolivian battalion was Francisco Villamiranoa, a descendant of an original Spanish *conquistador* in Peru and Bolivia, and distant relative of Pizarro through his mother. He was, obviously, on the path to much higher rank. He was introduced to the school cadre by Suarez. When he came to Scott, he was surprised to see his arm in a sling.

In very good English he asked, "How is your arm, sergeant? Did you fall over a log in the *selva*?" (jungle)

"No, *coronel*, I zigged when I should have zagged." The answer brought a knowing laugh, and the *coronel* made a mental note to ask about this tall young sergeant with flashing eyes.

Scott took more of an active part in the first two weeks of instruction than he anticipated. They were very short handed in this cycle, with a whole battalion to train. He found himself assisting a captain, and teaching some classes and demonstrations himself, which normally called for other captains and senior NCOs to instruct.

The *coronel* did ask Suarez about Scott and was told the surprising story of Sergeant First Class Scott, some of which was between the colonels on a confidential agreement. Colonel Bergeron had already filled Suarez in before he sent Scott over to the school. Now the Bolivian *coronel* was very interested for his own purposes in a much decorated enlisted man who had fought in the mountains with Castro's *barbudos,* personally knew two current presidents of Latin America counties, spoke fluent Spanish and French and was a college graduate. *Increible!* This was going to take help from someone on the State Department level.

The *coronel* was able to catch Scott when the schedule called for a day off from training. "Sergeant Scott, I wish to compliment you on your instruction and knowledge. I sincerely wish I had some NCOs with your competence. Do you know much about Bolivia?"

"Thank you, *coronel,* and I don't know much about Bolivia except it is very high."

"I understand you fought in the mountains in Cuba, *no?*"

"Sorry, sir, I am not allowed to discuss anything like that."

"Yes, yes. I understand, of course, but I would like to discuss some strategies of jungle warfare in a mountain environment. Let me tell you something about Bolivia. As your history books tell you, Francisco Pizarro conquered the mighty Inca, with fewer men than Hernan Cortes had in Mexico. I am a descendant of one of the original soldiers, who was a distant relative of Pizarro. I am also *mestizo,* because my family made an agreement hundreds of years ago that every other generation of men would marry into a royal family of the indigenous tribes. This way, we have always had an entré to both sides. Bolivia has the largest percentage population of Indians in all of Latin America with a very stratified class system, which frequently defies classification strictly on blood lines. Historically, the Spanish enacted the *encomiendo* system and allocated Indians as free laborers for Spanish owners. Bolivia was spared the worst of the abuses because the Catholic Church had declared parts of Southern Peru, now Bolivia, as a religious sanctuary for several hundred years. That was before the Jesuits were expelled from New Spain. We currently have a president, Paz Estenssoro, who is trying to liberalize restrictions affecting Indians and mine workers' unions, which are mostly Indians. In the background are strong military leaders, some of whom attended your School of the Americas. These men are my superiors. All of them have little tolerance for insurrection and strikes. Consequently, it is hard to keep the lid on the pot.

"Bolivia is a land-locked country thanks to some ill-advised wars with Peru and Chile, where we lost access to the Pacific Ocean. We also lost much land on the east to Paraguay in the Chaco Wars for the same reason. However, we have some of the richest mineral land in the world, but abuse of the workers has caused continuous strikes by the unions, and inhibited growth and effective use of mining. All of the miners are indigenous people and *mestizo* mixtures. The ruling class has never changed its attitude of superiority. As a result, we have always had revolutionary movements among the working class and farm workers. My family has always had a foot in each camp.

"At this moment on the eastern slopes and low lands far from the capitol, La Paz, a group calling itself *Los Originales,* and led by a very dangerous self-named, *Alfonso Tupac*, is raiding with terror tactics and playing on ancient grievances. *Tupac* has named himself after the last Inca king, *Tupac Amaru.* Our government is more appeasing than aggressive in dealing with the situation. As a result they will not request any assistance from the United States, even though they allow some of our soldiers and officers to attend your schools, including my own commander, General René Barrientos, who attended your School of the Americas. Things are about to change, but we need to eliminate this dangerous group before it can set the whole country on fire."

The *coronel* paused for a moment to let Scott absorb the situation. "Obviously, three weeks in the *selva* eating lizards and monkeys is not going to make my men experts in jungle warfare. We need more help, but our government will not ask for it." He paused again. "However, if I can create a school with a very, very little formal aid, it would be of great assistance."

Scott was thinking it was an interesting story, but why was he hearing it. It should be for Colonel Bergeron or Lieutenant Colonel Suarez. Maybe the *coronel* was just trying it out for size with an enlisted man.

"Now my $64,000 question, as you say in your country, is: Would you consider a temporary assignment to our army to help establish such training?"

That was a stunner. Scott stammered, "Sir, that is way above my pay grade. You need to talk to the colonel. I'm just a sergeant E-7."

"I will talk much higher than your colonel. You are a solution to my problem. You have the training expertise and the actual experience in the field and at war. You will not have to lead my battalion into combat. You will advise me and assist in setting up a school. I have already requested lesson plans from Lieutenant Colonel Suarez. My request will come from the highest military level, but not the government. You must see the logic in this. Requesting one sergeant does not appear as begging for your country's interference in our affairs, but it will solve my problem."

It still sounded crazy to Scott. "Sir, I am flattered that you think I can create a whole school, but under no circumstances could I go to my commanding officer with this, much less to the colonel. I am not exactly one of his favorite people."

"Au contraire, sergent" unexpectedly switching to French, the *coronel* persisted, "I have it from good authority that your colonel has a very high regard for you."

Now, Scott was really off balance. He could only beg off, in French, until the weekend to think about it.

In the interim, Lieutenant Colonel Villamiranoa put things in motion with a request to his superiors for this specific sergeant. He had already presented his outline for the program before he left Bolivia. The quiet, low level of the operation had appealed to the upper levels of the military who would be tasked to deal with the threat posed by Alfonso *Tupac*. They would not have to have permission of or consult with the 'untrustworthy' and vacillating politicians. Only a quiet word to the U. S. Ambassador, the CIA man assigned there, and the military attach would be required to set things in motion. He smiled to himself how easy this would be, *Just one lone sergeant that no one will notice could lead to a whole additional level of assistance in the future. He could even be assigned as an aide to the embassy military attaché. Bravo!* he thought to himself. Now he just had to make it work.

The training cycle ended and Tom was assigned back to his unit. He hoped he would not hear about the proposal again. He had said his goodbyes to Lieutenant Colonel Villamiranoa without any mention of it. He was even given a quart bottle of the best Panamanian rum in appreciation of his work. Only a slight smile by the *coronel* caused Scott to wonder if that was all there was to it. However, he had thought it might be interesting to see Bolivia. He had been to the port of Callao adjacent to Lima, Peru on his grandfather's ship, but he had never been high in the Andes. He had always wanted to see the land of the Inca in Peru, their ancient capital of Cuzco, and the lost city of Machu Picchu. What was about to happen, he had no idea.

Two weeks after the Jungle Warfare School assignment he was called into his captain's office. "Scott, I have another call for you from Colonel Bergeron. I hope you didn't screw up over at Ft. Sherman. Shine 'em and get over there."

'Shit,' Tommy was thinking, 'You would think the colonel had gotten even by now.'

The Sergeant Major was waiting with a smirk on his face. The sarcastic greeting of, "Welcome back, Sergeant Scott. The Colonel is waiting," didn't help matters.

He reported to the colonel. "At ease, Sergeant Scott. Why am I not surprised at the latest happenings with you? I am not sure whether I am relieved to get rid of you and your surprises, or sorry to lose a very fine soldier."

"I'm sorry, sir. I don't understand."

"No...no, I guess you don't. I have an interesting request here, like I have never seen before. It seems some back channel deal has been made with the State Department and the Bolivian army and the Pentagon involving one Sergeant First Class Thomas MacDougall Scott II. It is directed to me, as if I dared to reject a very high level request for a sergeant in my command. Is there anything you want to fill in for your humble group commander?"

Jesus Christ, they actually did it, was all Scott could think.

"Sir, I didn't think they would actually do this. I thought it was just training conversation." Then he related the conversation with Lieutenant Colonel Villamiranoa.

"Well, that is interesting. That government has resisted accepting our help for very political reasons. Now it seems the military wants to slip in by the back door, very quietly. You, my young sergeant, are now a pawn in a very big chess game. Fascinating. And again, why am I not surprised you are the one in the middle of it, willing or not willing? It's probably a good thing we couldn't get you to accept a 2nd lieutenant commission. I suspect they would not want a *last lieutenant* to move around their chess board. Anyway, I am going to give you a second palm to go on your Commendation Medal and a Good Conduct Medal. I think those, with a Purple Heart and a Silver Star, are quite enough for one tour of duty."

The colonel thought for a minute. "You will have to think of something to say to Denise. This is very classified stuff. My wife is going to blame me for sending you off, and I can't tell her anything except it is way above my pay grade. After our surprise meeting with you and the President of the Republic, I suspect she will get the idea of how high it might be."

Scott hadn't thought about that. He knew Denise didn't like his temporary duty disappearances in Panama. Now, he could not even tell her where or when or if he would come back. Oh, shit!

"I can only give you two days. I hope you can get your act together in that time. You'll have to or I get blamed, and I have enough problems. You're dismissed. Sergeant Major, give him his expedited orders. And, Scott, I can tell you that you are officially assigned as an aide to the embassy military attaché, Major Sean McCauley. He's a classmate of mine. Ever heard of him?"

Tommy could not help but smile, "Yes, sir. He was my old ROTC advisor. I'm glad to hear he made major."

"Damn, get out of here. I can't stand any more of your surprises!" the colonel shouted in mock horror. The Sergeant Major finally managed a grin.

"Yes, sir," he saluted and left the 8th Special Forces Group for parts as yet unknown.

CHAPTER 12

...to the mountains of BOLIVIA

Sergeant Scott sat in the first class section of the old Lockheed Electra turboprop plane operated by Bolivia's TAM Airlines, the civilian side of *Transporte Areo Militar*, trying to read a CIA country assessment of Bolivia, but he couldn't get his mind off his last meeting with Denise. They had never talked about getting married, but it was in the room between looks and between sentences, always in the room. He just had not faced it, and she could not say it. Now he was off again into what he could not foresee, and he could not tell her where or what or when. In fact, he didn't know. He needed *abuelita,* but she was fading fast after T.R.'s death and seemed to lose communication with the world. Maybe she was already in those other planes of existence she dreamed about. He had written her, his grandfather, and his mother, to let them know that he probably would not be writing for a while.

He and Denise had met by chance in Paris, met again by chance in Panama, and maybe they were destined to meet once again by chance...somewhere. Or as *abuelita* would say, it was already written somewhere on a different plane.

As the Lockheed crossed over the border of Colombia, he could see the smugglers' airfield at *Riosucio* and the hills and swamps along the border where he had spent time chasing bad guys. *At least there wouldn't be any swamps and mosquitoes in Bolivia*, he thought. He shook his head and went back to the report. It was a long flight to Bolivia on a slow plane.

As the plane descended into La Paz airport, he could see a landscape that looked like the moon. La Paz appeared to be in a crater made eons ago by some giant meteor.

The plane seemed to dive into the crater and level off for a long taxi. As it turned toward the terminal, he could see the grinning face of Major Sean McCauley in plain clothes waiting on the runway. Scott was also in plain clothes. He had replaced his army duffle bag with a businessman's suit bag and an expensive suitcase. It looked like, for all the world to see, two businessmen meeting in anticipation of a lucrative contract.

"Mr. Scott, welcome to the *Valley of the Shadow and the Mountains of the Moon*, I sincerely hope you are ready to *ride, boldly ride…if you seek the land of El Dorado.*"

Tommy thought, McCauley always did have a liking for the dark tales and poetry of Edgar Allen Poe. Some things don't change. Considering what he had lived through, it seemed appropriate.

McCauley gave him a big, very unmilitary *abrazo.* "Nice to see you again, Scott. You have a few more lines in your face. I see by your record you've gotten over the *Mickey Mouse* syndrome, but you still won't take that commission."

"Nice to see you again also, sir. I just wouldn't know what to do with all that extra money 2nd Lieutenants make."

That was a joke that made both of them laugh. A 2nd lieutenant O-1 with over six years' service (including National Guard service) actually made $70.00 per month more than a sergeant first class E-7 with the same service time. Considering the wealth of the Scott family, it really was a joke.

"Well, Scott, imagine my surprise when I got that message at the embassy. I thought, *Damn, my past was catching up with me again or Scott is being exiled to the moon.*"

"No, **Major**, I like the sound of that. Congratulations. I am here to enhance your military reputation and aid your promotion to general."

"Now, that would be more of a miracle than your landing here on the moon, but I am glad to have someone here with whom I can commiserate." More laughter as they walked to the terminal and an embassy car.

Waiting in the car was Liutenant Colonel Villamiranoa. "Welcome, Sergeant Scott, to the highest capitol in the world at 12,000 feet. It's going to take some getting used to after sea level Panama."

Already short of breath, Tommy gasped, "Roger that, Sir."

Laughter from both officers, "Don't forget to drink lots of coca tea, and don't worry. Cocaine is only one of the fourteen alkaloids in the coca leaf. It is insignificant unless mixed with other chemicals to release it. This country runs on the coca leaf and has from the beginning of time. You will even get used to chewing them when you are in the field."

Scott took this statement with some skepticism. He would learn the truth of it very soon.

"Scott, I was very pleased to find out that Major McCauley knew you as a cadet in college. This is even better than I planned. I think my stars are aligning. After a couple of days we will fly down to Cochabamba. You will see all of Bolivia does not look like the moon, and it is almost 2,500 feet lower in altitude."

Tommy was thinking, *Thank God.*

"But La Paz does have its redeeming features and places of interest. I believe the major has already found one at the French embassy. *Oui?*" as he turned to wink at McCauley. The major smiled. He had found a friend in the French military attaché and a companion in the attaché's secretary, Françoise.

"Ah, here we are, *sargento,*" as they arrived at the embassy. "I believe we have a briefing by the commercial attaché in the morning when you catch your breath. I will be back at 0700 for your American breakfast." The *coronel* got back in his staff car and saluted *hasta luego.*

The major and the sergeant ate supper with the embassy staff and talked about the University of Florida football team. They still could not win the SEC Championship. Scott was bunked in a guest room. Later they had a private conversation with the "commercial attaché" (CIA station chief), Jim Curren, as an informal *familiarization briefing* for Scott before the meeting with the *coronel* in the morning.

McCauley led off, "Scott, I have only been here nine months. At first, I thought I had been exiled to hell, but I have found their military very eager to talk to our military side. This has turned out to be the most fascinating assignment I've ever had, even if the

Army meant to bury me. The current government is not giving them much support, as I am sure you gathered from Villamiranoa. The French military attaché and I have been listening very closely. Your boy, the *coronel,* is one of General Barrientos' *fair-haired* officers. Barrientos is a graduate of your School of the Americas and a staunch anticommunist. He is the Chief of the Air Force, and, like Villamiranoa, is from Cochabamba and descended from both Quechua and Spanish. He and General Ocampo, the Chief of the Army, are pretty thick, and Villamiranoa is riding the wave.

"Barrientos has been playing his cards very cool for years with the party in power, and they have built up his image. Being fluent in both Quechua and Spanish has been a big advantage with this party, which has been successful in gaining favor with the peasant groups. At this time it is estimated that seventy-five percent of the population is Indian. Sixty percent speak only their native language, and two thirds of those are Quechua speakers. Now under President Paz Estennosso, the government is trying to court the leftist labor unions and miners. Leftist Juan Lechin is the current vice president, and wants to be president. The 1964 elections are in six months, and the military is getting nervous.

"As Jim will verify, it's a little easier for their military to talk to European military rather than to the *colossus of the north.* So, with Major Benoit at the French Embassy working with me, we find out a lot of things. The politics of this administration are very tenuous and the military is waiting for its opportunity. You will probably see Barrientos as president in the next year, one way or another, if you understand my meaning. Now, what does all this have to do with one lowly Sergeant First Class Thomas MacDougall Scott II? Well…, when the *coronel* picked you to come set up a school and pulled some very high level strings to do it, he had no idea what he was stirring up. Mr. Curren here, and his "employers" became very interested, and when they looked at your history, lo and behold, they really took an interest. Jim, you're up."

"Thank you, *general-to-be-after-we-pull-this-off* McCauley. First let me say, I was born and educated in the Canal Zone while my father was an executive with the Canal Zone. He knows your grandfather and the Panamanian President's family. Then I went to the Merchant Marine Academy, as a matter of fact, with the encouragement of your grandfather, and to sea for a couple of years, before the CIA picked me up. After your Cuban exploits and all the heat your family put on the agency from the inside and from the outside, you had dropped off our radar. McCauley filled in some of the gaps. Obviously, now we see all the dots connected. The agency has been very quiet in the background here. As far as the *coronel* is concerned, this whole show is his idea, but Major McCauley will be our connection with you and what you hear. "

Jesus Christ! This chess board is getting even bigger. McCauley just joined Villamiranoa as a white Knight on the board, Scott was thinking.

Curren continued, "I know this seems a little overwhelming, but if your side of this works the way the Bolivian military sees it working, we will be helping turn this government away from the communists. Then, I suspect, you will no longer be a *lowly sergeant.*"

They waited a very long minute for Scott to reply.

"Sir, I appreciate your thinking of me on such a grand scale, but I am a twenty-four-year-old enlisted man sent here to assist in a training program for which I am qualified. I am not qualified as a *spook.* I liked being a lowly sergeant who had a job to do within specific and definable limits."

Both officers laughed in sympathy with his predicament. "Scott, I was twenty-four when the agency sent me to Guatemala in the middle of a revolution just because I spoke Spanish. I survived and so will you. Any questions?"

"Sir, do you have any sleeping pills?" More laughter.

At 0700 hours they had the good ole' American breakfast of bacon and eggs and *quinoa,* which Scott thought tasted more like cream of wheat than good ole' grits. He didn't say anything to the *coronel,* because it was a grain whose origin was here in the high Andes Mountains where it was domesticated more than 7,000 years ago. The Inca called it *chisaya mama,* the mother of all grains. It was the staff of life for the native people. Anyway, it wasn't bad, just different, and he had a feeling that he better get used to it. He had definitely eaten worse things in the *Sierra Maestra.*

After breakfast they went to the situation briefing with the "commercial" attaché, with Villamiranoa contributing his part. It was the first time McCauley had heard the whole plan. The CIA had stepped aside, because it was to be strictly a Bolivian Army operation.

The *coronel* repeated for Scott that President Estenssoro had selected Juan Lechin as his vice president. Lechin was a *porista,* a leader in the *Partido Obrero Revolutionaria* (POR or Revolutionary Workers Party). The POR was an older Trotskyite group of workers allied with other left leaning groups. Scott was getting a flash back to college and studies in communism. Somehow, he thought that was all in the abstract. Now he was actually looking at it in the context of developing history. Estenssoro was trying to appease both the strong unions *and* the powerful Indian Congress of Aymara and Quechua speaking *campesinos.* This was causing the United States to see a communist under every rock, and there were lots of rocks in Bolivia.

The spark that could ignite a revolution was *Tupac* in the eastern mountains and valleys. He played on the historical abuses of the indigenous population and poor conditions of modern day miners by resurrecting the visions of *Tupac Amaru II,* the leader of a revolution against the Spanish during the 18th century, who had claimed direct lineage from the last Inca king, *Tupac Amaru.* Most revolutionary movements in Peru, Ecuador and Bolivia, seemed to adopt this link to history in one way or another. A later Indian leader had adopted the name *Tupac Katari* and had led a revolution in Bolivia in the late 18th century. If the "new" *Tupac* could unite these groups under one purpose against the ruling order, he could overcome a weakened military and possibly create a new order in South America. At the present time the government of Peru to the north had been overthrown and the United States ambassador had been withdrawn. The pot was boiling, and the traditional strong military had been gradually moved out of the mainstream. Weapons appeared to be flowing in from groups in Peru and Brazil.

The big question on the table was whether the Indian Congress would support the revolutionaries in the mountains and join the unions in antigovernment movements. Lieutant Colonel Villamiranoa had an ace up his sleeve. He was a cousin to the current president of the Indian Congress. He only needed to show that Tupac was not invincible and did not truly support the peasantry and miners as his rhetoric would lead the people to believe. This needed to be in actual combat to prove to the government that the military should be strengthened and more American aid should be accepted.

Just as Scott was thinking the black *King* was on the board and how right Colonel Bergeron had been about being a small *pawn* in a big dangerous game, the *coronel* looked up. "Good morning, Ambassador Stephens."

"Go right ahead, Colonel. Don't let me interrupt. I learn something every time I attend one of these," and the Ambassador took a seat in the back of the room.

The briefing was closed with a brief outline of Villamiranoa's jungle warfare school, which would actually prepare his battalion for a current and subsequent counterinsurgency role. This would be a school looking for a fight. But for the world to see, it was just a school.

"Very good, Colonel. Thank you. Now this must be the Sergeant Scott I have heard and read so much about. Well, Sergeant Scott, are you ready to win the war single-handed?"

Scott had not expected this greeting and was thinking fast. He paraphrased Colonel Bergeron, "No, sir, I'm just a small pawn in the middle of a very big chess board."

Laughter went around the room at this very accurate assessment. "Very good, Sergeant. Gentlemen, I'm going to surprise you with what more I know about this young man. As you have all heard me talk about my time on a PT boat with the President in the Pacific, Scott's father was the pilot who saved our asses when those Jap Zeros jumped us." And turning to Tommy, "I was very sorry to hear of his death in Cuba. You probably didn't know the Spaldings were friends and associates of my family in Boston. They told us, and I have met your grandfather at several Democratic Party functions."

"Thank you, sir. Jonathan Spalding was the CIA agent who got me out of the mountains in Cuba."

"Ah, that is something I did not know." He turned his head to the "commercial attaché" who nodded in acknowledgement. It seems there were things he still was not told. "Well, gentlemen, as you know the United States Ambassador has no knowledge of anything beyond Sergeant Scott being an aide to my military attaché in whatever liaison he may have with the Bolivian military."

"*Absolutamente, Senor Embajador!*" The *coronel* raised his coffee cup in salute.

"That reminds me, it is lunch time. We can now go into diplomatic silence and drink some of that very fine Bolivia wine," smiled the ambassador.

"Bueno," the *coronel* clapped his hands with a wink at McCauley. "Tomorrow we will fly down to Cochabamba, but tonight we will enjoy what La Paz has to offer, compliments of the French embassy. *Oui?* Ambassador, will you join us tonight?"

"Tempted as I may be, the sight of the United States Ambassador carousing with the likes of you rowdies could cause an international incident, or at the very least a scolding from my wife. Maybe next time." Another good laugh around the room. Scott was thinking this assignment may not be so bad after all. McCauley was thinking he ought to write to Colonel Bergeron just to give him one more surprise.

The French military attaché, Marcel Benoit and his wife Marie lived up to their reputation for hospitality. McCauley escorted Françoise, who brought along her cute Bolivian intern to accompany Tommy. Villamiranoa was assisted by his beautiful 'secretary' in this diplomatic mission. French and Spanish blended with the cacophony of nightclub sounds. Even McCauley got to exercise his West Point French. This was not Havana, but it sure was better than the NCO club and 'nightclubs' in Panama. But dancing a Bolivian version of a *salsa* at 12,000 feet was more than Scott could handle, even with *beaucoup* wine.

The *coronel* was mercifully late the next morning. Scott's introduction last night to *SINGANI,* the national drink of Bolivia distilled from muscatel grapes and classified internationally as a brandy, was still having a debilitating effect inside his head. Fortunately, the flight to Cochabamba was short. It was, as predicted, a world of difference from La Paz. Even at 8,500 feet, a flood of green spread out from the city. The still thin air finally convinced Scott to buy a handful of coca leaves from an Indian at the airport, which he dutifully stuffed in the side of his mouth like chewing tobacco. He had to admit it did moderate the altitude effect a bit, but he was careful not to buy the smelly ball of wax-like substance which the Indian also pushed to release the cocaine alkaloid.

"There! Didn't I tell you this was a different world? We call Cochabamba 'The Garden City' or 'City of Eternal Spring.' My Spanish family settled here in 1545, my Indian family, somewhere near the beginning of time," the *coronel* exclaimed with arms open to embrace the scene. It was a gesture Scott would see many times in the coming days.

He had to agree. And McCauley smiled.

"We will have a meeting with my battalion staff here to discuss our plans, then fly over to Montero across the continental divide on the eastern side of the mountains. Tonight we will stay in my house, and you will meet my family. My battalion is located here, and is preparing itself for more training outside Montero, where my family also has a plantation. You will learn more later today. Major McCauley already is familiar with our idea."

The Villamiranoas owned a house in the city, as well as their large house on the plantation outside Cochabamba. It was a classic Spanish colonial, two story home surrounding a landscaped patio, and the property was enclosed by a six foot high wall topped with broken glass. The conquistador atmosphere of portraits, suits of ancient armor and weapons was softened by touches of native culture, paintings, weavings and photographs. Scott had never seen anything in Cuba approaching this feeling of history and mixture of cultures. No visible traces of indigenous people remained in Cuba. Even though Cuba was the linchpin for Spanish conquest of the

New World after its discovery by Columbus in 1492, it had been completely affected by its modern neighbor to the north. Pizarro's final conquest of the area of Peru which became Bolivia was finally accomplished in 1538. Here was a mesmerizing step back into time. His grandmother's family history seemed to be entirely disconnected from this society on the top of the world.

In complete harmony with the house, the family members reflected the blending of cultures and races. Obvious European faces had become dominated with high cheek bones and narrowed eyes, very black hair became light brown or even blonde as the gene pools had mixed. Scott had thought of Villamiranoa as South American aristocracy. Now in this setting, he saw him as Bolivian history.

The evening was pleasant, and the food good. The parents of the *coronel* were the perfect example of the indigenous family connection. His father was a handsome man, but shorter with a darker complexion and higher cheek bones than his wife. Scott thought she must have come directly from northern Spain, but she was Bolivian from one of the more aristocratic families in Cochabamba. At this point he gave up trying to figure out the genealogy of Bolivia. Bolivia was Bolivia, and more fascinating than Cuba, even if it was hard to breathe.

The *coronel* interrupted his thoughts to introduce them to another member of the family. "Major McCauley, Sergeant Scott, this is my young cousin and outstanding Captain in my battalion, Francisco Gutierrez. Unfortunately, he had some illness at the time we went to Panama, so you did not meet him."

"*Mucho gusto*, Major McCauley and Sergeant Scott."

"*Un placer, Capitan,*" Scott replied for both himself and the major.

"Francisco is the son of the *Cacique* in this part of the world, who is also my cousin *and* the President of the Bolivian Indian Congress. Somewhere through the centuries they picked up the name Gutierrez and never changed it. The *Cacique* prefers to stay in his village with his people in the mountains rather than the bright lights of Cochabamba and the warm hospitality of this house. His brother, also my cousin, is the *gran shaman*. But we shall see them when we cross over to Montero tomorrow."

Looking at Francisco, Scott was thinking it had to be a long, long, time ago when they picked up the Gutierrez name. He was a classic guide-book handsome Indian, almost like he came from a movie casting studio for an Inca king.

"Francisco also speaks English and both Quechua and Aymara, but sadly no French."

"Not to worry, *coronel,* my sister speaks French very well."

"Ah…, yes. The lovely Maria Consuela. Scott, you have yet to see the more beautiful sights in Bolivia," as he winked at Francisco.

Scott wasn't sure whether this was going to be good or bad.

The *coronel* saw Scott looking at the bottles of Los Parales *singani* on the serving bar and laughed, "You won't have to worry about drinking much of that in the mountains. You are only going to get native *chicha."*

Scott wasn't sure whether this was going to be good or bad either. He remembered taking Denise out to the San Blas Islands off the coast of Panama to participate in a *chicha fuerte* celebration to "see visions into other dimensions…other levels of consciousness" with the Kuna Indians. He did not tell her that he had already visited those dimensions without any *chicha*, and he sure didn't tell the Army. She was never quite sure what she had experienced, except that it was very, very different. She gave him a questioning look out of the corner of her eye, then a good laugh.

'Well…this is bound to be *very, very different,'* Scott was thinking.

The next morning the *coronel,* part of the battalion staff, a company of soldiers, along with McCauley and Scott, boarded a C-123 for the flight. The aircraft was a little aid to the Bolivian Air Force that had managed to slip through. The C-123 was the twin engine, high tail, short takeoff and landing cargo plane popular with troops in the field needing resupply with minimum landing strips. It could also carry sixty soldiers. The flight took them over a wide area of the mountains as reconnaissance of the possible areas of operations. The most striking feature was the greenness on the eastern slope and the plains beyond as they became part of the Amazon rainforest. The warm northern trade winds blew over the Amazon rainforest and dumped their moisture as they rose up the eastern slopes. Hundreds of streams and rivers took the water back to the Amazon to continue the cycle. The *coronel* pointed out different settlements throughout the mountains, noting to his staff and NCOs where they might expect trouble. Several NCOs were from this area and added to the briefing.

Scott had jumped out of this aircraft many times, starting in airborne school at Ft. Benning. When he mentioned that to Villa-miranoa, he got another surprise.

"Scott, I meant to tell you we decided to set up a parachute school while we are at it. We will make my battalion a Ranger force modeled after your Ranger units. I already asked for the training schedule from the jump school at the Jungle Warfare School. That is where I and some of my officers received our own jump wings. You are going to be busy." He turned and winked at McCauley, who could not help but laugh. McCauley had earned his jump wings while a cadet at West Point, and suspected he would be down here more than he thought.

The thought crossed Scott's mind that he may never get out of Bolivia if these guys have their way. Colonel Bergeron was so right. He is a *very small pawn* in this game, and it is damn sure hard to see over the Knights and Castles on the chess board to the end game. He thought of one of his favorite poems by Rudyard Kipling,

> *"I keep six honest serving men*
> *(They taught me all I knew);*
> *Their names are What and Why*
> *And When*
> *And How and Where and Who"*

He just had not found all the *honest serving men* yet.

The C-123 landed on a dirt strip on the Villamiranoa's remote plantation in *Portachuelo* 10 km west of Montero and across the

Rio Piray. A big dust cloud was thrown up when the engines were reversed for the short landing. When they had flown over Montero it appeared about that dusty. The closest semblance of an airport was 72 km south in Santa Cruz, but this was good practice for things to come. 'Frontier town' would have been a good description of the rows of one and two story buildings and a few paved streets in Montero. Portachuelo could not even be called a town, even though it had been founded in 1770 by a priest and the army. They would not be seeing much of it anyway. The outskirts were not-very-organized farms growing soybeans, cotton, corn, and rice.

The population was completely Indian and *mestizo* mixture. Its strategic importance for the Army was its location on the east side of the mountains at 1,100 feet with access to the lowlands and the mountains. Guarani Indians from the lowlands added to the mix of Quechua speakers. The Guarani were the indigenous people of the lowlands and had fought both the Inca and the Spanish for hundreds of years and had been driven to the outer edges of civilization, even though 95% of the population of adjacent Paraguay had Guarani blood. These were an easy target for the propaganda of the *Tupac* movement. If they could also gain support of the Quechua and Aymara speakers and the mine worker unions, there was a strong likelihood of another leftist revolution like the one that brought down the government in 1941 and created substantial changes in 1952.

Ragged-looking, stake-body farm trucks were lined up to carry the soldiers to the training site at the foot of the nearby mountains to the west. No army trucks had arrived yet on the only paved road from *Cochabamba* south to *Santa Cruz*, then north through *Montero* to *Trinidad*. The local Villamiranoa plantation had served as a cover for the initial construction of the training facility. No signs announced the location of the 'school' and training site. The *campesinos* working on the plantation seemed to take very little interest in the army activities. They also had their own plots of land to work, thanks to the Villamiranoa family. Apparently, they were accustomed by now to the military part of this younger family member, but the sight of men jumping out of an airplane did prove to be a little bit of a distraction.

Scott's first sight of the 'school' proved that it had been in the works a lot longer than he had known. He could see buildings for barracks, offices, a rifle range, and a large building for indoor instruction with ceilings high enough for parachute rigging. That was another surprise. Two soldiers had been trained at the U. S. Army Rigger School at the insistence of Gen. Barrientos. In 1960 three Air Force parachutists under his command died when their equipment failed. Barrientos personally jumped one of the same parachutes to prove it was just bad luck. This had added even more to his popularity and legend. The riggers would also have to double as assistant airborne instructors. He could also see a 34 foot tower with a long cable extending at a 45 degree angle to a dirt mound for the simulation of exiting the aircraft. He winced at the memory of how that thing felt on his lower anatomy when the static line came to the end with a sudden jerk before the long slide down to the end. Fortunately, the actual aircraft exit was gentler on the body. McCauley saw him staring at the tower and laughed. He remembered too.

Spreading his arms wide in his favorite gesture, the *coronel* said, "Gentlemen, as you can see, we *have* been working on this. Let us take a quick tour while the troops are getting settled, and we can go to the office to go over the possible training program and the terrain maps." Behind the office building Scott could see an H-34 helicopter. It could carry sixteen troops and climb to 4,900 feet. He remembered the first time he jumped out of one of those. It felt like his parachute didn't open because he fell straight down instead of sideways from an airplane propeller blast with the speed of the plane forcing the 'chute to open. He guessed there would be a couple of tactical jumps from the helicopter for someone, in addition to reconnaissance.

The next two weeks consisted of a refresher of actual operation in the rain forest environment with the first company, not eating snakes. The native soldiers already knew how to do that, and there were seven species of monkeys in the rainforest to eat. Alternating platoons went through the parachute course. Gen. Barrientos had assigned the C-123 to the school for the duration. It would be flying back and forth to Cochabamba and La Paz to carry personnel and 'dignitaries.' The Jungle Warfare School lesson plans were camouflage for what was effectively Ranger training in a mountain rainforest environment, with the initial company training to be instructors. The *coronel* had also obtained lesson plans from the Ranger School at Ft. Benning. Scott had wondered why this initial company was so heavy in senior NCOs. It also looked like they had scavenged the whole Bolivian Army, from the amount of equipment he could see. Airborne school consisted of one week training with two jumps at the end. The last was with full equipment. Extensive physical training was not necessary and safety measures were cut to the bare minimum. This wasn't the U. S. Army where the minimum time was three weeks for enlisted soldiers and four for officers and senior NCOs. Here time was important. The drop zone was a ploughed but unplanted field.

Scott's assignment was as assistant to, and reporting only to, the commandant, Villamiranoa, which effectively placed him over the junior officers and NCOs. He was bunked in the plantation's main house with the major and his officers. He had to plan and schedule training with NCOs selecting terrain for him, while he modified and adapted the various objectives of the *coronel*, who also insisted that his young officers assist and learn to train. He had heard that South American officers were not as hands-on, but this group was going to be. It appeared that he had been promoted from *Pawn* to *Rook*.

At the end of the first week he had a status conference with the *coronel*. "How is it going, *sargento*?"

"Very well, *coronel*. You were obviously much farther along than I thought, and these men you selected are very motivated, if that is the correct word."

The *coronel* laughed, "Yes, this is a high priority item, and they are *motivated*. Scott, I have some reports of rebels over in the mountains causing some trouble with natives. They are using intimidation to get recruits, not humanitarian pleas to throw off the oppressive government, or as your Special Forces motto says, "*De*

Oppressor Liber." It looks like the bad guys are showing their bad side. I plan to run some *live fire* exercises in the area. Of course, this is just part of your training plan. *Si?*"

"*Absolutamente, commandante!*" Scott was beginning to see this was definitely going to be more than a training school, more like an operational base. That was fine with him. This is where he left off in Panama. He continued to modify and innovate his training plans based on his own experience as a *guerillero* in Cuba, and as a Special Forces counterinsurgency operator in Central America on the flip side of the revolutionary coin. This blend was exactly what Villamiranoa had been looking for. Once a week Major McCauley was flown in from La Paz to both contribute to the training and gather his own information for Curren. Occasionally, he even parachuted in. He said the Army had promised him his extra $110.00 per month jump pay if he made his monthly jumps based on his 'assignment' to the jump school as an extra duty. The Army was big on extra duty.

"*Bueno*, tomorrow you and I will go in the H-34 to take a look at the area."

At 0600 the H-34 lifted off to fly fifty miles west, deep into the mountains. They were accompanied by the battalion S-3 operations officer with maps, the senior NCO and two door gunners. Major McCauley had managed to schedule his training day to coincide with this 'training exercise.' He was surprised at his own excitement to be "back in the saddle."

The village was close to 4,000 feet with classic farming terraces down the mountain. It had a Quechua name which Scott could not remember, much less pronounce. No villager had ever seen a helicopter, and they scattered until the *coronel* coaxed them back, speaking in Quechua.

"Well, they were here five days ago. When conversation didn't work, they killed one of the young men and carried off his wife with threats to return if they did not supply the rebels with food." Villamiranoa stared off into the distant mountains in the direction the village chief indicated. No conversation could persuade the chief to ride in the helicopter to show them the way, and he could not understand the topographic map. But his son was convinced of the prestige he would gain by flying off into the sky with the soldiers.

With the chief's son pointing the way, they headed over the mountains. Scott was captivated by the views. He had obviously seen many mountains, but this continuing portion of the magnificent Andes viewed from a helicopter was a breathtaking collage of rocky, towering, mountain peaks, lush rainforest, and beautiful waterfalls into rivers rushing down to join tributaries ultimately emptying into the mighty Amazon River. The *Andes* Mountains split into the *Occidental Sierras* on the west and *Oriental Sierras* on the east. In between these towering mountains was the *Altiplano,* a large fertile plateau stretching from *Lake Titicaca,* a lake split between Peru and Bolivia, to the southern tip of Bolivia. Most of the population lived on the *Altiplano.* The eastern branch of the Andes they were flying over was the elbow where the eastern branch turned back south to become one range again in Chile. The military topographic maps had given him no hint of the sheer scale of this view.

The NCO who had some familiarity was busy describing landmarks. The metallic sound of "tink, tink" as rifle bullets hit the metal fuselage of the helicopter reminded everyone that it was not a sight-seeing trip. The *coronel* smiled "This must be the place!" and hung out of the door shouting to anyone below, "And *buenos dias* to you also, *mis amigos.*"

"Mark the map, *sargento.*" And to the pilot, "Drop off the *cacique's* son and take us to *Buena Vista.*"

"Scott, you are in for a treat. We're going to drop in on my cousin's settlement on the way back. Let us hope they do not shoot at us!" he said, still laughing.

It was late afternoon by the time they were on their way back to Buena Vista. The setting sun appeared and disappeared as they passed between one mountain peak and then another. Scott didn't know if it was his imagination or not, but looking west at the setting sun over these mountains this far south of the Equator the colors were different, the sky was different. It felt almost mystical; as if the alternating rays of the sun were reaching out for him, or asking him to see things he could not. *Abuelita,* he murmured to himself.

He could hear the coronel's voice over the engine and rotor noise. "There it is. Someone knew we were coming. They lit a fire in the large plaza."

On the ground he could see three figures standing by the fire. It was *Capitan* Gutierrez with two older men in native dress. The *Capitan* had been sent to the settlement several days before to gather intelligence from the surrounding areas.

Gutierrez was with his father, the *cacique or chief,* and his uncle, the *shaman* or medicine man or seer or whatever name people wanted to give him for his mysticism. He was named *Amboro'.* The name derived from the Indian legend of a young Indian, who was turned into a mountain as punishment by his father, the *cacique,* because he had allowed man to enter the mountains. That mountain was considered a magic place and could be seen from *Buena Vista.*

Francisco's father was named after the legendary *cacique, Grigotá,* who fought the Inca and the Guarani centuries before. It proved to be a substantial psychological advantage in dealing with the Indian Congress. Neither used their Spanish surname.

As the helicopter circled overhead Francisco turned to the shaman, "It is as you said, uncle, they are coming."

The old shaman continued to look up, "*He* is with them."

"*Who* is with them, uncle?"

"The one I have predicted. *He* will come to me."

The helicopter was starting to settle into the clearing and throwing a cloud of dust. The *shaman* never looked away.

Inside the H-34 Scott could not take his eyes off the figures on the ground. He felt pulled into the group, not physically but as if his mind was already there. He flashed back to his grandmother, thinking, *No, it is impossible. She cannot be there.*

As they dismounted the helicopter, the *coronel* turned to introduce Scott and McCauley to the Indians, "Major McCauley, Sergeant Scott this is my…" He could only see Scott's back as he was walking across the plaza towards the *shaman.* He called again,

"Scott…" Then turned to McCauley with a puzzled look.

"*Coronel,* you are going to learn not to be surprised at anything this young man does. I truly believe he is a bit of a *shaman* himself. In case no one has told you, his Cuban grandmother was considered a *bruja* (witch). In private moments he has told me of his nonverbal communications with her, and I believe it. Just watch."

Villamiranoa turned to watch this unanticipated scene. Scott had walked past the *capitan* and the *cacique,* neither of whom made any attempt to speak to him, and was standing in front of the shaman, not speaking.

Scott's mind was racing. This was not *abuelita.* Why was he drawn to this man? He was speaking, but not with words. Thoughts seemed to flow. He felt a welcoming. He said nothing, but he seemed to be communicating to the *shaman* that he was glad to be here at last. The *shaman's* eyes held him for what seemed to be a long time, then the old Indian turned and walked away without saying anything, seemingly satisfied that his vision was correct.

No one said anything. They only watched. Several Indian sergeants from the helicopter were kneeling, silently moving their lips as if in prayer. Most of the villagers had gathered on the outskirts of the plaza, and were standing silently, watching.

As the old shaman entered his lodge, *Capitan* Gutierrez broke the silence and the spell. "He was expecting you. We did not know who, but you seem to have fulfilled some prediction or premonition that we do not understand, yet. We have learned over the years to wait for his guidance. Now, Sergeant Scott, this is my famous father, the *Gran Cacique, Grigotá.*"

The *cacique* smiled, held out his hand, and in unaccented Spanish, "Welcome, Sergeant Scott, it is my pleasure."

Villamiranoa walked up to the group to exchange his greetings and introduce McCauley. "Well, cousin, that was a surprise. I suspect we are in for more before this is over. Are you OK, Scott?"

The moment had passed and Scott was back in the soldier mode. "Sorry, sir. Sometimes I just get fascinated by *shamans* and *curanderos* (healers). It's probably just a flash back to my grandmother." But he was thinking, *Now there is a white Rook and Bishop on the chess board.*

"No problem. We'll take it as a good omen. Now, Francisco, since you seemed to have been advised of our coming, what other surprises do you have?"

"A lot of food and drink, *coronel.* And some interesting reports from the *yungas* (fertile valleys) to the north."

"Bueno, I am hungry for both, especially the intelligence reports. And my pilots will only enjoy the food, because we fly back to *Portachuelo* tonight," he said as he smiled at his pilots.

His sergeants started to mingle with the crowd of villagers, "Remember, *sargentos,* tonight we return," he reminded them with a laugh. They waved in acknowledgement.

On the other side of the plaza, and beside the stone well that served the settlement, animal skins were being arranged on the ground for the guests to sit and pottery filed with *chicha* was being placed on low tables. The *cacique's* place was decorated with a jaguar skin as befitted his rank. The *shaman* was not in sight. No one asked where he was.

Scott didn't know what the protocol might be, but he sure was not going to presume to sit next to the cacique or the *coronel.* He calculated he should be on the far side of McCauley whatever anyone else did. McCauley whispered, "Scott, I think something else is in store for you. Before you pick a seat you better wait."

At that moment, a small group of women were approaching the meeting area. In the center of the group Scott could see who had to be the *cacique's* daughter, Maria Consuela. Villamiranoa's hinted description and her brother's good looks were not adequate preparation for this. She was taller than her brother with even sharper Indian features. As handsome as Francisco was, she was more beautiful. A casting studio could never find anyone for this part. The elegant, or aloof, air she carried only added to the illusion.

Her escorts stepped aside and she walked past her father and directly up to Scott. No one said anything. Her eyes were dark, piercing, and beautiful and fixed on him. He thought, *My God. She has the shaman's eyes. They are even more intense than abuelita's.*

McCauley stood, while the *coronel* and the *cacique* remained seated. The *cacique* smiled. He had seen his daughter dissolve men before.

She did not wait for him to speak. She started her conversation in relatively good French as if to challenge him to live up to some reputation. "*Monsieur*, my uncle has told me of your coming. You know who I am. It is my pleasure to meet you."

Scott thought this was an interesting development and picked up the challenge with his most formal, extended, and fluent French greeting by describing his enchantment with her unmatched beauty as complimenting these beautiful mountains while enhancing her heritage. She blinked. A little crack seemed to appear in her haughty disposition. The cacique smiled, and Villamiranoa ducked his head to keep from laughing.

As Scott had suspected, she had never before been the subject of a refusal to be intimidated by someone with a fluent, French, barrage of compliments. She quickly recovered and safely switched to Spanish by recognizing her father and the *coronel*.

McCauley whispered, "I think you just earned a place at the head table."

The rest of the evening was a pleasant get-to-know-you dinner, with Maria Consuela stealing short glances at Scott. When he caught her, he would wink. That would send color to her face and a swift look in the other direction. Whenever the *coronel* noticed this little exchange, he would turn to one of the people present and laugh loudly as if they had told a very funny joke. There was no suppressing his continuing amusement at this surprising turn of events.

The conversation at supper was primarily in Quechua and dealt with the reported rebel activity in the mountains and drawings on the map. Scott was free to continue his subtle teasing of Maria Consuela.

At the end of the dinner and meeting the *coronel* had his NCOs rounded up and formal expressions of appreciation were exchanged. Francisco also boarded the H-34 to return to the base. Maria Consuela stood silently in the background, and the *shaman* never appeared again.

After lift-off, Villamiranoa, turned laughing to Scott, "I have never seen anyone handle Maria Consuela like that. I thought I was the master of the wink, but..." he finished the sentence with his typical arms spread gesture and more laughter, joined by Francisco and McCauley.

"Well, sir, she just picked the wrong language to intimidate me." More laughter.

"You just have to forgive her. She is accustomed to having her own way. In case you did not notice, she has some *shamantic* qualities and will probably be the next *shaman* ...or if you please *bruja* after *Amboró* dies. *Vamos a ver.*" (We will see.)

Tomorrow would be a new day with real operations planning for a *live fire training exercise.* The battalion was at full strength because of the C-123 shuttle to and from Cochabamba and the units were rotating through the Ranger and Airborne phases.

Intelligence reports indicated the main *Tupac* group, consisting of approximately four hundred, was operating in the rainforest close to the Brazilian border. They were mainly trying to influence the Guarani Indians in the area. The location served as a rest and training site, and also afforded a quick escape into Brazil if attacked.

The activity reported by *Capitan* Gutierrez detailed a smaller unit in the fertile valleys of the *yungas* to the north, a rich agricultural area which had traditionally suffered from poor access to markets on the other side of the eastern mountains. This area had thousands of Afro-Bolivians who had migrated from the *altiplano* after emancipation in the 19th century. They were easily influenced by Tupac propaganda because of the historic and continuing discrimination in mainstream society.

This was a different group in a different location from the one who fired on the helicopter. It was an alarming fact that more groups in more areas were under Tupac influence than previously thought. It was decided that some plan must be developed to lure the main group out of the border lands and into an engagement with the advantage to organized military units, not guerrilla tactics.

Major McCauley had received permission to remain for a two-week period and had been discussing the pros and cons with the *coronel* and his staff, with Scott sitting in as a counterinsurgency advisor. He turned to Scott, "Tom, do you have an opinion?"

"Sir, it seems to me that these guys are doing more terror than talking. Maybe that is their philosophy. If so, they have not paid any attention to Mao Tse-tung or Che Guevara. I didn't know Mao, but I sure heard enough about him from Che. Mao said over and over, 'We must patiently explain, explain, persuade, discuss and convince.' Both Mao and Che were educated, intelligent men. These guys are stupid, more like bandits than idealistic *guerilleros*. They don't discuss. They just kill and take what they want. Why shoot at a helicopter and give away your position? Or they may just be a splinter group without a goal. From what I heard, the group in the *yungas* operates differently. They seem to play on Afro-Bolivian prejudice in society. The main group out in the lowlands is what we really want eliminated. They have read Mao. They are *'swimming in the sea of people.'* Out there we cannot corner them. They will run to the swamps in Brazil. Somehow we have to lure them out. In the mountains they are no better than our special unit and not as well trained or armed. We need to use the hammer and anvil and deny them the people. We have the vertical envelopment capability with our airborne units. We can jump in behind them and deny access to Brazil and its dense cover, if we can just get them far enough away from the border. It doesn't appear that they have convinced the Guarani to join forces with them in an actual fight...yet. The ones in the mountains remind us of the adage 'to fight a guerilla, be a guerilla.' We can do that."

Villamiranoa looked at McCauley, who raised his eyebrows in a return look, as if to say, "What did I tell you?"

"*Bueno.* Gentlemen, Mr. Scott has reminded us of what we have learned. We will plan this as a three phase operation." The *coronel* was thinking fast now, "First, we will launch a guerilla on guerilla operation on that group we located in the mountains. Second, we will create a bigger operation in the *yungas* to deal a blow to their hopes there. Third, that should be enough to draw Tupac in to fight when he sees his revolution being threatened in its early stages. I don't think he realizes yet how potent a force we have trained here and in Panama. I like that idea of an airborne assault behind him. We will indeed have an anvil and a hammer. Gentlemen, I will look for an operational plan in two days. Dismissed."

"Francisco, McCauley and Scott stay a minute."

"Francisco, old *Amboró* has something going on in his mind. I want to know what it is. Take the H-34 over there *now* and talk to your father. This is very important. You and I know this. The major and Scott will soon realize it. We will be there in the morning. That should give *Amboró* time to blow a little smoke, rattle some bones, talk to the spirits and whatever else he needs to do."

"Right way, sir," with that Francisco hurried out of the room.

The *coronel,* turned to the Americans, "Well, distinguished advisors you are about to see something they don't write in counterinsurgency manuals or teach at Ft. Bragg. Scott, that was well done. Let's see what kind of plan my staff comes up with." And smiling with another arm spread gesture, "Let us retire to my office and have a little of my father's finest *singani.*"

0630 the H-43 settled into the *Buena Vista* plaza. The clearing was just being flooded with sunshine with no mountains to the east to block it. To the west of the village, morning dew on the mountains was turning to a rising mist as the sun warmed the eastern slopes. Three men stood like statues in the plaza, neither ducking from rotor blades whirling overhead nor shielding their eyes from the downdraft. Scott recognized the same three as before, but he could not have expected anyone else.

On the ground they walked to the *cacique's* dwelling. Scott tried to see out of the corners of his eyes for sight of Maria Consuela to no avail. This was to be strictly business. A small table had been arranged for the military men's benefit and a topographic map was laid out on the table. Francisco had impressed on his father the importance of the meeting. The shaman sat off to the side awaiting his summons from the *cacique.*

The *cacique* nodded to Francisco to speak. "The *Gran Cacique* and I have discussed the situation and our purpose here. *Don Amboró* has spoken as to what the spirits have told him. I will explain. My father and the Indian Congress are very aware of the situation with *Tupac*. To this point they do not see that it is to their advantage to support what he wants to do. President Estenssoro already has the support of the Indian Congress based on his position on land reform in years past. The president's attempts to seek support from the mining unions and the known leftist positions of his vice president, Juan Lechín have no effect on the Indian Congress that they can see. The military has not caused any problems for the Congress in many years. The fact that I and our cousin Villamiranoa are allied with the military has little effect except for him personally. He wishes you to explain."

A polite pause and *Coronel* Villamiranoa spoke, "*Gran Cacique*, I do not speak only for the military or our families. I speak for our country. This so called *Tupac* impersonator does not speak for the people as he claims. He has no personal allegiances, only himself. He adopts causes like he changes clothes, espousing this one, then that one. He is not an Indian. He is not a farmer. He is not a miner. But he picks complaints of each group as he encounters them. All of this is to his own personal ends. In the military we wish to have stability and prosperity for this country, not just to turn it over to another despot. *Tupac*, with Lechin, will lead us to economic ruin while pretending to protect different parts of our society. We do not have a perfect government, but we are not trying to tear down the country. Young Sergeant Scott here had first hand experiences in Cuba with the great promise of 'revolution' to change a whole society. Scott, perhaps you can give us the benefit of your real experience."

This sounded more like an order than a request. He had not been expecting to be engaged in a sociological discussion, especially in a country he did not know. Where the heck did he begin? How did he address such an important person when he was just a sergeant?

McCauley sat quietly watching this play out. *Grigotá* shifted his eyes and expectantly tilted his head in Scott's direction.

Scott noticed the shaman intently watching from the background. He took a deep breath, "*Gran Cacique*, I am only a young sergeant from a foreign country, and I do not presume to give anyone advice, especially important leaders like yourself. My grandmother comes from a Spanish family as old as Villamiranoa's in a colonial society as old as Spanish Bolivia. Your society is far more complex than ours in Cuba. We only have statues to caciques who died hundreds of years ago and left no mark on our society. I have spent the last year fighting insurgencies in Latin America like this. However, I have seen and personally fought on the side of people like *Tupac*. Promises and more promises were made to the disadvantaged people. In the end it was only a personality cult and an ego to make a world in his own image. In the end a whole society was destroyed, not improved. I am only here as a low level military advisor, not a person qualified to advise on your level. But I can tell you my story and the story for which my father died ..."

As Scott continued his story, McCauley found himself spellbound in spite of swearing to never be surprised by Scott again. Villamiranoa found himself wondering if he should ever speak again, or just turn Scott loose to talk. The *shaman* was now leaning forward into the circle of men. The *cacique's* expression never changed nor did his eyes stray from Scott.

Scott was finishing, "...*Gran Cacique*, although I have no right to speak on this matter, I would sincerely request your assistance to eliminate this impersonator."

A long silence followed as the *cacique* digested this in his own manner and within his own experience. Finally, he turned to the *shaman*, who gave a slight nod of his head. "*Bien*, we will assist you. *Coronel*, we thank you for bringing this young man to us. He has experienced many life and death experiences in his young life with many powerful men and has accumulated much wisdom beyond his years from it. He is the one foretold by my *shaman* brother."

Villamiranoa concealed his surprise, but felt considerable satisfaction with himself. He was glad to take all the credit he could get. But he wondered why Francisco had not told him before.

McCauley felt a chill go through him at the thought of what could be next in this very alien setting. He couldn't even tell Colonel Bergeron about this surprise.

Scott was thinking, *Shit, another move was just made on the chess board, and I still couldn't see it. Why don't I just keep my mouth shut?*

"Mr. Scott, thank you for coming. My brother has told me that he has encountered your grandmother in whatever space she occupies in this or other worlds."

Now Scott was getting chills and thinking of those Cuban palm trees whispering and wondering what could be coming next. He couldn't say anything. He just nodded.

To everyone's relief, Francisco spread the map out showing pencil marks in the areas around the village they had visited, and started his briefing. Scott was only half listening. He could feel the *shaman's* eyes, but he didn't dare meet his look. The *shaman* still had said nothing.

They flew back to *Portachuelo*. Scott tried to say as little as possible. McCauley sat next to him, "Don't worry about it, Tommy. I've got your back. If anything weird happens, we'll get you out of here." He wasn't as sure as he sounded, but he hoped using Scott's first name was a little reassuring.

Villamiranoa's staff was anxiously waiting on the news. Their plan was just waiting on coordinates. Villamiranoa wasted no time getting into the details. He left Scott alone in consideration of what he just went through, but included McCauley. He also wanted to question Francisco further after the session.

In the privacy of his quarters he questioned Francisco, "OK, cousin, what is this really about? Your father could have told us about locations and his attitude anytime. *Que pasa?*"

Francisco looked at the floor and then the ceiling. The *coronel* was getting impatient, "Well, *digame, Capitan.*"

Francisco avoided his eyes and said, "The *shaman* believes that Sergeant Scott is or will become a *shaman,* and he is the one who *must* marry Maria Consuela to fulfill her destiny and her children's as the future *shamans.*"

"And your father believes this?"

"Yes."

"*Jesus Cristo,* do *you* understand that our family's future and our country is at risk with this *Tupac* situation? Does *he*?"

"Yes."

"And I suppose that he is going to use his assistance as leverage to arrange this?"

"Yes."

With that, the *coronel* slammed his fist on the desk and did some very serious cursing before he let Francisco out of the room, while threatening to send him back to live in a dirt floor hut.

In the morning he had reasoned that he did not have to deal with this situation immediately. First things first. He needed to gain some success in diminishing the nearby guerilla threat and some confidences of generals and politicians before he had to finish off *Tupac*. Then he could deal with this *other thing*. Cousin or no cousin, alienating the President of the Bolivian Indian Congress was a serious matter, but coercing a member of the United States Army to marry a relative was a *very big problem*, to say nothing of the fact that he had made him a critical piece in his own grand scheme. He tried to shut out the political repercussions with the ambassador and even the president.. However, maybe he will even want to marry her. She is beautiful and smart. That was a better thought. Now he needed to concentrate on the first phase of *Operation Tupac*. He needed another helicopter and support crew. Quickly.

He ordered Francisco to return to Buena Vista with the message that he understood the situation, but he suggested that for the minute they see what could happen naturally with the *other thing*. Meanwhile, he needed the *shaman* to go with Francisco to the last village attacked and do some *magic* with the villagers to enable his plan. He knew Francisco would phrase the "do some *magic*" in the appropriate manner to be acceptable to the *shaman* and the *cacique*.

Francisco did exactly that, and persuaded the *shaman* to spend the night in the village dispensing herbal and 'magic' cures to the villagers. It would be a great honor for them to have the *gran shaman/curandero* in their village.

With assurances from Francisco that he would truly soar with the condors and a stern *request* from *Cacique Grigotá*, *Amboró* boarded the helicopter in his finest regalia with bundles of assorted herbs and potions. Even with engine and rotor noise, *Amboró* did feel the flight of the condor. At Francisco's request, the pilot soared in and out of valleys like a bird to complete the illusion.

At the village Francisco exited first to announce that the *Gran Shaman, Amboró,* had chosen this village to bless and heal and had flown with the condors to reach them. *Amboró* stepped out blowing rich lowland tobacco smoke and shaking a rattle to clear spirits from his path and protect the villagers. The image of the shaman in his brightly colored clothing and brilliant macaw feathers did create the intended impression. Francisco stood to the side and had to admit this was a magnificent entrance. No one could fail to fall under his spell. The village chief came forward and fell prostrate at the feet of the great *Amboró,* begging his blessing of this village. The *shaman* was at his best in this setting. He turned and waved away the iron bird which had delivered him. At his gesture the H-34 rose into the air and soared into the distance. The illusion was complete.

From the shadows the chief's son watched the scene. Although he had also flown in the iron bird to show the soldiers the location of the rebels and had gathered much respect for his feat, he still felt weak at the sight of the *Gran Shaman. Amboró* was respected and feared throughout all the mountains and lowlands. He spoke to the spirits, knew their secrets, knew their cures for the sick and knew the way to lead the dead to the after-life. But no one knew that he, the son of the chief, had later spoken to the rebels, and he believed what they said about a new Bolivia where he could be the equal to any man.

Amboró was given a large stump of a tree on which he could sit. It was carved into a chair with many symbols and shapes of animals representing the mountain spirits presumed to rule the lives of the native people. From this position *Amboró* commanded the sick and suffering be brought to him. Francisco knew that there was no equal in all the mountains to *Amboró* diagnosing sickness and knowing what natural remedies would work. He had never seen a medical doctor the equal of the *shaman.* For those with sadness and hopelessness he could divine the spirits and lay his hand on the villagers, while he chanted and communed with spirits. No one felt that they were not cured.

Amboró granted the chief a special ceremony to see the spirits that night. True magic would be shown. Only Francisco and the chief's son were to be present.

The chief's lodge was much larger than the villagers' huts and served also as meeting hall and ceremony room. The walls were lined with cleaned and softened animal skins and woven blankets which were taken down for sleeping. The floor was composed of flat stones carefully shaped to fit into patterns. The roof of thatch had a hole in the center to let out the smoke from the fire pit which was surrounded by painted pottery and iron kettles. A raised platform served both as a bed and seat for the chief to conduct his council meetings. This night the *shaman* used the platform to place his ceremonial objects and containers of herbal mixtures.

The potion selected by the *shaman* for this ceremony was *San Pedro,* a cactus grown in the highlands (*Trichocerus Pachanoi*). It is the oldest known 'magical' plant in South America. It is used to experience heightened awareness and tranquility with the guidance of the *shaman.* Colorful visions and oneness with life through rapid thought flow enable the person to see his path through communication with human and animal spirits. These were the experiences promised by the *shaman. Amboró* had performed this countless times and led countless persons to understand the miracles of life and beyond. Tonight his object was to guide this chief to understand what he must do to help the *Gran Cacique* and his people by finding and visiting his spirit totem, either in animal or human form. He would chant and sing to the spirits to help this chief see what he must do. He also would drink his potion and travel with the chief.

Francisco would not take part. He would be witness to the enlightenment gained *and information revealed.* It was decided that the chief's son must take part in order avoid his feelings interfering with the spirits.

The spirit trip could not be explained or described. It was personal, intimate and deep within the participant. Only the *shaman* could interpret.

Francisco had participated many times before, but as he sat and witnessed, the effect was even more magical without the drink. The room seemed to take on a glow from the participants themselves. Their eyes were open, but they were seeing things he could not see. The shaman's chants and soft songs were lifting him into an avenue he had not expected. There were spirits here. He could feel them, but not see what they must be seeing or hearing. The hours passed until he had no sense of time. Gradually as Francisco watched, the air cleared, a feeling of well-being was apparent, the participants eyes cleared, and they smiled.

The chief's son left the ceremonial lodge with mixed feelings. He felt the magic of the spirit world and the peace of knowing, but the physical world was once again shoving its way into his conscientiousness as daylight came to the village. He looked about the village and saw only poverty and deprivation. Those were the words the *Tupac* men had used. It had to be the fault of the men in power. The *Tupac* men had said so. He wasn't sure where La Paz was, but they must be there. This shaman and his nephew were the agents of the soldiers who had come, and would come again to keep the La Paz men in power. He had flown in the iron bird. He knew it was not magic. He turned away and left the village to work in the terraced fields and to think. On the way he stripped leaves from a coca bush and stuffed them in the side of his mouth. This was *his* magic. He did not look up as the helicopter lifted off on its way back to Buena Vista with the shaman. It would pick up troops already ferried there in the night.

It was only a one hour flight each way. Francisco stayed with the chief to ensure there were no changes of heart in giving away the rebels location and plans. He had felt a little uncomfortable with the attitude of the chief's son. His hand-held radio only had a line of sight range in these mountains. He hoped the H-34 in the air would pick up any calls he had to make. Prearranged signals would notify the H-34 if it was safe to come in. No signal obviously indicated it was not.

Information and coordinates gained from the village chief were rapidly conveyed to battalion headquarters and as rapidly put into the Phase I plan. The second helicopter from Cochabamba had arrived and troops were loading within the hour to set up a blocking force (the *anvil*) in the valley the rebels would use for escape. Their estimated strength was twenty to thirty men. It would be far enough away with the H-34 hugging the ground to avoid detection by the unsuspecting rebel group. Fifteen soldiers, including a captain, with their weapons and equipment, including several light .30 caliber machine guns, were loaded, along with a hand-held mortar. They would establish fixed positions for the ambush. The group included more NCOs than normal, but everyone wanted to be on this first real action.

The H-34 from Portachuelo had been in the air for fifteen minutes when the second lifted off from Buena Vista headed back to the village to pick up Francisco. The *coronel* was in charge of the overall operation with another of his captains commanding this group of soldiers. Originally, eleven soldiers plus McCauley and Scott were planned. This would leave room for Francisco to be picked up at the village, but *Amboró* refused to leave the aircraft. He insisted that it was absolutely necessary that he return to the village. Villamiranoa didn't have the time to argue with him nor did he need the aggravation at this moment. So, off to the fight went this mixed group less one soldier.

The shaman sat quietly with his eyes on Scott, who was busy checking his weapon and equipment one more time. He rubbed his favorite M-2 carbine, worked the bolt even though he had already checked it a dozen times. McCauley was just happy to be there and feel the anticipation of combat again. A disproportionate number of .30 caliber BARs (Browning Automatic Rifle) were on board to be used as light weight machine guns. Soldiers carried the M-1 .30 caliber rifle with several having grenade launcher adapters to give the effect of artillery fire. There would be a lot of noise when this group commenced firing. Spotting from the air the H-34 could give covering machine gun fire with one of the soldiers assigned as a door gunner. The shock effect (the *hammer*) of all this could send a much larger group fleeing down their escape route to the *anvil*.

Francisco was in the aircraft before it touched the ground in the village. Villamiranoa physically forced the shaman off the helicopter. No time to argue. The pilot swung off to the given coordinates. By now the other H-34 would be on the ground and the unit emplacing itself to cover all angles.

Ten minutes later they were over what appeared to be a camouflaged campsite. *Tink... tink, tink* bullet hits confirmed this was the place. The *coronel* looked around. Only one soldier was creased in the leg. Not a serious wound. They poured machine gun fire into the area as the H-34 dove down to complete the shock effect. Rebels could be seen running into the surrounding trees. An apparent leader was trying to organize them. Scott shot him from the air as the helicopter closed in. More *tink, tink, tink, tink*, but the shots were wild with no damage. The *coronel* was first out of the right side directing heavy fire to the surrounding trees. Francisco was right behind him. Scott and McCauley exited the left side with the other captain and four soldiers, two carrying BARs. They could hear grenades being launched from the *coronel's* side and hear explosions in the direction of the woods as they landed. One of the BAR soldiers next to Scott went down. Before he could reach him McCauley had already picked up the BAR, slung the cartridge belt over one shoulder and his carbine over the other shoulder, and continued to fire it into the area where he could see and hear the rebels firing. Scott had the quick thought, *Damn, this officer really knows how to fight.*

The H-34 had lifted off and continued to fire at targets the soldiers on the ground could not see. Bullet holes were all over the aircraft but none disabling. The H-34 was one tough bird. The rebels were now in full flight leaving at least seven dead on the scene. The captain led seven men, chasing and continuously firing from a safe distance, just to keep the rebels running to the ambush. The remainder of the men set up a perimeter around the area where the helicopter would land.

Only two of the soldiers were wounded, one seriously. Scott

was trying to stop the blood flow. He was thinking how all that cross training in Special Forces always came in handy.

Villamiranoa walked over to McCauley, "How about that, Major?"

McCauley looked up at the sky and smiled, "Goddamn it, *Coronel*. I had almost forgotten how much I missed this shit." Villamiranoa laughed and turned to check on the wounded men.

Increased gunfire and explosions echoed up the valley as the rebels ran into the *anvil*. The H-34 returned. It had picked up the smiling *capitan* and his posse. The other unit would gather up any prisoners to be interrogated, while the *coronel's* unit searched the camp site for any intelligence they could use. This actual operation had taken only three hours from lift off. Villamiranoa was looking forward to writing his after-action report to Generals Barrientos and Ocampo, but the wounded had to be taken care of.

The closest medical help besides Scott was actually the *shaman/ curandero* left in the village. That was where they headed first, then to pick up soldiers left on the ground while prisoners were being transported to the base at Portachuelo for holding.

The *shaman* was waiting in the same spot where Villamiranoa had thrown him out of the helicopter. He seemed to have understood. He had his *curandero* medical sack still with him and immediately took charge of the wounded. Scott followed to where the soldiers were carried in the chief's lodge. He watched with fascination as *Amboró'* rapidly worked on the most seriously wounded by making him drink some strange smelling liquid and applied a poultice to the open wounds where the bullet had passed through. It somehow stopped the bleeding which Scott had been trying to do with pressure.

The chief's son watched in silence and wondered what had happened to the *Tupac* men. He soon learned. He turned back to the fields to think and chew his coca leaves. The juice was absorbed in his mouth and trickled down his throat until he felt strength and decision come to him. His magic was strong. He felt more powerful than the *shaman*.

The H-34 returned with the few soldiers who had been left

on the ground. Rebel bodies were left for the condors, whose high circles in the sky gave warning as to what had happened there. The sun was getting low in the western sky and would soon disappear behind the *Cordillera Oriental,* the eastern spur of the Andes, with its strange glow still fascinating Scott.

The chief's son climbed back up from the terraces striping fresh coca leaves as he walked. His short body cast long shadows from the setting sun. He did not need water or food. He had a purpose.

The H-34 returned to *Portachuelo* with the wounded and the additional soldiers from the other H-34, leaving Scott, Villamiranoa, McCauley, Francisco and two soldiers for the next day. *Amboró* sat on a large boulder staring into the mountains as the sun disappeared, not moving. The chief stood a respectful distance to the side. Scott wondered if the *shaman* was in a trance of some kind and started walking toward him. From the corner of his eye he saw a figure come up the trail from the terraces. It was the chief's son. He was now thirty feet from *Amboró,* who did not move. A knife appeared in his hand as he rushed at Amboró screaming, his face contorted. He reached Amboró before the chief could react and plunged the knife once, twice, three times into the *shaman,* before the chief could kill his own son. *Amboró* had made no sound and turned to look at Scott as his life's blood soaked into the mountain. Scott and Francisco dropped to the ground beside him, but he waved off any assistance. "It is my time." His voice became weaker as he looked at Scott and said, *"Casa Maria,"* and more faintly, *"casa maria,"* His last weak breath left him. Black *Pawn* eliminates white *Bishop.*

A stunned silence followed, except for the chief's soft crying over the body of his son. A soft blue light began to arise from *Amboró's* inert form. Scott thought it must be static electricity on the mountain top. He had seen St. Elmo's fire many times in the rigging of sailboats as static collected there, but there was no buzzing or hissing, only a slow rising of the light. He had heard of the life force of a dying person leaving the body and dissipating into the atmosphere in the form of a blue light. Some people said it was the soul leaving. He had never experienced it, never seen it. He was vaguely aware that a crowd of villagers had gathered and now quickly moved back to the perceived safety of their huts as the light continued to rise. However, this light was not evaporating, not dissolving into the atmosphere. It was surrounding him. He could see his hands outlined in a blue glow. The soldiers who were nearby took steps back, more in awe than fear. The villagers let out a mournful cry. Francisco knelt alongside and just watched his uncle.

Scott was still convinced it was static electricity. He had seen it before the lightning strike in basic training, but there were no storm clouds, only a darkening mountain sky. He turned to Francisco, who simply said, "He knew this would be his time. He told me. He wanted to be buried here on this mountain facing the rising sun."

Scott thought of the shaman's last words, "Where is the house of Maria he spoke of?" Scott was becoming confused.

Francisco looked at the distant mountains and the color of the sky then up at Scott, "He did not say 'house of Maria.' He said 'marry Maria,' my sister."

"What…?" Scott was stunned. He had confused the noun for house, *casa,* with the third person singular of the verb to marry, *casar.* Now he could feel a warming sensation. The universe was in its place. He could not describe the sensation, but everything seemed clear. Why? Was the world turning upside down? Nothing around him had changed. He just *knew.* He could hear Francisco's voice, "Sergeant Scott…, Sergeant Scott, are you OK?"

The glow was starting to dim, but it was still there. "Yes…, I'm OK. I guess it's just the mountain static electricity."

Villamiranoa had run to the scene, looked at the *shaman's* body and turned to Francisco, "Does he know?"

"Yes."

McCauley had followed Villamiranoa. He looked at Scott and also thought static electricity. "Tommy, Tommy, are you alright?"

Scott sat looking at his hands, turning them over and over. The glow was still there. He looked up, "The shaman is dead, but I feel his spirit."

McCauley turned to the *coronel*, "We need a medic!"

"No…no, we are seeing two souls merge, Major. We will never see this again."

"I'm sorry, *coronel*, but I think we are only seeing static electricity." But he could not convince himself.

"Come, Major. I need to tell you the rest of this story." As they walked, Villamiranoa related the Maria Consuela situation.

"Oh…, shit! You mean this whole operation, the whole plan to keep the Indian Congress from swinging away from the government depends on this marriage because a dead *shaman* says so? Tell me it's not so."

The coronel stared into the dark, "I am afraid it's true."

"Jesus Christ! How long have you known this?" McCauley was starting to get his Irish temper up.

"Yesterday. I thought we would have time to let it work itself out. The girl is beautiful, and he seems to like her. Time should have been on our side. Now…," he shrugged his shoulders asking for suggestions.

"And the *Gran Cacique*?"

"He is convinced it must be done to complete Maria Consuela's journey into *shamanism*. You told me yourself that Scott could very well be a developing *shaman* through his grandmother. In spite of my heritage, I really try to stay above this mysticism, but the more I see - and I have seen a lot - the more I wonder who is to say."

"I understand your dilemma, *coronel*. I don't think I agree, but I sure see the consequences for both of us. Let's think about it. I'll talk to Tommy. Maybe he does like the girl, but he can't stay in Bolivia forever."

Francisco came to talk to the *coronel*, speaking in low tones, "I think we can resolve the problem with the chief and his son."

"You have my complete attention, cousin."

Francisco looked around to make certain there was no one near, "*Amboró* told my father before he left that this was his destiny to die here. I have told the chief that his son was only fulfilling the *Gran Shaman's* most important prophesy, and he played a preordained part. Even the killing of his own son was the will of the divine spirits, and he will be blessed for his sacrifice. The *Gran Shaman's* grave in his village will be proof to the world of this truth. I need you to verify this,   even if we have to bring my father, the *Gran Cacique Grigotá,* up here. I believe this is true."

"I believe that is the easy part. Marrying your sister to Scott is the hard part. Let's bury *Amboró* and bring *Grigotá* up here tomorrow to bless this grave."

Amboró was buried that night under rocks on an outcropping facing east where the first rays of the morning sun would strike. Scott was left alone to sit by the grave. He did not feel the need to sleep nor eat. The faint glow and warm sensation remained with him. No coat or animal skin was needed to keep him warm through the cold mountain night. As the first light streaked across the grave, he stood and stared into the dawn. Everything was good. The white *Bishop* had just been sacrificed to move the white *Rook* forward.

The helicopter arrived in the early morning. *Grigotá* was on board. He had not needed to be told. He knew. Maria Consuela walked behind him to the grave. The villagers bowed and made way for the *Gran Cacique.* The prophecy was confirmed. Their village would be in the legend of the chief who sacrificed his own son to send the *Gran Shaman Amboró* into his final journey to the spirit world. Maria Consuela took her place beside Scott without looking at him or touching him. Neither said a word. There would be time later. The Cacique spoke only a few words, "My brother, the *Gran Shaman Amboró*, told me of this vision. It was his chosen path. His life was long and good." He sprinkled *quinoa* grain on the grave and left.

The ride back to Buena Vista was solemn with no conversation. On arrival Scott and Maria Consuela were left to walk in the woods and speak as they wished to one another. Villamiranoa requested an audience with *Grigotá,* while McCauley waited. *Grigotá* wanted one more unexpected thing. He wanted Scott to become an officer befitting marriage to the daughter of the *Cacique.* Villamiranoa had assumed this was a simple matter until he talked to McCauley. Now, he was really looking forward to the *singani* back in his quarters.

It took all night, but the *coronel* thought he had it figured out. The next morning he boarded the C-123 headed back to La Paz with the wounded, the prisoners, and McCauley. Both had to talk to their superiors. He hoped his report would put them in a gracious mood.

The ambassador's greeting was enthusiastic. He had received the reports. Then, McCauley gave his account to the ambassador and Curren.

"Good God, man. Are our governments being held hostage by some savage chief in the wilderness?"

Curren interrupted, "Mr. Ambassador, *Grigotá* **is** the President of the Indian Congress."

The ambassador pursed his lips, "Get Scott up here *tomorrow*."

McCauley spoke up, "Mr. Ambassador, may I make a suggestion?"

"Of course." The Ambassador wanted any suggestion he could get at this point. This had been a quiet tour in Bolivia and certainly not as bad as he had thought at first. Now he was facing an international incident.

"As you have noticed, Sergeant Scott is not stupid. He is obviously very smart, and the Indians out there are very strong in their beliefs. First, I would recommend him for a Bronze Star for his action out there. I will write it up. Next, I would get someone very high up to *suggest* that he take his commission. Then I can talk to Villamiranoa about having the *cacique* create some marriage that can be dissolved after the girl becomes pregnant. That could solve both problems. However, we don't know. Scott may really want to live in Bolivia."

The Ambassador looked at Curren and laughed, "Even the CIA couldn't make this one up. Major, show me some paperwork." He winked at Curren, "I think I know someone *very high up*. I believe I do owe one to this young man's family." McCauley and Curren smiled.

Scott was on the C-123 shuttle to La Paz the next morning. The airborne students would just have to jump out of helicopters.

Meanwhile, the *coronel* had met with Generals Barrientos and

Ocampo, who were very pleased with the report and had no problem making Scott an honorary major in the Bolivian Army Reserve. Things were moving well for the *coronel*. Now it was back to *Grigotá*. Trying to keep Scott in Bolivia was going to be a big problem.

The ambassador and McCauley personally met Scott at the airport. "Good job, Tom. The major has recommended you for a Bronze Star, and I am sending my own report to the State Department."

This looked like another chess move to Scott. He was very careful in his reply, "Sir, I appreciate your recommendation, but I didn't do any more than Major McCauley, and it was just a brief skirmish." McCauley looked down at the runway and smiled to himself.

"Well then, I will recommend him also. Nonetheless, you have been doing a fine job out there. We'll talk about it some more at the Embassy." Scott could feel the chess pieces moving.

At the embassy, the Ambassador had Scott come to his office for a private meeting. "Now, Tom, tell me about this Indian thing. We seem to have a diplomatic flap brewing." Scott could not help but notice the frequent use of his first name. "The major has briefed me, but I want to know what you think."

Scott had been thinking for a while about how he was going to respond to this. "Well, I think I understand the parameters of this predicament. This girl is knockout gorgeous in any setting, educated, and very, very smart. I just don't want to get married. I left a girl in Panama to come here. I should have married her then. Next, Maria Consuela cannot leave the country because she is the next *Gran Shaman,* hand-picked by *Amboró* in addition to being the *Gran Cacique's* daughter. Something happened out there that convinced the *cacique* and *shaman* that I was the one destined to marry her. I won't bore you with their spiritual beliefs, but I know they are serious, and their lives are ruled by them. I think this is a fascinating country, but I can't stay here the rest of my life. As far as being an officer, I don't really care anymore. I can leave the Army any time I want, as you already know money is not a problem.

My grandfather would love for me to come back and work in his company. I think my ROTC option expired a long time ago, and I have no desire to go to Officer Candidate School (OCS). That being said, if the other thing can be solved, I'll accept a commission."

The Ambassador was wondering if he was up to the task of handling young Scott. He decided to throw out one of his hole cards. "You probably have not heard yet, but the Bolivian military brass are so obsessed with this problem that they have made you a major in their reserve."

That *was* a surprise. He felt like he just peeked over the Knights at the Castles, but still could not see the next move on the chess board. He could only say, "Wow."

"Suppose we could negotiate a temporary marriage to satisfy the Cacique, but still let you out? I guess that would still mean she had to get pregnant." Damn, he hated to put it that crudely. He was beginning to feel like he was mediating a lawsuit again, and he hadn't even taken the other party out of the room to caucus yet.

"That seems a little insensitive to me, but I would like to see how she feels."

The Ambassador was thinking, *Now we're getting someplace. Maybe we can pull this thing off yet.* Then Scott dropped a bomb.

"I have another request." He related McCauley's story. "I hadn't thought much more about it until I showed up here, but that bit of injustice permitted by the Army has always bothered me. I would appreciate it if you could do something about it."

Damn, this kid is one hell of a negotiator, was all he could think. To Scott he said, "Let me check into it. I'll talk to you tomorrow." As Scott left he pushed his intercom, "Sally, send Curren in here."

Villamiranoa had presented his preliminary plans to lure *Tupac* out in Phase 2 and the final vertical envelopment in Phase 3. General Ocampo had promised him an additional battalion to match the strength believed to exist in the guerilla ranks in the mountains and the lowlands. Villamiranoa was also promoted to full colonel befitting a brigade commander. Additional troops would be sent for training via the C-123 shuttle over the next month. In recognition of Villamiranoa's success, his battalions would be designated as *Ranger*. All public information was kept to a minimum to avoid political fallout until their real mission had been accomplished. It was still a school operation which just had active training exercises.

Villamiranoa sat on the canvas seats along the inside of the aircraft thinking how *that other thing* could blow up all his plans, if he could not work it out. No conversation passed between them on the shuttle flight about *that other thing*. They talked about increased training to fit the larger push. He had thirty more troops aboard to add to the training roster that he needed to think about, and he had sent Francisco north in civilian clothes to gather intelligence in the *yungas*. He had also promoted him to major as his brigade S-2 intelligence officer. He couldn't help but gloat in the speed at which his *Ranger* concept was moving, but then there was always *that other thing*. Tomorrow he would go to Buena Vista to see *Grigotá* by himself. Without the advice of his brother, the *shaman*, the cacique must be feeling a sense of emptiness. Maria Consuela was now his main priority. This had to be adding to *Grigotá's* determination about *that other thing*. Hopefully, he was receptive to any idea that did not involve revolution. He looked down the row of seats at Scott and wondered, *What must he be thinking. Did he realize how serious this could be? How had Amboro's death affected him? Did something really mystical happen there? How did he feel about the girl?* Tomorrow he would present his idea of a marriage which would not be licensed or controlled by the government, only recognized and dissolved by the *cacique*.

0800 hours Villamiranoa arrived in the H-34 at Buena Vista and requested a private audience with the *cacique*. Maria Consuela was with the *cacique*. He could feel her eyes questioning his intentions. He tried to be polite, but he had known this girl all her life. She had lived with his family when she went to private school and college in Cochabamba. This was like some Iberian tragedy play where all the characters suffer.

In the privacy of the *cacique's* lodge the soft negotiations began. "*Gran Cacique,* I will not minimize the importance of what we must decide. I understand the meaning of *Amboró's* prophecy for our people and the destiny of Maria Consuela. We must also understand the extreme importance of your decision for our country. Please do not consider what I have to say as only a military man in the service of Bolivia. We are asking a citizen of a very powerful country to remain in Bolivia forever, because of your brother's vision. We also must think of your daughter and her future. If you force her to marry this American, she will be his wife forever and must go where he goes. He must leave Bolivia when his government orders him. He is a soldier. We cannot keep him here. I do understand the importance of Maria Consuela to our people."

Villamiranoa was trying hard to play his indigenous side in this meeting. He could see *Grigotá's* concentration - he hoped not intransigence - on the problem.

The *cacique* finally spoke without changing expression. "*Amboró* spoke the truth. She is the future of our people in these mountains and all native people of Bolivia. I know this, because I speak to all in the Congress, Quechua, Aymara and others. They know the importance of our *shamans*. She must continue our line. This man is the key to our destiny. We must have a solution, or we have no future. Then your concerns of the government will be of no importance."

Villamiranoa thought he saw an opening, "*Gran Cacique*, what is most important, the continuation of your line through your daughter as a *shaman* or keeping this chosen young man here in Bolivia?"

A long silence passed. Villamiranoa could see the turmoil going through the *cacique's* mind. Finally, "The young man is not important. His seed is what *Amboró* saw as the one for her."

Villamiranoa had to restrain his excitement. This had to be the solution. The Americans had also suggested it. "*Gran Cacique*, you are the one who makes marriages. Can you not determine how long they will last? The government cannot decide without long procedures." Villamiranoa could feel this within his grasp.

"I must talk to my daughter, but his government must make him worthy of this honor." The audience was over.

Villamiranoa was thinking, '*Gracias, Dios.* So far I am ahead of the game with the honorary major appointment. Now we need to have a long talk with Scott.'

He flew back to *Portachuelo* and found Scott was already ahead of him in this thought process. The long walk in the woods had been more than a discussion of the beauty of the mountains between Maria Consuela and Scott.

Ambassador Stephens had called Sally, his administrative assistant, into his office to personally call the President's office in Washington D.C. He wanted to know when the President was available. An hour later a call came back from the President's personal secretary requesting them to hold for the President. "Mr. President, Ambassador Stephens is on the line."

"Will, how is life on the top of the world? Enjoying being an ambassador?"

"Very prestigious being the personal representative of the President of the United States, but the top of the world is more like the surface of the moon. Actually, I had thought it more like going to the Court of St. James."

Laughter came through the phone, "That cost my father more like a million depression era dollars. You contributed considerably less to this noble campaign. What's up? Is this just a social call from my old shipmate?"

"Well, I have a little problem here that my *commercial attaché* tells me could be a big problem for our relations with this country."

"And?"

"As you know we are quietly trying to assist the military in preventing a left wing takeover with the labor unions and the *campesinos* uniting in what could be another revolution. You have already recalled your ambassador in Peru. I don't want to be next. It seems that the President of the Indian Congress wants my military attaché's sergeant to marry his daughter and…"

"Whoa, wait a minute. You're calling the President of the United States because some sergeant knocked up an Indian girl?"

"Damn it, Jack. This is serious. Let me finish."

A brief pause, "OK, shoot."

"First, this sergeant is not just a nobody. He is the son of, or was the son of, T.R. Scott, who we both remember well from the

Philippines. T.R. died in that Bay of Pigs mess. We both know his grandfather is a very big Democratic Party supporter."

Another pause, "I'm sorry to hear about T.R. I hadn't heard about him in the casualty list, and I have met old Tom. What does this have to do with the chief's daughter?

Stephens related the *shaman* story, "There is no way I could make this up, as crazy as it sounds. The kid is not so keen on getting married and staying in Bolivia."

"Is she good looking?"

"I'm told she is beautiful, educated and smart."

"And the problem is?"

"The chief wants him to be an officer. He's a college graduate and completed his ROTC, but he has refused his commission or OCS, I'm told, four times. We know he is independently wealthy. So, he can quit the Army anytime he wants."

With some disbelief the President asked, "So… you want me to order this?'

"Well, something like that. There is another problem."

"I can hardly wait."

The Ambassador went through McCauley's story and explained Scott's reluctance to trust any action by the Army. He also reminded the President what happened to T.R. in the Philippines for sacrificing his plane to save some sailors and a "wooden speedboat."

"Goddamned Army. Alice, get my Army aide in here *now*."

"Right away, Mr. President."

Very quickly Brigadier General Jerald Atkins appeared, "Yes, Mr. President?"

"General, do you know a major named Sean McCauley?"

"Yes, sir. He was a classmate of mine at West Point. He received a Medal of Honor in WW II, and we served together in Korea."

"General, he is now a military attaché at the embassy in Bolivia. The ambassador is on the speaker phone, and he just told me a very ugly story about the Army's treatment of the major. Would you care to further enlighten the Commander-in-Chief?"

Atkins swallowed hard and related the same story, adding that he has had to live with silence about that incident by an unspoken threat of the now retired Army Chief of Staff.

"Goddamned Army. Can you verify this?"

"I can get two general officers, three colonels and a half a dozen sergeant majors to swear to it, Sir. We all owe our lives to him for what he did."

"Get the statements on my desk in two days, and I want one Sergeant First Class Thomas MacDougall Scott II promoted to 2nd lieutenant...*by order of the President.* I have a lot to do before I go to Dallas next month."

"Yes, sir. It will be my pleasure to rectify this travesty," the general said as he hurried out of the Oval Office.

"Goddamned Army," he muttered again. "Call me again in two days. Anything else I can do for you today, *Mr. Ambassador?*"

"Well, while we are talking about the Army, Colonel Bergeron the CO of 8th Special Forces has been extremely helpful to this embassy in this situation, and he is up for general."

"I got it."

"Thank you, Mr. *Presssiident!*"

"Screw you, Will. Go keep us safe from the communists." Stephens heard that familiar laugh as the line went dead.

Stephens said to himself, "That wasn't so bad after all."

Two days later Gen. Atkins had his affidavits, Department of the Army findings and recommendations, and Scott's direct promotion to 2nd Lieutenant, in a neat folder on the President's desk. The President had read it still mumbling, "Goddamned Army."

Now Gen. Atkins stood before him. "Atkins, I have read this sorry situation, and I am very disappointed that you were involved."

Atkins could see his own career going down the drain. His stomach tightened and he could only say, "Yes, sir."

"You are an outstanding officer or you would not be assigned here. Now, here is what you are going to do *by order of the President.* 1. Draft these findings for my signature. I will not assign blame to any of you. The SOB responsible for this is beyond my reach now. 2. Process a Distinguished Service Cross instead of this Bronze Star and correct the record to reflect what really happened that day. 3. Have him immediately promoted to Lt. Colonel with a date of rank backdated to when it would have been for an officer on the fast track. 4. Put him on the short list for full Colonel. 5. Send him my personal apology for this injustice.

"With great pleasure, Sir."

"And, General, *make sure* the Secretary of the Army and the Chief of Staff are *very clear* on how I feel about this… and I want you to mention Colonel Bergeron in Panama, also."

The Vice President had walked in as the President again muttered "Goddamned Army." "I'll put an Amen on that, Mr. President," as he looked at the report the President handed him. The Vice President had also served in the Navy during the war.

That afternoon everything was signed, sealed and delivered.

In La Paz a priority message was delivered to the Ambassador, who notified "Attaché" Curren and asked him to bring in McCauley for a little surprise ceremony.

As McCauley entered the office, the ambassador said, "Well, Sean, I told you I might know someone *in high places.* Your young sergeant is probably the only 2nd Lieutenant to ever be *ordered* to accept a commission by the President of the United States, who personally signed his commission."

"Outstanding, sir. I wish I could see Colonel Bergeron's face when this processes through his command."

"Oh, there is something else." He flicked the intercom, "Sally, come in."

She came in, followed by the rest of the staff with a very large bottle of French champagne compliments of Major Benoit, who stuck his head in the door.

The ambassador smiled, "It seems the Army has corrected a mistake made in the heat of battle a few years ago. You are now a Lieutenant Coronel and your old Bronze Star has been upgraded to the Distinguished Service Cross. You better have a seat before you fall down."

"I think I will. Thank you, sir." McCauley could say absolutely nothing else.

"Sally, pin on his new rank. These will have to do until the plane arrives tomorrow with the real ones." She had cut out silver oak leaves from paper and pinned them on his collar after removing his gold ones. McCauley still could not talk as Benoit stood laughing at him. Behind Major Benoit stood a smiling Françoise.

McCauley was gritting his teeth now to keep from crying, but even that did not work when Françoise laid a very long kiss on him. That set the stage for every woman in the embassy to cover him with lipstick before anyone could shake his hand. McCauley had to start laughing too.

With Françoise sitting on his lap, the staff sang, "For he's a jolly good fellow." The tears came again.

All embassy business closed down as the party kicked into gear with another magnum of champagne. Even the off-duty members of the Marine Security Guard Detachment joined the party. The phone rang and the ambassador answered. To McCauley he said, "Someone wants to talk to you." The ambassador smiled and handed him the phone.

An unmistaken nasal sounding voice came over the phone, "Colonel, I just wanted to add my congratulations and apologize for a grateful nation. Hey, it sounds like my embassy in Bolivi*er* has just closed down."

"Thank you, Mister President." The room got just a little bit quieter, then erupted again.

A laugh came through the phone, "Have a good time, Colonel. I have a feeling we will be talking in the future …and tell 2nd Lt. Scott I already talked to his grandfather." The line went dead.

More congratulations and more champagne.

After half an hour the door opened again. *Coronel* Villamira-noa walked into the room followed by new 2nd Lieutenant Thomas MacD. Scott with Maria Consuela Gutierrez. News really traveled fast. Champagne was flowing and everything was coming as a blur. News had reached *Portachuela* earlier and the C-123 shuttle was in full operation. They looked at McCauley's lipstick covered face and laughed.

The suggestion was too much for Maria Consuela, and she leaned over and put some lipstick on Scott. Fortunately, the crowd noise and champagne covered the slight blue haze that reached between them. But the *coronel* saw it with great pleasure. Then the ladies converged on Scott to complete the paint job.

Sally was ready for Scott also. She used scissors to cut off his sergeant's stripes and pinned paper gold bars on his collar. Scott could never have asked for a better promotion party.

Villamiranoa was smiling ear to ear. He had everything he wanted for his friend McCauley, and Scott with Maria Consuela was the *pièce de résistance*. He whispered to the Ambassador and excused himself to go to the front gate to meet a car, followed by the Ambassador.

The Ambassador came back to the party and announced that General Barrientos was on his way up to join the party. After a moment of silence more revelry. The General entered to a loud applause and accepted a glass of champagne. McCauley accepted congratulations and thought this party was getting out of hand. He had only met Barrientos once before at a reception. Scott was introduced next with Maria Consuela at his side. The general's smile broadened as he glanced at Villamiranoa. Scott smiled to himself and thought, *The white King just appeared on the chess board, and I have the white Queen.*

Food, Bolivian style, was brought in by caterers, and more champagne…and, of course, *singani*. Sally had outdone herself.

Hours later the party broke up, and Françoise dragged McCauley off to her place. Scott and Maria Consuela walked around the grounds talking before she had to leave for Villamiranoa's townhouse in La Paz. They had breakfast together the next morning in a small restaurant in La Paz. They were just another young couple enjoying each other's company in the city on top of the world. They had come to an agreement that they would do what needed to be done and see what would happen. Both were smiling at the prospects.

At Ft. Gulick, Canal Zone the sergeant major handed Colonel Bergeron a letter. "Letter from General Atkins, Sir."

The colonel quickly read the contents. "Goddamn it."

"Problem, Sir?"

"Yes and no. Scott did it again."

"Sir?"

"The U.S. Ambassador in Bolivia has requested the President personally look into my promotion. General Atkins is a classmate, and he is "unofficially" telling me that I have been selected to go to the War College, and he would not be surprised if a promotion followed. I know Scott is behind this." Then the colonel smiled, "This surprise I like."

Back at *Portachuela,* Villamiranoa always found a reason to send Scott by helicopter to Buena Vista. Training was now being done in the nearby mountains on a regular basis. Troops were rotated in and out of the settlement on an increasing rate. Scott was on site most of the time directing training. He and Maria Consuela had never touched each other before the promotion party until one day upon his arrival she had reached out to greet him as her father stood by. At the first touch in the clear mountain air a brilliant spark arched between the two. Scott had felt that static electric spark before while sliding across the car seat in cool weather and shuffling his feet on a wool carpet or other surface. It had leaped across the gap as he leaned to kiss a girl or shake someone's hand or touch a metal object. But this time it lit up the immediate area around them with no accompanying buzz or sizzle, just that blue light again. He thought this was not going to do, if it happened every time they touched. *Grigotá* had been startled out of his usual lack of expression, before he smiled and nodded his head. More sign of *Amboró.* Villagers had been frightened. He and Maria Consuela laughed. It became less the more they touched. Perhaps they were becoming a part of each other.

CHAPTER 13

MIAMI

After the second month of training in *Buena Vista* Scott received an emergency message relayed from Ft. Gulick. His grandmother was dying. He was allowed to fly back to Miami on the next Pan American flight with the reminder that he was still on a confidential assignment in Bolivia. In Miami the air was hot and humid. It felt thick compared to Bolivia. It should have felt familiar, but it didn't. Familiar places didn't seem so.

His grandmother was at home in bed. The hospital had discharged her to die at home. She brightened as Tommy entered the room. He could feel it more intensely now. She smiled and said, "Finally, you have reached your destiny. I felt it when it happened. I am at peace now. I told your grandfather. I met your cousin. I can see your grandfather in him. It's good." Her sentences were shorter and shorter as if she were trying to condense all her thoughts to get them out quickly. His grandfather stood silently at the foot of the bed. Tommy didn't want to leave her. She read his thoughts, "It's alright, *Tomasito*, I am going to join your father. I will be waiting for your grandfather when his time comes. Come see me in the morning. I am going to sleep now." Old Tom stayed in his chair by her side. Tommy could not see through his tears and stumbled against the door frame as he left the room.

As daylight poured through the open window, a soft salt air breeze blew in from the bay stirring the curtains. She was still smiling and his grandfather held her hand, but she was no longer breathing.

He had felt her go during the night, but could not bring himself to see her until, as she had said, "in the morning."

A nice church service was held in Spanish with many old

friends from Cuba attending. She wanted to be cremated so her ashes could be returned to Cuba someday. Tommy sat with his mother, sister, nieces, and grandfather. He could only tell them that he was promoted and was stationed as an aide in the U. S. embassy in La Paz, and he had to fly back in a week. Big Tom had flown from Ft. Bragg for the funeral. He had volunteered for Special Forces based on *all the wonderful things* Tommy had written to him about the *Forces,* a private joke between them.

All three Toms spent the night at the house. They had moved from Coral Gables years ago to a house on Bayshore Dr. in Coconut Grove where Old Tom could see and smell Biscayne Bay from his front porch and bedroom window. Old Tom talked to the boys about the pioneers he had known in Miami and how Coconut Grove was the original settlement, because it was the highest ground where fresh water springs flowed down to the bay and bubbled up again in the middle of Biscayne Bay. His house was actually built on an ancient coral rock outcropping. They sat on the open porch, rocking in old wooden rockers and enjoying the sea breeze. He looked down the street where he could see the old Coral Reef Yacht Club of which he was a founding member. "Boys, let's have breakfast at the club and go sailing tomorrow." He kept a 30' sailboat, cutter rigged with two head sails and a short bowsprit there. He let the club rent it and maintain it in exchange. He didn't use it like he used to when he was younger. Tommy felt like he was raised on that boat. Big Chicago Tom had never been on a sailboat, even though he was born and raised in Chicago. They didn't do any of that on the South Side.

The next morning was clear with a light ten knot breeze, perfect for lazy cruising. Big Tom got the job of hauling up sails as Old Tom headed up into the wind and turned off the little diesel. But when the sails were up, Tommy had to cleat the halyards for him. As the boat heeled over, Big Tom turned a shade paler. Old Tom assured him it wasn't going to turn over and that he should take a deep breath of that salt air, because it would cure everything. He thought back to those days at sea with his uncle and when he was wounded at Santiago. Salt air did cure everything. It had been a very good life. Now he had two big grandsons to carry on, and he was back on the bay.

Tommy pointed out the old Pan American sea plane base, now City Hall, and the Coconut Grove Sailing Club where he first learned to sail in a little 6' dingy. The mountains were beautiful, but this was home. The salt spray as the bow sliced though green waves matched the mountain mist anytime. Sea gulls squawking close overhead brought a friendly feeling. Condors silently gliding high in the mountain thermals were a perfect contrast to these two lands. He had to laugh at the memory of the ugly buzzards that always circled and rested on the twenty-eight story Dade County Courthouse on Flagler Street built in 1925-1928. The joke about their location was obvious.

They tacked out to Stiltsville, a group of vacation houses built on stilts south of the old Florida Lighthouse on the south end of Key Biscayne. Old Tom used to have one until a hurricane blew it away, and he pointed to some barnacle encrusted pilings still visible above the water as all that remained. The government had decreed that you could not rebuild once they were blown down, but a dozen still remained on the sand flats dividing Biscayne Bay from the Atlantic Ocean. The ocean had sliced navigable channels through the sand in its determination to pour water into and out of the bay with the tides.

Old Tom smiled and said, "Tommy, get the fishing rod out." Tommy knew what he was thinking. Large barracuda hung out among the pilings. Chicago Tom was in for a treat. Tommy came up with a deep sea rod and reel with a yellow feather lure, sure-fire barracuda bait. "That's a really big fishin' pole you got there," Chicago noted.

"Here you go, Sergeant. Catch us something to eat." Tommy teased as he let the line out and set the drag. As soon as the line tightened, a large splash erupted around the lure and the rod nearly bent double. Line was singing and jerking off the reel. Chicago's eyes went big as he stumbled trying not to be pulled overboard. Old Tom turned the boat away to get more room for the fish to run, laughing all the time. Tommy slacked up on the drag to keep the big fish from snapping the line, and Chicago held on. Steering a sailboat with a big fish on the line was an art Old Tom knew well. He loved it. "Tommy, pull down the forward jib and get Tom on the foredeck."

"Oh, shit!" Big Tom hollered as the fish changed direction and more line screamed off the reel while he tried to keep his balance on a moving, heeling sailboat. There was no nice fighting chair like on a sport fish boat. A six foot barracuda sailed out of the water like a rocket tossing his head and snapping his large teeth. That was the first Chicago realized what was on the end of his line. His eyes got bigger. "Son of a bitch!"

Old Tom laughed, "That's a tough old bastard you got there, Tom. Hang on, cowboy. "

Tommy was doubled over laughing as his grandfather steered for deeper water.

"Hey, I think he got off." Chicago yelled as the line became slack.

"No, Tom. He's just swimming toward the boat. Keep reeling in, faster."

"Shit, is it goin' to jump in the boat?"

"Maybe," confirmed old Tom, while trying to hide a smirk.

"Shit."

Tommy had to turn away. This was just too funny. The 'cuda decided he had enough and took off on another run. The slack whipped up out of the water throwing a spray into the wind.

"Shit." More laughter from the spectators.

They were headed down the bay now. Old Tom could anticipate where the fish would turn away from shallow water. The dance continued for forty-five minutes with Big Tom awkwardly trying to hang on to the rod and the rigging at the same time. Gradually he gained on the fish and could take in line. "Shit, how much line is on this reel?" They could tell the excitement and strain of staying in the boat while fighting the fish was wearing the big man out. It looked like time to give him some help.

"He's tired out now, Tom. He's just dead weight on the end of your line. I'll pump the rod. You reel in the slack." With that they begin a little team work. The big barracuda slowly was dragged alongside the boat.

"Stay away from the edge of the boat, Tom. He can still jump and bite your hand off."

Big Tom peered carefully over the edge of the gunnel at the gaping mouth full of sharp teeth opening and closing. "Shit. He's an ugly son of a bitch. Man, look at those teeth." Tommy had the long gaff ready to hook him, while keeping the gaff hook looped against the steel leader to keep him from jumping "I got you, you motha. I'm the *man*." The barracuda gave a big swish of his tail and came half out of the water as Tommy shoved down on the leader wire with the gaff to keep him down. Big Tom leaped backwards, his eyes widening even more. "Shit!"

Old Tom looked over the side, "OK, boys. This old guy has been around this bay for a long time. We've probably even seen him before. What say we cut him loose?" Tommy reached in his pocket for his wire cutters and snipped off the leader. He understood his grandfather looked at this old fish as part of the life of the bay, a part of himself.

Chicago looked up, "You just goin' to turn him loose?" As it swam away it rolled on its side with an eye looking back at the boat. Big Tom drew back a step.

"Yep. He's no good for eatin' anyway," Old Tom turned his head and sniffed the wind. "Tommy, get sails up. Let's get back before these afternoon thunderstorms roll in. I want a real big fish dinner at the club." Tommy knew it was more than the eating part.

The grouper and wine were good, and the club staff treated Old Tom like the legend he was. Afterward they walked down the street past the former Pan American Clipper seaplane-hangers and trendy waterfront restaurants. Their large ramps into the bay now served the public and private boat yards. Behind the old Pan Am terminal building, now Miami City Hall, was the Dinner Key marina with hundreds of sail and powerboats. Tommy remembered walking these docks with his unfulfilled mental wish list. *God, what a long way from the towering Andes Mountains with fertile valleys... and things that awaited him.*

"Boys, lets go to my office in the morning and I'll show you around." With that they strolled past quaint Coconut Grove shops on Grand Ave. and Main Highway, stopped at the old drug store on the corner and had a milkshake at the lunch counter. Tommy stared at the small octagon tiles on the floor and wondered how many times he had done this over the years. They returned to the porch and the rockers, swapping stories, the boys about the Army and Old Tom about the sea and Cuba.

The twenty-one story Alfred I. Du Pont building was built in 1939 and was the second "skyscraper" built in Miami, after the 1928 courthouse. It was an award winning example of *Modern* architecture and the home of the Florida National Bank, St. Joe Paper Company, and the Florida East Coast Railway, all owned by the Du Pont Estate . Ed Ball was the chairman of them all and the brother of Mrs. DuPont. Old Tom just happened to be on their Boards of Directors. Scott Enterprise, Inc. occupied three floors of the building, and, of course, one floor for Spalding, Whitman and Sterling, whose door still read *Security Dealers, Miami and Havana Office.*

As they entered the lobby of the bank, all the polished brass doors and trim gave a golden glow like the rising sun. A short, heavy-set man with a broad southern accent approached across the lobby with another taller distinguished man. Tommy recognized them as Ed Ball, Chairman of all the DuPont Florida enterprises, and Fuller Warren, former governor of Florida and now a lawyer in Miami. Both men spoke, "Tom, how are you. Nice to see around. We were very sorry about Graciela, a lovely lady."

"Thank you, gentlemen. I believe you both know my grandson, Tommy."

"Absolutely, how is the Army treating you?"

"The Army never changes. Good thing you were in the Navy, Governor."

"Amen to that," the governor said. "Well, it's always nice to see a fellow Florida Blue Key member, Tommy. Have you finished reading my *Book on Bombast?* I am sure it won't help in the Army though." A little laugh.

Ed Ball looking up at Big Tom said, "And who is this big, good-looking gentleman?"

"This is my long lost second grandson, also named Tom. The two of them met in the Army, and they are both in the Army's Special Forces."

The governor looked at Big Tom, "Now that has to be a fascinating story. I can see he has your eyes. I look forward to it at cocktail hour at the old Urmey Hotel down the street."

"Tom, we have to go make sure these county politicians stay honest…at least for our side." Ball winked at the governor and they walked out through the light of polished brass. Ball looked back and hollered, "Tom, don't forget the Board of Directors meeting next week." Old Tom waved in acknowledgement.

"Boys, you just felt the ground under the State of Florida shake as those two walked by."

Big Tom was mesmerized. He still had not realized the reach and depth of this family.

"Now, let's go to my office for a minute and then down to Spalding, Whitman & Sterling."

Old Tom's office on the 20th floor looked east over the city, the old hotels along Biscayne Boulevard, Bayfront Park where an assassination attempt was made on Franklin Roosevelt when he spoke there, and Pier 5 marina where Old Tom kept his 40' sport fish boat. They could see over Biscayne Bay, the dog race track at the end of Miami Beach, and all the way out to the Atlantic Ocean with the deep blue Gulf Stream flowing north. Tommy even imagined he could see Bimini Island in the Bahamas, where he had sailed so many times.

Spalding, Whitman & Sterling were on a floor above the bank with a movie theater-like room for customers to watch the stock flash by on the electronic board, executive offices and conference rooms. A warm greeting came from the Manager when he saw Old Tom come in the door. There was also a small office labeled *Thomas MacDougall Scott, Director.* "Boys, let's go see what the stocks are doing."

Tommy turned to Big Tom, "You remember the Spanish War

where grandpa got the medal. The other man up there was old man Spalding. You can see their pictures in grandpa's office. That's the connection."

"Oh," was the only thing he could think to reply.

Charts were given to them and they watched the stocks flow. "Granpa, I think you should buy more Xerox. Even the Army is getting away from that damn mimeograph."

Old Tom gave him a curious look, "Your grandmother told me that a couple of years ago. I bought it to humor her, but I made a lot of money. She sent it to the church in Cuba. How did you pick it, Tommy?"

"I really don't know. I know what it is, but I never studied it."

Old Tom waived at the Manager, "Buy me 1,000 shares of Xerox."

"Right away, Mr. Scott."

The next time it flashed on the screen it had gone up ten dollars. "Well, you just made $10,000, Tommy. Chicago, you want to try?"

"Oh, no, sir. Let MacD do it for me." Tommy did, and another $5,000 was made. "Shit." Big Tom whispered from his cushioned seat, eyes as wide as when he had a barracuda on the line.

"Tommy, are you sure you want to stay in the Army? Your grandmother kept telling me you had a gift that your father could never fully develop in his life. It was one of the last things she whispered to me, that you had found it. Now I believe her."

"Well, I love you, Granpa; but I have a lot of unfinished things in my life before I come home."

Old Tom thought for a minute, "Chicago, you too?"

"Yes, sir,...Granpa."

Old Tom smiled, "Thought so, but I tell you what I'm going to do. I'm going to set up an investment fund with both your names on it for a half a million dollars. Let's go do the paper work. What do you want to call it?" He called the Manager over to start it.

With no hesitation Tommy spoke up, "*The Valor Fund*, granpa."

"And, Chicago, I have asked your grandmother to come down

next week before you boys leave. Tommy's grandmother wished me to."

"Shit," even softer came from the cushioned seat. Big Tom was now really speechless.

US ARMY FORT GULICK, Canal Zone, Panama

At HQ 8th Special Forces Group, Scott's promotion had arrived from the Department of the Army. "Sergeant Major," Colonel Bergeron hollered from his desk.

"I saw it, sir."

"I am not surprised it happened, but, by God, I am surprised it came direct from the President. What the hell has Scott stirred up down there?"

"Well, sir. Since we don't have any slots for 2nd Lieutenants in Special Forces, I thought I would pass it back to Ft. Bragg, and let them deal with it."

"Good idea."

FT. BRAGG, NORTH CAROLINA

Major Guillermo L. Rodriguez was now Lieutenant Colonel, S-1 Personnel for the Training Command. He looked at the communication and laughed. "Very simple, Sergeant Major. Wait one week and promote him to 1st Lieutenant, since we have no 2nd Lieutenants here. He has more experience and decorations than a hundred 2nd Lieutenants. We won't even need the President to do that."

In Miami the leave time was up. Goodbyes until next time were said. Big Tom's world had changed beyond those brief prior meetings. His grandmother stayed in Miami for a week to try to absorb what was happening.

CHAPTER 14
BOLIVIA

On arrival back in La Paz, new 1st Lieutenant Scott was greeted by McCauley. "That was a fast promotion. I understand Special Forces does not like 2nd Lieutenants."

"No, it's just a TO&E problem for them, *Lieutenant Colonel.*" Scott smiled and they both laughed at the strange circumstances of the past month. On the way to the embassy he told McCauley about the *Valor Fund.* "Colonel, I have been thinking about the meaning of the fund, and I would like to make you an equal partner in future earnings. My grandfather retains the principal, but I make the investment decisions and my cousin and I share the earnings. Now, you make three."

A very long pause. "Tommy, I know your family has a lot of money, but that's more generous than I can accept."

"Not so, Colonel. The name *Valor Fund* just popped into my head thinking of you with your medals and my grandfather. I talked about it with my grandfather. He agrees completely. If I lose money, he writes it off his taxes. If I make money, it's found money anyway. Maybe someday my cousin and I will be worthy of being in your company."

There was no way to respond to that. "OK, I'll feed you all the hot stock tips I get in La Paz." They both laughed.

"Now back to the war at hand and *that other thing.* Maria Consuela is waiting. She seemed to know when your grandmother died. I am not even going to try to figure this *shaman* thing out. I'll just accept it, and never mention it again…at least not in this man's Army. Next, Francisco, brought back some intel from the *yungas,* and Villamiranoa is planning a big operation. Ready to get back in the saddle, 1st Lieutenant Scott?"

"Roger that, and I'd like to get out of this altitude. I'm already used to sea level again."

"By the way, Colonel Bergeron sent a pair of silver 1st Lieutenant bars and said he was now surprised, but promised nothing else would surprise him. I'll bet he hasn't heard of the Bolivian Army Reserve commission to major." They both laughed.

Scott thought that it was a nice gesture from the colonel, but it gave him a twinge about Denise. It seemed a very long time ago.

A second C-123 had been added to the shuttle, and they were back into *Portachuelo* the next morning with another company of soldiers on board. Activity had definitely picked up. New barracks were under construction and open hangers for the aircraft. Some troops were quartered in squad tents and everything seemed in a hurry. A new sign had been erected announcing the school, as if no one had noticed soldiers falling out of the sky. The plantation house was now completely full of officers.

As they carried their gear through the dust kicked up by the C-123, a familiar voice shouted over the engine noise, "It's about time you got back here 1st Lt. Scott." The smiling face of *Coronel* Villamiranoa appeared through the dust. "Let's go to my office and shake off this dust with some good *singani."* He was definitely in a good mood.

Extra generators had been added and light was everywhere. Ceiling fans stirred the cool evening air and the *singani* was a perfect fit. Maps with marked-up plastic overlays were scattered across the conference table. Topographic maps overlapped each other around the walls. Something big was definitely being planned.

"Gentlemen, Francisco has returned from the *yungas* areas with excellent information. Our friend, the false *Tupac,* has organized a small band of *guerilleros* to right the wrongs that our country has continued on the Afro-Bolivian community. The other groups of Indians, *mestizos,* and even the Jewish communities are not interested in revolution."

1st Lieutenant Scott tilted his head, "I'm sorry, *coronel,* did you say Jewish communities?"

"*Si,.. si.* I guess you have not heard of that part of our history. During the Nazi persecution of the Jews, before and during World War II, many thousands of Jews were welcomed here as a haven from the Nazis. They added many skills and professions to our society, but many were not able to work. They had to learn different skills and settle in outlying areas. The rich *yungas* valleys were one of those areas. They also recognize the type of tyrant-in-the-making like *Tupac.* They have frighteningly vivid memories of Hitler."

"Yes, now I remember. My friend, Jacob Stern, in Miami had a doctor uncle who was able to escape to Bolivia from Germany and another to Cuba before Castro. I can understand what they must be thinking now."

"*Exactamente,* and they will be a very valuable source for us. *Tambien* (also), one of my best sergeants is an Afro-Bolivian who will infiltrate that community for us. *Tambien,* one of my sergeants is a Guarani from a village near the border of the Brazilian rainforest. We have them, as you say, *boxed in.*" The *coronel* went on to explain how they planned to draw *Tupac* into the *yungas* by creating a small competitive revolution group sufficient to make him feel that he had to intervene. Once *Tupac* had moved in close to the mountains, the Army would drop a battalion of *Rangers* by parachute behind him to cut him off as a blocking force then search and destroy the safe refugee camps near the border. "*1ˢᵗ Lieutenant* Scott, I suspect you can see part of the plan you suggested in the beginning has now been adopted by the Bolivian Army." The *coronel* had a big smile and held up his *singani* in a toast. "*Tambien,* after a formal staff meeting, a helicopter will fly you directly to *Buena Vista* to discuss *that other thing.* Since you are already a reserve major in the Bolivian reserves, you will also be executive officer for the company stationed there for their part of this operation. As befitting your exalted rank, a small house has been constructed for you." Scott saw this chess move coming before it was out of the *coronel's* mouth. He had no doubt this house was built for two people.

At 0830 hours, immediately after the staff meeting, the H-34 lifted off for *Buena Vista.* Maria Consuela was waiting. The *cacique* had conspicuously not met the arrival. They took their walk together in the rainforest at the base of the mountains. This morning a troop of Bolivian red howler monkeys were in the trees nearby. They were unusually close to the settlement. Scott had seen and heard a different species of these monkeys before in Nicaragua and Panama. Normally, they were at some distance where only the calls could be heard echoing across the forest. He could only describe the "howl" as a deep a throated growl echoing out of a 55 gallon drum. This resulted from enlarged bone and gland structure. They are described as the loudest land animal. The "howls" can be heard for 4.8 kilometers. Here he could see them scampering through the tree tops less than one hundred meters away. The noise was thunderous.

He smiled at Maria Consuela, "You know, when he saw them at Mayan ruins, the American diplomat and explorer of Central America, John Lloyd Stephens, described them as *grave and solemn, almost emotionally wounded, as if officiating as the guardians of consecrated ground.*' I always thought of that when I saw or heard them. Did you call these magnificent monkeys?"

"Yes, I did. When Alexander von Humboldt was exploring South America and our ocean currents, he said *'their eyes, voice and gait are indicative of melancholy,'* but today they are happy."

He looked at her and wondered how so much could be combined in this girl far away in the South American mountains.

She smiled and reached up to kiss him. Amid the blue glow surrounding them, the noise from the trees became louder.

Scott felt his heart keeping up with the monkey howls. "Let's go tell your father it is time."

"Yes."

They were met by a smiling *Gran Cacique* with the howling still going on in the background. He knew and had planned a great ceremony to invite many *caciques* from the Indian Congress to celebrate. All Bolivia would know the line of *Amboró* would continue. However, his son Francisco had cautioned that there were plans for Scott which would not allow a big announcement. Scott had known since the staff meeting and had told Maria Consuela on the way back to the settlement that any ceremony had to be small and quiet in order to keep his name hidden. She was happy with that.

As though on cue, Villamiranoa arrived in the second H-34 with McCauley. He smiled,

"I see the love birds have arrived at an agreement. Is there any reason we should delay this wedding past today?"

A simultaneous answer from both, "Today is good."

Grigotá had already agreed to perform the short, private ceremony, where he spoke his words of union of these two spirits. He had also previously agreed to dissolve the marriage when a child came and Scott's government needed him. But there was time.

Villamiranoa threw up his arms and scowled into the trees, "Well…,Scott, you have *twenty-four hours* before I need you, and can you turn off these damn monkeys now?"

McCauley smiled as he watched them laughingly run to their prepared and well-stocked *Honeymoon House.*

Twenty-six hours later Scott's head appeared out of the door, and he joined a staff meeting in progress in the *cacique's* quarters. No one said anything. The mission he was being sent on was going to be the key to the whole operation.

On paper he was to be a Cuban revolutionary sent to Bolivia to organize a guerilla band on Castro and Guevara's orders. This was a part he could play well. In his group would be the Afro-Bolivian sergeant to convince men and women in the *yungas* that Scott was really Tomas Rodrigo Echeverria from Cuba. Francisco, now a major, would represent a *Quechua* speaking Indian, who was disillusioned with the government and would lead ten other sergeants who spoke *Aymara* and *Quechua.* Their weapons and equipment would all be Russian, quietly provided by 8th Special Forces Group, to complete the illusion. They would supplement their armaments as U.S. Army weapons and equipment was "captured." This scenario came straight out of Che Guevara's book, *Guerilla Warfare.* To complete the illusion, they all grew long hair and beards, as best they could.

Their mission was to seek out and destroy any competing guerilla groups and cause enough havoc to draw *Tupac* into the fight to eliminate this competition. Classic guerilla-on-guerilla tactics. Scott was thinking how similar the scenario was to the field exercise in Special Forces School at Ft. Bragg, but there would be no umpires marked with arm bands to *tell* you when you were killed.

They spent two days familiarizing themselves with weapons and equipment. Peruvian Army maps would be used. Scott had no problem regaining his Cuban accent. The Afro-Bolivian, Sgt. Gomez, would infiltrate to seek out friendly assets and determine locations of competing guerilla groups. Designated infiltration points and signals were arranged. Communications would be a problem.

They would have to chance using their 'captured' Army radios, set up codes, radio net monitoring and broadcast times.

Scott smiled to himself about how many US Army Operation Orders he had written and helped write; if only civilians could learn to plan this way:

1. SITUATION...
2. MISSION...
3. EXECUTION...
4. SERVICE SUPPORT...
5. COMMAND AND SIGNAL...

The next day Sergeant Gomez was inserted at night into a remote area of the *yungas* near *Coroico* by a short eighty kilometer helicopter ride from La Paz, because the distance was too far for the H-34 from Buena Vista. *Coroico* was one of the areas where Afro-Bolivians had settled after their emancipation in the 19th century. He had a long range radio and hand-operated generator to communicate with Headquarters in La Paz. The 'guerilla' group continued its preparation modeled on the typical twelve-man Special Forces A-Team. All members had some competence in communication, but Scott had to adjust to sending and receiving Morse code in Spanish. A relay communications team was on its way from *Portachuelo* on the eastern slopes to set up, disguised as a government agricultural inspection unit. Communication with La Paz on the west would be easier. It was considered very unlikely that the rebels had any devices to triangulate by radio direction finders on their locations.

The howler monkeys were gone, but the *Honeymoon House* was still there...every night.

Two days later word was relayed from Gomez as to a time and place for the team and equipment to be inserted by parachute into the field of a friendly farmer. The aircraft would continue north to confuse anyone taking notice. This maneuver had been practiced at night in nearby fields. Scott remembered night jumps in Panama where he could see the ribbon of light from the canal crossing the isthmus, an extraordinary site sight before the trees reached up for him, not nice level ground. He hoped this field would fit the formulas he had been teaching from his U. S. Army Pathfinder manuals, which provided a wind drift and descent formula for the T-10 parachute and a dispersion pattern across the drop zone (DZ). These would be marked by burning clay pots on the ground, not ground fires which could be seen for miles. Gomez would also have a homing beacon to guide the aircraft to the DZ.

Once on the ground a concealed base would be set up in a friendly area where food and shelter were available. As an additional part of the deception, part of the Ranger battalion would be sent to an Army base northeast of La Paz where they would create a decoy convoy into the *yungas* from the west toward *Coroico*. This convoy would be *ambushed* by the friendly guerillas on a narrow mountain road. The troops *escaping the ambush* would return with terrible tales of slaughter by many *guerilleros* shouting revolutionary slogans. The *killed* soldiers would actually join the *guerilleros* and substantially increase their numbers.

All this would be exaggerated by the newspapers to indicate that a real threat existed. Presumably, this would get the attention and concern of *Tupac's* main group to the east.

Two companies of soldiers with their heavy weapons, approximately two hundred in each group, would be sent from *Portachuelo*. They would set up a camp for 'resisting' this guerilla group 400 kilometers north on the east side of the *yungas* area in the village of *Yucumo* at a junction of the cross mountain road from *La Paz* known as "the road of death" which passed through *Coroico* to the west, and the road to the city of Trinidad to the east. This would essentially block *Tupac's* access to an easy route into the mountains. However, this group would be ready for any actual attacks from the *Tupac* group in the *yungas* and the main group to the east. The Army's main body would remain in Portachuelo in preparation for the airborne assault once Tupac's main force had been drawn out beyond his safe areas. Presumably, Major Francisco and Lt. Scott would be keeping *Tupac's* groups in the *yungas* preoccupied.

Portachuelo had retained the illusion of a *training school* and encouraged this appearance by transferring troops in and out as in training cycles, but substantially tightening security. Meanwhile, Villamiranoa and his staff, including McCauley, continued to expand their plan to draw *Tupac* out into the open without broadcasting the real purpose of the 'school.'

One day before Scott and Francisco and their group were to leave for their mission, a C-123 arrived. As Villamiranoa and the school cadre watched, three parachutes emerged out of the plane. The *coronel* smiled and went to greet them. It was General Barrientos and his adjutant with Major Marcel Benoit of the French Embassy making one of the general's famed and flamboyant entrances.

The general disconnected his parachute, dusted himself off, and laughed as he greeted a laughing Villamiranoa. "My dear *coronel,* how are you this fine morning? I thought I would just come to see what you were doing with my aircraft."

"I see you have not lost your touch, *General*. It is our pleasure to have you inspect us. You have arrived just in time to see our first group of '*guerilleros*' before they start the action."

Scott laughed to himself. The white *King* had just floated down to the chess board from the sky.

McCauley stood in some amazement at the fact that a commanding general would arrive unannounced...and by parachute. But he had heard of this general's flair for the dramatic. Coming from behind the general he heard a familiar laugh, "Hey, *mon ami,* did you think you could have all the fun, *non?* Thanks to you and Gen. Barrientos, the French ambassador was shamed into making me a Lt. Colonel also. Now we show them the might of the allied forces. Q*ui?*"

"*Absolument, mon colonel,*" McCauley replied and laughed as the C-123 circled to land with a new load of troops.

General Barrientos was given a quick tour and taken to the conference/map room for a briefing where the insertion team was assembled.

"*Bien,* nice to see you again, Major Gutierrez and Lieutenant Scott. I almost did not recognize you with those beards and long hair. Ah, I see you are in good company with these other *barbudos.* " He turned and greeted each member of the team in fluent *quechua,* then walked to the map for his briefing. He turned and said, "*Tambien*, my intelligence officer has discovered some interesting facts. This so-called new *Tupac* is actually from the city of La Paz and has no empathy for *campesinos* or Afro-Bolivians. His real name is Alejandro Matamoros. The name *Matamoros* itself should not ingratiate him to Afro-Bolivianos. He is just another glory seeking despot. *Tambien*, we have a doctor under government contract to travel the *yungas* providing the people with medical treatment and providing us with information, Dr. Isaac Stern."

Scott was thinking the word *Matamoros* literally means *he kills moors*. The word *moor* was used to describe the Africans who occupied Spain for hundreds of years, "This guy is something else. No wonder they say he will be president." The news about Dr. Stern was fascinating. He would get to meet the third Dr. Stern.

Word had spread that the general had parachuted into the camp, and soldiers had formed up outside the building to show their respect as the general exited.

The general smiled and saluted the soldiers as he left. "Colonel Villamiranoa, is the H-34 ready to go to Buena Vista We have some politicking to do with the President of the Indian Congress…and the next great *shaman*…before I return to La Paz."

"It's standing by, General."

At 2330 hours the C-123 took off carrying the insertion team and its equipment for the two and a half hour flight to *Coroico*. At 0200 hours the team exited the aircraft. As they descended they could see all lights being extinguished on the ground and the exhaust flames of the C-123 disappearing to the north. Some lights from the small town of *Coroico* could be seen in the distance until they dropped below the edges of the mountain. The only sound was air rushing through the parachute and thin nylon lines with a figure dangling beneath it. Even in the darkness, there was the feel of the ground rushing up to meet them. There were no trees, only bushes and the ground cushioned by relaxed legs and the rolling motion of a well-rehearsed parachute landing fall. Scott had been the second out of the aircraft door behind Francisco. He could hear other members now landing roughly in line with the line of flight and Francisco quietly "rolling up the stick of jumpers" just as practiced. Scott could not help but feel a little pride at the efficiency. A dim outline of Gomez appeared whispering the password.

They had landed in a relatively flat coca field of Gomez's farmer friend on the side of a mountain. Scott found himself stripping a handful of leaves along with the soldiers to store in his jacket for use later when the altitude and physical strain begin to show. He thought of the Inca warriors marching to conquer this same area over five hundred years before who probably had done the same thing.

Gomez had selected a well concealed camp site on the side of the mountain and a spot for his radio farther up. His radio antenna was strung between trees with the long axis facing toward La Paz for better reception. Food supplies, explosives and ammunition were stashed in secure places. Alternate routes of exit and return had been planned. In four days the Army convoy would leave La Paz on the *Camino de las Yungas,* known as the *Death Road,* on its way to *Coroico.* The road was one lane carved out of the sides of mountains which could be easily blocked with no room to turn around, and was the frequent site of deadly accidents.

Gomez had coordinated the convoy to occur two days after an Afro-Bolivian ceremony in which he would introduce Scott as Tomás Echeverria of Cuba, a revolutionary who wished to assist them in seeking better treatment from the government and assistance in preserving their African heritage.

A small village of Afro-Bolivians was five kilometers northeast of *Coroico* in the heart of the coca growing region. Even though the altitude was only 4,000 feet, the use of coca leaves during the march through the mountains was an assistance. Scott, as planned, was introduced as sent by Castro to the head man, Augusto Pinedo. Pinedo was in line to be the "king" of the Afro-Bolivians in maintaining their African heritage.

Pinedo looked for a full minute at this tall man with a beard before speaking. "Why do you come so far to help us? Another group has already offered the same things, but they are Bolivians."

Scott launched into the revolutionary speech he had heard so many times from Fidel, while adapting it to Bolivian history. He reminded Pinedo that a large part of the Cuban revolution and its heroes were black men, and that Che was in Africa leading similar revolutions.

"Also, our excellent Cuban intelligence people have learned that this *Tupac* is really named *Matamoros* and is proud of that name." Scott noticed a small change in expression by Pinedo. Scott pressed the point, "He is only a city person who seeks power for himself, not the people. A true revolution is why I am here."

Pinedo held up his hand, "Enough. We are here for a ceremony. We will talk later."

Scott had heard of Afro-Bolivian *saya* music and dance but had never seen it. He could identify typical Andean musical instruments, but they were played to drums and rhythms passed down through generations of African slaves. Scott could feel drums dominating the native instruments as if Africa was alive here in this distant land, in this alien culture centuries later.

The leader of the dance, the *Caporal*, commenced with the ringing of a small bell. Jingle bells were tied near his ankles. He began to dance to the drums leading the dancers, with whip in hand. The villagers were dressed in Aymara style clothing. The women wore brightly colored blouses with ribbons, a multicolored skirt, a black *manta* or cover, in their hands, and a bowler hat. The native string and flute-like instruments joined the drums, rattles and shakers.

Scott felt the drum rhythms. He had been here before. These were *Yoruba* drums he was hearing. They were even shaped like the Cuban *batá*. He had heard them and played them with the workers on his grandfather's plantation. His father had helped teach him. It had been a part of the African culture of Cuba for hundreds of years. Santeria ceremonies in Cuba had almost the same rhythms. 'Of course,' he thought, 'these people are part of that same slave trade from the same parts of Africa from which the Spanish enslaved them. Even the drums and bells are similar. This has helped them hold on to their culture through the centuries. I have even heard the echoes in the Bahamian junkanoo parades.'

The headman offered him more *chicha*. The feeling of the firelight, the dancing, the swaying bodies, several drums now mixing the beat, the women waving their hands and shaking their hips while taunting the drummers, was sinking deeper into his memories, deeper into his soul. He was almost unaware of picking up a drum and joining the primal throbbing. The headman smiled. Gomez thought that it must be true that this man is a spiritual leader. Hours drifted by with echoes of drums through the valley until all the participants had melted away or slept where they fell. Scott slept with the drum on the ground. Fortunately, someone had covered him with native blankets.

Daylight began to creep through the valley in advance of the first rays of the sun skirting the sides of the mountain. Scott awoke with Gomez shaking his shoulder. He was cautious not to move his head too fast, but the throbbing told him it was definitely there. The cold morning temperature reminded him of the *Sierra Maestra* in Cuba, but he didn't have that nice, captured sleeping bag now.

"*Teniente* (lieutenant) Scott, the headman will be here in a minute to talk. He was very impressed by your knowledge of the drums and ceremonies. I think he is ready to help us. I don't think he cared much for the name *Matamoros* either," Gomez laughed.

Scott could smell fresh mountain coffee brewing somewhere in the village mixed with something cooking that he could not identify. Whatever it was he need some this morning. Then he remembered he was in the *Andes*, and he still had the coca leaves in his pocket. That should do the trick for a hangover. Gomez had already anticipated the need as he handed Scott some of his own, and smiled as Scott quickly stuffed them in the side of his mouth. By the time the headman walked up, the world was good again.

"*Buenos dias, Jefe Tomas.* I am glad you enjoyed our *saya.*"

"More than you know, *cacique*. It brought many memories to me. I thank you for allowing me to join you."

"*Bueno,*" Pinedo clapped his hands and women appeared to serve them. Scott's mouth watered at the smell of food, but it just created more coca juice. He had to turn and spit out the leaves to the amusement of the headman and the women. Gomez smiled. He was becoming more impressed every minute with this young *teniente.*

Scott continued his story and answered Pinedo's questions. He told him that his group would soon cause a big problem for the government and make many demands for the people.

At the end of 'breakfast' Gomez and Scott went back down the mountain promising the headman they would return again with great news and renew their new friendship.

Climbing back up the next mountain Scott asked, "Gomez, do you have the impression that Pinedo knows where *Tupac's* men are? And will he help us?"

"Absolutamente, Teniente. After that show you put on last night, he will believe anything you say. *I* almost forgot you were not black."

Scott laughed, "Our problems are what he does after we leave, and what the government does for them when this is over. You come up with a good solution and you're going to be the *teniente*. Actually, I think you are the only one who can. You understand their problems. I'll be gone, but you will be here. Think about it."

They walked in silence the remainder of the return. There was no doubt in Scott's mind that Gomez was very deep in thought, and that was good.

At the camp Francisco had coordinated the convoy 'ambush' with La Paz at noon the next day. Civilians would be blocked off the road for five hours to avoid any undue complications. A perfect spot had been selected at a wider place in the road which permitted them to put on a show without getting anyone injured. It was reasonably close to the camp, no more than two kilometers. They did not need alternate return routes, because they were not going to be followed or ambushed in turn. It would be good practice. They just needed to make it look good.

Scott thought the plan was good and should actually be fun for the men.

The tricky part would be to make sure that the explosive charges did not destroy the road or cause landslides on the mountain. The demolition sergeants were sure they had the answers with small open charges on rock not tamped down with weight and several suspended in the air. A lot of noise and no damage. The explosives would ignite with enough noise to carry sound and echoes for many kilometers down the valley and up the mountains. Small arms and machine gun fire would sound like WW II in the valley's natural echo chamber. One of the soldiers had come up with the idea of using animal blood thrown all over the area. It would be a gruesome site smelling of cordite smoke and blood. The fact that no bodies would be found could be accounted for by setting a truck on fire and pushing it off the road and down several thousand feet into the valley. A second truck would be shot up enough to look real, but not enough to destroy it. The remainder of the convoy would back down the road in mock fright. Francisco had not told the convoy commander that he was actually going to destroy one truck. That should make him adequately angry.

1000 hours: Francisco's men were in their ambush mode. Explosives were set, and a lot of ammunition ready to fire down the valley and up the mountain. It would all be replaced by airdrops. The play was set to begin.

1200 hours: Amazingly the convoy was on time. A jeep with a small trailer was in the lead of three trucks followed by another jeep.

Francisco looked at Scott, "I hadn't thought about the jeep leading."

"I like it. We can use it to carry supplies back up the mountain. No one is going to track us. We'll hide it. Maybe we can use it later. I remember Castro did the same thing."

Francisco nodded. He liked the idea. He instructed the demolition sergeant to let it pass and detonate a safe distance in front of the first truck, which would be loaded with soldiers who in turn would make a lot of noise shooting the mountain to death. Hopefully, there would not be a lot of ricochets flying around.

The first explosion went off loudly, followed quickly by a second and third. The sound froze the soldiers, momentarily surprised by the reality of it. Francisco started firing into the air, the machine guns followed. The shock of the soldiers in the trucks was overcome, and they put up their own "defense." It did sound and smell like a war was happening. The jeep driver had surged ahead in fright until the lieutenant could slow him down and back up.

"No laughing," Francisco was shouting as the shooting died down. "Unload the supplies. Shoot holes in two trucks. Set the first one on fire and shove it down the mountain."

The lieutenant started to object, but one look at the deadly serious camouflaged and bearded faces looking down at him changed his mind.

Two sergeants carried large containers of pig blood and liberally spread it around among piles of empty shell casings and on trucks until it did look like a slaughter. Scott stood on a large boulder looking down on the scene thinking how really gruesome it looked.

Francisco looked at his watch. Only fifteen minutes had elapsed. *"Excelente, muchachos! Vamanos."*

Scott had to admire the discipline and planning. The new *guerilleros* followed the plan with preselected loads of supplies and silently fell in line as the group moved back up the mountain with more than a few smiles. He looked back when the truck exploded as it careened halfway down the side of the mountain. A few explosives placed on the gas tanks gave a spectacular effect. Perfect. Thirty new *guerilleros* were added and the new 'revolutionary' band had made the headlines. *Tupac* was definitely going to hear about this. Time to get down to business.

The jeep gave some relief in carrying supplies. Gomez rode with the still shaking driver to show him a rough trail up the mountain.

News spread quickly about the "massacre" in the newspapers and radio about the wild, bearded revolutionaries who shouted slogans while they killed soldiers and looted weapons and supplies.

The explosions and gunfire had echoed down the valley and up the mountains to *Coroico* and across the valley to the Afro-Bolivian settlement. Smoke caused by the burning truck and trees could be seen from great distances. The Army had closed the road to traffic, but transported reporters to the scene to have a good look at the massacre site. Some officers were instructed to 'admit' that the Army did not have adequate resources to patrol farther into the *yungas* and the helicopters had very limited range. The story was that the Army had recovered the bodies which were not burned in the truck explosion. Only the blood, areas blackened by explosions, the burned out hulk of the truck 2,000 feet down the mountain, and empty shell casings could be seen. Blood had pooled on the sides of the road and dried into a sticky mass with swarms of flies competing to get their share. Reporters were sufficiently sickened and asked fewer questions.

Curious civilians had walked to the site and spread their own exaggerated stories. The Army appeared on full alert. Helicopter patrols made regular searches through the mountains and valleys, but at night they secretly delivered supplies. It was a perfect excuse for helicopters to be in the area.

The following night Scott and Gomez returned to the settlement with two more sullen, bearded *guerilleros* to reinforce the illusion. The trip was a lot easier and quicker in the *captured jeep,* which had a little pig blood smeared on it and a few bullet holes for effect. Francisco continued to stay with the main group to avoid any future recognition. He would have to deal with the results as a representative of the government after this revolution was crushed.

Pinedo was waiting, "Tomas, you have poked a stick into the bee hive. The Army is everywhere. A helicopter even landed here. We told them we know nothing. Where are you hiding?"

"*Cacique*, I cannot tell you that, but we have many men and must keep moving. We have shown what we can do. We are the true revolutionaries who can help you. Perhaps we can convince the other groups in the mountains to join us and become an even stronger force for change."

"Ah, *sí*, but I have heard the *Tupac* group is not happy you are here."

Scott was thinking, 'Well, well that's good news in a hurry.' To Pinedo he said,

"*Cacique*, can I meet with the *Tupac* group?"

"*Quisás* (maybe), but they are very dangerous people."

"*Cacique*, I believe we have just proved that we are very dangerous people against the Army, not small outpost police and farmers. We do not steal and threaten people."

"*Sí*', I see that is true. They are far to the north from here and deep in the mountains, but my messenger can reach them in two days. We hear they are planning something big."

"We have little time. We must move now to keep the Army off balance. We have started to send our demands to the government."

In the eastern forest regions *Tupac* Matamoros had indeed heard the news and seen the newspapers. The city of Trinidad newspapers were full of very convincing pictures of blood and bullet holes.

Matamoros had grown a beard more for effect and to disguise his very non-Indian features than to imitate Fidel and Che. In fact he wanted absolutely no Cuban influence in *his* revolution and glory. He already had in place groups in the always restless mining unions and now in the mountains. He needed more time to consolidate and influence the Indian Congress. This new Cuban-led group needed to be co-opted or neutralized. He turned to his second in command, "Manuel, my people in La Paz and Trinidad know nothing of this new group. They seem to have come down from Peru and picked up support from people we have not reached. They have made the Army start acting. The Army has sent some troops from Trinidad to go over to the mountains from the east to Yucumo. Start sending fifty men in farm trucks to the mountains disguised as farmers to reinforce our units. Avoid the Army by going north to Rurrenabaque then up the *Beni* River. We will attack these new isolated Army units in *Yucumo* before they can organize. Then I will follow you. We must make the Cubans join us, or we must kill them. We must now make bold moves while the Army is occupied with this new group."

Two days later in *Portachuelo,* Villamiranoa was keeping track of movements in the mountains and the Guarani sergeant in *Trinidad* had reported the movement of Tupac's men on their way to *Yucumo.* He stood smiling in front of the maps on the wall, drawing red lines on the plastic overlay. His Afro-Bolivian sergeant at *Coroico* and his Gurani Indian sergeant in his village east of *Trinidad* were performing beyond expectations. He could track *Tupac's* movements in the east and information was flowing in from Francisco in the west. He stroked his chin and turned to his staff with his arms spread gesture, "*Perfecto,* we have to send these two sergeants to officer school when this is over. *Caballeros,* let's have a *singani* toast to the brave men out there. I trust our airborne operation is prepared when *Tupac's* main body moves on *Yucumo?*" he asked turning his head toward his S-3 Operations Officer and S-2 Intelligence Officer.

"*Absolutamente, Coronel.*"

"*Bueno,* make that two toasts of singani."

Near *Coroico,* Francisco had received word that Dr. Stern was returning from the north on his government medical rounds. It was common knowledge that the *Tupac* men in the mountains extorted medicines and supplies from Dr. Stern in exchange for safe passage to the outlying villages. They knew better than to take everything and disrupt the continuous rounds of the doctor. It was not suspected that Dr. Stern and his nurse assistant, Hilda Hindman, were gathering intelligence for the government. They traveled in a jeep and trailer painted white with a red cross in order to avoid any confusion as to the purpose of the vehicle.

Hilda was the daughter of a German Jewish refugee from Nazism and an Aymara woman. Her looks were so dramatic that if you looked at her as a European, you saw a beautiful European, but if you looked at her as Aymara, you saw a beautiful Indian woman. Such was the extraordinary mix of races. All this enabled her to communicate and collect information from men in the mountains when the doctor could not.

This day they were returning from *Guanay,* one hundred kilometers to the north along the brown and silty waters of the Tupani River before it enters the Beni River. *Guanay* was along the old *Gold Digger's Trail* where residents still panned for gold. This remote area with its *Wild West* attitude had been perfect for Tupac's group.

Francisco and Scott had been alerted as to the day when Dr. Stern would pass by on the old road. They sat out of sight in the trees along a wider part of the road. Two hours later their wait was rewarded with the sight of the white jeep with a red cross descending the dirt and gravel road. Francisco walked out in the road, pretending to ask for assistance for some injury to a friend up the mountain as other travelers passed by.

When they were alone, "Dr. Stern, I am Major Francisco Gutierrez. We have been expecting you. Please follow me up this trail." Dr. Stern shifted into four wheel drive and followed the rutted trail out of sight of the road. Francisco had glanced at Hilda and now could not take his eyes off her. He knew there would be a nurse, but not one like this. They stopped at a small clearing about fifty meters off the road and out of sight.

The doctor and the nurse nervously looked around to see what was happening to them now. A tall bearded young man stepped out of the trees and said in Spanish, "I am very glad to meet you Dr. Stern. Your nephew, Jacob, is my best friend. I also know your two brothers. My father helped them escape Cuba. My name is Thomas Scott."

The doctor could only stare at the unrecognizable bearded young man who looked exactly like the *Tupac* bandits. Francisco could only stare at Hilda, who stared right back. Shyness was not one of her qualities.

"*Mein Gott*, is it true? I heard of the Scott family from my brothers. Is Jacob here also?"

Scott laughed, "No, after our Cuban escapade your brother has Jacob's nose firmly to the grindstone of medical studies."

Now it was the doctor's turn to laugh. "*Sehr gut.*"

Francisco was surprised at their familiarity with Scott, but he still could not take his eyes off Hilda.

Two more bearded *guerilleros* stepped out of the trees, breaking the spell. Francisco became the major again. "Doctor, I assume they have told you why we are here dressed like this. We need whatever information you can give us."

"I must admit, I was surprised when you stepped out of the trees. You can imagine we have had some unpleasant appearances like that before, but, yes, I have been told that you needed information on these bandits calling themselves revolutionaries. In truth, my nurse has been much more effective than I. She speaks Aymara, and the men do like to brag to her." He turned to her, "Hilda, tell them what you learned, in Spanish please."

She again stared straight into Francisco's eyes. "Major, the doctor is right. They talk to me about how brave they are, and they let secret information come out while they speak in Aymara. Perhaps they think it is safe from the doctor. Do you have maps?" Francisco pulled a map out of his pocket and she began to show locations and directions they intended to take. It was like she had been in their meetings or intercepting messages.

Scott sat against a tree listening and wondering where these beautiful and intelligent women could possibly come from far out here in the mountains away from everything that seemed civilized. Obviously, his thoughts had turned to Maria Consuela. He tried to concentrate on her face as if to communicate that he was OK, but somehow he knew that she knew.

By the time Hilda finished her briefing, Francisco's and Scott's attention was entirely focused on surprising news. She not only had learned of the intention of the local group to destroy the "Cuban" group on its own initiative, but also that another group was supposed to be coming up the Beni River to reinforce them. She did not know how many.

The doctor and nurse were given some much appreciated food supplies and allowed to go on to *Coroico*. Unspoken words between Francisco and Hilda said they would meet again. Scott was thinking that this woman just got promoted from white *Pawn* to white *Queen* for reaching the back row on the black side of the chess board with the *Tupac* men. Obviously, her information was going to eliminate a lot of black *Pawns*.

Word needed to be passed to *La Paz* and *Portachuelo* quickly. Clearly, the *Tupac* group around *Guanay* had no friendly intentions in spite of Pinedo's attempts to arrange it. Their strength was estimated at forty without the reinforcements headed up the Beni River. They would be using confiscated trucks moving slowly along the dangerous mountain road. Messages flashed back and forth. Two H-34s were sent to *Coroico* to refuel at prearranged sites for a flight to an ambush site between *Coroico* and *Guanay*. The H-34 had a maximum range of 293 kilometers. This was pushing it roundtrip overloaded with twenty soldiers, with equipment. The H-34s would have to return empty for supplies while an Army convoy started from the outskirts of La Paz almost 80 kilometers away on the winding mountain road. They had to destroy the first group before reinforcements arrived.

Scott and Gomez had already moved toward a potential ambush site with two men and a vehicle mounted radio in the "captured" jeep to set up a landing zone for the H-34s far enough to be out of sight and sound, approximately halfway to *Guanay*. With the long whip antennae they were able to relay communications through helicopters to La Paz and on to *Portachuelo*.

At *Portachuelo*, word had been received about the group moving up the Beni River from *Rurrenabaque*. The staff was quickly trying to alter plans to meet both threats. McCauley and Benoit were clustered with the staff to offer any suggestions they could.

"*Hijo de puta!* He has split his forces north and south," growled the *coronel*.

Apparently, the sergeant had only seen *Tupac's* forces leave the heavy forest areas and had not seen them split.

McCauley looked up, "*Coronel*, it looks like he intends to attack *Yucumo* at the south road intersection and has bypassed *Yucumo* with a smaller force to the north at *Rurrenabaque*. With that force added to the local group near *Guanay*, he intends to crush Francisco. May I make suggestion?"

"Sean, all suggestions are welcome. We seem to have missed a twist here."

"Sir, I suggest that we reduce the main airborne assault behind him at *Yucumo* and plan another drop at *Guanay*. The aerial photos show a relatively flat river plain around it and a bridge crossing the river. Give me a couple of soldiers and we'll do the pathfinding to guide you in. You will probably find *Tupac* in this group instead of assaulting your garrison in *Yucumo*. He's not much of a frontal assault guy. "

"I will go. I am trained in pathfinding," shouted Lt. Col. Marcel Benoit, a little too eagerly.

McCauley looked at Villamiranoa and smiled.

"Why not?" laughed the coronel, "You two allies can die together," more laughter. He turned to his staff, "Split our forces and plan two airborne assaults, quickly. Do not forget to assault to the east from Trinidad also, to clean out his supply bases. Pilots, get over here and memorize this. We only have four hours to move, and… Sean, you are probably correct about *Tupac*. So, I shall be there to greet him."

McCauley and Benoit took aerial and topographic maps to another table, selected two soldiers who had some pathfinder training and started planning the airborne drop, equipment, and the variables of what to expect on the ground. Back to the good old Operations Order.

Halfway to *Guanay* Scott had selected a possible ambush site and radioed back to Francisco. Thirty minutes later Francisco's *barbudos* were loaded and lifting off in two H-34s. The area residents were accustomed to seeing helicopters and tanker trucks by now, but no one could see where they landed to pick up the *guerilleros*. Across the mountain and over the second valley, Pinedo and his Afro-Bolivian villagers watched H-34s fly north, and wondered who was going after whom.

In an isolated valley two kilometers away from the road to *Guanay,* the H-34s dropped the *barbudos*. They were quickly led by Scott to an ideal site over the road. Unlike the fake ambush, this spot was narrow. Lookouts were posted high and around the curve but in sight. The rear element of the *Tupac* group would be attacked first to block retreat, then the lead element. The remainder of the group would be in a clear fire zone.

Two hours later the unsuspecting Tupac group came down the road with two trucks loaded with approximately thirty men. As planned, the heavy weapons squad fired a 57 mm recoilless rifle into the second truck causing it to burst into flames while it was raked by rifle and machine gun fire. Some were able to leap from the truck and return reasonably accurate fire while they ran to some shelter under the side of the mountain. The first truck reacted sur prisingly fast with its occupants exiting before another recoilless round could be fired. Scott thought to himself that this was a pretty disciplined bunch. They must have some former army sergeants leading them in a counterattack. They were not like the group of bandits they had wiped out down south where Amboro' had died. Automatic weapons fire was now raking leaves and branches over his head. He could hear cries of wounded men nearby, but he couldn't tell whose. He concentrated his own fire where he could see movement and bursts of fire. The firing died down. Some revolutionaries held up their hands in surrender and others tried to run back down the road only to be cut down by machine gun fire. Scott looked down and thought how eerily familiar it looked to the 'fake massacre' they did. This time there were real bodies and real blood.

A shout came from the lookout. A car had been trailing the trucks just out of sight. Now it had turned around and was speeding back the way it came. Long range shots may have put some holes in it, but it didn't stop. Someone was going to be warned, but this group was finished. By now, Villamiranoa should be assaulting from the air behind *Tupac's* main group for the *coup de grace*. No one suspected that *Tupac* himself and fifty heavily armed men were at this moment on the Beni River headed their way.

The previously sent radio relay team sent on back roads toward *Yucumo* disguised as an agricultural survey team had been ambushed by elements of the *Tupac* force. Only the civilian agricultural engineer and one wounded soldier were still alive. R. Rudolph Brandl had been sent from Germany before WW II to assist the Bolivian government in agriculture. He stayed in Bolivia rather than return to the chaos in Europe. With two Rs as initials his friends delighted in calling him R. R. with the prolonged roll of the Spanish "r", *Erre Erre*. He had accepted various clandestine assignments for the Bolivian military. *Like this crazy stunt,* he was thinking while driving as fast as he could on a rutted dirt road in order to get out of range and into the nearby mountains. The wounded soldier was frantically using the radio to let *Portachuelo* and *Yucumo* know the assault was coming out of the heavy forest southeast of *Yucumo*. Brandl had reached a point on the side of the mountain where he could look down on *Yucumo* and the forest. A small river ran between the forest and *Yucumo* which the enemy would have to ford or come to the edge of the mountain to skirt it. From his view he could see that in the night they had already crossed the river and were within two kilometers of *Yucumo*. He could also see trucks coming down the road to attack from another direction. He was trying to aid the soldier, who kept fading in and out of consciousness, and keep communications going. The inside of the van was a mess of bullet holes, blood and the bodies of two other soldiers. Fortunately, the radio was still working. He had warned *Yucumo* of the two pronged attack and relayed the urgent information to *Portachuelo*.

At *Portachuelo*, Villamiranoa was receiving broken transmissions, but the message was obvious. Reports were coming in from the besieged garrison at *Yucumo*. Villamiranoa made his decision. He directed the pilots to visually select drop zones behind the two groups of attacking revolutionaries. There was no time for formal plans. He needed to attack quickly before his garrison was overrun. He ordered the C-123s into the air with sixty paratroopers in each plane. The drop zone would have to be determined from the air depending on the direction of attack. Fancy plans were unraveling. The first plane would have to drop troops and return to load the group to be dropped in *Guanay*. It would take three hours flying time minimum to go and return to *Portachuela* from *Yucumo*, and another one hour and a half to Guanay. Timing was close. With a range of over 1,500 kilometers the C-123 would not have to refuel. It could fly the shorter return to La Paz after the *Guanay* drop. The radio team was trying to reach La Paz to relay to Francisco the latest developments.

Communications with La Paz had somehow been scrambled. Francisco and Scott were unaware of *Tupac* heading their way with superior numbers on the river.

There would be no time for pathfinders to go first to *Guanay* either. That one they would literally have to do *on the fly*. At least the C-123 could communicate over the mountains when in the air to warn Francisco… if they were not down in a valley.

At the ambush site the helicopters had returned from *Coroico,* fueled and ready to evacuate the unit. They had also received relayed information about the battle in progress in *Yucumo* to the east and the proposed airborne assault on *Guanay,* but no information on the Tupac group coming up the river.

Francisco was worried about the car that had escaped. With a helicopter he could quickly bypass the car and reconnoiter *Guanay* before the hastily planned paratroop drop. "Scott, pick fourteen men to go with us in this H-34, quickly!" He instructed the pilot to fly directly to a spot on the road overlooking the Beni River approximately two kilometers from *Guanay* and out of sight of the town. It was only fifty kilometers as the crow flies and in easy range of the H-34. The second pilot he instructed to carry the wounded back and notify the unit in *Coroico* to send an extra truck to pick up prisoners and the troops left to guard them, also to pass on the information to the units on the way from La Paz by truck to continue to *Guanay.*

Scott was thinking, *This guy is good. He has to be a general someday.*

It was 1500 hours by the time the H-34 landed on the road out of sight and hearing of *Guanay* on the opposite side of the river. The men jumped out, and the helicopter quickly departed at a low angle to minimize noise and visibility. They climbed about two hundred feet up the side of a small mountain overlooking the river and the town. The obvious drop zone was below them on the flat plain adjacent to the river. They settled into hidden positions to rest and eat some combat rations from their packs.

On board the C-123 Villamiranoa and fifty men, including McCauley and Benoit waited in their parachute harness for an anticipated green light in forty-five minutes. They were one hour later than anticipated, and the *coronel* was not happy. He already knew about Francisco's ambush, and had just received a relayed message from the H-34 that Francisco and only fifteen men were somewhere on the south side of the river with no communications. He passed the word down to watch for them. McCauley suggested that they would probably be at a high vantage point to watch the drop and the town.

On the ground the lookout had spotted *Tupac's* group coming around a bend in the river where they were disembarking from the small fleet of confiscated boats with outboard motors. They were deploying below Francisco's small group on the same side of the river, and seemed to be waiting for some communication from the town.

Scott whispered to Francisco, "Damn, that's a lot of armed men. If Villamiranoa jumps onto that plain, they are going to be cut up before they know what hit them."

"I am afraid you are correct, Scott. Let's get our men deployed where we can hit them and distract them away from the drop zone. At least we have one 57 mm recoilless rifle to make a big noise and grenades to throw down on them. That should disrupt them and let the airborne unit know where the enemy is. We are not many, but we can make a lot of noise. I hope." Francisco smiled.

Scott agreed. "They will probably have to jump at 1,000 feet to avoid the low mountains. That means they will probably only be hanging in this thinner mountain air for less than thirty to forty seconds. We should be able to create a lot of noise in those seconds. At least it's enough for them to get on the ground and assault these *comemierdas.*"

They had a good position in heavy growth and a sharp incline below them. It would be hard for *Tupac's* group to determine how many men were above them and even more difficult to assault up the mountain, especially with more men landing on the ground in front of them.

The *Tupac* men had settled into concealed positions watching across the river toward *Guanay*. Apparently, they did not know that the *Guanay* group had been wiped out earlier, and they were waiting for a meeting with someone.

Behind Francisco's small unit they could hear the distant engine noise of the approaching C-123. *Tupac* had not paid any attention to some plane flying in the distance. He was focused on the other side of the river. As the plane approached closer and lower, he shifted his attention to this low flying plane, trying to recognize what it was.

Francisco was cautioning his men to hold their fire until just before the first jumper left the plane. Hopefully, they could distract and disrupt the *Tupac* group long enough for the paratroopers to get on the ground. His men had preselected fields of overlapping fire to concentrate maximum kill zones.

"Hold, hold, my good soldiers… *Fuego!*" he shouted. All weapons opened up on full automatic fire and the recoilless rifle fired into the center of the group with a tremendous explosion. The effect was of a much larger group in ambush. Grenades were being tossed down the mountain adding to the shock value.

Twenty seconds after the firing began Scott could see the first paratrooper exit the aircraft. It was probably Villamiranoa followed by his company commanders, leading their respective companies out of both sides of the plane. He was sure they had the complete attention of Tupac focused on the mountain ambush. His men were wildly trying to return fire up the mountain at men they could not see.

By the time *Tupac* noticed the paratroopers, they were all out of the plane and halfway to the ground. He frantically tried to direct the fire of his men at the airborne assault while ducking fire from above. Francisco's men didn't try to conserve ammunition or grenades. They kept pouring it on. It did sound like a whole army was firing down.

Villamiranoa had a bird's eye view of what was happening. From his angle and the different sounds of the weapons, he could clearly determine where the enemy was. His fingers were gripping his own carbine strapped along the side of his body. He switched to full automatic while he waited impatiently for the ground to come up. He could see some of the last men to exit would drop into the river. He hoped they remembered to release their parachutes before they hit the water. *Thump.* He rolled into the ground with what he thought was a perfect parachute landing fall, but something hurt. He had landed on a small bush, and he could see a branch sticking out of his leg. He released his 'chute, pulled out the branch and looked for his company commanders. '*Perfecto,*' he thought,

'Thank God the H-34 pilot had warned us that Francisco was in the area.'

His unit commanders and sergeants were organizing their men and beginning an assault up across the riverbed plain toward *Tupac*. They also had been able to determine where Francisco was and the direction of fire from *Tupac,* whose men were now starting to direct more fire on the paratroopers. The *coronel* could see some of his men fall under the increasing fire from the bottom of the mountain, but he could tell from the sound of rifles and grenades that Francisco had not let up. He hoped they did not run out of ammunition. Bullets were now whining and cracking overhead and kicking up sand all around him. His staff assembled around him and he started the hundred yard dash toward enemy positions. One of his staff went down and something banged off his helmet. Russian made AK-47 rounds cracked across the plain and M-1 and BAR 30 cal. rounds banged their answer. He had forgotten about the hole in his leg. The adrenalin covered any pain. *Zziip.* Something burned his left bicep. "*Hijos de putas!*" he shouted and kept running.

Different colored tracer rounds flashed back and forth as machine guns fired. Army units had now entered the woods at the foot of the mountain, and *Tupac's* men began to break and fall back under the assault of the paratroopers.

Francisco ordered his men to cease fire and watch for enemy trying to escape through the woods.

Scott felt a moment of confusion as the firing slowed, then he could see five men running along a narrow trail fifteen feet down the mountain side, but there was nothing visually. He could only see them in his mind. "Francisco, can you see those five men below us? Can you see that ledge they're on? It's *Tupac.*"

Francisco turned to him and shook his head, "There is no one I can see. There is no ledge."

"I see them. They're escaping."

"Are you OK, Scott?" Francisco was getting worried that the strain was affecting him in the middle of a firefight.

Scott jumped up and sprinted five meters past startled soldiers to the edge of the apparent cliff and leaped over the edge. Francisco looked on in horror at this obvious suicide.

As Scott went over the edge he could see the men directly under him. He shifted his carbine in front and fired as he was falling. Two men fell and he landed on top of a third. He could feel and hear the man's bones breaking as he cushioned Scott's fall. The fourth man spun in confusion, but Scott scrambled to one knee and shot him before he could fire his rifle. Behind him he felt and smelled a hot, rancid breath on his neck as a rough hand grabbed his head. The flash of a blade made him force his chin down into his chest. A sharp burning sensation traced his jaw bone as the knife sliced across his face instead of his throat. He instinctively jammed his rifle butt into the face now on his shoulder. He heard a groan and more bones breaking as his rifle butt shattered the man's face. Scott spun around to face his attacker. The man was kneeling with one bloody hand on his face and still slashing out with his knife. Scott kicked him in the face. Now the man was down and unconscious. It was *Tupac* Matamoros himself. "*Checkmate!*" was the only thing he could think to say.

Francisco had rushed to the edge and stood looking down at the mini massacre Scott had just created. Blood flowed down Scott's face and clothes, but he only stood looking down at the man who, until now, had terrorized Bolivia from the *yungas* to the border of Brazil. Francisco could hear other men running down the path and turned to fire, but they stopped and only stared at the scene, then up at Francisco and his men aiming at them. Some began to throw down their weapons as they realized what had happened. The others did the same as the word was passed back.

Scott still stood staring at Matamoros and wondering how he knew these men were there and what made him leap into space before he could see them. The sun was dropping behind the mountains, but he could feel a warmth flow over him and see a slight blue glow in the fading light. He knew.

Of the fifty men Matamoros had led up the river only fifteen had survived. Scott had accounted for ten percent of the entire force by himself in his high-flying act and probably all the surrenders by capturing Matamoros, who was now in substantial pain but still defiant. Francisco's unit had suffered no casualties except a few nicks and Scott's slashed face. They were in a very jubilant mood as they filed down the mountain with their prisoners.

A bloody but grinning *Coronel* Villamiranoa sat on a large rock by a fire surrounded by his staff and the two military attachés as he greeted them. He tried to use his signature arms wide gesture, but his bloody left arm kept sagging down. "Ah, my brave soldiers you have spared my units many casualties by your action. We only lost six men in that assault across an open field, and the wounded will recover. Now, my good Major, you must tell me all that has happened." He noticed Scott's blood covered uniform and hastily bandaged face. "Ah, *que pasó?*"

Francisco related the story as best he could as the *coronel's* eyes opened wide, "*Dios mio!*"

"I'll be goddamned," was added by McCauley, and "*Scare bleu,*" by Benoit.

Francisco had the bloody and bandaged Matamoros dragged in front of the *coronel,* who growled, "*Hijo de puta.* We have a special place for you." Matamoros spat at the coronel, who quickly kicked him in groin. That was the end of that bit of defiance and gave the *coronel* a great smile of pleasure to the laughter of his men.

Scott slumped on a rock on the edge of the group, thoroughly expended. The always alert Gomez came to his side with a canteen of water and discreetly handed him some coca leaves. Scott looked up and painfully smiled his thanks as he slipped them into the un-injured side of his mouth.

By midnight the convoy from La Paz arrived with food and extra troops to provide security and relieve tired paratroopers. Dr. Stern and his nurse had returned with the convoy for medical support. The doctor had wanted to suture Scott's face but Hilda convinced him to let her use a native poultice under a tight bandage. It would reduce the scar and heal faster. Dr. Stern knew better than to argue with her.

At daylight they awoke to the sound of two helicopters landing with additional medical support, newspaper reporters …and both

Generals Barrientos and Ocampo, to inspect the battlefield. The capture of *Tupac* Matamoros was going to be a very big deal.

Villamiranoa limped to meet the generals and related the story out of hearing of reporters.

After relating the part about Scott he motioned to McCauley to come over. "Sean, I have been discussing Scott's role in this. I think we all can agree that this has to be handled carefully, especially the vision part. The generals understand, but feel that the capture of Matamoros should be attributed to Francisco's unit with recognition of valor to Scott due to the somewhat secret role of Scott in his assignment here. We will leave higher decorations to your discretion and the Ambassador's diplomatic approach. Of course, we will endorse to your government in the strongest terms whatever you decide." He noticed the blood on McCauley's fatigue jacket for the first time. "Looks like you got nicked a little yourself, Sean."

"Not as bad as you, Sir, but I completely understand the problem. I will discuss it with the Ambassador." McCauley was thinking if anything deserved a Medal of Honor, this would be it. Now, they couldn't even talk about it.

Helicopters evacuated the wounded, including Scott, McCauley and Benoit. Villamiranoa took some pain killers and stayed with the generals for the photographers. He had to be here for this. Matamoros' wounds were not life threatening so he was kept there for the show.

In La Paz, Scott, McCauley, and Benoit were quickly shuttled off to the United States Embassy while wounded soldiers were sent to the Army hospital. The ambassador, Maria Consuela, and a doctor were waiting.

"Good Lord, Sean, you two look awful. Are you alright?" exclaimed the ambassador.

"No problem, Mr. Ambassador. Just a little battlefield grime," McCauley laughed.

Maria Consuela didn't think it was funny as she rushed to Scott. Benoit requested a ride to the French Embassy.

Maria Consuela inspected his face while the doctor cleaned the wound in McCauley's side.

"Who did this bandage?" she demanded.

"Dr. Stern's nurse, Hilda Hindman. She is half Aymara." It was becoming painful for Scott to talk so he just blew her a kiss.

"She is very good. I can smell the poultice. I would have done the same thing. You will have less scar. I have to meet her. You need a bath and a careful shave."

McCauley looked up and smiled, "I need a bath too. I think I'll call Françoise." Scott tried to keep his mouth shut and still laugh. The ambassador did laugh loudly. Maria Consuela gave them a blank look.

"Oh, McCauley, a message came in from the Pentagon. You are to report to Command and General Staff College at Ft. Levenworth next month. Looks like you are moving right along, and I have a couple of Purple Hearts and some more dangling things to recommend. Which reminds me, I need a new military attaché. Any suggestions?" the ambassador grinned and tilted his head in Scott's direction.

"*Absolutamente, embajador,* and I need an appointment with you in the morning."

"I'll be here."

Maria Consuela took Scott to Villamiranoa's townhouse and dropped off McCauley with a waiting Françoise. She deposited Scott in the care of the housemaids, and left for the "witches market" for her own choice of medicinal herbs.

The next morning McCauley arrived to find the ambassador waiting with the 'commercial attaché,' Jim Curren. He related the Scott story as he heard it directly from Francisco and confirmed by Scott.

"Jesus Christ, that's incredible. Is there a problem?"

McCauley looked at Curren, who had already picked up on the problem. "The problem, if I may presume, is the Bolivian military cannot admit that Scott did what they had not been able to do. He is technically just an aide to McCauley, not a quietly handpicked advisor to Villamiranoa, who has greatly aided their government by marrying the daughter of the President of the Indian Congress."

"Hmmm, damn. Doesn't seem fair does it? They are going to

make me a believer in this shaman business before I leave this land."

"I have a suggestion, Mr. Ambassador," McCauley started slowly explaining what he had been thinking. "Scott was assigned here on a classified mission. That means that we don't have to explain everything openly, just the basic facts, not any visions, to the pentagon. A Medal of Honor is well deserved but politically not possible. It would expose too many things and take away some well-earned credit due some fine Bolivian officers. However, for this extraordinary action we can recommend him for a Distinguished Service Cross, which is only one step down *with a lot less investigation.* In addition, for his actions earlier in the day and previously with the Afro-Bolivians he should receive another Bronze Star. He already has three Commendation Medals and a Silver Star. Besides, the Bolivian Army is going to give him some medal for valor anyway, even if they don't mention his flying act."

Curren was listening and nodding his head said, "If I may make a suggestion, we should also look at what he was asked to do on a national scale. We asked him to influence the political balance of the whole government. That was something *we* were unable to accomplish. He did it both militarily and politically with the Indian Congress. I think one more "dangling thing" is in order. The Legion of Merit, as I recall, is awarded for *"service and achievement while performing duties in a position of responsibility."* No question in my mind that both Scott and McCauley did exactly that. Normally, junior officers are not awarded this normally noncombat medal, because they are not put in positions like we did to Scott. In your report to the president about this significant turn of affairs in Bolivia you might mention it. It should also make him feel better about what he did for both of them. Also, the Legion of Merit is designed for foreign personnel. That should be a nice reciprocal award for the Bolivian officers to put on their uniforms."

The ambassador stared at the ceiling, "You know, Jim, sometimes I think there actually *is* something in the designation Central *Intelligence* Agency. Consider it done." The ambassador did exactly that with the endorsement of Gen. Barrientos. It took about *two* days for the awards to be completed once the report and recommendations hit the President's desk directly from the ambassador.

Two weeks later an awards ceremony was held at the Presidential Palace with the president of Bolivia in attendance. Generals Barientos and Ocampo presented some of the highest decorations and promotions to Villamiranoa, now Brigadier General, and Francisco Gutierrez, now Lieutenant Colonel. Lower decorations for valor were awarded to various soldiers, including McCauley, Benoit and Scott. Medals for distinguished service were presented to civilians R. R. Brandl, Dr. Stern and Hilda Hindman. Colonel Bergeron had flown in to receive a special medal recognizing his quiet logistical support for the training and operations of the new 'school.' Parachutes, weapons, ammunition and medical supplies had quietly been provided by the 8th Special Forces Group.

Francisco was trying to watch out of the corner of his eye as Hilda received hers, but she caught him and smiled. Villamiranoa saw it and raised an eyebrow at him. Maria Consuela saw it also, as well as their father. The *Gran Cacique*, President of the Indian Congress was not going to miss this.

As for Matamoros, the false *Tupac,* he was put in an iron cage dressed in convict stripes on the sidewalk outside the Ministry of Defense with a sign saying, "**Do Not Feed The Animal.**" His now grotesque face and nasty demeanor completed the lunatic image as he shouted and spat at passersby and the two guards posted there.

Another reception was held afterward at the U. S. Embassy. Before the start of the reception Scott was invited into the Ambassador's office for a private conference. As the door opened Scott could see his grandfather talking to the ambassador, Jim Curren, and Colonel Bergeron.

With big smiles they gave each other a very big Cuban *abrazo.* He was still tall and straight with clear blue eyes. Only the cane was a reminder of his leg.

"Granpa, how did you get here?"

"Well, I bought one of those new executive jets. It goes like a bat out of hell and carries six passengers. After all those years on ships, it's about time I got somewhere in a hurry. We'll take it for a spin tomorrow." He laughed. His southern drawl had never changed. Even after so many years speaking Spanish, it came through. "This is like old home week. I haven't seen Jim Curren since he was a teenager in the Canal Zone. Colonel Bergeron was explaining to me what you did to him in Panama." More laughing from everyone except Scott. He was still antsy about that reception in Panama.

The Colonel was still laughing, "Every time I thought I got even with him, it turned into more awards. Well, excuse me gentlemen, I need to talk to my old classmate McCauley. Nice to see you again, Scott."

"I'll join you," added Curren.

"Tommy, the ambassador has brought me up to speed on these incredible events in Bolivia. I brought you a new set of dress blues and formal mess coat for these diplomatic affairs. You'll have to order the miniature medals and probably have to have the uniforms tailored a bit."

Damn, Tommy was thinking, *He never forgets anything.*

"I assume I get to meet this extraordinary young lady?"

"Inmediatamente, mi abuelo distinguido." Tommy turned to the door. Maria Consuela was waiting outside. She entered uncharacteristically subdued, staring at the tall, distinguished gentleman who could only be the grandfather.

"Wow, Tommy, you hit the jackpot." Switching to Spanish he said, "Come here, my daughter," as he held open his arms. Nothing had ever felt more natural to her. The room seemed to light up. Only the ambassador was surprised.

Old Tom looked up at the formidable Indian figure standing in the doorway watching the scene.

"This must be the *Gran Cacique Grigotá* of whom I have heard so many glorious things. It is my honor to meet you, *Cacique Grigotá.'* Both men stood looking at each other appreciating the power each man represented.

"The honor is mine, Don Tomas Scott. I too have heard of your many accomplishments."

Old Tom turned to the Ambassador, "Will, this is wonderful. I truly appreciated your letting me come."

"What? Are you kidding? I could lose my job if I left you out. The President and I owe your family more than we can repay." Maria Consuela and Grigotá did not understand the exact meaning of this exchange, but it was clear that Don Tomas was an important person.

The Ambassador brought the ceremony to order and awarded McCauley and Scott their higher decorations without any fanfare except more lipstick from the ladies. The United States Legion of Merit was also presented to Villamiranoa, Gutierrez, Benoit and General Barrientos with appropriate diplomatic protocol and the Bolivian Foreign Minister in attendance. A special Legion of Merit on a neck ribbon was given to the *Gran Cacique* for his efforts in keeping the Indian Congress out of the resistance. Humanitarian service medals were awarded to Stern and Hilda. All citations had been signed personally by the President of the United States, a special touch the ambassador had arranged.

Old Tom was standing in a group with General Barrientos, Col0nel Bergeron, Villamiranoa, the Foreign Minister, Curren, and McCauley, and, as usual, leading the conversation and asking questions. The military men were very much aware of the miniature Medal of Honor in his lapel and the one around the neck of McCauley.

Maria Consuela beamed standing next to Scott, as her brother and father had received the American awards. She was prodding Scott to introduce her to Hilda. There had been no time at the military ceremony.

Francisco beat her to Hilda, but there was no way his sister would be ignored. She insisted that he introduce her. Scott stood off to the side with an amused smile. He felt someone beside him. It was the *Gran Cacique* wearing his medal. He too was smiling at this scene. Dr. Stern had walked up and got the drift of what was occurring. After some very serious looks from Francisco, Maria Consuela arranged breakfast in the morning with Hilda and excused herself. A look at her father's smiling face and she started to quietly laugh.

"I think we all need to go have some champagne and leave

them alone." Scott ventured, to quick agreement from everyone.

Scott's assignment as Military Attaché had also come through. It was unusual for a First Lieutenant, but this was a most unusual circumstance in a most unusual country. To solve any diplomatic niceties, an *acting captain* promotion was approved as long as he was the military attaché.

Maria Consuela had to hurry the breakfast with Hilda in order to catch the plane ride. However, the bond was made. Talk about medical school to augment their natural remedy training would be the next meeting.

Colonel Bergeron, McCauley and Old Tom were waiting on the tarmac when they arrived. Maria Consuela had even talked her father into coming along.

"Well, gentlemen, here she is, the *Sabreliner 40*. This is how the *four stars* ride in the military version. She cruises at 500 mph. at 40,000 feet with a range of 3,000 miles. Step this way." A long appreciative whistle came from McCauley as he entered the specially appointed cabin.

A course had already been determined in order to show everyone where the action had occurred in *Coroico, Guanay* and where *Amboro'* was buried. The pilot had to slow down and circle *Guanay* lower so everyone could match the map with what they could see from the window. *Grigota'* even forgot his nerves as they banked back south to give everyone a view of Buena Vista and *Portachuelo*. Round trip only took one hour and forty minutes, but the mountains and valleys were spectacular.

As they taxied up to their assigned spot, they could see the Ambassador waiting. Obviously, something had happened. Old Tom stepped down first. The Ambassador walked up close. "Tom, the President has been shot."

"Jesus! How bad?" Old Tom turned and motioned to the two colonels.

"Reports are still coming in. All embassies are on alert. I need to get back, but I thought Colonel Bergeron should know. I didn't want to announce it from the control tower."

Tommy watched the colonels hurry to the ambassador's side

and saw the looks on their faces when they talked to him. He excused himself from Maria Consuela and her father, and joined the group.

By the time they returned to the embassy, it had become obvious the president would not recover.

Old Tom instructed his pilot to fuel the plane and be ready to fly in the morning to Panama to drop off Colonel Bergeron then to Miami. The ambassador would fly with them to Miami then catch a flight to Washington D. C. Curren would be left in charge of the embassy.

Tommy and McCauley would also join the group. The ambassador had even persuaded *Cacique Grigotá* to allow Maria Consuela to attend the state funeral, provided that she return immediately after. A very quick diplomatic passport was arranged for the daughter of the President of the Indian Congress.

CHAPTER 15

WASHINGTON, D.C.

By 0700 hours they were off the ground in La Paz and only landed in Panama to refuel and deliver Colonel Bergeron. The condor's eye view of South America, the breadth of the former Inca Empire and the Caribbean kept Maria Consuela glued to the window. Her books on geography had come to life.

Old Tom was able to point out the islands and where he traded. The sky was clear enough for the pilot to veer over Jamaica to the east end of Cuba for a high altitude view of the Sierra Maestra Mountains, Santiago de Cuba and the old Scott plantations. The excitement of explaining their past in Cuba to Maria Consuela overcame the melancholy of a lost life. Tommy was able to show McCauley where he fought alongside Castro in the mountains and, sadly, back to the west where his father died at the Bay of Pigs. Old Tom recounted the day he earned his Medal of Honor on the cliffs below, and pointed out their old plantation with so much history as they skirted the eastern tip of the island.

The pilot made his approach to Miami International Airport from the east over the Bahamas at a lower altitude. To the Scotts, the sparkling, clear, green, and dark blue waters surrounding the 700 islands of the Bahamas were memories of happy days sailing and fishing, away from the crowded streets of Miami. To Maria Consuela it was mesmerizing. After this trip, her view of the world outside Bolivia would never be the same.

With the Ambassador in their party, customs and immigration was fast. The Ambassador caught his connection to Washington D.C., and the Scott limousine took the rest of the party to the residence in Coconut Grove.

Maria Consuela stopped at the front door and looked at Tommy. He knew she could feel *abuelita's* spirit in the house and needed reassurance to enter.

"It's OK, *mi amor*. She would welcome you," he assured her. Old Tom smiled and nodded. The big smiles and greetings of the Cuban maid and cook swept her into the house. They had been part of the household for many years in Cuba, and they delighted in telling embarrassing stories about Tommy when he was young. Tommy's mother and sister were waiting inside to greet this miracle of a wife.

The wide front porch with wooden rocking chairs and large slow-turning ceiling fans looked across flowering bougainvillea, gumbo limbo trees, and coconut palms to Biscayne Bay. The setting sun was behind them, and the light sea breeze blew in from the bay. To Maria Consuela this was a truly magic place that no book could describe.

Old Tom had been watching McCauley daydream. He turned to him and said, "Sean, why don't you go call that French girl and ask her to fly up here with the compliments of Scott Enterprises."

Caught off guard, McCauley stammered, "I couldn't let you do that."

Tommy added, "OK. You pay for it. You've earned enough money in *The Valor Fund.* That's a great idea. Maria Consuela and my mother will have someone to speak French with." He turned and explained in French to Maria Consuela. "*Oui, Oui,*" was her excited response.

Old Tom waved his hand, "The company telephone is in the den. It works all over the world."

The next afternoon Françoise arrived, and they all went sailing on Biscayne Bay…without catching very large barracudas. That evening the Scotts and Maria Consuela flew to Washington D. C. for the funeral procession and burial at Arlington Cemetery on Monday, November 25, 1963, three days after the assassination.

McCauley and Françoise remained guests at the house looking over the bay for the next week until he had to report to Command and General Staff College. Old Tom had instructed his personal assistant that McCauley should not be allowed to pay for *anything* in Miami.

In Washington the Scotts rode with the Ambassador in the funeral procession and to the cemetery. The tremendous amount of emotion surrounding them made Maria Consuela feel very weak… or maybe it was something else.

The next day, courtesy of the Ambassador and Old Tom's influence, they attended a brief reception in the White House to wish the new President well. Tommy wore his dress blue uniform with captain's silver bars and a lot of "dangling things" which turned more than a couple of senior military heads, who also saw the Medal of Honor in Old Tom's lapel. Tommy noted the miniature Silver Star in the President's lapel.

Maria Consuela had a brief conversation with the Bolivian Ambassador before she was introduced to the President.

"Well, my, my. This must be the young lady I've been readin' and hearin' about, Mr. Ambassador."

"It is indeed, Mr. President."

Maria Consuela did not exactly understand what the President said, but she liked his smile.

The President waived to the White House photographer, "Make sure you get a picture of this pretty girl." Turning to Old Tom, "Hello, Tom. I would guess this is your grandson with all that fruit salad on his chest."

"Absolutely, Mr. President. Best of luck to you, and may God bless you, Sir."

"Thanks, Tom. I expect I'll be needin' both. Young Scott, keep up the good work. We have our eyes on you." The President turned away to greet the next person in line.

As Tommy exited the reception line, a tall brigadier general approached, "Captain Scott, I'm General Atkins. How are my old friends McCauley and Bergeron?"

Tommy recognized the gold "rope" or aiguillette on the general's right shoulder as a military aide to the President before he recognized his name. His own "rope" as a military attaché to the Ambassador was worn on the left shoulder.

"General, they are doing fine. Thanks to you. Colonel McCauley is at my grandfather's house in Miami with a friend from the French embassy. This is my wife, Maria Consuela."

The general laughed, "I heard about the *French connection.*" He turned to Maria Consuela, "*Enchanté, Madame* Scott."

"I wish I could take credit, but we all know up here that it was you and the Ambassador who instigated that correction of a great injustice to McCauley. What are your plans after Bolivia?"

"Well, Sir, I'm sort of playing it by ear."

"If you need any help let me know. We'd like to keep you in the Army." The General looked over Scott's shoulder and said, "Wait right here. I want to introduce you to the Army Vice Chief of Staff, General Jaworski." He walked to a group of officers around General Jaworski and brought him over. It was a bit of an unusual breach of protocol to bring a four star general to meet a captain.

"General, this is the young Captain I was telling you about, and his wife."

"Well, young man, you certainly know how to get noticed."

"Sorry, Sir. That has never been my intention."

"Relax, Captain. I meant that as a compliment. Oft times in this Army it is easy to be overlooked." He noticed the long thin scar on Scott's jaw and laughed, "You know, Scott, Napoleon's officers would have paid a lot to have that saber scar." In French he turned to Maria Consuela, "Madame, it is my pleasure to meet you. The United States Army is very proud of your husband. You will excuse us now. I need the attention of the President's Aide for a few minutes." On turning away he noticed the Ambassador and Old Tom standing off to the side. "Mr. Ambassador, my compliments on your choice for an attaché." The Ambassador smiled and nodded his thank you. "Mr. Scott, it's an honor to meet you, sir. You have a fine grandson."

"Thank you, General." As the two generals walked away, Old Tom turned and looked at his grandson, tilted his head and raised his eyebrows. "Very impressive, Tommy."

Maria Consuela had been almost speechless with the display of powerful men and enthralled with senior officers speaking French. No one had told her about the United States Army's heavy involvement in Europe with NATO (North Atlantic Treaty Organization).

The reception was short without any celebratory effects, for obvious reasons. The next two days were spent showing Maria Consuela the sights of Washington as it settled back into its routine. She was able to go to the Bolivian Embassy to show off her picture with the President. Tommy was also able to show her the "sights" at Spalding, Whitman and Sterling, where he explained the stock market and let her pick several stocks, with surprising results. He again wondered about the potential of "shamanism."

By the end of the week Old Tom and the Ambassador had both finished their business meetings. The Ambassador's wife had joined him in Washington and would fly back with them to Bolivia in the Scott Enterprises' jet.

The return flight to Miami was filed as a route that would take them a little to the west over the Smokey Mountains to show Maria Consuela the scenery and their house on a mountain top in Banner Elk, N.C. At the end of November the trees at 5,000 feet were almost bare, but lower down the burst of autumn colors was still spectacular. The pilot made a low altitude circle over the clearly visible estate. The caretaker waived as he recognized the plane, and the pilot dipped his wings in answer.

During the three hour flight the Ambassador explained the protocol of each ambassador offering his resignation to a new president. This allowed each president to select his own choices. It would usually take a few months, but Bolivia would have a new ambassador, who would probably want to select a higher ranking officer as attaché. "Meanwhile, *Captain* Scott, enjoy the diplomatic ride without the combat."

The group spent the night at the Coconut Grove house and flew to Bolivia the next day, with Françoise as an additional passenger, via the Scott executive jet.

Captain Thomas MacDougall Scott II bought a very nice townhouse in La Paz, became accustomed to the altitude, didn't need any more coca leaves, enjoyed the diplomatic scene, and waited it out.

As anticipated, Maria Consuela and Hilda received scholarships to medical school in La Paz to start in January. One little fact had been sneaking up on Maria Consuela...morning sickness.

Also as anticipated, a new ambassador was appointed after two months. It was decision time for Scott. With pregnancy and medical school, relationships were already changing with Maria Consuela.

In the Ambassador's last week, he called Scott in for a final conference. "Well, Scott, decision time is here. The new ambassador is requesting his own military attaché. He will soon learn that he made a big mistake, but he *is* the new President's man. I'll be going back to some cushy, influence peddling law firm spot in Boston. The Kennedys are still controlling things there. It's been quite an experience here. I, sort of, hate to leave. Barrientos has been selected as the next Vice President, and who knows what will happen. Got any plans?"

"My grandfather wants me to come home, but I've been thinking about staying in the Army. Special Forces wants to send me to some schooling at Ft. Bragg in preparation for sending me to some old French colony on the other side of the world, South Vietnam, where I can use my French. Maria Consuela can have the townhouse. She has plenty of help around the house, and she's very busy with medical school. I guess we will see what happens the rest of the year." Scott looked out of the window at the surrounding mountains and thought about the incredible events of the last year.

"My young friend, I just happen to have your orders here on my desk, if you want them. Of course, you will have to drop back to 1st Lieutenant with that terrible loss of income." That was good for a big laugh from both.

Maria Consuela had always known this would happen, and Scott promised to fly back after his school for the birth of the next *Gran Shaman*.

Scott flew to Ft. Bragg with a stop in Miami to explain the situation to his grandfather and his mother, then to the other side of the world.

CHAPTER 16

GOING WEST TO BE IN THE EAST…
to the shores of Vietnam

Ft. Bragg, NC, Smoke Bomb Hill and the BOQ (bachelor officer quarters) were pretty shabby looking after La Paz and the Andes Mountains, but it did feel like coming home. Special Forces was a lot busier now with the new 5th SF Group taking on heavy involvement in Vietnam. Scott had been assigned to a little reorientation as an officer and a short language course in Vietnamese, because he already was fluent in French, the leftover language from colonial days. The 5th Group was the place if you were looking for action. Scott wasn't so sure he was ready for much more action after Panama and Bolivia. He already had two Purple Hearts.

On his way to report to Training Group he met Lieutenant Colonel Guillermo Rodriguez coming out of the administration building. "Hello, Scott. Good to see you made it back in one piece."

Scott saluted, "Thank you, Sir. Congratulations on your silver oak leaf, Colonel."

The colonel laughed, "Thanks. I see they have already demoted you back to 1st Lieutenant."

Scott laughed in turn. "It was nice while it lasted."

"I'm on my way to 5th Group HQ in Nha Trang, Vietnam. We're still phasing in with the 1st Group out of Okinawa. Since I see you are assigned to the 5th, I suspect I will see you around. Good luck."

"Thank you, Sir." As the colonel walked away, Scott wondered where he was headed and how big a country this Vietnam place was.

Officer orientation seemed to be a waste of time considering his prior assignments, but country orientation and language class was interesting. He doubted that he would ever master an oriental language where the different sounds of the same word meant different things. However, almost a century of French occupation and bilingualism had influenced a pronunciation level that helped more than the straight conversation.

At the end of his brief training, he called Maria Consuela about taking a quick trip back before he deployed again. She was in the middle of exams and didn't have time to take a break. So, he just saved some leave time and flew out to San Francisco where he had orders to take a slow boat from Oakland Army Terminal to Vietnam, because he was deployed as an unassigned individual and not part of a team. His report date was still forty days away.

San Francisco definitely had its sights, and he was temporarily quartered in a BOQ at old Ft. Mason. It was conveniently located a short walk down the hill to Fisherman's Wharf and a skip up the hill to the popular Buena Vista Café where the cable car turned around. The sights wore thin quickly with no one to share them.

Over breakfast at the Ft. Mason officer's club he met several officers who were headed to "Nam" by air from nearby Travis Air Force Base. He related his future "slow boat" voyage.

"Scott, you like long boat rides?" asked Alan, a 1st Lieutenant in the artillery from Brooklyn, and the talkative one of the two.

"Hell, no. I spent too many weeks as a common seaman," and he related his shipboard experiences.

"Well, come with us to the "O" Club at Travis AFB tonight and wear all those medals. I guarantee we can find some pilot who will be happy to fly a hero to war. Besides the US Air Force does have the best food, the best entertainment and the best women, and we know a guy over there. He is in operations, and he is the Officer in Charge of the Officers' Club."

Scott looked dubious, "How do you know this guy will be there?"

"Man, he's always there watchin' things and holdin' court over in the corner with a bunch of good lookin' honeys. He's got a Warrant Officer runnin' the operation. He just keeps the place flowin'. Lot of guys passin' through who might not come back. They call him *Rocco*. Nobody seems to know why, because he has a Scot name. I know a few Roccos back in Brooklyn, and he does look a little like 'em.

"You sold me, but how do I get my orders changed?"

"*No problema, amigo.* Tomorrow we will take a couple of bottles of good Scotch down to Oakland Terminal and *presto change- o.* You will fly with the eagles."

Alan's buddy, a 1st Lieutenant in the Signal Corps, spoke up, "On that happy note of just passing through, let's go put on some aftershave and start driving."

TRAVIS AIR FORCE BASE, CALIFORNIA

True to form and accurate description, Captain MacLachlan, USAF, aka *Rocco,* was at his table with the prescribed number of good looking women. He looked up as the three Army officers approached.

"Gentlemen, gentlemen, a big welcome to the humble hospitality of the United States Air Force for our Army heroes," he said with a very mischievous grin.

"Evenin', Rocco. We brought a real hero with us who needs a little help." He nodded toward Scott.

MacLachlan looked up at Scott's row of *decorations* with a *Combat Infantryman Badge, Master Jump Wings with two combat stars and Green Beret* and realized he wasn't kidding. He stood up and held out his hand. "It's an honor, Lieutenant. What can I do for you?" His grin got bigger as he swept his hand toward the girls.

"I need a ride to Vietnam."

Rocco stared for a moment. That was definitely not what he was expecting.

The other Army officer explained the "slow boat" problem.

Still a little surprised, MacLachlan raised his eyebrows and looked at the girls. "You mean you really want to get there early?"

Scott smiled. "Yes, Sir."

"OK, hero. Let me see what I can do. Take a seat with your buddies and *my friends.* I'll be back. Have a drink on me."

A few minutes later he returned with a young 1ˢᵗ Lieutenant with pilot's wings.

"Scott, this is Jim Williams. He's flying an empty KC-135 tanker to Tan Son Nhut Air Base in a

couple of days. He can squeeze you in a jump seat, if you can get some orders. I would not be surprised if he had some mechanical problem that forced him to spend a night in Honolulu."

Alan's grin got bigger, "No problem, and Scott is buying drinks and dinner."

Scott laughed, "Absolutely no problems, my friends. Ladies, let's dance."

Rocco smiled and thought he needed to check for rooms in the Guest House, probably better a local motel. This group was never going to be able to drive back to San Francisco.

They took *four* bottles of 12 year old Scotch over to Oakland Army Terminal the next day.

The KC 135 was primarily a fuel tanker to provide an airborne gas station for the Air Force, but some had been converted to troop carriers. Like the one Scott had flown from Ft. Bragg to Panama. There were only two small windows, the seats faced backwards and ice formed on the cabin ceiling. However, this one was a fuel tanker with limited seats for the crew and some makeshift arrangements for the crew's comfort. It was definitely not his grandfather's executive jet, but it was much, much better than a C-123 with sling mounted seats along the sides. Overnight in Hawaii made it even better.

Tan Son Nhut Air Base was originally built by the French in the 1920s as a small unpaved airport only six kilometers from Saigon. In WW II the Japanese occupation forces used it as a transport base. By mid-1964, the Americans had expanded it to not only serve the small Vietnamese air force and civilian international terminal, but as a base for supersonic fighters to old C-47s and everything in between.

Scott's first breath of Viet Nam air was very different from Miami, Cuba or Panama. One of the crewmen noticed Scott wrinkle his nose at the smell. "Hey, Lieutenant, welcome to 10,000 years of Asian civilization soaked into the ground and flowing down the river for a few thousand miles. You hope you never get used to it." The crewman had loosely used the word *civilization,* as if civilization was a reality 10,000 years ago. Scott figured it was obviously a line he liked to use on everyone they delivered here, judging by the way he laughed and went on about his duty unloading. The thought did occur to him that he wouldn't like to get used to it; and thinking about history, the Vietnamese were actually part of the original ethnic Chinese who appeared 20,000 years ago. The Vietnamese had primarily remained ethnic Chinese because the Annamite Mountain range had served to seal off the groups historically flowing down from India on the west side of the mountains. The blending of cultures and people only began where the great Mekong River crossed over from Cambodia in the southern delta.

Scott thanked the pilots, shouldered his duffle bag and went looking for a way to get to the C-Team company headquarters in Nha Trang. They weren't looking for him this soon. So, he headed for the air-conditioned terminal looking for anyone in a Green Beret. The first ones he saw were pretty bedraggled looking and were headed to the bar. Perfect. He needed a drink. They were an A-Team just finishing a six month tour and headed back to Ft. Bragg.

He noticed there were only ten, not twelve, including one 1st lieutenant. "Mind if I join you, lieutenant?" The closest members turned to see who was talking and conspicuously stared at the left pocket of his fatigue jacket. Seeing the sewn on Combat Infantryman Badge (CIB) and Master Jump Wings, they were satisfied enough to smile and offer their hands.

"Jack Crawford," the lieutenant offered his handshake. "First time here, Scott?"

"Yeah. I was with the 8th in Panama and elsewhere. I was an SFC until they coerced me into being an officer." They all knew what "elsewhere" meant and smiled a knowing smile. Having been an enlisted man struck a chord with the sergeants.

"You with a Team? Where you headed?"

"No. I'm solo. Don't know where until I get to the C-Team in

Nha Trang."

"Looks like you are probably headed for some B-Team some-where if you're solo, but they're not losing men like A-Teams. So, I wouldn't be surprised if you end up in an A-team.

"Been there, done that. I'm ready," Scott smiled.

"Well, I haven't been to Panama, but here we have to work with the Vietnamese forces and local men recruited as irregular forces. Some of 'em are even Cambodian bandits. Most of the time you can't tell if they're Viet Cong until you get into a fire fight. We lost our captain to an infiltrator before we knew it and could kill him, and the politics of their officers is insane. Some of 'em fought with the Viet Minh against the French, some fought with the French and a lot of 'em are just useless political appointments. They don't tell you all of this stuff at Ft. Bragg. Hell of a screwy war."

"Crawford, I appreciate any advice you can give me. The next *two* rounds of drinks are on me."

A collective, "Aw right!" went around the team.

The next two hours were full of war stories, women and advice. Scott bought two more rounds before their plane was ready for boarding.

"Scott, see that REMF (Rear Echelon Motha Fucker) over there. He's with the transportation unit up at Nha Trang. He can get you a ride. Been a pleasure meeting you. Hope to see you again." Each member echoed their team commanding officer and shook his hand as they shouldered their duffle bags and headed for the plane.

The REMF turned out to be a friendly and very helpful guy. He fixed Scott up with a ride on an Otter U 1A, returning to Nha Trang. The Otter was built by DeHaviland in Canada and was the favorite of "bush pilots." It was a very rugged 41 foot single engine airplane with STOL (short landing and takeoff) capability. It could also be equipped with pontoons for water, and skis for snow. In order to parachute from it you had to sit on the deck and slide out, but it did get soldiers in and out of tight places.

The pilot took a quick fly over the beach at Nha Trang. The bright white sand beaches and clear blue water would put to shame any post card from Miami Beach was Scott's first thought. The surrounding mountains that hovered over the beaches reminded him of the Windward Islands in the Caribbean. It certainly did not look like a war zone.

Scott thanked the pilot and caught a ride into the HQ compound. A big sign over a long, one-story, part concrete block and part wooden plank building with a tin roof, announced "Headquarters 5th Special Forces Group."

Scott found a door marked C-4 HQ and entered. A small electric fan was blowing on a Specialist 5 clerk, who was busy typing, with a Sergeant Major looking over his shoulder. The sergeant major looked up, "Can I help you, Lieutenant?"

"Yes, Sergeant Major. I'm 1st Lt. Scott, Thomas M. reporting. I'm a little early."

"Are you sure you're in the right place, Lieutenant?"

The clerk looked up, "I saw his name come through, but he's more than thirty days early."

"Kind of an eager beaver aren't you, Lieutenant? How'd you get here?"

"Well, I'm tired of slow boats. So, I wore my beret, pinned on medals, went to the "O" Club at Travis AFB and caught a ride."

By this time the sergeant major had noticed the CIB and Master Jump wings and his tone softened a bit. The clerk handed him a sheet from Scott's file listing his decorations. The sergeant major laughed, "That will do it every time. Welcome to Vietnam, Lieutenant."

The sergeant major turned and knocked on an open door. "Colonel, we have a lost sheep out here in the form of a 1st lieutenant." The voice came back, "Send him in."

Scott entered a room covered with maps with different symbols drawn on acetate covers and colored pins sticking in them, saluted and stared at Lieutenant Colonel Guillermo Lazaro Rodriquez.

"Scott, how the hell did you get here?"

The sergeant major titled his head, "You know this one, Colonel?"

"Hell yes. I promoted him to Sergeant First Class *and* 1st Lieutenant. Scott, you looking for a third Purple Heart so soon?"

"No, Sir, I just didn't have anything better to do." At that the sergeant major laughed and left the room, and Scott related the Travis AFB story again.

"Well, you just happened to walk into the right room in the right building at the right time. How would you like to be in the United States Navy for thirty days?"

"Pardon, Sir?"

"I have an old friend from the Bay of Pigs training time. He's an old Navy "mustang" that came up through the ranks from a seventeen-year-old seaman landing craft operator in the Normandy invasion to Navy Lieutenant in charge of some beat up old small boats on the river patrolling out of Saigon. He has been asking me for someone to fill in until he gets replacements. The Navy apparently has some big plans for river operations but the paperwork is moving slow. I can't officially use you for thirty days, and you have slipped in under the six month tour limitation. In September everyone gets one year in paradise."

"I like small, fast boats, Sir."

"Good. This will be an experience, and you are based out of Saigon, tough duty. Sergeant Major get Scott a luxury suite for the night with permission to eat at the mess, and get Lieutenant. MacDonald in Saigon on the phone."

"Right away, Colonel," said a smirking sergeant major.

"Scott, report back at 0700."

"Colonel, Lieutenant MacDonald is on the line"

"Jim, how's the river rat?"

The quick answer came back "This river is full of shit. How's the snake taste up there, Guiillerrrmo?" MacDonald liked to drag out the name Guillermo instead of calling him just Bill or colonel.

"Delicious when you put a little chili sauce on it."

"What's up, amigo?"

"Well, you asked me if I had anyone to loan you for a few weeks. I have a new lieutenant who needs something to do."

"Are you shittin' me? What the fuck am I going to do with a new lieutenant? Does he even know the bow from the stern?"

"Well, let me see. It says here he has a 50 ton U. S. Coast Guard License…and a Merchant Marine Able Seaman ticket…and some offshore racing experience…and…"

"Alright, he knows boats. Has he ever been under fire?"

Well, let me see…"

"Why do I think I'm being set up?" exasperation was starting to creep into MacDonald's tone. "Are you enjoying this?"

"A little, but seriously you need to hear this. I know this kid personally. He was in the mountains with Castro in the *revolution*. His decorations are *Good Conduct Medal*…"

"Whoopee."

"Wait one. He was an E-7. You should relate to that."

"I'm listening."

"Three *Commendation Medals*, two *Purple Hearts*, two *Bronze Stars* with V,…"

"That's enough!"

"Oh, no. I'm not finished…*Soldiers Medal, Silver Star, Legion of Merit,* and…*Distinguished Service Cross.* Now I'm finished, and it's not Audi Murphy. It's Thomas MacDougall Scott II.

"Screw you. Just send him down with orders for thirty days."

"Jim, one more thing. You remember when we were down at *Puerto Cabezas* the last day of that goat-fuck in Cuba. The pilot who flew Somoza's F-51 to Cuba was his father."

"Damn. I'll look for him tomorrow. At least he has an acceptable name," was MacDonald's last word.

At 0700 the next day Scott reported.

"*Tomás*, my young friend, you are "*in the Navy now,*" as the expression goes. Your orders will be cleared in time to catch the 1200 hrs. flight to Tan Son Nhut, and you are authorized to take civilian travel to Saigon. Lieutenant MacDonald will meet you at the Continental Palace Hotel at 1600 hrs. You *will* recognize him. Anchors aweigh! *Buena suerte.*"

"*Muchas gracias, Coronel.*" As he left he wondered why all sergeant majors had that same smirk on their faces.

He met the same transportation officer at the airfield. "Leaving already, Scott?"

"Yeah, Jeff. Just too much luxury around here. I'm going to Saigon to rough it for a while." Both laughed.

"Well, you have a little better transportation this time. You get to ride the Caribou."

The CV-2 Caribou was the third type of rugged Canadian "bush plane" the Army had purchased from de Havilland. It was a larger, twin engine, high tail airplane with STOL capability, 72.5 feet long, and could carry 32 soldiers for 1280 miles at 180 mph. Scott remembered parachuting out of one at Ft. Bragg from the rear loading ramp.

CHAPTER 17

SAIGON

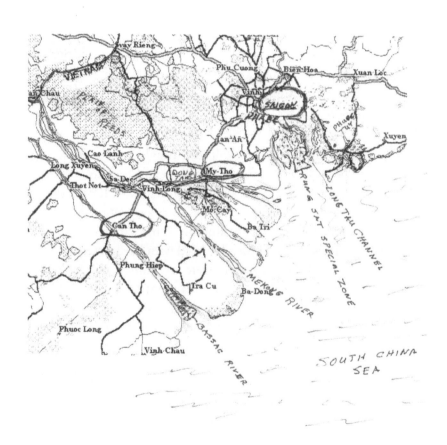

He arrived at the Continental Palace Hotel (formerly the Continental Hôtel in French Colonial times) in the center of Saigon's business district. He stood on the sidewalk in front and stared at this classic old French colonial building, as he waived off the bell hop who had rushed out to take his duffle bag. It had been built in 1880, only two years after its namesake, the Hôtel Continental in Paris. For a moment, he was back in Paris on the corner of the *rue de Rivoli* and *rue de Castiglione* about to escort a pretty girl to the hotel bar. The chatter of French along the sidewalk tables only enhanced the illusion, until loud American voices and laughter drifted through the open door.

The spell was broken. He went to the front desk to ask if the French desk clerk knew Navy Lieutenant MacDonald. On hearing a very Parisian accent the clerk was delighted to tell everything he knew about *Le Lieutenant,* which was substantial. The clerk even suggested he take a stroll down *Duong Tu Do* (Freedom Street, formerly *Rue Catinat*) while he waited. The clerk put Scott's duffle bag behind the desk for safekeeping.

As the cab had sped and dodged through Saigon traffic with its mixture of cars, motor scooters, trucks and bicycles, he could only glimpse the scenery and smell food mixed with car exhaust. Now he could walk along the tree-lined streets with the shops and restaurants and watch pretty young girls in their colorful *ao-dai* dresses split up the sides. French blended with Vietnamese cooking smells, as well as language. There were few uniformed Americans and bars catering to the military at this point in time, and he enjoyed a quiet coffee at an outdoor cafe. He made a mental note to come back and buy Maria Consuela a silk dress for the great sum of less than $10.00. If there was a war going on somewhere out there, he couldn't tell.

By 1600 hrs. he was back at the hotel desk while the clerk checked in and out an assortment of tourists, businessmen and reporters. The clerk looked up and over Scott's shoulder. A large grin spread across his face.

"*Bon jour, Jean Pierre.* This must be the famous Lieutenant Thomas MacDougall Scott."

"*Absolument, Lieutenant MacDonald, c'est le homme.*"

Scott turned around to see a short, husky, dark-haired man in a Hawaiian shirt, jeans and deck shoes. "And this must be the infamous, if not notorious, goat-fucking, French speaking Scotsman, Lieutenant James MacDonald."

"Now that's a hell of a way to talk about your new commanding officer, MacDougall, but it's all true. I can see this is going to be '*the start of a beautiful friendship,*' just to quote a line from *Casa Blanca.*"

"Aye, aye, SIR. You do know that the Clan MacDonald is just an offshoot of the older Clan MacDougall?"

"I heard that from a Limey sergeant once…before I knocked him on his ass." Both men laughed as the clerk stood opened-mouthed at this confusing greeting.

"Come on, Scott. Let's go down the street and get a drink before these reporters start asking you for an interview just so they can file a story without leaving that bar in there they call *The Continental Shelf.*" He turned to the clerk, "*Merci, Jean Pierre,* for babysitting my friend." The clerk looked puzzled but his grin widened.

The two men strolled down the street. Shop keepers and waiters called out their greetings to MacDonald, and he to them. Scott was thinking this lieutenant is really living up to his reputation. A rain squall swept down the street and Scott ducked under a restaurant awning. It was the rainy season now. MacDonald seemed to ignore the rain, as if it was just spray over the bow, but he did sit down, and they had a cup of coffee with chicory.

"So, MacDonald, how do you know French?"

"Short long story. My father immigrated from Scotland. I joined the Navy in WW II. During the war I met a French girl in England. She was a county girl. That's why my French is not Parisian, like I heard from you when I walked up. It was true love. She did love America, but she didn't like being a Navy wife. I still have two kids back in the states. Now, what is your story? Rodriquez told me about your father. I didn't personally know him, but I did see him fly out that last day. I couldn't figure out whether he was the bravest sonofabitch I ever saw or the craziest."

Scott looked at the rain for a moment. "No. He was just Cuban."

"Well, that does say it all. I trained a lot of 'em in those old landing craft who never came back. But how about you? Are you just a Cuban? I understand you don't have to do this shit, if you don't want to. Are you looking for more glory, crazy, or both?"

"Don't know. Maybe I'll find out watching you. You're still here after Normandy."

Now it was MacDonald's turn to stare at the rain. "We may both find out on this shit-filled river soon. Let's go take a look at your new home. We're all quartered in a little hotel down by the river."

They walked to where the Navy jeep was parked. Scott reached in and swept off the puddle of water on the seat. MacDonald just sat in it and gave his introduction spiel.

"The Navy got more than a little upset a few of months ago when *Charlie* sunk the carrier escort *USNS Card* right here in Saigon. I guess they told you why we call him *Charlie* from our phonetic alphabet *Victor Charlie* for VC, Viet Cong. Anyway, the VC just swam out there from the sewer, attached explosives and blew a 12 foot hole in her side. The Navy refused to admit it was sunk. They said it was damaged and repaired. But the Navy has been worried about ships being sunk in the 20 mile long shipping channel coming in from the sea. The majority of the country's commerce comes up this river, to say nothing of the war material coming in. So, the Navy wants to see if we can make it secure with small boat patrols. They promised the best boats, but sent junk. We had to send a couple to the Philippines for repairs the other two we fixed up here. Look down there. They are designated LCPL, Landing Craft Personnel Large, 36'x 10' powered by a Detroit 6-71 diesel engine. They're just glorified crash boats. They only "land" at docks. The old WW II LCPL had a different bow and actually shoved up on the beach to land marines. But we fixed them and begged, borrowed and stole what we needed."

Scott looked down on the docks at two boats rigged with two .50-caliber machine guns mounted fore and aft, .30-calibers on each side amidships, a radar mast and shark's teeth and eyes painted on the bow.

"Why the shark's teeth?"

"Well, they sent me up here from coastal patrol in the Mekong delta. Would you believe, they use old sailing junks down there. Nobody goes up into the rivers. All the junks have dragon eyes painted on them for superstitious reasons. So we went one better. It's also good for morale."

Scott took another look and smiled. "I like it."

"Good. Tonight you'll be an armed passenger."

"You patrol at night?"

"Yep. That's when the VC like to move around and the government has a curfew time, but today we'll leave in the daylight so you can see this mess of rivers, canals and mangrove islands they call the *Forest of the Assassins*. I've already told everyone that you know the pointy end of the boat from the flat end, and that you know how to fight, and you've been shot before…and once upon a time you were an NCO. So, they know not to fuck with you too much. It just happens we are short one enlisted man and one officer. The ensign assigned to me got some kind of bad fever, and they sent him to the hospital. The EM took a slug in the gut and was evacuated back to the states. I also try to rotate men for a day off once a week, just to give 'em a break.

We have a crew of eight   on each boat including a couple of Vietnamese to translate…and fight. Let's get you situated with quarters. We have weapons on board."

By 1730, with an hour of daylight left, the two boats pulled away from the quay and headed downstream. Scott was in the lead boat with MacDonald for his "orientation." Without taking his eyes off the river MacDonald said, "We'll just throttle up the engines to 14 knots and drive down the main shipping channel in the Lòng T⊠u River to the entrance. It'll be dark by then, and we'll work our way back by radar in one of the side rivers that split off and come back to the main channel. Officially, the Vietnamese Navy covers the main river. We never tell anybody where we're goin'. We usually catch some VC sampan trying to slip supplies around, but most are just fishermen violating the curfew. The VC are supposed to have a hospital and supply dumps back in that maze, but the Vietnamese Army and Navy prefer not to go in there. Probably smart of 'em. They don't call this the *Rung Sat* **Special Zone** for nothin'."

The next twenty minutes Scott spent matching spots on the chart as MacDonald called them out. "That's *Nha Be*. It's the last friendly place." Turning to his crew, "Everybody suit up. Uncover your weapons."

Scott noted everyone put on their armored vest and checked the four machine guns. He put on the one a sailor handed him. He could hear bolts of the machine guns slamming rounds into chambers ready for action. He was thinking about the tremendous amount of steel that could be flying off this boat at the enemy, plus the assortment of other small arms and an M 79 grenade launcher, which looked like a giant single-shot shotgun that fired a 40 mm shell.

MacDonald seemed to read his mind. "Yep, we can tear up the countryside with this stuff, but they have some too…and 57 mm recoilless rifles sittin' in concealed positions. We had to learn to recognize what to look for along the trees and grass."

"Jim, what are you using to trade for this equipment when you can't requisition it?"

MacDonald laughed, "Now you're startin' to sound like a sergeant. We trade whatever we can capture from the VC. The REMFs like to show it off like they captured it themselves."

"I saw a VC flag below. Did you capture that?"

"Yeah, but my guys like to keep those."

"Well, I bet if you go to one of those dress shops they can make plenty of them. All you have to do is dirty them up some and shoot a few holes in them. I also bet I can get you some of those brand new night scopes from the army supply depot in Saigon."

"Shit, why didn't I think of that. Sonofabitch!" was MacDonald's reply.

The helmsman, Petty Officer 1st Class Jason Uszkowski, standing at the wheel next to the officers volunteered, "That's a hell of an idea, Lieutenant. We could sure use something besides radar to look on the dark banks of these rivers. Welcome to the boat, Sir." Several of the gunners were listening to the conversation and nodding their heads.

"Thanks, Ski. Mind if I drive for a bit? Looks like you're going to need a break before this night is over." Uszkowski looked at MacDonald.

MacDonald shrugged his shoulders, "Hell, Ski, he knows the *pointy end* goes forward." They all laughed.

The wheel felt good in Scott's hand, and he had a better feel of the engine vibrations. "Brings back a lot of memories. Keep narrating, Skipper. I'm all ears."

Scott was gaining popularity fast. He had already helped the engineman adjust the injectors and shown his knowledge of the big machine guns. The crew was forgetting he was Army not Navy.

Saigon was disappearing as the river twisted and turned through the palm and mangrove covered banks. The church steeple was the last thing to disappear. Only a glow in the sky from the city remained as evening and rain clouds closed over the river. Ships had continuously passed in the channel coming and going both to Saigon and across the Cambodian border farther west to Phum Daung. The LCPL stayed out of the main channel, because the boat only drew three feet or slightly more when heavily loaded with ammunition.

MacDonald interrupted his thoughts, "It's easy to understand the Navy's concern if the VC sunk a ship in the channel, but the VC have their own interest in allowing small ships to come in to and down from Cambodia. A lot of VC supplies were unloaded or dropped overboard at convenient spots on this twisting river. Occasionally, we catch 'em. Then somebody in the government cuts a deal, and the ship goes on its merry way. *En Viet Nam c'est la vie et c'est la guerre.*"

"*Et c'est la pomme de terre (and that's the potato)*" added Scott.

MacDonald laughed, "Damn, I haven't heard that in a long time." He looked in his radar scope. "About twenty minutes and we'll be in *Ganh Rai* Bay opening onto the South China Sea and turning to starboard around the point at *Can Gio* and back up the *Dong Tranh* until it doubles back into the shipping channel. Ski, take the helm so I can show Scott on the chart. We'll turn off our lights when we're out of the shipping channel and *see* what we find in the dark. You just got the cook's tour. Now we get down to business."

Rain made it even darker as the radar tried to pick up objects on the river. The green glow from the radar screen reflected off the edges of MacDonald's face as he tried to sort through what the screen was picking up. "Ski, ten degrees off the port bow. It looks like a fisherman's sampan. About 100 yards. Ease it down. Let's see what he's up to."

Scott could see men moving to their positions and guns being checked. He heard MacDonald order "Lights." The rain had stopped and the makeshift searchlight seemed to light up the whole river. Two surprised fishermen threw up their hands in surrender. One Vietnamese sailor questioned them and checked their documents while another searched the sampan. They were just fishermen violating the curfew. The same scenario was duplicated four more times before the river merged into the shipping channel.

As they started to turn the corner MacDonald nudged Scott, "Looks like we got some activity up here. They're pickin' up something from the river, and it ain't fish. Ski, throttle up."

The bow lifted up as the engine rpms suddenly increased. The searchlight came on, but these fisherman picked up rifles instead of raising their hands. The forward .50 cal. started firing a hail of steel on the first boat as Ski angled the boat so the midship .30 cal. could bring his machine gun into action. The second LCPL kept out of the light and in the shadow behind the lead boat in support for any surprises. MacDonald's boat was now firing on the second sampan trying to get into the mangroves. From the shore green tracers arched out at the lead boat. That was the surprise the second LCPL was waiting for. Its red tracers tracked into the source of the green ones. Scott had picked up the M-79 grenade launcher and popped one into the tree line. Everything went quiet except for the whining roar of the diesel engine. By the time they reached the sampan, nothing was left except splintered wood. A fisherman's float was tied to a line, which turned out to have a bundle of weapons tied to it.

"Well, well, more gifts from our friendly Cambodian sailors. Wilson, throw the grappling hook around down there and see if any more *gifts* are there." The sailor came up with one more wrapped bundle with ammunition. MacDonald turned to Scott, "Hey, MacDougall, looks like we did earn our keep tonight after all." Over his shoulder he called, "Andretti, break out the British rations for good work, but don't tell the admiral."

"Aye, aye, sir. White Horse coming on deck. Shall I signal the number two boat?"

"Absolutely! They have their own Horse."

Scott could see in the faint light that Andretti appeared with a bottle, and he could smell the Scotch. MacDonald turned to Scott, "Don't worry. Everybody only gets a swallow as we head for the barn. Best damn thing I remember about the old British Navy. You're the guest. You first," as he handed him the bottle. Scott smiled in the dark, took his swallow and handed it to Ski, who passed it around.

'No wonder they love this guy,' Scott was thinking as he listen to the chatter and laughter of the sailors. The night's tension was fading, and they were full speed ahead for Saigon before the dawn started to creep in behind them.

The crew spent an hour servicing the engine and cleaning weapons for the next time. There was no grumbling about being tired and sleepy. They knew what had to do, and it would save their lives.

Scott and MacDonald left to take on their scavenger hunt and to order some VC flags made. MacDonald knew where the Saigon Depot sergeants ate breakfast. It was easy pickings until it came to the new night scopes. One Master Sergeant E-8 wanted to ride along so he could verify the *war trophies* he was trading for. The officers knew he just wanted to say he had been in the action and would get his picture taken to prove it.

"Why not? We can have you back in time for breakfast. Can your fire a .30 cal. machine gun?" MacDonald watched his reaction closely.

"Hell yes, Lieutenant. I'm a Master Sergeant in the Army. I handle those guns every day."

Scott smiled to himself. Probably the last time this sergeant had to fire any weapon was in basic training years ago. His required qualifications were most likely just more forms he filed. Scott couldn't resist, "Sergeant, what do we tell your commanding officer if you're killed or seriously wounded? You know the VC doesn't just hand us this stuff."

The sergeant's eyebrows knotted together. He hadn't considered that possibility. "I'll think of something. That's what supply sergeants do," he said very carefully.

"Good. We can always use an extra hand. 1830 hours at the Navy dock. You know where we are. We need to go get some sleep now," MacDonald said as they stood up to leave the table.

On the way out Scott asked, "Do you think he'll really show up?"

"Don't know. I just hope he has a good excuse for being on board. We do need those night scopes. You're going to take the number 2 boat and the rest of the Army with you. Let's go buy some flags."

At 1830 boat engines were warming and crewmen were checking weapons...again. US Army Master Sergeant Lehberger, George F. showed up in new starched fatigues with a Colt Model 1911A1 .45 cal. pistol on his hip and *ready for action*. He did have an excuse for his CO...sort of.

This trip was the reverse of the previous night. The radio started to hiss *Ssssshhhht* "Commo check. This is Rat 1 to Rat 2. Come in."

Ssssshhhht "Rat 1 this is Rat 2. I hear you 5 by 5. Over."

Ssssshhhht "Roger. Rat 1 out."

Master Sergeant Lehberger asked, "What other weapons do you have on board?"

"We have a BAR (Browning Automatic Rifle) and several M 2 Carbines. You're assigned to one of the .30 cal. machine guns in the Number 2 boat. The crewman will be loading for you."

Scott had the crewman subtly check him out by pretending something was wrong with the gun. Scott could see the sergeant was already breathing hard. Everyone in the crew understood the purpose of this charade…except the Vietnamese sailors.

"Well, I'm glad you don't have any of those new AR-15s they call M-16s now. Guys in the field have been having a lot of problems with them malfunctioning. Give me an old M 1 rifle, a .30 cal. machine gun and a carbine anytime. They've already been tested in two wars."

One of the crewmen chimed in, "Yeah, the Navy sent us AR-15s. We traded 'em to the Vietnamese Army. They like 'em, because they're new and light weight. Our government sent 'em lots of ammunition and Korean war stuff that works a lot better for us in this salt water."

Several fishermen were searched in the next two hours before live contact was made. Rainclouds and darkness had completely enveloped the boats. The sergeant was wiping more sweat off his eyebrows than from just the heat. "Jesus, how can you see what is happening?" he whispered to Scott, who explained they had to rely on the radar to keep their interval with the Number 1 boat who was sweeping the river ahead. He had already explained the backup duty and support of the Number 2 boat. "I think you can understand why we need night scopes."

Ssssshhhht "Rat 2 close up. Contacts on port bow." Lehberger wiped his sweating palms on his now unstarched fatigues. The spotlight lit up the sampans making for the shore as the engines throttled up. The sailor next to the sergeant put his hand on the sergeant's shoulder, "Steady, Sarge. Don't fire until we see what's on shore. We're hidden behind the Number 1 boat's lights." Small arms fire came from the sampans at the lights. Return fire from the .50 cal. in Number 1, then the .30 cal. as the helmsman angled the boat. Immediately green tracer rounds arched toward the Number 1 boat. The light went out and the .50 cal. on the bow went silent but the stern and port midship guns were still firing.

"Shit," came Scott's voice. "Open fire."

The .50 cal. on Number 2 opened up at the source of the tracers. A second source of tracers streaked over the Number 2. "NOW, Sarge, track your fire to the source of the second tracers." Lehberger grasped the trigger and forgot everything he knew about firing in burst. He just needed to release some tension in that direction in a continuous stream of fire in the area of the enemy. Tracers streamed back at Number 2 sending wood splinters as some rounds tracked across the deck. Lehberger dived for the deck, as if the wooden hull would offer protection. He hit his head on the motor box on the way down and lay stunned on the deck. The Navy gunner kicked the sergeant's limp body out of the way, stepped back to his gun and poured accurate fire on the VC second gun, along with the stern .50 cal. Hot brass from expended rounds rained down on Lehberger's now bloody face. The cut on his head made a puddle of blood among the empty shell casings.

Firing stopped. The five minute engagement seemed to have lasted all night. Number 1 boat was inspecting what was left of the sampans. *Ssssshhhht,* "Rat 2, you OK?"

Scott looked back at the gunner and Lehberger, who was leaning against the motor box as he sat on the deck. "He's OK, Lieutenant. He just bumped his head when he dived for cover. He did get off a few rounds."

Scott chuckled and turned back to the radio, *Ssssshhhht* "Roger. OK. The sergeant bumped his head."

Ssssshhhht "Andretti got hit pretty bad on the bow. We need to get him back full speed."

Ssssshhhht "Roger. We're following. Out."

An ambulance was at the dock by the time they arrived. They were fortunate to be in Saigon with a major hospital close. Lehberger was still groggy, but he had his head bandaged and salve on his face burns acquired while on the #2 boat. He was taken to the hospital for observation and a couple of stitches. A 'ragged VC flag' was stuffed in his jacket by Scott before they loaded him in the ambulance, and the crew told him what a good job he did.

MacDonald stood watching the flashing lights of the ambulance disappear down the street. "Well, Scott, that turned out pretty good, except for Andretti."

"Yeah, short another man, but I bet we get some night scopes, maybe even through proper channels. He's definitely going to remember how dark it was and those green tracers coming out of the dark. I say we give the master sergeant. a Purple Heart for all those *battle injuries.* I'm sure all those tracers must have burned his face and grazed his forehead," Scott said with a wink.

"Shit, Tom. We might even recommend him for a Bronze Star, if that insures us of a steady supply of our needs. He's goin' to remember this as we tell him, and be bragging about it for the rest of his life."

Other members of the crew stood around them, laughing and nodding their heads.

And so it went for the next three weeks. Some active patrols and some quiet. The Army's new generation of night scopes which utilized ambient light from the moon and stars magically appeared. The shore looked a lot different at night with the new scopes. A few new men were assigned including a brand new ensign just out of the Naval Academy (Ensign Polk, Travis J.).

During the last couple of weeks the Navy had decided to insert their new commando types, SEAL units, for reconnaissance and ambushes to disrupt the VC in their *Rhung Sat* sanctuaries. They were delivered by LCPL to a designated point and picked up the next day at another spot. Meanwhile, they were on their own to move and hide in the enemy's back yard. On Scott's next to last day on the river they received an urgent *Mayday* message from one of the units relayed by a Navy helicopter flying over the area. The unit had been ambushed and had retreated to a peninsula. The boats were already headed in that direction for a scheduled pick up in a different spot. The coxswains throttled to maximum rpms and the radio man tuned to the designated radio channel.

Sssssshhhht "Snake 3, Snake 3. This is Rat 1, over." The radio operator reached over and twisted the squelch knob to reduce the static.

Sssssshhhht "Rat 1. This is Snake 3. Do you read?"

Sssssshhhht "Snake 3. We got you. What's your situation?"

Sssssshhhht "Rat 1, we are trapped on peninsula at *one zero niner five three one* by company size Victor Charlie unit, 1 kia, 2 wounded, low on ammo. I say again *one zero niner five three one.*"

Ssssshhhht "Snake 3, we'll be there one five minutes. Hang on."

Ssssshhhht "Rat 1, don't stop for beer."

MacDonald laughed in spite of himself, "Fucking SEALs."

Ssssshhhht "Scott, you hear all that?"

Ssssshhhht "Roger, I'm checkin' my map for those coordinates."

Ssssshhhht "Just follow me, as they say in the infantry."

Ssssshhhht "Roger that."

Ten minutes later. *Ssssshhhht* "Rat 1. This is Rat 2. We picked up some trash on the prop. Need to clean it off."

Ssssshhhht "Shit. Come as soon as you can. I'm goin' in."

Ssssshhhht "Roger, understood. "

Scott cut the engine and sent a seaman over the side to cut the trash off the propeller.

Ssssshhhht "Rat 2, this is Snake 3. Rat 1 just took a recoilless 57 round through the hull. Goin' down by the stern."

"Goddamnit!" *Ssssshhhht* "Snake 3 can you see the gunner?"

Ssssshhhht "Rat 2, I can see the smoke. He's just around the last bend waitin' on you in the palms."

"Polk, check the chart for a spot where he can't see us before we get there."

"Aye, Aye, sir … About three hundred meters port side, sir."

Scott, was thinking, 'Here's where I get to play soldier again and practice my Vietnamese.' He turned to the starboard gunner. "Rader, get out that BAR with five magazines and give it to the strongest Vietnamese and find me a smoke grenade, any color."

By now the crew understood what he intended to do. They all volunteered at once.

"No. The boat needs you guys, and I need a Vietnamese. Polk, you're in command. Here's what I need you to do. When you see me pop smoke, come barreling around the corner guns blazing. I'll have Snake 3 put smoke on his position. Everything in between is free fire. Got it?"

A wide-eyed ensign shouted, "Aye, aye, sir. Everything between the smoke."

Scott slapped him on the back. "Good man. Now, get me two M 2 carbines with ten clips and four grenades for both of us ... and a canteen. I'm goin' to be thirsty after this." The nearby crew members smiled and shook their heads.

Scott turned to explain to his Vietnamese sailor with the BAR and the magazines of 20 rounds each in a back pack. Scott hoped the adrenaline would help him through the weight. It weighed almost sixteen pounds without ammunition. Plus he had two grenades.

Sssssshhhht "Snake 3, when you see my smoke, mark your own position with any color you have. We'll be on the ground behind ours. Understood?"

Sssssshhhht "Roger, wilco, Rat 2. There are Rat 1 survivors hiding behind the bow sticking out of the water."

Sssssshhhht "Hang in there, Snake 3. Watch smoke. Keep firing to cover the noise of our approach."

"OK, Polk, ease into the bank. Remember, not until you see smoke."

"Aye, aye, sir." Polk's eyes were narrowed and his mouth was a fine line.

Good, he's settled down, thought Scott.

The bow nosed into a tangle of vines stretching between mangroves and Nipa palms. One of the sailors jumped off and parted them for Scott and his *attack partner.* Mud sucked at their boots until they could reach firmer ground beyond the mangroves. Gunfire was closer now with rounds cracking overhead as branches were clipped off by friendly fire. Adrenaline was definitely helping both of them.

Sssssshhhht "Snake 3, shift your fire to the right."

Sssssshhhht "Wilco."

'Good boy,' Scott said to himself. Polk had realized what was happening and reacted.

The sun was going down. Scott realized he had to get where he could see the recoilless rifle gunner as quick as he could wiggle through the tall grass. He watched the tree line overhead for any indication of higher ground where the gunner might be. The

Vietnamese struggled along in his wake trying to keep the BAR out of the dirt and untangled from the thick brush. Scott could see a stand of palms twenty yards off to his right. A little closer he could make out the form of a soldier crouched in a half dug bunker ready to fire at the second boat. They knew LCPLs always traveled in pairs. Sweat was clouding Scott's vision and mosquitoes around his head sounded as loud as gunfire. He needed to eliminate this man without attracting attention to himself. The VC and SEAL rifle fire covered his last rush onto the man. His knife did the rest. He signaled his gunner to move off and get ready to fire. He pulled the pin on his smoke grenade and tossed as far as he could behind the line of VC trying to close on the SEALs, then fired the already armed recoilless rifle into the VC. He tossed one of his grenades and started firing both of the carbines at the same time. His man tossed a grenade and started firing his BAR. The effect sounded like a whole army had arrived at the rear of the VC skirmish line. The SEALs popped their marking smoke and Polk came roaring around the corner pouring steel between the two columns of smoke. Scott could barely make out the *poop* sound of the M-79 grenade launcher, but the explosion among the VC was definite.

MacDonald had a ringside seat as he peered around the hull of his half sunken boat. "Sonofabitch!" was all he could say.

As the remnants of the VC company tried to escape past Scott and his man, they fired wildly on them. The machine gunner was hit in the leg, but he and Scott continued to fire and throw grenades. The VC turned away from what they were sure was a large body of men and veered back into a hail of fire from the boat. The fading evening sky was lit up like the fourth of July with tracer rounds from the boat.

It had taken five minutes from the time Scott fired the 57 mm recoilless rifle round into the VC ranks. He could see the SEAL squad leader out among the dead searching for any intelligence that could be useful while his men were loaded on the boat. "Damn, that is some kind of training and discipline," he said to no one in particular.

"Mac, are you trying to live up to your "river rat" reputation swimming around in that shit river?" Scott kidded him.

"Fuck you, you crazy bastard. If I'd had a gun I'd probably have shot you up there thinking you were the VC. But thank you, kind sir, for your timely appearance. I really walked right into that one."

"Oh, bullshit. You were trying to save this crazy bunch of guys the Navy doesn't even talk about."

"I'll vouch for that, Lieutenant. The VC were about to over-run us when you came around the corner blazing away. We should have located that gunner before he shot your boat," volunteered the SEAL squad leader. He added, "Sorry about your men, sir."

The three men slowly turned and looked down at the bodies on the deck, one SEAL and four sailors. One sailor's body could not be found even in the sunken boat as they stripped off the weapons to prevent the VC from salvaging them.

The diesel engine proved its worth that night as it plowed up the river with two boat crews and a SEAL squad on board. The SEAL medic was examining the rest of the boat crew after treating the obvious wounded. He flashed a light on Scott. "Lieutenant, is that your blood or someone else's?" He moved the light up to Scott's face. "It's yours."

Scott felt his face. What he thought was sweat was now a sticky sheet of blood down his neck and soaking his fatigue jacket. He heard one of the sailors laugh, "Shit, Lieutenant, that's how my pappy marks hogs." He felt his ear and sure enough a nick was cut in the top of his ear.

"Ha. We finally got a name for you. *Hog man.*" gloated Mac-Donald. "That'll go with the scar on the other side of your face."

Scott glared at him, "Mac have you checked inside of your pants for blood-sucking leeches from that river?"

"Shit." MacDonald jumped straight up to the amusement of everyone who heard it.

The ambulance was waiting at the Navy dock for the wounded.

"Well, Scott, looks like your time in the Navy is up tomorrow. Sorry to see you go. It's been an experience. I think you better get that ear fixed. You got a lot more country boys in the Army who would recognize that ear marking. And…since you are officially in the Navy, your Purple Heart additional award is going to be a bronze star on your medal instead of an oak leaf. That ought to be worth a lot of conversation."

"*Merci, mon ami.* Your advice is well taken. I'll try to stay out of the mangroves." Both laughed with the crew members standing near.

Scott turned to Ensign Polk, "Looks like you are going to have a scar face like me with that nick in your cheek. Now you know what an AK 47 rounds looks like coming at you. Not many Navy officers do. Travis, you're going to be a fine officer. I'll look for you on the admiral list one of these days."

"Thank you, Sir. It was an honor to serve with you."

"It was my pleasure. You saved my butt and your commander's. Turning to MacDonald he said, "In addition to your Purple Heart, I am sure your CO will have a recommendation for valor."

MacDonald smiled. "Damn right."

Scott shook hands with each smiling member of the two boat crews and SEALs. "You guys almost make me wish I was in the Navy, but between this experience and long days on my grandfather's merchant ships, I think I'll stay on land for a while. Tonight the drinks are on me, wherever the Skipper says. Let's go get cleaned up."

"*Immediatement, mon heros.* I am sure you realize how much sailors can drink, and no duty tomorrow."

"Not a problem, *mon ami.* My company American Express card is good in Saigon, and my grandfather loves sailors. Throw in the food, too. And get that master sergeant there... and his CO. We'll give 'em something else to remember."

A loud cheer went up, and the lights of Saigon would get brighter.

CHAPTER 18

MEKONG DELTA

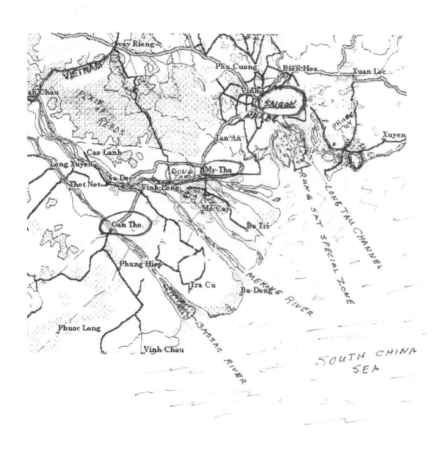

Scott reported back to Nha Trang and C-4 Team headquarters. "Good morning, Lieutenant. You got an earache there?" was the greeting from the sergeant major as he walked to the colonel's door. "Colonel, the lost sheep is back."

"Enter, *oveja perdida* (lost sheep.)

"Good morning, Colonel."

"Well, would you like to be in the Marines next, and collect some more Purple Hearts?" the colonel asked with a big smile.

"Thank you, sir, but I would like to stay in the Army for a while."

"*Bueno*, I need an S-2 Intelligence Officer. Since you have just had your experience in the delta, you'll do. We're finally going to get out of Group HQ and move down to *Can Tho* in the Mekong Delta. It's a captain slot. So, I put the paperwork back in to promote you. This time it won't be temporary. However, I do have this application for you to be a Regular Army officer, not a Reserve Officer. Sign here."

Scott smiled, dutifully signed and accepted an additional obligation of service. "Thank you, sir."

"Hell, if you hadn't kept turning down that ROTC commission, you'd be a captain by now anyway. I see you already did the Infantry Basic Course and almost finished the Advanced Course by correspondence. *Excelente.*"

The colonel looked down at a file and tapped his pencil. "One other thing, Jim MacDonald called and personally told me the story of your latest escapade." The colonel shook his head. "Damn, Scott, I can't send you anywhere without you getting in trouble." Rodriguez paused, gave a sigh and said, "He is putting you in for the *Navy Cross*, since you were officially assigned to the Navy, and making sure the Vietnamese give you, Lieutenant Polk and your Vietnamese gunner their *Gallantry Cross*. Lieutenant Polk is also going to get a Silver Star for following your orders. Mac sends his sincere thanks again for saving his butt. Congratulations. Special Forces *is* proud of you." With that the colonel stood up and offered his hand. The sergeant major came in with a smile and offered his hand, followed by the company clerk. They all laughed and slapped

Scott on the back.

"Scott, go get settled. Tomorrow you and I are going to fly down to *Can Tho* in the Otter. *Can Tho* is the largest city in the delta with a history of almost two hundred years and has a decent little airport. The 1st Group already has a B-Team there which is about to transition out on their six months tour. I sent my adjutant, Major Mario Thibodeaux, down there to start squaring it away. He was in the 8th. Did you know him?"

"Yes, sir. We met before I went to Bolivia."

"Good. He is a fine Special Forces officer, even if he did go to West Point. I think he likes it down there in the delta. It must remind him of the bayou."

Scott smiled at the memory of the 'Cajun Captain who spoke *good* French, but spoke like a bayou 'Cajun the rest of the time, at least out of the colonel's hearing.

The flight in the Otter was like a scenic tour over the *Rung Sat Special Zone* and the *Mekong Delta* to the south. The pilot let Scott fly for a couple of hours, and he circled over the routes and firefight locations he had experienced with MacDonald to show the colonel. It felt good to be flying again, and he could feel how strong this plane was. It was no wonder the *bush pilots* loved it.

The old city of *Can Tho* sprawled out from the south bank of the *Bassac River* and was larger than Scott expected. The shape of the adjacent Special Forces base and the Air Force improvements to the airport were clearly visible.

Major Thibodaux stood up from his desk, saluted Rodriguez, and spotted Scott behind. "Hey, looky heah what dat Mekong done wash up, and he done got dem silva ba's too."

"Hey, *Majah*, I see you got dem mosquit' bite down heah. I done call 'Cajun Pete ta brung u dat bottle Dr. Titchena' ta rub all ovah yo body," was Scott's quick reply.

The colonel looked at one then the other. "I understand you two know each other. If I hadn't spent time in the Louisiana bayou training Cubans for the Bay of Pigs, I wouldn't know what in the hell you were saying." They all laughed.

"Yeah, Colonel. Dis heah Scott boy done save my ass in Nicaragua."

"He has a habit of doing those things," the colonel said with a straight face. "Now, Mario, how are we doing on this transition?"

The 'Cajun accent suddenly disappeared and Thibodeaux became a serious Army officer responding to his commanding officer. "Sir, we will have quarters, such as they are down here, expanded to accommodate the C-Team HQ next week. Not fancy but adequate. The communications net is ready. I have visited the A-Teams in this area and the other B-Teams in IV Corps will be expecting you this week. The B-Team from the 1st Group will be outbound in two weeks. I have my recommendations for our B-Team. The Air Force is building a pretty complete facility on the other side of town."

"Very good, Major, because you are now this B-Team's commanding officer."

Thibodeaux hesitated for a second with surprise, "Thank you, Sir. I have scheduled a visit to one of our A-Teams up on the Cambodian border along the Mekong River. A lot of activity seems to be going on, both on the land and river. They have a small dirt airstrip up there that can handle your Otter."

"Excellent. Now let's take a tour of this military resort, before we retire to the exclusive officers' club for some serious planning."

The SF facilities were typical military-temporary, Viet Nam construction with half sand bag and concrete walls, then screen up to a palm thatch roof. Machine gun emplacements were located at corners and everything was surrounded with barbed wire. The "club" was only distinguished by the salvaged bow of a small sailing junk serving as the bar. Its painted dragon eyes glared at everyone who entered. It seemed appropriate.

0700 the Otter was off the ground headed for the A-Team two kilometers from the Cambodian border and seventy-five miles from Can Tho. From the air they could see the small dirt airstrip alongside the village and a helipad closer in. The compound was bordered on one side by the Mekong River and with river irrigated rice paddies on three sides, bordered by stands of trees. The village was on the east side of a rice paddy. The open fields of fire looked good, but the tree lines and village offered some concealment for heavier enemy weapons.

The A-Team commander, Capt. Fritz Nitschke, met the Otter as it taxied to a stop in a cloud of dust. "*Bonjour,* Thibodaux."

"*Guten Morgen, Fritz.* This is Col. Rodriguez and his S-2 Tom Scott."

"*Buenos dias, Coronel y Capitan. Bienvenidos a nuestro palacio,*" was the captain's greeting with a surprisingly good Spanish accent.

"*Ja, heute ist ein guter Tag, Hauptmann.* (Yes, today is a good day, Captain)" Rodriguez replied in German.

Scott was thinking Thibodeau and Nitschke had done this routine before, and he wondered if this was going to be some sort of European language convention with this German captain. You never knew what nationalities you could encounter in a Special Forces unit anywhere in the world. He hesitated to chime in with his skimpy Vietnamese. So, he waited.

The colonel turned to Scott, "Tom, I know you speak French and Spanish. No German?"

"Colonel, I didn't meet that many German girls in Paris. So, I only know the appropriate words and phrases for the sensual occasion." That was good for a laugh.

"Fritz, let's show the colonel around and you can give him a briefing."

As they started toward the compound a familiar deep voice boomed across the field. "I'll be goddamned. You never know what the hell they're going to send out here next."

Scott smiled and turned toward the voice. "How you doin', Cuz?" His cousin, Big Chicago Tom Scott walked up, and they gave each other a big *abrazo,* which was more like a bear hug, to the surprise of the other officers.

Big Tom stood back and noticed the long thin scar on his cousin's face. "Hey, cuz. That's a nice looking saber scar you got there. How much you pay for that? In Chicago that's worth a lot more than any tattoo, but that hog marked ear ain't worth nothin'."

"Colonel, this *really is* my cousin. We even went to basic training together. We haven't seen each other for a while, and I didn't even know he was in this A-Team. Unfortunately, his name is also Tom Scott. I guess I'll be MacD again."

"I'll be damned. Now, I have to contend with two of you. Shit! *Hauptmann* Nitschke, you are in for a real experience," was the colonel's laughing response.

"Amen!" echoed Thibodeaux, who had thought his Scott surprises were over.

The two Scotts talked and walked behind the three officers as they entered the barbed wire gate. MacD stopped before the gate. Something had triggered an old feeling that he hadn't had since Bolivia. "What's that building, Cuz? It looks like some kind of temple."

"Yeah, that's an old *Cao Dai* temple with that one big old eye watching you. Not many people go there anymore. Just one old priest does his thing there."

MacD remembered reading that *Cao Dai* was supposed to be the only religion native to Viet Nam and incorporated elements of Buddhism, Christianity, Islam, Taoism, Judaism and an eclectic assortment of historical individuals as saints like Joan of Arc, Thomas Jefferson, Victor Hugo, William Shakespeare, Sun Yat-sen, etc. It was on the sensitivity list put out in Army guidelines in order to avoid offending the native population. They had rebelled once against the predominantly Catholic government, which resulted in considerable suppression of the religion. He hadn't paid much attention in *Can Tho* as to whether there was a *Cao Dai* temple or not, but something here was bothering him. He made a mental note to come back for a closer look.

The two Tom Scotts walked into camp with Chicago Tom explaining the layout. "We have a pretty basic plan here in this 100 yard rectangle, 30 cal. machine guns on the corners in between and up in the 30' observation tower, two 81 mm mortars in pits in the middle of camp. Some 50 cal. heavy machine guns would be a big help to reach out there, but the powers-that-be figure we are going to get overrun and the VC will get the 50s and shoot planes down. That's some kind of stupid thinking. Shit! The VC already have heavier stuff than we do, and they have a regiment running around out there somewhere with about 1,500 men. We've trained two companies of Civilian Irregular Defense Group (CIDG) with about one hundred men each, a small Luc Luong Dac Biet (LLDB) Vietnamese Special Forces unit to help train the CIDG, and fifty Cambodians. The Cambodes are good fighters but we lost a lot of them when the Army took over from the CIA. The CIA used to drop in a shit pot full of counterfeit Cambodian money to pay them. It looked real good too. Our lieutenant XO had to be evacuated because of some kind of infection from a shrapnel wound. So, we got eleven Green Berets here with less than three hundred Vietnamese troops, and we are sure some of them are VC. So, the VC got more men and more guns when they decide to do something serious. We usually get a few incoming mortar rounds at night just to keep us awake. This *strategic hamlet* thing ain't working out so well. We're getting reports of all kinds of units comin' up the trails from southern Cambodia just like they're comin' down the Ho Chi Minh Trail from the north. We call it the Sihanouk Trail. Our intel ain't so good way out here. But, shit, that's just *me* talkin' to *you*, cuz. You're goin' to hear it from the CO in a few minutes."

"What kind of weapons do you have out here, Tom?"

"Man, we got everything you can imagine left over from WW II and Korea. The CIDG like the light weight M2 carbine like you're carryin', but the LLBD have new AR 15s. The Army is gettin' the bugs worked out and they call 'em M-16s. We're supposed to get them, but I guess you already know that."

MacD nodded.

As they walked to the command center bunker, MacD could see the sandbagged and dirt wall around the camp with sharpened stakes facing out toward the rows of barbed wire. He knew somewhere hidden out there were Claymore directional antipersonnel mines detonated by remote control. It sprayed 700 1/8 inch steel balls like a shotgun out to one hundred yards in a 60 degree arc. It was named after the large Scottish medieval sword. A "fire arrow" was in the middle of the camp, which could be filled with gasoline to ignite and turned to indicate the direction of an enemy attack for air support. The problem was it could take forty-five minutes to one hour or more response time for air support, depending on action in other areas. In a large scale attack it could be over in a matter of minutes, depending how many casualties the enemy was prepared to accept.

In the command center, which was a sandbagged bunker with a thatch over log roof, Captain Nitschke started his briefing. It seemed to be simply a more formal scenario of what Chicago Tom had already said, with a more dire warning of what may be forming across in Cambodia.

At the end of the briefing Major Thibodeaux made a request, "Colonel, I would like to stay here for another day. A resupply helicopter will be here tomorrow afternoon, and I can catch it back. You can fly straight back to Nha Trang then without stopping at Can Tho."

"Very well". The colonel turned to look at his S-2, Capt. Scott, "And I know my intelligence officer is itching to stay here with his cousin to gather some useful first hand intelligence, which needs to be sent to me one hour after he returns to Can Tho."

MacD was thinking this colonel was getting too good at reading his mind. "Thank you, Sir. I think it would be very helpful."

"All right, gentlemen. Let's take a stroll around this palatial estate before I have to go back to shuffling papers around."

By 1400 the tough little Otter was on its way northeast over Saigon and on to Nha Trang 300 miles away, but not before the colonel had laughed and reminded the A-Team captain that he had two Tom Scotts in camp to cause excitement.

On the way back from the landing strip MacD again stopped in front of the old Cao Dai temple. Through the open entrance he could see the flicker of candlelight in the dimness of the interior. "Tom, I need to check this out."

"Not me, cuz. That place is too spooky for me. That big eye keeps lookin' at me."

Scott's eyes adjusted to the dimness in the temple. It was cooler inside, but the musty smell of years of darkness and humidity overcame the incense arising from the altar in a spiraling smoke spreading across the single room. He could feel more than see the rough stone floor. Candles flicked light and shadows on faded colored paintings on the ceiling and walls. He could make out a solitary figure of the old priest kneeling before the altar. Above the altar was a statue of Buddha, the primary influence in Cao Dai, and nearby a crucifix to symbolize the influence of Christianity, and writings in Chinese to celebrate Confucius. Symbols of Islam were scattered on the walls. Scott remembered that everything was to remind the worshiper that there was one God and all religions celebrated that God. Scott's mind wandered for a moment on the thought that it must be true. He had also read that there were still shamans in this religion all the way on the other side of the world from Bolivia, and they often conducted séances to talk to spirits.

The priest raised his head as if to acknowledge Scott's presence but never turned. He again lowered his head. Scott felt the tingle on his skin and a warmth spread over him. He could not tell if it was the excitement or his imagination…or the same things he experienced with *Amboró* at his death in the mountains…or what he felt with Maria Consuela…or what he felt with his grandmother. He sat on the cool stone floor, crossed his legs and closed his eyes, trying to feel something… anything that could make him understand. Words, phrases, colors flooded through his brain. Where was the clarity, the knowing he had felt not so long ago? Now silence came, not the silence before meditation comes, nor the shocked silence after an explosion when all senses are momentarily stunned. Confusion came. He had to get out. He stood up. The mustiness and dimness returned to his senses as he turned and left.

"Shit, man. You look like you saw a ghost. What happened in there?"

MacD shook his head and inhaled the hot, humid air outside. "Nothing, Tom, it's just the bright light after being inside. Just an old man in there. Let's go check the radio traffic."

Major Thibodaux was waiting. "Captain Scott, I want you to go out on a patrol today for a couple of *klicks* (kilometers) to get a feel of what's happening. You and your cousin will be the American advisers with a platoon of CIDG. You know the drill. Captain Nitschke is the only A-Team officer, and he needs to be here. Your counterpart with the CIDG will be Lieutenant Tri. You have an hour to get briefed. You should be back before dark."

An hour later the patrol filed out the main gate and passed the Cao Dai temple. MacD was surprised he felt nothing. He was interested to see that march discipline was pretty good. They walked single file on the dike separating rice paddies to the edge of the tree line. At the tree line he felt that combination of tingling and warmth. Then he noticed the old priest sitting quietly under a tree watching him. Even in his robe he looked more like a beggar with his tired eyes and scraggly white beard. The troops paid no attention, but he could feel the priest's eyes on his back as they walked down the trail into the trees.

The point man was now out front scanning for any signs of booby traps the VC may have set up in the night. Noise discipline was good, but they were not carrying extra equipment like they would for an all-night ambush patrol. The trees thinned out some and a foul smell came from the side of the road. A few pigs ran away as the patrol approached. It was obviously a pig wallow where they rolled in the mud and defecated while they were there. The smell seemed to cling to his clothes. Even on his grandfather's farms in Cuba and Homestead he had never gotten used to that smell. Out here in the delta it seemed worse. He did notice that the CIDG troops moved a little farther to the other side of the trail. Big Tom wrinkled up his nose and tried to get even farther away.

The patrol stopped short of the Cambodian border. MacD had been continuously taking photographs as they walked, while Big Tom oriented him. It definitely was not a stroll in the park. Strict noise discipline had been maintained and no one took their eyes off the trees and the terrain ahead. Now he walked to a rise in the land to take a series of panoramic views across the border and back toward the Mekong. He would later match them with the aerial photos he had been supplied for approaches and changes in patterns. Evidence of a lot of ground movement had been seen along the patrol, but no contact had been made with any VC. That indicated that the enemy did not want any notice. They certainly had not given up the area, but, more likely, they were planning something bigger than ambushes. The return was equally uneventful, but the same vigilance was kept up.

MacD noticed the priest was not sitting under the trees now, but in the fading light he could see a flickering of candle light inside the temple. "Tom, do you ever see that priest ever come or go or eat or even sleep?"

"No, man, I just stay away from that place. That damn eye keeps watching me."

"Tom, did you ever look at the back of a one dollar bill?"

"Why?"

"The same 'all seeing eye' is watching you. Here they say it is the left eye of God."

"No shit?"

"No shit."

Big Tom looked thoughtful.

They went into the command bunker for a debriefing of the major and A-Team CO. MacD had taken the unusual step of bringing a small amount of chemicals to develop his film in the field. Meanwhile, they went over the latest aerials delivered by the Air Force. Everyone agreed the lack of contact meant something big was coming. The team intelligence sergeant gave his assessment of enemy troop movements and strength. The operations, weapons, demolition, commo, and medical sergeants gave their readiness plans.

"Fritz, has anyone tried to talk to the old Cao Dai priest?"

The intelligence sergeant spoke up, "Captain Scott, he's just not very communicative. So, we leave him alone. We are pretty sure he's not VC, and the Army tells us to keep our hands off the religious people and places." The Team CO, Capt. Nitschke, agreed.

MacD looked at the major then the captain, "Is there any objection if I try. I dealt with a few shamans in Bolivia, and I married a girl who will be one soon."

Nitschke looked at the major, who took a deep breath. "Tom, I heard about Bolivia from Colonel Bergeron in Panama. I guess you may be the only man in the United States Army who could do this. OK." The team sergeants looked at each other, waiting to be told "the rest of the story."

"Thank you, sir. I think I will make a preliminary visit tonight. My photos should be developed when I get back." He left to walk back to the temple. The officers turned to the maps and the sergeants walked outside.

The intelligence sergeant turned to Big Tom, "Scott, is this guy for real? Is he really your cousin?"

"Will, I know this cousin. The major has been in combat with him and gave him a Silver Star. I heard the story about how he got the DSC down in Bolivia dealing with those shamans in combat. If he says so, by me it's true. I met his grandmother. She really was like a medicine woman. She had visions and all that stuff. Let's see what he says."

A silence went around the small group of sergeants. It was obvious they were thinking, *only in Special Forces.*

The candlelight seemed brighter in the evening, and the faded paintings were more visible. The priest was at the same place in front of the altar. The only difference seemed to be new candles beside the melted ones. Scott wondered if they ever scraped off the old melted wax. This time he selected a spot much closer to the priest before he sat down cross-legged again, on the stone floor. Once again the priest slightly raised his head in recognition of another presence.

Scott tried to focus his thoughts and energy on the priest without verbalizing his questions first in Vietnamese and then in French. "May we speak in the morning? May I communicate with my guardian spirits? May I see beyond the village?" A slight nod of the head was the answer he was looking for, and he left quietly. As if to reinforce this communication, several rats scurried out of his way to hide in dark corners. Their eyes glowed in the candlelight as he slipped into the humid night. It had been an hour of intense concentration.

Big Tom was waiting at the gate. "Did you learn anything?"

"Tomorrow. Tom, do we have any food that we can leave at the temple for him?"

"Yeah, I'll get the Vietnamese cook to fix him somethin' he'll eat."

MacD entered the command bunker and finished developing and drying his film. Then they compared it to the recent aerials. The major shook his head, "Damn, Scott. I have never had an S-2 do this before in the field. It sure looks like there was a lot of recent activity. Do you think you can get any more information from the priest?"

"Yes, sir. I do. It won't be in any format you will recognize, but I think I can interpret it for you." I'll go back at sunrise. I think we need a patrol out before dark tomorrow. I have an idea."

Captain Nitschke was rubbing the back of his neck and intently listening. "I have been all over the developed and the undeveloped world, and I always thought that there must be a way to communicate with these holy men. Now, I need to see this play out."

At sunrise Scott entered the temple with Big Tom guarding the entrance. This time the priest sat with his back to the altar and an empty food bowl in front of him. Several rats ran for the corners. Scott couldn't tell if it was the rats or the priest who had eaten the food. At this moment it was the least important thing. He carried with him his photos and aerials. He didn't know if they would be any use, but he needed to try. In Bolivia the CIA agent had told him that he had heard about a secret psychic program they were exploring called Remote Visualization with subjects who showed a particular psychic ability. To Scott it had sounded like out-of-body experiences to specific locations. His grandmother had told him that he had the ability, but he had never tried, nor had she tried to guide him.

This time Scott sat directly in front of the priest where he could look into his expressionless eyes. He placed a picture of his grandmother on the floor and his photographs and aerials beside it. For a long few minutes he stared into those expressionless eyes, concentrating his thoughts on his grandmother.

The priest finally moved his hand to cover the photo, and closed his eyes. Scott closed his. He felt the priest's other hand on his. The sensation was warmth and comfort. His grandmother appeared in his mind and said, "I am here, Tomasito. Everything is fine. This man can help you." Then the vision faded.

The priest placed Scott's hand on the aerial photo. He could see the camp and the river and the rice paddies with wavy lines, some thick, some thin, some near and some far. Some lines were doubled and tripled or spaced. Soldiers appeared and disappeared. Smoke and noise cluttered his mind. The squealing of pigs was mixed with voices and more loud noise and silence and more noise, then silence. He opened his eyes to find that the priest was again facing the altar with his head bowed. The only movement in the temple was the thin column of smoke rising from the incense straight toward the ceiling. There was no movement of air and no sound; only the shadows of candles dancing on the walls stirred the stillness.

Slowly regaining his awareness, he wondered what the confusing images could mean and what could *Abuelita* mean saying the priest could help. Scott quietly gathered his photos and stood up to leave. The priest never moved nor made a sound, and no rats scurried in the shadows.

The sun was up and bright in his eyes. In the distance rain clouds were gathering. Big Tom said nothing and followed him back to the command bunker. Major Thibodaux, Captain Nitschke and the intelligence sergeant were waiting. MacD held up his hand to indicate they should wait. "Pencil and paper, please," he asked. "Overlay, grease pencil?" He was trying to hold in his mind the images he had just seen and get them written down.

The sergeant put them on the rough table top that served as a conference table, and Scott began to draw. The group stood in silence while he drew lines and symbols, alternately closed his eyes then drew some more when he opened them. After ten minutes he stood back staring at the maps and markings on the plastic overlay. He made a few notes in pencil on the paper beside the maps and photos. Still staring at the overlay he asked, "Anyone have an idea on what we are looking at? I think we are looking at troop strength, locations and timing, but how much and when?"

"Jesus Christ," muttered the major.

"I'll be a sonofabitch!" exclaimed the intelligence sergeant as he gaped at the table.

Nitschke held his hand on top of his head and repeated several times, "I *knew* it. I *knew* it."

Big Tom had been guarding the door and now craned his neck to see what had happened.

Nitschke turned to Sergeant Scott, "Scott, get the LLDB commander in here quick."

Captain Tran Cung was an experienced soldier who had fought with the Viet Minh against the French, but as a Catholic he had fled south after the country had divided and the communist gained control of the north. He hurried into the command bunker, urged on by Sergeant Scott's excited summons.

The major looked up, "Captain Cung, we have come into some intelligence which needs your expertise. Take a look at this and tell us what you think."

Cung stared at the map overlay "Sir, this looks like a VC order of battle. How did you get this?" was his surprised response.

"We'll go into that later. Please tell us what we are looking at when we overlay it on our camp."

Cung leaned closer. "This symbol indicates a Main Battle VC Regiment with over 1,500 men with some heavy weapon elements added. The heavy dark lines I would guess are battalions, the lighter ones are companies and the dotted lines are probably skirmishers of platoon size. I do not see any date here or unit numbers, and I do not understand the spacing." He looked up from the overlay and spread his hands to ask for answers.

Nitschke spoke first, "Captain, do you believe the Cao Dai priest is VC?"

"Never, sir. The communist try to eliminate all religions. That is why I am in the south. But this could not come from a priest. He would not know these symbols or such an order of battle."

The major ignored the statement. "Do you have any idea about the spacing?"

"In my experience, Major, I have never seen this. Something makes me think there is regular North Vietnamese Army mixed in or guiding this. We are close to the Cambodian border and there are many NVA advisors there."

The major turned to Captain Scott, "Tom, got any feelings?"

"Yes, sir. The more I think about it, the more I think the spacing is a time element. Look at the very heavy lines behind the dotted skirmisher line. Compared to the other dark lines, that's more than a battalion, and you don't hold your largest unit in reserve. The platoon of skirmishers seems to be some sort of feint or to make us think it is a feint in order to concentrate our forces on the other side, because the density of fire would be weak. If we weaken this side too much this larger force would overwhelm it quickly."

Cung's eyes widened. "Yes, yes I see it. The space is timing. The extra heavy dark line has to be a reinforced battalion which will rush in when we move our men to the other side."

Nitschke was slowly shaking his head. "Excuse me, sir. If this unit is as big as Cung says, there is no way we can hold them off with the resources we have. We have always known that they could take us if they wanted to take the casualties."

Major Thibodaux titled his head and asked, "Are you suggesting we make plans for evacuation, Captain?"

"No, sir. I am only stating the facts. Our air support cannot stay in the air just waiting for an attack. The question is can we hold them off long enough once it starts. It will probably be in the dark also."

Captain Scott had been standing over the drawings, slowly tapping his finger on the spot where the larger battalion would be poised. "Major, I have an idea."

"We are all ears, Tom. These are your doodles."

Cung's head jerked up on that. He had heard that Scott had been in the temple. "It is you and that priest!"

The Americans ignored him. "Go ahead, Tom."

"If it is time you need, I recommend you alert the air support to be on standby *tonight* for movement on immediate notice. Maybe they can keep one aircraft in the air after midnight very slowly orbiting nearby for immediate support. I realize this is putting you on a very difficult spot, but if I can get in there after dark I may be able to create enough confusion that they will start shooting at their own elements in a cross fire. That should slow them up. There is going to be enough noise it will be hard for them to tell their own weapons from ours. With a couple of rifles and a lot of grenades I can create a lot of noise right in the middle of them."

The major rested his elbow on the table with his hand on his forehead. He slowly wiped his hand down his face and took a deep breath. "Tom, I know you are notorious for doing crazy and impossible things, but that is the craziest fucking thing I have ever heard. One man in the middle of a heavy battalion? Shit!" The room stood still.

"Sir, hear me out. There is a nice big, stinking pig wallow out there on the same danger side. Sergeant Scott can verify that the Vietnamese avoid it like the plague. I am sure Captain Cung knows it." Cung had to nod his head to that unpleasant fact. "It is nasty and you may not even let me back in the camp with the smell on me. But nobody in their right mind would go in it. As you remind me, that category fits me. All I have to do is stay low in that mess and nobody will come near me as I lob grenades and fire a couple of carbines at both sides. Besides, maybe all this is just a bunch of crap and the VC have just moved to another area. In that case you have lost nothing except some aviation fuel and one stinking captain in the camp."

From the corner Big Tom spoke up, "I volunteer to go support him, Major."

The major walked around the room rubbing the back of his head. "Fritz, now you see what the colonel was talking about with these Scott boys? What do you think?"

"I'm at a loss for words, Major. Maybe it is crap, but we cannot ignore it. Captain Cung you have my blessing if you want to take your LLDB out of camp tonight."

Cung looked straight ahead. "No, sir. I will go prepare my men and the CIDG for a real fight. I will be back to plan our defenses. Lieutenant Tri will take the patrol out tonight with Captain Scott and Sergeant Scott."

Thibodaux shrugged his shoulders. "Well, that seemed final. Tom, go get your act together. Fritz, gather your team and let's get to work. Like we say in the bayou '*Laissez les bon temps rouler*'." (Let the good times roll)

Outside Big Tom walked with MacD to the sandbagged quarters. "Damn, cuz. We really goin' to get in that shit hole?"

"Not *we,* just me. I need you for support with an M-79 grenade launcher. *We go makum big noise, chief.* Let's go take another look at the aerials and my close-up photos."

The enhanced aerial photographs clearly showed the extent of the pig wallow to be about forty-five meters wide and seventy-five meters long with the long axis toward the camp approximately one half kilometer to the east. MacD clinched both fists and stood up. "Beautiful. This gives me plenty of room on each side to move without being too near the VC. The tall marsh grass is even better. This location matches exactly where the battalion will be waiting to go into action when the camp has sent most of its men to the other side to defend the heaviest attacks. The length of this cleared spot gives them plenty of room to kill each other without trees in between. Man, these pigs have been using this for a long time. No wonder it stinks so bad. Look at this. There is even a trail worn into the ground by these pigs for me to crawl out."

Big Tom had been slowly shaking his head. "There're a lot of people I would like to throw in that shit, but I never thought I would be buryin' my cousin in a damn hog sty."

"Don't worry, cuz. I'm not done yet. This looks a lot better than I thought. Now let's find you a concealed place to lob one hell of a lot of grenades with that M-79 on both sides of this wallow. All the shooting should cover up that stupid little sound it makes. You're going to carry a pot full of shells out there. With all the noise from you and coming from the camp attack, I don't think they can even recognize the sound of their own AK-47s shootin' at themselves. There it is. See that little rise off the trail? You need to dig a rabbit hole to get in and cover it until they are all past you. When I start shooting and throwing grenades, you start poppin' 'em in there on both ends of their line."

Big Tom scratched his head. "How the hell are you goin' to see in there?"

MacD reached into his rucksack. "A little magic I picked up

from a supply sergeant in Saigon." He pulled out a night scope.

"Sonofabitch. They don't even let us have those out here on the edge of the world. How the hell did you get that?"

"Trade secret, but it did cost me three Viet Cong battle flags. The only trouble is it won't be much good when there are a lot of muzzle flashes messing up the starlight. Once I get out of the firefight it should be good again. Remember, we only need to keep enough confusion goin' until air cover can get here. When that happens we need to get way out on the trail and away from bombs and napalm. We might need to spend the night as guest of Cambodia. OK. Let's get back to the command bunker and see what they have set up."

The crowd around the maps on the table included the two American officers, the Team Sergeant, Intelligence Sergeant, and the two Vietnamese officers, Captain Cung and Lieutenant Tri. The two Scotts stood off to the side until they were called.

The major looked up. "Tom, you got your end figured out?"

"Yes, sir. We'll wait until you're finished."

"We're done. I hope. Captain Cung, Captain Nitschke will go with you now to start working with you on your defenses." He turned to the intelligence sergeant. "Will, wait with me for a minute. Fritz, I'll talk with you when you get back." He turned to Scott with a smile. "Now, Captain Scott, since we are assuming for safety sake that you are correct in your *intelligence*, let's see what you two characters are going to do to win the war."

Scott outlined his plan, with the request that the patrol return to camp in a group that would confuse any VC in the village counting heads of troops going out and coming back. The intelligence sergeant just stared at the map. The major started rubbing the back of his head again looking at the ceiling.

"You men understand what your chances are of getting back here, even if you screw up their plan."

MacD nodded, "What I do know is that if we can't screw up their attack and this battle plan is correct, it's not going to matter, AND if my *information* is wrong you will have a story and a stink to hold over my head the rest of my time in the Army."

The major laughed. "You got dat right, *garçon*, an' Colonel Bergeron gon be dah firs' mon ta heah it." Scott had to smile at his reverting to a 'Cajun accent.

The sergeant was still staring at the map and shaking his head. He offered a few helpful suggestions, including taking an HT-1, a small, black plastic, hand-held radio the CIA had developed for paramilitary units in Viet Nam. It used eight flashlight batteries and had a one mile range. It could also be used just to send prede-termined *clicks* to avoid voice transmissions and increase the range. He nodded to Big Tom and left.

Big Tom was relieved he didn't have to carry the 26 lbs. AN/PRC-10 back pack radio, considering the amount of 40 mm am-munition he was going to carry for the M-79 barrage that he would need to lay down. He could fire six rounds per minute, and there might be a lot of minutes.

"Gentlemen, I suggest you go get some sleep. It's going to be a long night whatever happens." The major then turned to the ra-dio sergeant to send an encrypted message on the situation expect-ed. Obviously, the reference was to a *good intelligence source*, not a priest and remote viewing.

Evening came quickly, and Lieutenant Tri and his LLDB ser-geant hand-picked twenty of the best soldiers for the patrol in or-der to avoid any possibility of VC infiltrators. Several carried bags of extra M-79 ammunition for Big Tom. For anyone watching it looked like a typical patrol with the usual two American advisors. The patrol would bunch up in the dark as they returned into the camp in order to make it impossible to count how many returned.

The walk out for two kilometers was uneventful in a fading light. The quiet only served to heighten tension. It was a sign that the VC were avoiding contact until they were ready. There was just enough light for MacD and Big Tom to identify the locations of where to drop out of ranks. They carefully picked their way out to the extent of the patrol area then returned. The Scotts dropped off a little more than a kilometer from camp. There was no moonlight, but there was enough starlight to operate the night scope. MacD was always impressed with how clear the sky was out here. The stars looked like you could walk across them. It had been the same, sailing in the Caribbean between islands. He had to push his memories aside and concentrate on the uncertain job ahead.

Big Tom's spot behind a small rise had to be quietly scooped out and camouflaged. Brush needed to be arranged to hide, as much as possible, the muzzle flashes from the M-79. Hopefully, there would be so many flashes from rifle fire and exploding grenades it would not be noticeable.

"Well, cuz, try to drop your grenades on the outside edges and work in. That way you won't illuminate the ranks firing at each other. I hope they won't recognize who they are firing at until it's too late. You know where I'll be crawling out of the shit before any air strike comes in. Remember these guys in the back are going to sit quiet for the first part of the attack until they think the camp's focus is on the other side. At first you are only going to hear the thin line of skirmishers on this side trying to fool the camp. So don't get itchy. I'm only going to start firing when they start to move forward."

Big Tom noticed that he had been squeezing his M-79 so hard his hands were hurting. He thought to himself, *Shit, man. Relax.* To MacD he whispered, "Just get your ass back here before that napalm starts comin' down. We got to get the fuck over into Cambodia."

"No sweat." MacD bent low and slowly made his way one hundred meters down the trail to the wallow. There was no mistaking its location. It was almost 2300 hrs. before he reached the edge. There was no sign or noise indicating any troops in the area. He sat on the edge to put off going in as long as possible and took out his night scope. The bright image was magnified so much by the starlight he had to put it down for a second. He looked again and scanned the area around the wallow as far out as the image would show. Nothing showed but trees and tall grass around the wallow. An hour more, and no sound. He was beginning to think this may be bogus. A slight splashing came from the wallow. His heart jumped a couple of beats at the thought the VC was already here. He heard an unmistakable grunt of a pig. Raising his scope he could plainly see a large pig exiting ten meters away. It stopped and raised it ugly snout into the air to determine what the different smell was in his wallow. Obviously, he determined it was an unpleasant human smell, gave a disgusted snort and trotted off.

The pig had trotted off about fifty yards when it gave a squeal and ran in a different direction. A Vietnamese voice gave a low curse. His heart skipped more beats, and he cursed himself for not continuously scanning. He eased into the stinking mess trying to keep his two M-2 carbines and bandoliers of ammunition magazines out of the knee deep water and ooze, less aware of the smell than what was coming. He could see in his scope what was an advance scout easing through the woods, more soldiers were coming down the trail. The pig had momentarily distracted the scout and probably made him more aware of the stinking wallow. He veered off at an angle away from the stink. Scott shifted his scope to the trail again. The column coming down the trail also angled away from the smell. It would have been funny under any other circumstance, Scott thought. It had to be the advance line of skirmishers for the first feint. Several were carrying 57 mm recoilless rifles. The thought flashed through his mind that he had locked in on the imagined plan so much that he was losing flexibility. He tried to focus back toward the border for the main body. He hoped Big Tom had sent some quiet radio klicks back to the camp signaling that the attack was coming. He pushed up the sleeve of his fatigue jacket to look at the luminous dial of his watch. It was 0130 hours.

Fifteen minutes later he could make out a much larger group moving into position on both sides of the wallow. He could hardly believe this was the same scenario he had seen and put on the overlay.

0230 hours in the camp, defenses were set on all four sides while they waited for indications of an attack. The CIDG companies were spread evenly. Sentries were set on the river bank in order to watch up river and for any landings along the bank out of sight of the tower. Claymore mines were set on all sides. There were never enough to satisfy the demolition sergeants. Captain Nitschke was in the 30' tower in order to command all corners and direct the machine gun from its sandbagged protection. Captain Cung and Lieutenant Tri each commanded a CIDG company with their LLDB personnel scattered in the ranks. The 81 mm mortar crews had their aiming stakes and coordinates set for any direction needed. The LLDB had their 60 mm mortar ready to support. Nothing more to do but wait.

In the command bunker Major Thibodaux, the intelligence sergeant and one of the communications sergeants sat sweating in the heat under a sandbag covered roof. The sergeant reached for the HT 1 radio. A series of clicks were clearly audible. "Major, Sergeant Scott is signalling that a small force is headed this way and a much larger force is waiting at the designated spot."

"Shit, this thing is actually playing out. Get the message out quick for air support. Will, let the captain know." The commo sergeant turned to his AN/GRC 109 radio and rapidly tapped out preset Morse code messages. A series of rapid dots and dashes flashed back. "Major, they say it will take an hour to get air support. The reconnaissance plane just returned to refuel."

"Goddamn it. Tell 'em we don't have an hour."

A loud *whoosh* and whistling noise signaled incoming mortar fire, sending men into holes and hugging the ground. Then two more, followed by sharp *whaamm* explosions in the middle of the camp. Sand filtered down in the command bunker and the single electric light bulb swung violently over their heads. The commo sergeant frantically threw a poncho over his radios as explosions were even closer. The tower personnel tried to determine the direction. Simultaneously, small arms fire erupted from the west side and the distinct *swoosh* of rocket fire from 57 mm recoilless rifles, followed by explosions in the middle of the barbed wire. Large gaps were opened. Everything but the volume of fire indicated an attack from the side facing Cambodia.

Nitschke was shouting from the tower that he could see flashes on the other side from mortars. Captain Cung had climbed the tower to the sandbag machinegun emplacement and was shouting in Vietnamese for one platoon of CIDG to move to the east side. He had also determined that this was a feint. Now gunfire was coming from the river side as sentries tried to get back into the camp behind the relative protection of the dirt and sandbagged perimeter walls. Machine guns had started to fire on all sides as the full attack began. Mortar shells still rained down while men ran from one side of the camp to the other, alternately throwing themselves flat as mortar shells signaled their incoming flight. The Special Forces men remained focused, popping rounds out of their 81 mm mortars from sandbag emplacements as fast as they could pull powder increments and drop in shells. The attack across rice paddies was relatively easy for them to cover. Recoilless rifle rockets flashed over the camp and crashed into the defensive walls. Demolition sergeants waited beside the Claymore electronic firing devices watching for enemy troops trying to advance through the wire.

BAMM, a Claymore had detonated sending a spray of steel balls toward a VC group trying to get through the wire. VC on the west side kept up small arms and some recoilless rifle fire, but made no move to breach the wire. Small boats with machine guns appeared on the river to support an attack on that side. The machine gun in the tower sank them quickly. Somehow rocket and mortar fire were missing the spindly structure of the tower.

One kilometer away, MacD Scott squatted in the middle of a stinking pig wallow listening to the gun fire and the muffled booming sounds echoing through the trees. No movement was evident in the group waiting in the woods. A whistle sounded and men begin to stand up. It felt like ten chills ran up Scott's spine as he reached into his bag of grenades. Now the stinking mess felt like protection, and he didn't want to leave. He suddenly wanted to crawl back out the pig trail away from this stupid idea. Too late. The VC started to move. His hands were frozen around two grenades which he had already unconsciously pulled the pins. He couldn't turn them loose. He had to throw them as far as he could. The realization jolted him to action. He couldn't smell the stink anymore. His senses were all tuned to throwing. He threw the first to his right then quickly the second to his left. The *ping* of the safety lever flying off of the first was followed by the second within seconds. He was sure they could hear that *ping* all the way to Cambodia. It only took five seconds to explode in the middle of the group closest to the wallow followed by the second on the opposite side. The explosions were deafening in what had been dead silence. Before the sound of the second had subsided, Scott had both carbines firing on full automatic in one direction then the other. He didn't care if he hit anyone. The combination of grenades and rifle fire should cause sufficient confusion. He ducked and moved ten meters back toward the trail throwing two more grenades. Simultaneously, he could hear and see explosions on both ends of the VC line. Big Tom was doing his job. He raised his carbines over his head while he knelt in the ooze firing in one direction then the other. The VC were starting to fire back blindly in the direction they thought the firing was coming from. Big Tom was pouring in a rapid barrage up and down their lines. He had been right. With all the explosions, it was hard to tell what kind of rifle was firing. He threw two more back towards the edges of the wallow. The VC fire intensified and Big Tom's M-79 grenades were squeezing in from the edges. Directions of fire were becoming hard to determine and the surprise had caused the VC to fire wildly at flashes from the other side of the wallow.

"Keep firing, Tom." He shouted out loud in the middle of the noise. For good measure he raised up and emptied the twenty round magazines of both carbines. He felt sharp stinging pain in his back driving him down into the muck. He gasped for breath trying to hold his head above the water. One carbine was lost in the ooze. He tried to hold on to the other and crawl to the trail. Stinking water ran down his face as he tried to spit it away from his mouth. He had no idea how bad he was hit. The water was shallower and rounds were cracking and whistling over his head. He had a brief thought that at least his grandfather didn't have to crawl through shit in Santiago de Cuba, followed by a mumbled, "What the fuck am I thinking about?"

He could feel solid ground under his hands and knees. He wanted to just lay there whatever happened. Big Tom's grenade explosions were still numbing his senses. It felt better on his back by taking pressure off his arms. He tried to stand, but collapsed in a dizzy heap. *No. no. I can't die here in this shit.* He thought about

Maria Consuela and *Abuelita*. That was the answer. He had to concentrate on their faces, feel their strength. It was working. He could feel that warmth again. He couldn't see any blue glow, but strength was coming back. He turned to look back at the fire flashing back and forth over the wallow. Big Tom's fire was slowing but still effective. He felt in his bag. Good, the night scope was still there. They would need it. He lurched forward getting more strength each step. Only one hundred meters to the rabbit hole was his thought.

At the camp, mortar fire continued to rain down. One round made a direct hit on an 81 mm mortar emplacement killing the LLDB crew and an A-Team sergeant. Somehow it didn't set off the ammunition stored in a bunker alongside.

Captaim Cung had left the tower and was crawling along the CIDG lines directing fire. *Swoosh whamm* a 57 mm round hit the west side of the dirt wall near him throwing him back, killing several CIDG soldiers and leaving a hole in the wall. The sharpened stakes in the wall flew in the air and landed inside camp. Their sharpened points had missed any soldiers as they fell back to earth. Cung crawled out of the dirt and rushed more men to cover the breach.

Bamm another Claymore exploded on the east side where the VC were trying to enter a hole in the wire. A couple of machine guns went silent as the gunners tried to change the overheated barrels.

Major Thibodaux tried to exit the commo bunker to assess what was happening. He saw the tower slowly falling as recoilless rifle fire finally found its mark. He could see men around the tower trying to scramble away from the direction of its fall. He thought he saw Nitschke jumping from the far side, but a mortar round exploded near the entrance to his bunker. The blast force blew him back inside as shrapnel whistled through the bunker. He lay on the floor stunned with blood coming from holes in his arms and legs. The commo sergeant was shouting in his face. "Major, can you hear me? HQ says air support is on the way." The major nodded through the ringing in his ears. He was still alive and feeling was returning, but the wounds were starting to burn as the hot metal fragments seared the entry points. A team medic crawled through the entrance, cut the major's uniform where shrapnel entered and bandaged the blood flow. Thibodaux was fully conscious now. "Sergeant, get back to the serious wounded. I had worse than this when a goddamned 'gator bit me down in the bayou. Just help me up. Can anybody see Captain Nitschke?" *Bamm, bamm,* two more Claymores went off on the east side, clearly distinguishable above the rifle fire.

"Sir, we haven't seen him since the tower went down. Captain Cung has that machine gun back firing. I saw Lieutenant Tri go down. We've lost two team members and three wounded. We can hear explosions off to the west and no push has come from that side. Sounds like Sergeant Scott and his M-79 working on that group back in the woods. A push came from the village side, but we beat it back with machine guns and the LLDB 60 mm mortar. We only had to use two Claymores there so far. The attack from the east seems to be slowing some. They must be waitin' on that group in the woods to do somethin'."

The major had to smile in spite of his wounds. "Goddamn, it's working. The air cover should be here soon. Let's get out there and give some encouragement to those brave sonofabitches. *Laizzez les bon temps rouler!*"

MacD had run and crawled about seventy meters. He was feeling better every time he looked back to see firing back and forth across the pig wallow. A voice came out of the dark, "Cuz, is that you, you stinkin' sonofabitch." The strong hands of Big Tom grabbed him and drug him back to the rabbit hole. "You alright?"

"Yeah, but something got me in the back."

Big Tom ran his hand under MacD's fatigue jacket and across his back. "Shit, man. I can feel a piece of frag' stickin' out. Grit your teeth and I'll pull it out."

"Do it. ...Aahh, shit. That hurts."

"Grit your teeth some more. First take a drink of this. I ain't got any antiseptic. Just bandages and rum for antiseptic. Have a swig first, before I pour it on you."

"Jesus Christ, Tom. What the hell are you doin' with rum out here? ...Aahh, that burns."

"Have another swig. I figured you'd need it, and if you didn't make it I'd just get fuckin' drunk before they got me."

MacD laughed in spite of it all. "What the fuck would I do without you, cuz?"

"Be damned if I know. I just hope the air cover gets here before those dumb shits realize they're shootin' each other. My M-79 barrel is damn near melted."

"I hope you have one more illumination round to mark 'em for the Air Force."

"Got it. Sounds like the camp firing has slowed some. You were right. With all those flashes in the woods nobody seemed to notice my muzzle flashes in this hole. But I think there is some kind of command element back about one hundred meters and off to the left. I could hear shoutin' and radio static."

MacD pulled out his night scope and wiped off the lens. "Damn, you're right. Let's see if we can catch a prisoner."

"Shit, man. Are you fucking nuts?"

"Well, they are between us and safety.

Big Tom thought about it for a moment. "Fuck it. Why not?"

They began a slow crawl in the dark with MacD periodically checking his night scope. "Jesus, Tom." He whispered, "One of 'em is a damn North Vietnamese general. We need to shoot the other four."

"I'd like to shoot the fuck out of all of 'em."

"Negative. Let's get within twenty meters. The general is on the right. The little light they have while they're looking at their map will give you an outline of the others."

Thirty seconds later, "Ready, cuz?"

"Fuckin' A."

Both rifles fired knocking down all except the general, who was startled into inaction.

MacD had forgotten about the hole in his back as they rushed forward. Big Tom knocked down the general with the butt of his rifle. Three of the soldiers were killed and the fourth was seriously injured.

The map light flashed on MacD's face. The general's face flashed in recognition. "*Tomasito, no me mata.*" (Tommy, don't kill me.)

The sound of Spanish and his name startled MacD. He took a closer look at the general. "François de Rousseau?"

"Si."

"*No es posible*," was MacD's response.

"*Si, si y este es mi hijo. Por favor ayudale.*" (Yes, yes, and this is my son. Please help him.)

Big Tom looked around. "What the fuck, cuz? You know this sonofabitch?"

"Unfortunately. I'll tell you later. Tie him up with the others' belts. I need to check out this one. It's his son."

"Shit, man. We got to go."

"Wait one!" MacD responded in a surprisingly strong manner while he turned to the young captain moaning on the ground. He had an apparent chest wound with air bubbling out of his chest. He tried to think back to his combat first aid cross training. He had only seen this once before. "Tom, give me a compression bandage. Do you have any syringes?"

"No, man. Just a morphine syrette in case you were hit bad."

"Hit him with it and give me the empty. This guy's got a sucking chest wound."

"Shit, man. Leave him. Let him die."

"Can't do. His father saved my father's life, your uncle."

"Oh, fuck."

MacD took the empty syrette, tore off the back and inserted the sharp pointed end as far as he could in the chest to release the pressure built up from the punctured lung. "OK, help the general carry him and let's get out of here."

The sound of airplanes could be heard. "Tom, fire an illumination round over those VC."

They hurried as fast as they were able toward the Cambodian border. Behind them the world lit up with the orange and yellow flames as napalm and thick black smoke spread over the wallow MacD had just escaped.

They moved as far from the illuminated area as they could.

There was no more strength to make another kilometer to the Cambodian border. The general remained quiet with the threat that they would let his son die if he shouted to the remainder of the VC troops fleeing past and back into Cambodia. Some had their backs still flaming with napalm. The smell of napalm and burning flesh on the wind blowing from that direction was nauseating.

In the camp the fire arrow had been turned from the east and was now pointing to the VC on the west side under Big Tom's illuminating round. The napalm bombardment was clearly illuminated in the west in the beginning morning twilight to the cheers of the troops in the camp. Captain Nitschke had been found grinning and grimacing among the tangled pieces of the tower with a few shrapnel wounds and a broken leg. An urgent message had been received from Big Tom in a clear voice over his hand radio requesting immediate medical assistance. Captain Cung personally led a CIDG platoon out for security until a medivac helicopter could arrive.

The helicopter briefly landed at the camp to drop off the Scotts and their main prisoner and pick up more wounded before it flew back to Can Tho.

Major Thibodaux sat staring at General de Rousseau. He hadn't changed from his bloody and cut fatigues, but he was grinning. He had already been told by MacD that the general was half French and had been a friend of his father. "*Bonjour, general.*" A relatively friendly and courteous conversation flowed in French. While being complimentary to Captain Cung, Thibodaux had refused to turn the general over to the Vietnamese interrogators. This one was a matter for senior US military intelligence as soon as another helicopter could arrive.

MacD had tried to wash off the smell and thrown away his fatigues and boots. The medics shot him up with antibiotics, cleaned the hole in his back and gave him a fistful of pain killers. He stood in the morning light looking at the wreckage and still smoldering holes where mortar rounds had landed. The CIDG dead were laid out near the gate and covered with ponchos, waiting for relatives to claim them. The VC dead were still piled in rows where they fell trying to get through the wire. He wondered how anyone could have lived through it on either side. He looked beyond the gate at the smoking pile of rubble that used to be the Cao Dai temple. He was told no one had survived when a VC mortar round made a direct hit. He suddenly felt very, very tired. It seemed even Death had its fill and left the area.

Colonel Rodriquez received the message that the camp was under full scale attack by what appeared to be a regiment size unit. He rounded up his sergeant major and the Otter pilot. By sunrise they were in Can Tho and caught a ride on a medivac helicopter to the camp. They were met by the team operations sergeant and escorted through shell holes to the now ragged command bunker where Major Thibodaux sat stiffly on an ammunition box. Pain pills had helped but moving was a problem. He had refused to be evacuated.

"Jesus, Mario, what a mess."

"Ain't it the truth, Sir, an' dat Scott boy done save my ass *ag'in.*"

Rodriquez smiled at the return of the 'Cajun accent. "OK, tell me about it."

Thibodaux related the whole story "...but he still stinks. I think you should leave him out here until he smells better, besides they need a team CO. Fritz won't be back."

"Consider it done." The colonel sat quietly for a full minute staring at the floor and slowly shaking his head. "Mario, are you thinking what I am?"

"Absolutely, Colonel. No way they could deny him the Medal of Honor, and we don't even have to talk about the priest."

"Agreed. How about the cousin?"

"Distinguished Service Cross all the way."

"Done. Where do you have this general?"

"He's over in the officer's quarters with Scott and two A-Team guards. Capt. Cung's got the red ass because I won't turn him over."

"Good. We'll give him a medal. That ought to pacify him."

The major laughed and flinched with pain at the same time. "Roger that, Sir. He actually deserves a good one. He held the defense together."

"Get your shit together, Mario. You're going back to Can Tho on this medivac."

The colonel entered the room that served as sleeping quarters. The first thing he saw was a tall man in ill-fitting Vietnamese black pajamas with sandals on his feet speaking Spanish. "Tom, is that you?"

Mac.D. stood up and tried to salute but the pain in his back only allowed him the raise his arm half way.

"At ease. Sit down before you fall down. What happened to your uniform?"

"Sorry, sir. I had to burn it and my boots, or they would have run me out of camp from the smell. I only came out here with one uniform, for a one night stay."

The colonel smiled. "I heard about that. This is the famous general of Cuba and North Vietnam? I've heard the story." Turning to the general he said, *"Buenos dias, General."* They exchanged greetings in Spanish with a pleasant conversation about the beautiful Cuban countryside and assured the general that his son was now in an Army hospital and would survive. Now was not the time or place for high level interrogation. Both knew it.

The colonel turned to leave. "Tom, get a uniform and boots from one of the sergeants. I'll send your things. You look ridiculous in that outfit. Besides, you are now the A-Team commander."

Fortunately, life at this Special Forces camp continued to be relatively calm, because the A-Team was short four members. It seemed the loss of a VC Main Battle Regiment and a general had substantially reduced activity in the area. His A-Team, with Big Tom, from whom he had extracted a promise to continue picking up college courses, had rotated back to Ft. Bragg when their six months was up, and he had gone back to the C-Team in Can Tho to finish his tour. He had learned several weeks later about being recommended for the Medal of Honor. By that time it was being fast tracked through the Pentagon and up the chain of command. Lieutenant Colonel Rodriguez had already taken affidavits from most of the A-Team, Captain Nitschke and Major Thibodaux. Old Tom had let several war decorated Florida congressmen know about it, including the Chairman of the Armed Services Committee. Everyone who had ever met him was acknowledging it, including the Army Deputy Chief of Staff. Colonel (soon to be General) Bergeron continued to say, "I'm not surprised," when he read it in the US Armed Forces newspaper, *Stars and Stripes.*

CHAPTER 19

STAYING IN THE EAST

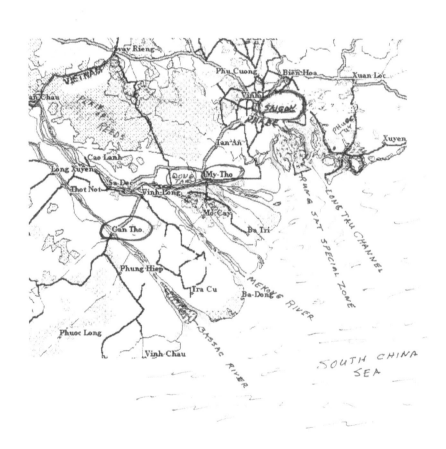

Mail had finally caught up with now permanent Captain Scott. He learned he was a father of a son in Bolivia. Maria Consuela and Hildegard were doing well in their second year of medical school. General Barrientos, who had been elected as Vice President, had effected a coup with General Campos, and they were co-Presidents of Bolivia. The latest letter was a surprise. Lieutenant Colonel, (soon to be full colonel) Sean McCauley and Françoise were getting married in Hawaii before McCauley deployed to Vietnam. Maria Consuela had even suggested that they go to the wedding in Hawaii, since it would be at the same time his tour was finished. Scott thought she must be getting pretty independent from the *cacique* to suggest that. Bolivia was a long, long way from Hawaii, over 5,000 miles and no direct flights. The rest of the letter seemed a little formal to him, as if she were trying to tell him something. But he liked the idea and said so.

Scott was able to locate McCauley through Françoise and arranged to meet in Honolulu before the girls arrived. Flying back to Hawaii had a very different feeling than coming over. It was much different than returning from Bolivia. There was no feeling of stabilization or accomplishment. In Vietnam the people were either numbed by hundreds of years of one group or another marching through and turning their rice paddies into battlegrounds, or simply felt resignation while waiting for this group to pass. In this land, derived from the same people who spawned the ancient civilizations of South America more the 15,000 years before, there only seemed to be perpetual war-enabling corruption in the name of stopping an ideology not native to the land and supported by a western civilization unable to understand any of it, but willing to send its young men to war. Scott made a mental note to have a little philosophical discussion with McCauley based on his talks with de Rousseau after his capture and insights gleaned from the Cao Dai priest and the farmers trying to live their lives. The farmer wants to farm, the politicians want power and money, and the North has an idea…and a determined patience.

Scott arrived a day before McCauley and arranged with his grandfather to have a penthouse suite in the Royal Hawaiian Hotel reserved for McCauley and Françoise. The girls would arrive the day after. When McCauley arrived Scott gave him the now obligatory *abrazo*. Both were in civilian clothes, and no one paid any attention. "Well, Tommy, that's a nice Hawaiian shirt you got there. You don't look any worse for the wear in Viet Nam. From what I see in *Stars and Stripes,* you still can't stay out of trouble. I just wish I could see Bergeron's face. Actually, I'm sure he's proud of you."

"Thank you, Colonel."

"Ah, quit the colonel crap. No uniforms here, and after what we've been through you're like my little brother. In fact, I do have a little brother about your age…in the Navy."

"Thank you…Sean."

"Better. Now, I never got to Hawaii when I was coming and going from Korea. Show me some of the sights and give me a briefing, so I can sound like an expert when Françoise arrives."

"Roger that. First, let's check you in. Grandpa changed your dinky room for something more befitting a French bride."

McCauley looked suspiciously at Scott.

"Not to worry, big brother. It's his wedding present. You're going to love the view of Waikiki Beach and Diamond Head… whenever you come up for air." Scott couldn't help but smirk a little. "But we have a couple of hours left in the business day. Spalding, Whitman and Sterling have an office in downtown Honolulu where we can go make a couple of dollars."

McCauley looked very dubious. To him the stock market was like the crap table in Las Vegas where the house always wins. "Are you doing that shaman stuff to the stock brokers?"

Scott laughed, "Just a little bit. Sometimes I can pick 'em good and sometimes not as good, but I always look at the company and the industry first. I guarantee we'll make enough to have a good supper,"…and they did. McCauley could not miss the photograph of the company board of directors with a smiling Thomas Mac-Dougall Scott, the elder, in the middle.

Later over drinks at the Royal Hawaiian Hotel outdoor bar with fading sunlight reflecting off the breakers on Waikiki Beach and the great Diamond Head Mountain in the background, they had that philosophical discussion.

"What kind of assignment did they give you? Did you get much briefing on the country or the people or the politics?"

McCauley looked thoughtfully at Scott for a moment. "Why do I feel like I'm going to get a lecture in the guise of a briefing by a captain?"

"*Non, mon ami.* I'm just trying to understand what our government is thinking and planning, and give you a first-hand account of what I saw and heard."

"Well this shouldn't come as a complete surprise to you, considering the last two assignments you've had in the delta. Understand that all I know about what you did I read in *Stars and Stripes,* but you apparently had a good orientation in riverine warfare on the water and on the land alongside the Mekong on the Cambodian border, which does bring me to my assignment. It's no secret. Viet Cong infiltration and recruitment in the delta containing four-fifths of the population, including Saigon, and their resupply in the breadbasket, or I should say *rice bowl,* of Viet Nam is a substantial problem. Gen. Westmoreland and the powers in Washington have decided that we have to cut off this VC lifeline. It looks like they have read their history books on the Civil War riverine operation in the Mississippi delta. As you know, the Navy has been patrolling and interdicting in the delta and its navigable waters, but Washington thinks we need to infiltrate from the rivers onto the land in a joint Army-Navy operation. It's called *Mekong Delta Mobile Afloat Force,* but I'm sure we'll shorten that label to something workable. We'll have a reinforced brigade to go up river, land, fight and return to Navy boats, which will add covering firepower. The land is too soggy for traditional Army operations with tanks, armored personnel carriers, self-propelled artillery and trucks. I have the advance unit of one battalion to coordinate and give it a trial run to work out the details with communications, logistics and fire support with live combat operations...and, if I don't screw it up, I'll be a full colonel before the end of the year, thanks to you and the ambassador. Of course, the Army of Viet Nam will have to be integrated somehow, since they already operate in the area. As I understand, the Navy has been developing and testing a lot of new equipment to deal with the delta environment. You've probably seen some of their new stuff when you were at *Can Tho*."

Scott nodded his head, "Yeah, I've seen some strange looking watercraft. With all the guns and armor they look like porcupines. The French left their old *dinasault* boats with the South Vietnamese. Most of those had been given to them by the USA after WW II. Now the Navy is reconfiguring its old landing craft and putting faster small boats and armed mine sweepers in the water. The old PCLPs I served on in the *Rung Sat* are looking very out of date, but they proved a point." Scott went on to tell the stories of trying to coordinate with the ARVN and their political appointed officers and lack of motivation after years of war. He was careful to point out his experience had been with good professional Vietnamese soldiers.

McCauley sighed, "I have heard the reports of avoiding a fight for political reasons and misrepresenting defeat as success and political sensitivity. I heard the story of that Ap Bac debacle by the ARVN. Hopefully, creating a combined force of US Navy and Army supporting each other will be a more effective fighting group, utilizing, but not requiring, ARVN in critical roles."

Scott thoughtfully rubbed the back of his neck, "Well, these people have been at war for centuries while just trying to make a living. They just seem to be waiting for this one to pass also." With that he related the feelings and insights he had gathered from the farmers, the priest, common soldiers, and most of all, his conversations with General de Rousseau and his own father's experience with the Vietnamese guerillas in WW II, including Ho Chi Minh and Vo Nguyen Giap.

McCauley stared at the tops of the coconut palms for a minute and turned to Scott. "Tommy, I have been thinking about your experience in the delta all the way here. Would you consider coming back to the real Army and staying for another six months? You are exactly the person I need to give me and my staff the insight we need to put this together."

Now it was Scott's turn to stare at the palm trees. "I was afraid you were going to ask something like that. I don't think the Pentagon is going to like it. I was only wounded twice, but I understand they want to make some propaganda about awarding The Medal in Washington."

McCauley smiled, "Well, thanks again to you and the ambassador, I have a lot of people in the Army who think they owe me a lot of favors. I certainly could not and would not order you to do it, but changing orders, even for a hero, is not a problem. Just think about it. From now on this is my honeymoon, we won't talk about it anymore."

"OK. I'll think about it, but I need to have a long conversation with Maria Consuela."

McCauley looked out to the ocean for a moment. He had been told by Françoise what was coming, but that was for Maria Consuela to tell Scott. "Fine. That's all I can ask." He did not add that he had already put in an urgent request with his brigade commander to be forwarded to the appropriate parties in the Pentagon for Scott's reassignment.

The next morning they stood at attention and saluted as the bugler played "Colors" and the flag was raised over the USS Arizona Memorial in Pearl Harbor. Scott had seen it before, but the sight and feeling never failed to move him. They both looked down silently as water in a falling tide splashed over the rusting deck and against the remaining gun turret. Sea weed growing on the submerged hull waved in the current. After more than twenty years, oil still bubbled to the surface spreading a collage of colors as if the ship was weeping for the 1,102 sailors still entombed there. A brief tour of Honolulu sufficient to make McCauley an "expert" followed.

By late afternoon they were at the airport awaiting the flight from Los Angeles. It had been a long, long flight from La Paz to Mexico City to Los Angeles to Honolulu, but Scott had made sure they were flying comfortably in the first class section. Customs had been cleared easily in Los Angeles with both traveling under diplomatic passports. The first sight of the girls was at the head of the first class passengers moving rapidly down the concourse. Maria

Consuela sprinted the last fifty feet with Françoise immediately behind her.

Maria Consuela leaped the last five feet into Scott's arms and a bright blue flash lit up the concourse. Lights flickered out in the terminal, alarm bells sounded and emergency lights flickered on.

"Jesus, here we go again," laughed McCauley. "Break it up you two. Let's get out of here before they figure out who caused this mess."

That evening a wedding was held at the Royal Hawaiian Hotel's outdoor bar on Waikiki beach with the sun setting to their west and behind Oahu's mountains. Hotel guests were invited as they appeared, including several French couples who added to the pleasure of Françoise and Maria Consuela. "Here's to Françoise and Sean," toasted Scott and all the *guests,* "May they get up early enough for us all to go surfing in the morning."

Eventually, the next day the new couple did appear. Scott already had Maria Consuela and himself in the waist high surf, taking lessons. The surf in South Florida had not prepared Scott for this. He was surprised to see how well Maria Consuela could swim, but dipping her board into the face of a breaker to let it pass over her did prove a problem. Before the end of the day they were all able to ride small waves in an acceptable manner, much to the girls' delight and McCauley's surprise. The night was filled with nightclubs and a walk on the beach while Scott related his experiences in Viet Nam to the only people on that side of the planet who could understand his encounter with the *Cao Dai* priest.

The next day was spent sight-seeing with the "expert" narration by McCauley and a one hour drive to view the famous Hawaiian Pipe Line with winter surf of thirty feet and more at Waimea on the north shore. No one volunteered to try those breakers.

The next day they flew to "The Garden Island" of Kuai, with its beautiful valleys and cliffs. The Scotts left the honeymooners by themselves for a few days. Scott and Maria Consuela returned to Honolulu where they had some things of their own to sort out. Maria Consuela was quiet on the flight back to Oahu while tightly gripping Scott's hand and watching island paradise pass below. He knew she had something to say, but he waited for her. A long walk on the beach brought it out.

She started, "*Mi amor,* with you I have known love that I could not imagine, and experienced a spiritual fulfillment beyond my dreams. I have seen the outside world as I never thought I would. Nothing in my life will ever be the same. It will always be better. I have your child to love and teach. I have medical school to expand usefulness to my people and more influence in my country than I ever could have expected. All of this was because you came into my life. Now the time has come that we all knew would come. You have your life in the Army and your country, and I have my destiny. My father has stated a procedure to end our marriage, but we will always be tied to one another by bonds only the spirits can understand." She looked up with tears in her eyes, but that bright light still glowed behind the tears.

Scott could only look into those beautiful eyes, unable to speak, but he knew he did not have to speak. Between them everything was always on a higher plane. He nodded his head and they walked back hand in hand with the soft sea breeze in their hair with the sound of the ocean's approval … slow breakers swishing and bubbling over the sand and around their ankles.

Scott smiled at the moon coming up over Diamond Head. "*Bien, Luz de Mi Vida,* I will always love you. Now, let's go have a drink and light up the night." She giggled and put her head on his shoulder. They did light up the Waikiki night.

The girls left at the end of the week. Scott told McCauley, yes. New orders arrived for Scott and a C-135 arrived with McCauley's advance party of staff officers and senior NCOs for an overnight stop-over before heading to *Tan Son Nhut* Air Base over 6,000 miles away. The main body of the advance battalion would arrive in ten days. McCauley never admitted that he had requested Scott be transferred weeks before. He just left Scott to wonder how orders could be shuffled through the Army bureaucracy so quickly.

"Scott, I believe you know my Executive Officer."

Scott looked behind McCauley at the smiling face of Major William Jameson, his old basic training company commander.

"Indeed I do. Nice to see that oak leaf on your collar, Sir, and that you are back in the *real Army*."

"Well, that show you put on back at Ft. Jackson probably helped. I am very glad to see those silver bars on your collar. Colonel McCauley tells me that it took some pretty high powered influence to make you take off those sergeants strips, and I see you keep collecting fruit salad over your pocket. It's a small world in this Army. How is your grandfather?"

"He's fine and still ordering people around. I'll have to tell him you're here. I guarantee he'll say the drinks are on him, and I have the credit card."

McCauley turned to the rest of his group. "Gentlemen, on that high note let's get over to the Royal Hawaiian bar and take young Scott up on that offer." Scott walked to the hotel desk phone and called Old Tom in Miami to confirm it.

"Grandpa, I hope I didn't wake you up, but I'm in Hawaii with Sean McCauley and Major Bill Jameson. You remember Bill Jameson from Ft. Jackson. We're headed back to Viet Nam. Maria Consuela was here for the wedding, and we drank and ate a lot on your ticket. I'll write you about it. Now we're about to take the whole advance party to do more drinking. I love you. Here are Sean and Bill."

"Mr. Scott, nice to talk to you again. Françoise and I cannot thank you enough for your wedding surprise."

"Sean, that's one of the great pleasures of an old man to see his good friends get some enjoyment out of life. Give Françoise my love and be careful...and tell that grandson of mine that he can stop being such a hero."

"Roger that, sir. I'll try, but we all know he inherited that trait. Here's Bill Jameson."

"Mr. Scott, long time no see. It's an honor to speak to you again and thanks for the drinks you are about to buy these not so humble servants of our country."

"The honor is mine, Bill. Glad to see you are moving along in your career. You boys have a good time, and tell my grandson I am waiting on his letter."

"Roger that, sir."

McCauley grinned, "Well, I guess that confirms our license to be licentious for the night before that long plane ride tomorrow."

Over drinks and the sound of breakers on Waikiki Beach, Scott was introduced to all members of the advance party, which included artillery, engineering, medical, transportation and signal officers, as well as infantry, and senior NCOs. Then he gave them the "delta briefing," as he experienced it, while trying to downplay his own medals. But no one forgot that they were in the presence of two recipients of the Medal of Honor and the drinks were being bought by a third. After the third round before dinner McCauley could not resist relating the *Bolivian experience* and some of the more humorous and absurd escapades of *Sergeant* Scott and the natives. Scott just had to grin and bear it. No one knew him better than Sean McCauley. The dinner ended with a toast by McCauley to the absent patron of the night's food and drinks, "Here's to Thomas MacDougall Scott, the elder, recipient of the Medal of Honor in 1898 at the age of sixteen."

The long flight to *Tan Son Nhut* allowed sufficient time for recovery from the night before. The airbase with its large number and mixture of aircraft he could see on approach never ceased to amaze Scott. He had to laugh along with the aircraft crew at the group's initial reaction to their first smell of Viet Nam and the hot, humid blanket of air that enveloped them. It definitely was not Kansas. He had to admit he had *almost* forgotten the smell.

He turned to McCauley, who still had his nose wrinkled. "Not like that clean Bolivian mountain air. Eh, Colonel?" McCauley just shook his head and headed down the ramp. A truck was waiting on the tarmac.

A voice boomed across to the aircraft. "Goddamn it, Scott. Why don't you go home and give the VC a break!" McCauley looked up at the Navy Lieutenant Commander standing next to the truck.

"Looks like someone knows you, Tom."

Scott was grinning, "Yes, sir. It's that crazy-ass Scotsman, MacDonald, who swims in the shit filled river, and the damn Navy has even been crazy enough to promote him," he said loud enough for MacDonald to hear him.

"Fuck you, you insolent junior officer. Give your better an appreciative hug."

McCauley laughed. He knew this *abrazo* scene well. The remainder of the advance party looked on in some amazement, even though they had heard the story of *le lieutenant* over drinks in Honolulu.

MacDonald turned to McCauley, "Afternoon, Colonel. Don't mind us, we just went through some crazy shit together. I'm your liaison officer to get you down in the delta."

"Not a problem, Commander. I know Scott from way back. Glad to finally meet you. Tom does talk about you in a great deal more reverent tone."

"Damn, I'm sorry to hear that. Let's get you loaded and over to that Caribou at the end of the runway. We'll be flying 70 km down to *My Tho,* the province capital, then trucked over to *Dong Tam* where the Navy is dredging out a turning basin and filling in for a base. Your men will be quartered on a modified barracks LST (Landing Ship Tank) with hot food and showers. It will house 1,100 personnel…with air-conditioning, compliments of the United States Navy… that is when you aren't sloggin' and sleepin' in the rice paddy and Mekong mud with mosquitoes."

Scott was still grinning. "Jim, what the hell are you still doing over here?"

MacDonald grinned back. "They gave me a promotion to stay. What's your excuse? You already got more medals than you know what the hell to do with."

"Well, I promised the colonel's wife I would look after him, and my wife is getting a divorce."

MacDonald whistled and threw up his hands. "That'll do it every time."

The flight and landing in *My Tho* were uneventful and the truck ride to *Dong Tam* was hot and dusty, but short. The truck stopped in front of a long low building made from plywood and surrounded by sandbags and screened up to a palm thatch roof.

Scott laughed to himself, 'I've been here and done this before.'

MacDonald turned to the group, "Gentlemen, this will be a base to eventually hold twelve thousand Army and Navy personnel. You can see out in the river that beautiful old LST. I believe that is the same one I was on before the Normandy invasion. That is where you will be in air-conditioned comfort for the next week until your advance battalion arrives. We will have enough of these to create a mobile force afloat base for 5,000 personnel. They will move up river, along with support and attack boats, as we push the enemy out." Scott knew these ships were more of a treat than anyone in the party realized.

MacDonald and McCauley were becoming fast friends. Both had served in WW II combat as seventeen-year-old kids and a few years later in the Inchon, Korea landing.

They were transported out to the LST in the well deck of a modified LCM 6 (Landing Craft Mechanized) bristling with two .50 caliber machine guns, a 40 mm grenade launcher and a 20 mm cannon turret. "Gentlemen," MacDonald continued, "this landing craft was used in WW II somewhere. I know it's not the one I drove ashore at Normandy, because the Germans blew that one out from under me. As you can see, we have made a few modifications in armament. The metal rebar you see welded in a web along the sides is designed to explode VC rockets before they reach the hull or superstructure. Our armor is thick enough to withstand the fragments but not a direct hit. The canvas over your head is strong enough to bounce any hand grenades back into the water. She will carry forty troops at 6 to 8 knots, depending on the current, and only draws 2-1/2 feet. It will be the work horse of your brigade and will carry a platoon of soldiers. We call it an ATC (Alpha Tango Charlie) or Armored Troop Carrier, a *Tango* boat for short and radio designation." A little hesitation in his voice was not noticed by his audience, but soldiers in the well deck brought back too vivid memories flashing through his mind with German machine guns ripping his landing craft apart, men dying at his feet and the water swallowing him amid clouds of blood and swirls of beach sand.

But McCauley noticed, understood and spoke. "This same

sturdy boat took a lot of us ashore in a nice quiet ride at Inchon. They have really changed her with all this armor and weapons. S-3, you will need to develop a training program for loading and unloading here on these muddy river banks. At least you won't have to be climbing down cargo nets in a pitching and rolling boat in an open sea to get in these boats. This river looks pretty calm."

MacDonald smiled his appreciation for the break, and recovered his composure. "Better than that. You can see the pontoon platforms alongside the LST. On a smooth river loading is a piece of cake, unless you are clumsy and fall overboard in that river current. Then our Navy divers have to go swimming after you."

As he watched the Navy dredge pump up river bottom over dikes and muddy water flowing back into the river, one of the Army NCOs asked, "Do you see any action back here?"

MacDonald cupped his hand around his ear. "I think I hear the answer to your question." The whistling and swooshing sound of a 60 mm mortar round incoming was clearly heard above the dredge noise. Muffled explosions and large water spouts erupted in the freshly filled area. The next group exploded louder as they landed on dry land closer to the sandbagged buildings.

"Does that answer your question?" he said, looking down at the NCO taking cover behind the side of the boat. "That's why your orientation and training is going to be live. We need to keep the sons-of-a-bitches away from this operation. The Marines and helicopters try to keep 'em away, but they sneak in close enough to lob in small mortar rounds."

The barrage was short and did no damage except to the nerves of the men new to Viet Nam. MacDonald, McCauley and Scott stood topside among the guns as the ATC motored out to the LST. The sun had set and white clouds in the west glowed pink and red. Scott said more to himself than anyone else, "Red skies at night, sailors' delight."

McCauley turned to Scott, "What did you say, Tom?"

MacDonald gave a short laugh. "He's just quoted old sailors' lore. We tend to forget he was a seaman long before the Army. It's a truism frequently more accurate that the weather report. It means that when you see that red sky at sunset it will be good sailing in the morning, but if you see that "red sky in the morning, sailors take warning."

Scott smiled and nodded his head.

The formal briefing was conducted after supper in what served as the officers' mess or dining area. The food confirmed for the advance party the old saying, *The Navy gets the gravy, and the Army gets the beans.* A tall, thin Navy Captain with a tidewater Virginia accent and a Naval Academy ring on his slim finger turned and pointed to a map of Asia, then a larger one of the Mekong Delta. "Gentlemen, you are now floating on the end of a 2,600 mile journey this river started in the mountains of Tibet. The velocity has decreased from a rushing torrent through Tibet and China to a calm tidal river here. The river split into the Mekong and the Bassac near the Cambodian border then into eight exits into the South China Sea. The Vietnamese call it *Cuu Long Giag* or the River of Nine Dragons. They use nine because eight is an unlucky number. We have been patrolling the exits in Operation Market Time in order to intercept VC supplies coming in from the sea, and Operation Game Warden to patrol rivers. Washington has now decided we go beyond intercepting junks and sampans and carry the fight up the river and on the land all the way to Cambodia."

Scott and McCauley smiled at each other thinking of all the streams and rivers flowing down the Andes Mountains and ultimately into the mighty Amazon River on the opposite side of a continent on the opposite side of the world.

The captain continued, "Close cooperation between our services will be critical, and I am sure both of us will come up with novel ideas. I understand Commander MacDonald and Captain Scott have already worked together in the *Rung Sat* portion of the delta. The success of that experimental operation on the river and the commander's extensive experience with these landing craft has confirmed to the Navy that this operation will be a success in putting a crimp in the VC's operations. You noticed some strange craft as you came aboard in addition to our ATCs. The 'battleship' of our little river armada is the 'monitor' you see below, which will lead you into battle. It also is a conversion of a landing craft. Some will even have 105 mm cannon on the bow in addition to the assortment of smaller cannon, machine guns and mortars. Some will have twin flamethrowers on the bow. As a native Virginian, to me it looks more like the Confederate *Merrimac* combined with the Union *Monitor*.

"Don't be alarmed by the occasional explosions you see and hear in the surrounding water. We are not under attack. Our circling security boats throw grenades in the water to discourage VC swimmers from trying to attach mines to the hull. They were effective in sinking an auxiliary aircraft carrier in the river in Saigon. We learned how to prevent it.

"Now my staff will breakout with your Army counterparts while Colonel McCauley and Commander MacDonald and I have a chat. Oh, Captain Scott, stay a minute. I want to shake the hand of the only Army guy I ever heard of with a Navy Cross."

Captain Davenport, McCauley, MacDonald and Scott walked out onto the open deck. The moon was starting to rise and reflected off the river in a ribbon of light. The deck light was almost obscured by a cloud of insects.

"Well, gentlemen, I think this moon river is pointing to a very interesting time starting tomorrow. We'll split your party into two separate APCs with a monitor escort. I don't want to lose all of you in one boat if we hit a mine or heavy VC rockets. On that happy note, I'll see you at 0700 for breakfast. No need to get up too early for this joy ride. You can draw weapons after breakfast."

The river was calm with an ebb tide and the morning was a *sailor's delight,* as predicted. The little convoy of two APCs, a monitor and two river patrol boats on the flanks set out for a twenty mile orientation cruise. A Navy helicopter slowly orbited overhead. After this the cross service conferences would have more insight.

Approximately five miles upstream both APCs pulled into the banks of the river and let the ramps down. A Navy SEAL squad had formed a perimeter defense to allow the Army personnel to have a walk around on the ground where they would be fighting.

MacDonald hollered down to the SEAL squad leader, "Hey,

Bielecki, you remember this Army guy?"

"Hell yes, Commander. Nice to see you again, *CAPTAIN* Scott."

Scott grinned down at the squad leader. "Glad to see you're still doin' the job, Bielecki. Congratulations on your promotion to petty officer 1st class. I see you have your own squad. *Please* protect us today." A laugh came back from the nearest squad members.

MacDonald briefly related the *Rung Sat* story again from his perspective to McCauley and the Army personnel. Then he had Bielecki talk about his mission to reconnoiter the area around the base and what to expect as they walked about 100 meters into the mushy ground and rice paddies. When they returned the other SEAL squad members found spots to lie down in the well deck to sleep for the first time in twenty-four hours.

McCauley and his party listened to the Navy boat crews describe how they had to learn to recognize signs along the river bank that would indicate an ambush, everything from paths down to the river to dead or disturbed vegetation. Some of the canals were so narrow the APCs could barely turn around. Mangroves and Nipa palms reached out into the water. At one spot an obvious fire fight had taken place. Broken tree trunks and branches were scattered at angles where machine gun fire had cut a swath searching for the enemy. Large holes had been blasted in the bank by cannon fire and grenades.

As they slowly motored past one spot of blasted bank and cleared vegetation, twisted bodies of VC still floated in the water where they were caught in branches or dangled from blown up river bank. Flies swarmed over exposed and bloated flesh only disturbed by the boat's wake as it splashed against the bank. No explanation was necessary. The smell seemed to be sucked along behind the boat mixed with the diesel exhaust until a slight breeze blew it away.

Scott was silent and thinking about the first time he had seen the Mekong River after he had been on the Saigon River with its raw city sewage. This was less polluted and smelled different even after a millennium of countless villages emptying their refuse into it. He had been thinking about the muddy red rivers in Georgia and North Carolina as they emptied down from the mountains and through farm lands. This had a more green tint and darker color. It was in the tropics and always had the rotting smell, but now increasingly the smell of death clung to it. Scott was thinking it was fortunate that the monsoon season had not started with its continuous rain and deeper mud.

As the canal turned back into the river, McCauley asked about the lack of vegetation in some areas. MacDonald answered, "The Air Force has been dropping those defoliants along here for two years. I'm damned glad I wasn't under it. That's wicked stuff, but it does the job. You can see how this vegetation gives good ambush spots. They call 'em *Rainbow Herbicides*, because they come in barrels with different color-coded bands; Agent Pink, Agent Green, Agent Purple, Agent White, Agent Blue and Agent Orange." He looked away thoughtfully for a moment, "I understand they are even destroying the peoples' rice crops now to deny the VC supplies. After they drop it hundreds of dead fish float on the surface and wash ashore increasing the stink. Birds die from eating the fish, and they wash ashore."

The river tide had now become an outgoing rush to the sea and slowed the APCs speed to below five knots. As they reached the twenty mile limit and turned to ride the outgoing tide, speed increased to almost ten knots. No one noticed that the patrol boats had moved to the rear of the column. On a prearranged signal all boats opened fire at an imagined enemy ambush on both sides of the river. The Army personnel had not been warned. The thunderous noise and tremendous power of 20 mm canon, .50 cal. machineguns and 40 mm grenades fired from the APCs and monitor caused the unsuspecting soldiers to scramble for cover. The SEALs and Navy boat crews just laughed.

After thirty seconds the firing stopped. "Well, that's about as realistic as we can get today, and that's about how quick it happens out here on the river," grinned MacDonald. Even Scott had to just shake his head at the sudden display of Navy firepower.

At the end of the week the main force of the advance battalion was met by Major Jameson when they arrived at *Tan Son Nhut* for the flight to *My Tho,* and the shuttle to *Dong Tam.* As the companies unloaded they formed up for a brief inspection by Lieutenant Colonel McCauley, accompanied by Major Jameson and Captain Scott.

When they walked down the neat lines of soldiers in combat gear with weapons, Scott had the feeling of how, after Special Forces, this regular Army unit felt so organized, predictable and comfortable…yet restrictive.

At the last company in line Maj. Jameson started to smile, and ordered the company commander to have his company *Stand At Ease.* The company First Sergeant had his back turned as he gave the order. When he did an about-face, he was staring at Scott. Both the smiles on Jameson and McCauley turned to grins. Scott found himself staring into the face of First Sergeant Mario Tartaglia, his old basic training Drill Sergeant.

Scott had to turn his back, put hands on his hips, look at the ground, then the sky before he started to laugh.

McCauley motioned for Tartaglia to step forward as he and Jameson started to laugh, "I believe you know my S-2, Captain Scott."

"I sure as hell do, Colonel," as he stepped forward with his hand out. Scott grabbed it and turned it into an *abrazo.* A cheer went up from the men of Alpha Company, who had been told the story of Ft. Jackson and the recruit who had saved Tartaglia's life, led the training after, and now was a recipient of the Medal of Honor.

Jameson smiled, "It's a small world in this Army."

The battalion spent the next two weeks working out procedures and methods with the Navy on communications, loading, landing, sweeps through the rice paddies, fire support, and coordination with air and ship support. Occasionally, they encountered a sniper or small group of VC.

Scott, as Battalion S-2 intelligence officer, was busy continuing to gather intelligence from air reconnaissance, SEALs on the ground, boat patrols, ARVN reports, and even scattered Special

Forces camps throughout the delta. On more than one occasion his helicopter was struck by those familiar metallic *tinks*, including one crash and a fire fight with a small VC group before they were rescued. For the number of flights into enemy territory and his command of the defense of the downed helicopter he was recommended for the Air Medal with V...a little more color in the fruit salad.

The first live operation was a sweep within the five miles to the west of the base to clear out some VC units which had been harassing the camp with sniper and mortar fire. A SEAL squad had been out for twenty-four hours tracking and reporting VC movements. Estimates were that a VC company was operating in the area adjacent to the base in approximately a ten mile square. It would be a simple search and destroy mission with one Army company and two ARVN companies driving VC into a blocking force of two Army companies and an additional company in mobile reserve in the river.

At 0400 the next morning the small fleet of APCs, a monitor, a command and control boat, and fast patrol boats set out up the river. The Navy would supply fire support where needed and disrupt any canal crossing groups along canals surrounding the operational area. Helicopters would be overhead.

On the edge of the operational area the command and control boat picked up the SEAL squad to coordinate the latest intelligence. A company of VC had been operating in the area with their small mortars and machine guns.

By 0530 the driving force was landing with no opposition on the north side of the area. The two Army companies were dug into dikes along rice paddies and tree lines on the south side of the designated zone. The first action heard was from somewhere in the middle of the designated zone when heavy machine guns opened fire on the command helicopter with several rounds striking the underside of the helicopter with that metallic clunking sound. The pilot juked his aircraft sideways.

McCauley and Scott smiled at each other remembering their time in Bolivia with Colonel Villamiranoa shouting obscenities at the enemy below as rounds struck their helicopter.

The pilot cursed in the intercom, "Goddamn it. They have heavier stuff down there than we do. *The powers that be* think that we are dangerous to the population if we carry .50 cal. machine guns. The VC can reach us, but we can't reach them. They can drive us up out of range."

However, the firing was what the ground forces were look-ing for as they closed in through the rice paddies, mud and tree lines. VC mortars and machine guns shifted to the units closing on them. Overwhelming numbers became obvious, and the VC began to abandon their dug-in positions and heavier weapons. Soon it became a rout directly into the blocking force. Some VC managed to reach hidden sampans, only to be blown out of the water by patrol boats.

The command helicopter had swooped back into the fight add-ing its own machine guns. McCauley had taken one of the ma-chine guns himself. He smiled, "That felt good. It's been a while. That was a classic 'hammer and anvil' with a Navy twist. Let's hope they all go that well."

The after action report indicated sixty dead Viet Cong, ten wounded prisoners, and twenty American wounded. More impor-tantly, the dual service concept had worked as planned. The Navy commander was pleased, as well as McCauley.

Scott's intelligence gathering had included reports from ARVN sources which indicated a substantial retaliation was being planned by the VC, and units were moving into the area twenty-five miles west, and more to the north. This was corroborated by Navy patrol boats which were encountering more contacts as troops and sup-plies moved into the area.

Captain Davenport stood in front of his large map of the delta. It was now overlaid with acetate showing red arrows and rectangles indicating VC movements and unit sizes. At his side were ARVN Colonel Lat, Scott as Army S-2, and his Navy intelligence counter-part. "Gentlemen, here comes the real action. Captain Scott and Lt. Wilkinson have pieced together what is evidently happening out there. Apparently, Charlie wants to get rid of us before we get any stronger and really do him some harm." Slapping his map with a pointer for emphasis, Davenport continued, "Indications are that he intends to strike us from two fronts and pin us against the river, then come after the base. We need to drive both of his prongs into the middle where we can pound all of them and chase them back to the river and into our blocking force of three companies, keeping one company as a mobile reserve in boats. Major Jameson will be in command on the ground and Colonel McCauley will be in the command helicopter. We are going to use two ARVN battalions commanded by Colonel Lat to supplement our forces and drive the VC with a lot of airpower. They know the area and the enemy. The best we can determine is Charlie has a reinforced regiment out there. It's going to be hard for him to hide. So, we will have him spotted. All your training has developed some pretty good communications and joint tactics, including Army artillery and mortars on barges and good coordination with our mobile boat firepower. I'm going to turn this over to Colonel McCauley and Commander MacDonald and their staffs to develop a plan. Unit commanders get your men and equipment ready."

After the meeting McCauley called Scott aside. "Tom, Capt. Jennings in Alpha Company has come down with a fever and his Executive Officer, the only 1st Lt. in the company, was wounded last time. You know the 1st Sergeant, Tartaglia. How would you feel about taking over his company in this operation? I hate to ask you, but I need somebody on the ground I can depend on. You'll be in the blocking force, and you know the drill."

Flashes of stinking mud and the smell of cordite and napalm went through Scott's mind. "Sure, Colonel," was his simple answer. "But I would like a pile of Claymores."

"You got 'em. All you can carry."

After reporting to Major Jameson, Scott went immediately to the Alpha Company section of the ship. "Sergeant Tartaglia, gather the company up with the platoon leaders. I have the dubious honor of being your company commander."

Tartaglia laughed, "I knew it would happen someday. Better now than any other time. I'll round 'em up."

Five minutes later he had all the platoons and their officers crowded into the sleeping quarters.

"Gentlemen, I am your new company commander. As you all know by now, this gorilla you have for a first sergeant was my drill sergeant in basic. So I know what it's like to have him yelling at me." A confirming laugh went around the room. "This operation should be very much the same as your first one except much bigger and more significant in chasing Charlie out of the Delta. From my own experience I know he is not dumb. He learns each time we do something to him. This will not be a cake walk. I know what it's like to have him coming through the wire, but we don't have any wire. And I damn sure don't want my ass hanging out without a lot of shit protecting me. I have four purple hearts, and I do not intend to make this my final one.

"On that score, I have asked for as many Claymore mines as we can carry. Colonel McCauley said no problem. I don't care what other companies do. I want every man here, including me and all the officers, to carry so many we can hardly walk. I have some bad memories of human waves coming at me. I want to blow their asses up one hundred yards away from me, then fifty yards, then twenty-five yards, if they get that close. Do not panic if some don't work. That's why we are going to put out three or more rows. Sometimes these bastards even sneak in and turn them around. Here I think they will not have time, but keep alert. Seven hundred whistling steel balls is one scary sound, and I want 'em going right at *Charlie*. You men have all been under fire on this assignment. Just keep cool and remember to aim…at least in Charlie's direction. Machine gunners stay disciplined. Your platoon leaders and NCOs will set up your fields of fire, and we will be dug in on dry ground. I'll be there with you. Officers meet me up in the mess hall in ten minutes. That is all."

The First Sergeant called **ATTENTION,** and Scott left the area to his subordinates.

When Scott was gone, Tartaglia turned to his men, "Gentlemen, now you know why I think we got the right guy."

At 0330 all units were in boats and underway. The tide was

coming in and the twenty mile trip to the deployment area could be made before daylight. Soldiers would have to makeup sleep in the well deck of the ATCs. The ARVN battalions would be coming up a parallel canal on the north side of the area and divide into two elements to shove the VC prongs inward and back.

The Army blocking area was a peninsula 1,200 yards across and anchored on each end by the river. A former village had occupied the area until it had been destroyed by the VC. The village had been built on higher ground which had been built up over many years. Now it offered dry ground to dig machine gun emplacements and foxholes. The command element with Major Jameson, the sergeant major, medics, and radio operators were dug in fifty yards to the rear. The three company commanders with medics and radio operators were on the left and right slightly to the rear of their companies. An unloading area on the river bank with the Battalion S-4 officer, supply sergeant, and support was set up for APCs to land ammunition and evacuate the wounded. The fourth infantry company in the battalion was held in reserve in their APCs in the river to be deployed as needed. The abbreviated headquarters company was onboard the Navy modified monitor communications and command boat with MacDonald. McCauley would be overhead in the command HU-1 helicopter.

Daylight was spreading over the destroyed village and rice paddies when Alpha Company finished setting their rows of Claymore mines. Some good natured kidding by the other companies had taken place about the amount of mines loading down the soldiers.

Flashes from explosions could be seen beyond the operational area in the still-dark distance to the west. A radio message was relayed by the Vietnamese translator with the Navy command boat that the ARVN base where the two battalions were stationed was under attack while they were away. No enemy contact had been made in the ARVN sector designated to drive the VC in the direction of the Americans. ARVN Colonel Lat had made the decision to release one of his two battalions to return to relieve the base, and directed air support be concentrated there on the presumption that it was the real thrust of the VC not the unit they were trying to drive to the Americans.

An hour passed as the sun began to rise with no contact as the remaining ARVN battalion continued its sweep in search of the VC units believed to be in the area. By 0730 a light rain had begun to fall making soggy ground even worse for foot soldiers. The ARVN battalion had spread thin to make up for the battalion withdrawn back to relieve their base. At 0745 intense automatic weapons fire and mortars from VC units suddenly appearing from concealed positions forced the ARVN battalion back into a defensive perimeter. Urgent radio calls went out for air and naval support, but available air cover was occupied with relief of the ARVN base. The ARVN commander on the ground refused to move out of his defensive position. Heavy mortar fire continued to pound them.

No activity was happening in the American sector. Patrols had been sent out 200 meters with no sightings. APCs with the reserve infantry company and monitors continued to slowly patrol around the peninsula. McCauley was in the air conferring with MacDonald in the command boat while Major Jameson and his company commanders listened on their radios.

MacDonald was urgently calling for information from the air, "Land One, Land One, this is Water One. Do you read me? Can you see what's happening?"

"Water One. This is Land One. I hear you, Mac. I can see a lot of firing around the ARVN. The VC have a lot of heavy stuff keeping us very high. It looks like they sprung a trap on the ARVN. Their commander refuses to move forward, and we have no air support up here. What's your situation? Over."

"Land One, everything is too quiet here. Did you see any activity in our area when you flew by? Over."

"Water One, I didn't see anything from up here. Looks quiet. I can hear the ARVN commander calling for Navy fire support on his end of the peninsula to take some pressure off his flanks. Can you spare some boats for fire support? Over."

"Land One, I'll send a monitor and a couple of ATC's to dump a lot of shit on 'em. Get me some coordinates. It will take three zero minutes to get up there. Let him know help is on the way. Your mortar barge will be set in three zero minutes. Out."

Scott turned to his 1ˢᵗ Sergeant, Tartaglia. "Mario, let me see your map. I don't like this. Make sure those platoon leaders have all their Claymores rigged correctly and have the machine gunners get more ammunition while they can. I've got a feeling Charlie is out there watching us."

The radio crackled, "Land One, this is Water One. Over."

"Go ahead, Water One."

"Land One, the ARVN commander is asking for your reserve company to commit. Over."

"Water One. That's a negative until this side develops some more. Suggest you move the ATCs to the other side of the peninsula to be ready."

"Wilco, Water One. Out."

"Land Two. This is Land One. How does it look down there, Bill?"

"Not a creature is stirring, Colonel. Patrols see nothing."

"Water One, this is Land One. Mac, go ahead and start my reserves up the river to help the ARVN."

Meanwhile Scott was concentrating on the map showing his position. He stared at each feature on the map surrounding the battalion's position, then put his hand over it and closed his eyes. Only blurred unidentifiable images came. He shifted to the other side of the river on the map behind their position. Same blurred images which would not come into focus. He looked up at Tartaglia who had been standing nearby watching him. "Mario, bring me those aerial photos."

The 1ˢᵗ sergeant dug into the map case and handed the aerials to Scott.

Scott repeated the process with the photos. Something was there, but he could not see it. He put one hand on the map and one on the aerial. Fifteen minutes went by with Scott alternately staring and closing his eyes. Tartaglia was beginning to worry. Another fifteen minutes went by.

"Captain, are you OK?"

"Mario, give me your hand. I need your energy for a moment."

"Sir?"

"Don't worry. I'm just concentrating on some details and slight differences."

Tartaglia tentatively held out his hand and almost drew it back when he felt a slight static electric charge tickle his hand. Now he was mesmerized watching what he could not understand.

Time seemed to melt by as the two knelt over the map and photos. Suddenly Scott drew back and released the sergeant's hand.

"Jesus Christ!"

Startled, Tartaglia jumped back. "Sir, what's happening?"

"Mario, get Major Jameson on the radio quickly."

Now thoroughly frightened, he fumbled with the telephone hand-set and switch on the ANPRC-25 radio. "Land Two, this is Land Three. Over."

"Go ahead Land Three."

Scott took the hand set. "Major, has our reserve been released?"

"Roger. About an hour ago. Things are quiet here and crazy on the ARVN side."

"Sir, request permission to speak with the colonel. I think something is happening here that needs both of you and Water One."

"Wait one."

"Land One, are you reading this?"

McCauley's voice came back. "Affirmative. What's goin' on, Tom?"

"Sir, I believe we have almost two battalions of VC dug in and camouflaged in the tree line and dikes."

Tartaglia's eyes went wide open, "Holy shit."

"I don't see anything like that from up here, Tom. Bill, you see anything funny?"

"Negative, Sir."

Scott's voice was getting desperate. "Colonel, do you remember *Tupac?* I see them."

A long pause on the radio. "Shit. Goddamn it. Mac, do you hear this?"

"Roger, Colonel. I understand, and I just ordered them to come back. They are half an hour away."

"Bill, I'll explain later. Get ready. Now."

As if on cue, the whistling, air-rushing sound of VC mortars filled the air. The first set straddled the battalion headquarters killing the sergeant major and the radio operator and wounding the major. The second group destroyed the resupply ATC on the river bank. The third landed among the dug-in companies. They had, obviously, been sighted and ranged onto the exact spot the battalion was located. Trails of rockets could be seen from the other side of the river, reaching out to the support boats and mortar barge. Still no enemy soldiers could be seen.

Tartaglia's eyes grew even wider. Scott glanced at him. "I'll explain later. Right now get your troops fighting." He turned to the radioman. "Jackson, see if you can reach anyone in the battalion command post."

Looking across the rice paddies and tree line, nothing was moving. The mortar fire was coming from much farther up in the peninsula. Scott looked at his map and then at his radioman.

"No answer from the major, Sir. The radio must have been knocked out when the mortar rounds hit them." A mortar shell landed forty yards away. A moment of silence from deafness followed. "Oh shit. A frag hit my arm."

The company medic crawled over to him. "Not bad, Jackson. I'll wrap it."

"Jackson, send these coordinates to Water One for their mortars, and tell them to concentrate on the tree-line."

McCauley's voice came over the radio trying to reach Jameson, with no answer. Finally, "Tom, are you there?"

"Affirmative, Colonel. Looks like the CP was wiped out."

"Understood. I'll be overhead in ten minutes. You are commander on the ground. Water One, are you there?"

"Roger, Land One. We're putting Navy 81 mm mortar fire where Scott directed, but we are under heavy rocket, machine-gun and RPG attack from the other side of the river. We can't direct fire over your troops because of the low tide and the elevation of the old village. So, we're trying to clean out the river ambush site with direct fire. Your mortar barge has been destroyed. Looks like Charlie was waiting on us. We're going to try to come around the side and flank Charlie with direct fire from our 50s and 20 mm."

McCauley could hear enemy rounds hitting the sides of MacDonald's boat over the battle noise.

"Keep your head down, Jim. The ARVN still won't move, and we lost two HUEYs shot down and into the river. Scott, see any movement yet?"

"Negative, Sir, but my read is Attila's hordes will be coming shortly. Thank you for the Claymores."

"Just kill the bastards, Tom."

"Roger that." Scott and Tartaglia smiled at each other.

"All companies, this is Scott. Train your machine guns on the dikes. They will be coming out of the ground there. Then in front of the tree line." He hoped his communications were going through over the continuing barrage. He could see large craters all over the village site. "Send me a damage report. Sergeant Tartaglia is now Battalion Sergeant Major."

The mortar barrage was slowing as Navy mortars begin to find their range.

"Captain Scott, Bravo Company lost its company commander, one platoon leader, four men KIA, five wounded, and a machine gun with its crew. Charlie Company lost its 1st sergeant, three KIA, six wounded, and one machine gun. We lost one machine gun crew and one platoon leader KIA. The machine gun is serviceable," was Tartaglia's report.

"Not good, but could be worse. Get someone on that machine gun."

Scott picked up the radio hand telephone set and pressed the key. "Gentlemen, we are still in good shape. I just got word that Major Jameson is wounded but alive. Any minute you are going to hear whistles across your front and men will start coming out of the ground that you did not think were there and over those dikes. There will be a lot of them. Aim low, machine guns fire in bursts, and don't set off your Claymores until they are within fifty meters of each row. Fix bayonets. Do not let them break through your lines. Good Luck!"

"Mario, we're going to get the heaviest attack on our end position. They are going to try to break us and flank around the other companies from behind. I can see it. Go steady our second lieutenants. And get that gun back in service."

Tartaglia had stopped wondering how Scott knew all this. The colonel and the Navy commander believed him and they knew him the best, much better in combat than he did. He also knew those *last lieutenants* did need some encouraging. He moved down the line of platoons encouraging and demanding attention to their weapons. As he turned to go back, six Rocket Propelled Grenades (RPGs) flashed out of the tree line trailing smoke over the entrenched soldiers with two landing in the village high ground in loud explosions, blowing craters in front of the line. Then what seemed like hundreds of whistles sounded. He looked over his shoulder, shouted "Jesus Christ!" then jumped into the closest fox hole. It happened to be the machine gun for the 1st squad in the first platoon, which was anchoring the right side of the battalion line and covering the river bank.

"Shit, Sarge, look at those sonofabitches coming out of the ground just like the captain said. There must be thousands of 'em."

Tartaglia caught his breath. "Now you do what the captain said and fire low, and don't set off any Claymores yet." He looked down at the ammunition boxes and saw they had done as instructed to draw extra two hundred round belts. He quickly calculated they had 2,000 rounds to fire. If they could just get one VC every ten rounds, it could turn the battle. Machine gun and AK-47 rounds were now cracking overhead, the other platoons were starting to fire at the fast approaching mass of VC. He felt a wet splatter on his face and saw the machine gunner next to him had just been killed. He saw the opened mouth stare of the assistant gunner. "Just keep loading. I'll knock 'em down." With that, he grabbed the M-60 and set up a rhythmic fire while the loader crouched beside him and fed belts into the gun.

Scott was on the radio to McCauley. "Land One, we have a full assault coming with what looks like two full battalions of VC. Water One, if you can bring down your mortars one hundred meters you'll catch them in the middle. They seem to be bunching on my end to break through."

"Roger, Land Three. As soon as we can break up the ambush on the other side of the river we will be on your flank."

"Water One, don't stop for a beer!"

MacDonald had to laugh remembering the same SEAL transmission in the Rung Sat in the middle of a firefight.

Scott looked down the end of his line where Tartaglia was manning the machine gun, then up and down the rest of the companies. They seemed to be holding. ***Bamm, Bamm.*** Two Claymores went off in his company indicating that the VC had reached within one hundred meters. He could see by the density of VC that approximately three hundred were now assaulting his end of the battalion line. ***Bamm, Bamm.*** More outer Claymores from different squads exploded, then more. Then inner lines of Claymores started exploding. He could see rows of VC fall as the 700 steel balls from each mine ripped through their ranks. Only a few mines went off from the other companies, indicating to him that the VC were just keeping the other companies occupied while they overran Alpha.

He could hear several of his machine guns go quiet. Either they had been destroyed or they were changing hot barrels. He was collecting reports from the other companies which confirmed what he thought. He climbed out of his hole with his radio operator to check on his line and reinforce the far end. He could see his medic lying flat on the ground while he reached down to a wounded soldier in a fox hole. ***Bamm, Bamm.*** More mines were set off by his company. He calculated the first two rows were gone. Fortunately, he had two more rows with the last one five meters in front of his line. After that it was bayonet time.

Scott ran crouched as low as he could, trying to use as much of the high ground as possible for protection while rounds zipped over and around him. Somehow the noise and adrenaline of combat felt familiar and almost comforting. "That's nuts," he said aloud, more to himself.

The first platoon leader he came to he ordered to send a machine gun crew to Alpha Company where the heaviest attack was occurring. Then he returned to the heaviest part of the action which was happening in front of Alpha Company. Suddenly he felt a sharp burn in the only part of his anatomy exposed, his buttocks. "Goddamnit."

His radioman was following close behind. "Sir, I think you need a medic."

"In a minute, Goddamnit."

"Yes, sir."

Scott was thinking this wound was going to be a worse joke than his ear.

Halfway down his company line he met his medic, who had a shrapnel wound of his own.

"Jenkins, patch this and don't laugh."

"No, sir. It looks like it just passed through one cheek and no serious damage. It won't feel so good tomorrow."

"I'll be delighted to be here tomorrow. How many casualties?"

"Three KIA, twelve wounded and still fighting. You better look at the 1st sergeant, sir. He took one in the stomach and his loader is dead."

"Shit."

Tartaglia was still manning the key machine gun on the right flank.

"Mario, can you still load?"

"Hell yes. You mow down the little fuckers and I'll load."

Scott could see a pile of bodies in front of the machine gun and two more Claymores were still left. The bodies of the machine gunner and his assistant lay on the ground behind the gun emplacement.

"You got it, Sergeant Major. Jackson, get down low in this hole with your radio. I want to know what's happening along the line, and fix your bayonet."

Jackson's eyes went wide, but he reached around and found his bayonet to attach to his M-16.

A group of ten was closing within 40 meters of the emplacement. Scott reached down and flicked the switch to the Claymore's wire. 700 metal balls screamed into the group. To his left he could see the soldiers could not fire their Claymores and four VC reached them tossing grenades into the foxhole and toward Scott, who grabbed an M-16, and with his radioman, killed them. The VC grenade exploded twenty meters from the machine gun and down in front of the embankment. Scott felt tiny pieces of hot steel piercing his arms and chest outside his flak jacket. He looked back at Jackson who was staring at his bloody hands and arms. Blood ran down his face where more shrapnel had hit him. Shock showed on his face, but he nodded and shook his M-16 in the air. Tartaglia had more shrapnel wounds, but nodded he was still OK, and loaded another belt into the machine gun. More than one hundred bodies lay in front of his machine gun, some within ten meters. One more group of ten came rushing toward the emplacement. Scott continuously fired, screaming as he fired. He could taste blood in his mouth. He was bleeding somewhere else. He fired the last Claymore and was vaguely aware of more Claymores firing in Alpha's line. One VC fell dead in the emplacement on top of Scott with a grenade in his hand, which rolled into their fox hole. Jackson shouted, "Grenade!" Scott saw it and shoved the dead VC on top of it. The body was just enough to keep shrapnel from spreading, but not the gore it created in the explosion. Some shrapnel managed to hit all three men in the legs but with lessened force.

Pain from multiple wounds was starting to set in on all three. "Mario, if you still have your morphine, hit yourself. Jackson, you OK?"

"I'm OK, sir, but it looks like you took one in your shoulder."

Scott reached out to one of the dead soldiers and took the unused morphine syrette from the first aid pouch and stuck it in his thigh. He suddenly realized the concentrated attack had shifted to the middle of the battalion line onto Bravo Company, which did not have as many Claymores. The front of Alpha was now empty except for several hundred dead and dying VC.

Relief started to spread over Scott's body as the morphine took effect and a feeling of well-being took over. Wounds were forgotten. "Jackson, can you get the other company commanders on the radio?"

"Roger, sir." He turned the volume up in time to hear McCauley's voice come through.

"Scott, Scott, can you hear me. Are you alive?"

"Affirmative, sir. Just a little shot up."

"I'm overhead. I can see our battalion is starting to break in the middle."

Scott looked again. He could see hand-to-hand fighting one hundred meters down the line in Bravo. "I got it, Colonel. Jackson, let the platoon leaders know we are attacking the VC flank."

Scott looked for his M-16, but found it jammed in the mud. The closest weapon he could find was an AK-47 with a broken stock and a fixed bayonet. "This will do." he said to nobody.

He felt indestructible as the morphine continued working, but climbing out of the hole proved his legs were weak. He felt nauseated. Then he seemed to gain strength as his reserve adrenalin kicked in. Waving the broken AK-47 over his head he shouted to his platoons to follow him. Slowly at first, then with screams and shouts his men came out of their holes and charged into the flank of the VC breakthrough after Scott. Uninjured men picked up M-60 machine guns with ammunition belts over their shoulders. The remaining second lieutenant was waving his M-16 and yelling "Follow Me," the motto of the Infantry School. Wounded men moved forward the best they could. Seventy men of Alpha now followed Scott into the VC flank.

The enemy was caught by surprise by this sudden attack on its flank and soon became disorganized and started to retreat. Scott stumbled into the middle of it. Blood loss had taken what reserves he had left. His last vision was of a young, frightened VC lieutenant in front of him as he shoved the broken rifle's bayonet into him, then lost consciousness.

McCauley was overhead in the HU-1 watching the action. "Jesus Christ, look at that." He could see Scott leading the charge into the VC, then the VC breaking ranks in retreat. His crew chief was busy taking pictures.

"Goddamnit, it looks like they killed him. Pilot, get down

there. Medic, get ready."

"Sir, there is still a battle going on," was the pilot's quick reply.

"Get down there. Give me that damn machine gun." McCauley began to fire into the rear of the VC line, causing more panic. "Water One, are you hearing this?"

"Aye, aye, Colonel. We are coming in on their northern flank with fire and your reserve company to sweep 'em up. It looks like the attack on the ARVN base was just a distraction and air support returned to clean up the other side. Looks like your battalion was their main target."

The battle had cleared from the spot where a blood-soaked Scott lay. The helicopter landed. McCauley and the medic leaped the last six feet and ran to Scott.

The medic's first reaction was, "Jesus, Colonel. This man has no blood left. I can't even get a needle in a vein. He's gone." A light blue haze suddenly floated up from Scott's body. "Holy shit. Did you see that?"

A scream pierced the night, high in the mountains on the other side of the world. A bond had been broken.

As the medic sprung backwards in confusion, if not fright, he felt the hard barrel of a Colt .45 pistol in the middle of his back, and a low, angry, shaking voice in his ear. "Get some plasma in him, or, so help me God, I will shoot you right here in the middle of this fight."

Now more frightened, he pleaded, "Sir, his veins are collapsed. There is no way. He's…"

"*Do it now,* and get him in the chopper back to the Navy hospital ship. I'm staying here. This fight is not over yet."

CHAPTER 20

Ft. Benning, Georgia

Everything seemed a blurry white. He could hear voices in the distance and things being moved around. Nothing was clear or familiar. A voice seemed to say "call the doctor." What doctor? Where was he? He couldn't speak. Was he alive or dead?

"Oye, comemierda. Welcome back from the land of the spirits," a voice seemed to say, close-by, in Spanish…Cuban Spanish.

Slowly the room and the figure came into focus. "Jacob?" His voice was scratchy.

"A tu servicio, Capitan."

"Where am I? How long have I been here?"

"You are the guest of our extraordinary hotel, Martin Army Hospital, Ft. Benning, Georgia. You have been unconscious for three days."

"Why are *you* here?"

"Why…I, too, am a captain in the service of the United States Army… Captain Jacob Stern, Medical Corps, if you please. Once again we are equal in the service of yet another army. Did you have pleasant dreams of all those beautiful maidens in Cuba? Also, since we have the same blood type, you now have some good Jewish blood."

Scott had to smile. Jacob gave him some water and continued with his personal narration.

"You know, you are one lucky *cabrón.* We counted no less than twenty-seven holes in you. The Army medic and those Navy doctors got to you just in time and most of those hot grenade fragments cauterized themselves and sealed off the blood flow. You are going to be picking pieces of steel out of your body the rest of your life. Fortunately, I am good friends with a nice Jewish plastic surgeon here, and I got him to fix that ugly ear job while he was disguising a lot of other ugly holes. However, there are two things that are puzzling us. How did you get a bullet through your cheek and no teeth are missing? We figure you must have had your big mouth open hollering for help at just the right angle."

Scott gave a painful smile, "Something like that."

"The second is that thin scar running along your jawbone. Dr. Horowitz says he could not have done better. *Que pasó?*

"A Bolivian *curandera's* magic herbs. Ask your uncle. He was there. I'll tell you the story later. How did you know I was here?"

"When I heard that a famous *HERO* checked in to our establishment, I knew instantly it must be you. *Coño,* I heard they are even putting you in for a *second Medal of Honor.* Speaking of Medals of Honor, your grandfather is here, with your mother. I called them when you showed up. Are you ready? Then I have another surprise, your own personal pretty nurse."

"Please give me a few minutes to adjust to my arrival from the land of spirits. And can I eat without all these tubes?"

"*Absolutamente, mi heroe.*"

"Screw you, smart ass. Just unhook me," Scott laughed.

"Oohh, nurse. Would you please come in and unplug this cranky captain?"

Scott looked up at the starched white uniform as she entered the room. 'A pretty blond,' he thought. Then he was speechless.

This time she spoke first. "You look a little worse for wear this time, *CAPTAIN.*"

Scott recovered, "This time you changed *your* attire, *First Lieutenant* Denise Johanson."

"Well, after the last time you abandoned me for the good of the service to parts unknown, and classified, I thought I would do something for the service. I figured I would catch up with you in a hospital somewhere. So, I went back to nursing school. I already had a Bachelor of Science. So, it didn't take long, and the Army paid for it."

Jacob waved his hand, "Excuse me, people. I'll see you later. I'll send up his family in ten minutes." He left and closed the room door.

Denise took Scott's hand and began to disconnect IVs. "Happy to see me, CAPTAIN?"

"You have no idea. Waking up from the dead to see your face is beyond imagination."

She laughed and kissed him on the forehead.

Ten minutes later Jacob knocked on the door, followed by Old Tom and his mother.

"Goddamnit, Tommy, didn't Sean and Bill Jameson tell you what I said about not being such a hero?" said Old Tom, with tears in his eyes.

"Yea, Grandpa, and I heard him tell you that I inherited it."

Jacob laughed from the corner, "He's got you there, Mr. Scott."

His mother rushed to the bedside, "Tommy, are you in pain?"

"Not a bit, mother. This is Denise…"

Old Tom cut him off and turned smiling, toward Denise, "We all met yesterday. Now I know the rest of that Panama story Colonel Bergeron was telling me down in Bolivia, and she now knows the whole Bolivian story."

Tommy looked at Denise.

"Not a problem, *mon cher*. I understand what happened." Denise smiled back.

Jacob interrupted, "Mr. Scott, is that Major Bill Jameson you are talking about? He's just arrived here in Martin Army. He was pretty banged up, but he will be fine. He would probably appreciate seeing you. Small world in this Army."

After thirty minutes Jacob called an end, "Sorry, folks, we need to change some dressings and let the honorable captain get some rest, dreaming about beautiful Cuban girls."

Denise shot him a dirty look. To which he laughed.

"Denise, may I talk to Jacob alone?"

She hesitated, looked him in the eye and said, "Sure. He is the doctor…and your friend."

When she left and closed the door, "Jacob, I need to call Bolivia. I have a son down there that I have never seen, and I don't know if I'm divorced or not."

"I'll take care of it. Actually, your grandfather said the same thing when we were alone."

"Damn, he thinks of everything."

Jacob nodded his head, "He certainly seems to. I'll try to arrange it in the morning before Denise comes in."

"Thanks."

Scott did have that phone call. Maria Consuela did confirm the divorce and was grateful he survived, but something in their connection was no longer there.

Afterward, Scott had Denise push him in a wheelchair to Jameson's room where he was joined by Old Tom and Jacob.

Old Tom looked around and out of the window at the busy post activity and the active 200 foot towers of the airborne school and many helicopters. He asked, "Jacob, why are there so many helicopters around here?"

"The 11th Air Assault is training for a new type of warfare. They call it "airmobile." So, here at Benning, we have the old *airborne* and the new *airmobile*."

Old Tom thought there was no question, the Army was very much at war.

Jameson looked up in surprise at both Scotts in his room, "Well, I'll be damned. I never thought I would see you two again."

"We just heard you were here. Dr. Stern made the connection. He was with me in Cuba with Castro."

Old Tom stared at the ceiling trying to ignore the reference. "How are you, Bill?"

"I'll be fine, Mr. Scott. I may need your walking cane, but all the other holes will heal."

"Oh, with all this new surgery and equipment you won't be needin' my cane. They did the best they could for me back then under the circumstances. We would like to hear the rest of the story of that day in the Delta. To Tommy it was a blur, and he never saw the end."

Denise took a deep breath and said, "Gentlemen, you will have to excuse me. In this place I have heard too many of these stories," and she left.

Jameson related the scene as he saw it from lying wounded in a fox hole, crawling around behind Bravo Company with his Sgt. Maj., medic, and radioman dead, Scott leading a flanking charge, to McCauley jumping out of the helicopter to lead the remainder of his men in chasing the VC. "It was all a ruse to draw off the ARVN and eliminate us with their main force. The Americans were the objective the whole time. They were ready. They had to know our plan before we got there. Very smart. Fortunately, they didn't figure on Alpha Company's resistance to their main assault to break through, nor Tom's leading a flanking attack with a bunch of crazy wounded men when they finally gave up attacking Alpha. I had a grandstand seat view, and all I could do was bleed, shoot when I had a clear target and keep Bravo and Charlie companies in the fight. A medic from Bravo finally got to me with a radio, but by that time I could see Tom and Alpha Company coming. After they cleaned up the VC, McCauley came back and told me about Tom. Nobody knew if he made it. And now here you stand…I mean sit."

"Dr. Stern, sorry I didn't make the connection. Tom had told me about you in Cuba, and here you are again playing doctor to shot-up soldiers."

Stern looked thoughtful for a moment. "Well, I guess I got a taste for it. I lost track of Tommy, and when I had an argument with my father about ROTC, I just got the Army to pay for med school. Now here I am. I requested to be sent to Vietnam. We will see."

A deep voice came from the doorway, "This looks like a family reunion."

Everyone turned to see a very big master sergeant in a Green Beret looking down on them.

"Hi, granpa. Hi cuz. Major, nice to see you again. Don't stand up. Dr. Stern, I'm Tom Scott."

Old Tom reached out for an *abrazo*. "Good to see you, Tom. Where did you come from?"

"They have me training people up at Ft. Brag, but I got a three day pass when I heard there were some regular Army types down here that I knew, who let themselves get all shot up," he said as he patted his cousin on the back and shook hands with Jameson.

Captain Scott looked at Stern's puzzled face. "I'll explain later."

Jacob stared at the ribbons on the sergeant's chest, starting with the Distinguished Service Cross, Bronze Star with 'V' and Purple Heart down to the Viet Nam Gallantry Cross and Service ribbon, Combat Infantryman Badge and Master Jump Wings. The realization dawned on who he was, but not the 'grandpa' part. He had read the Medal of Honor story. Stern thought now would be a good time to mention a conversation he had with the Commanding General of the Infantry School. "Gentlemen, I had a call from the Commanding General over at the Infantry School inquiring about Captain Scott and the possibility of awarding his Medal at the school since he never came back to the States to get it, and the President is a little busy at the moment. Additionally, a little lecture on riverine warfare to the current basic and advanced classes would be in order. Now that we have Maj. Jameson and Master Sergeant Scott here, a lesson on warfare in the Mekong Delta would be a great asset to the school. Excuse me. I'm going to go call him now." Without waiting for any response he turned and left.

Jameson looked up, "This sounds interesting and better than sitting here eating hospital food. I suspect Sergeant Scott is about to get his pass extended...*By order of:*"

Scott was thoughtful for a minute. "What happened to my first sergeant, Tartaglia?"

Jameson smiled. "He made it. The last I heard he was in a military hospital on Governor's Island in New York Harbor wearing a Purple Heart and a Silver Star on his pajamas and a lot of girls from his old neighborhood hanging around."

Scott smiled. "Good. He earned it."

The Commanding General of the Infantry School was in Scott's hospital room with Dr. Stern the next morning. Maj. Jameson had been wheeled in also.

"Good morning, Major, Captain. Obviously, no need for you to stand. Captain Scott, you may not remember, but we met at the White House reception when I was a deputy to General Jaworski and you were there with your grandfather and the ambassador."

"Yes, Sir, I remember. A lot of water down the Mekong since then. I understand you have already been to 'Nam and back."

"Roger, I had a brigade up in II Corps, but we don't have anyone on staff who was in the Delta. We could use some help. Dr. Stern tells me both of you should be able to be wheeled over to the school and talk. We also get the honor of awarding you the Medal. My G-3 will speak to you about a lesson plan for a presentation in a week or two.

"Also, Captain Scott, I understand that you are almost finished with the Advanced Course by correspondence. I would like for you to complete the last two weeks with the current class. You will receive the certificate as a resident student. Any questions, gentlemen?"

"Sir, about Master Sergeant Scott..."

"Already done. He is assigned to the Infantry School for thirty days TDY. You might speak to him about Officer Candidate School. I understand he is getting close to a college degree. That Distinguished Service Cross will look good on his application. Well, that is all. I'll see you in one week. Oh, by the way, my old classmate, Lieutenant Colonel McCauley, sent me some photos he had taken of you two from his helicopter during that fight in the delta. Very interesting." With that, the general turned and left.

"Jacob, do you actually know that general?"

Stern grinned. "I delivered his last baby. His wife loves me."

Jameson and Scott looked at each other, shaking their heads.

Scott thought for a minute, "We need to get a set of greens. All my uniforms are in storage or destroyed. I don't want to show up in this hospital gown."

Stern laughed, "Gentlemen, your every need has been anticipated. You will be wheeled to the uniform shop by two beautiful nurses this afternoon, where Mr. Scott will be waiting with a tailor, compliments of Scott Enterprises, Inc."

Scott and Jameson again looked at each other, shaking their heads.

At 0630 two days later Scott and Jameson were wheeled into the Officers' Club by Denise and another blond nurse to have breakfast with the Commanding General of the Infantry School. They were joined by Scott's mother, grandfather, Dr. Stern, and, by special invitation, Master Sergeant Scott.

"Ladies and gentlemen, we are about to be joined by General Jaworski and one of his deputies, General Bergeron." The Commandant of the Infantry School smiled.

Jameson looked up a little incredulously, "The Army Chief of Staff?"

"The same. It seems both generals are acquainted with Captain Scott and his grandfather, and it is not often the Army, instead of the President, gets to present the Medal of Honor to one of its own. The White House staff was a little miffed when Scott didn't come back to the States for a White House ceremony. They don't like missing photo ops, particularly when they are taking so much heat. Now they don't have time."

He looked at the door and stood up, "Good morning, Sir."

General Jaworski put his hands on the shoulders of Scott and Jameson, "Don't you boys even think about standing up. Good morning Mrs. Scott, ladies. Mr. Scott, I haven't seen you since the White House, it's again an honor. I understand you all know General Bergeron. Dr. Stern, thank you for arranging this with the Commandant."

Bergeron smiled and nodded as he looked around the table until he came to the nurses. "Denise, is that you?"

"Yes, sir," she said, with a smile barely disguising a smirk.

"Hey, Bergeron, I'm impressed. You even know the pretty nurses. Does your wife know?" the Chief of Staff laughed.

"She knows this one, Sir. Denise was our daughter's French teacher in Panama when I had the 8th Group."

He still could not suppress his surprise, "Denise, how in the world did you end up in the Army? And a nurse?"

Now it was Denise's turn, "Well, sir, when you sent *Sergeant* Scott away and would not tell me where, I decided to join the Army to look for him." Scott just stared down at his coffee cup.

General Jaworski was beginning to enjoy Bergeron's discomfort. "So that's the rest of the Panama story, eh?" he laughed.

To Denise he smiled and said, "Don't be too hard on the general. I remember that came to the Pentagon from a pretty high State Department source. I was under the impression that Scott did not want to go. In fact, he is the only soldier I ever heard of who had to be ordered by the President to take his ROTC commission."

He turned to look at Big Tom, "I see the third Tom Scott here. Sergeant, the Chief of Staff of the United States Army wants to know why you haven't made application for Officer Candidate School."

Big Tom was stunned being addressed by the Army Chief of Staff, "Sir, I…"

"No buts. You do it, and I will personally endorse it. We'll talk about it later." He winked at Old Tom and took his seat.

0800 all current classes of the Infantry School were assembled in the auditorium. The School Sergeant Major called, "**Attention**, the Army Chief of Staff," as the generals entered.

General Jaworski was first to address the students, "At ease, gentlemen. Take your seats. I always enjoy coming back here. I have a lot of memories on this post over two wars. Now we are engaged in a different kind of war, a war of no front lines, a war where the enemy is mixed with and part of the population, a guerrilla war and a counterinsurgency war.

"Today I came down here to recognize two infantry officers, who have just experienced this war as infantry officers do, close up, hand to hand and looking the enemy in the eye, Major William Jameson and Captain Thomas Scott. It should be noted that Major Jameson was the company commander of Captain Scott's basic training company at Ft. Jackson. Therefore, he will take credit for all things accomplished by Captain Scott. Including the Medal of Honor that I am about to present." A laugh went around the room.

"First, I have a Silver Star to present to Major Jameson for his actions on the day you are about to see on slides and hear him narrate. These good looking nurses have already pinned on their Purple Hearts." More laughs around the room.

The Chief of Staff walked over, leaned down to the wheelchair and pinned a Silver Star on a surprised Major Jameson. "Now the major will give a little background on Captain Scott and read his citation before I present the Medal. Both of these officers will also receive the Republic of Vietnam Gallantry Cross and the Joint Service Commendation Medal with V as recommended by the Navy."

Jameson wheeled his chair to the microphone and started to laugh, "Gentlemen, you are not going to believe all this, but it is all true." He then related the story of former sergeant Scott and his decorations from Good Conduct Medal to Distinguished Service Cross, Navy Cross and medals for valor from Nicaragua, Bolivia and Vietnam. "That's a lot of moving around in four years, and he speaks Spanish, French and Vietnamese."

Jameson read the Medal of Honor citation,

"While serving as S-2 for his Special Forces C-Team in Can Tho, Vietnam and inspecting an A-Team on the Mekong River near the Cambodian border, Captain Thomas MacDougall Scott II ... "

General Jaworski took the medal on the blue ribbon with thirteen white stars from the sergeant major and placed it around Scott's neck. "There is no question of *'conspicuous gallantry and intrepidity at the risk of his own life above and beyond the call of duty.'* Captain, it looks like I will be saluting you from now on. I believe you have something to say." The general stepped back, saluted and added his applause to that of a standing audience.

Old Tom leaned over and explained to Denise that it was tradition for even officers of higher rank to salute any recipient of the Medal of Honor.

With Big Tom's help Scott was able to stand behind the lectern, look out at the assembled infantry officers and speak. "As all of you out there wearing a Combat Infantryman Badge know, you are never alone on the battlefield, someone is with you, trying to get to you or supporting you. That day I was not alone. This man supporting me now was there supporting me then, and help was on the way. That is why you see that Distinguished Service Cross on his chest below the CIB. He fired his M-79 at both ends of the VC ranks until it melted and caused so much confusion within the VC that they did not know which way to shoot except at each other. He gave me the time to crawl out of that stinking hog wallow."

He turned to General Jaworski and the Commandant and said, "General, I hope you will forgive a bit of combat humor, and not hold it against my best friend here." General Jaworski smiled and nodded his head. "When I crawled back to the sergeant with a grenade fragment in my back, he dug it out and poured antiseptic on the wound. I could distinctly smell rum. I asked him what the hell he was doing out there with rum. He nonchalantly said, 'Shit, I figured if you didn't make it, I'd just get fucking drunk before they killed me.' Then we had a long drink." He waited for the laughter to die down and said, "Then we got the hell out of the way of that incoming napalm and captured an NVA general along the way." More applause. He noticed out of the corner of his eye the generals laughing and clapping. Big Tom just looked at the floor shaking his head.

"I'll have some more to say with Major Jameson, but I would like to recognize my personal hero, my grandfather. Please stand up, Granpa. He was the recipient of the Medal of Honor as a sixteen-year-old sailor in a land engagement that probably saved the landing on Cuba in the Spanish American War." More standing applause. "Thank you."

The Commandant took the lectern. "Gentlemen, we'll have a fifteen minute break while we set up a slide presentation as an introduction to an added section on riverine warfare to your courses, as experienced by these two officers." The sergeant major ordered, "**Attention!**" as the generals left.

During the presentation Tommy's mother sat holding hands with Denise. Their conversation had been in French since she had realized Denise was *the girl in Paris*. They had been joined by General and Mrs. Bergeron, who were Denise's longtime supporters in the Canal Zone.

"*Attention!*" ordered the Sgt. Major.

The generals re-entered and the Commandant ordered, "At ease, gentlemen. You have noticed in your handouts that we have altered your training schedule, because of the unusual opportunity to show the revival of a use of infantry not seen since the Civil War, *Riverine Warfare*. Fortunately for us, not so fortunate for these two officers in wheelchairs, they are here. This short presentation will be developed into a section of our curriculum in two weeks. It promises to be very instructive and very timely for the current action in Vietnam. Major Jameson will narrate as slides are shown. He was the Executive Officer of the advance battalion sent to the Mekong Delta by his brigade to develop on the ground, and in combat, procedures for combined operations with the Navy."

Jameson wheeled to the microphone. "There are many more photos, but these will give you the story. Sergeant Major, the first slide please."

The first slide was an aerial of the delta showing the maze of waterways, mangrove swamps and rice paddies. He briefly explained the significance of the area food supply and dense population to the enemy war effort, and the difficulty of the terrain.

"This second slide shows the Navy support contingent and their weaponry. We will go into detail later in your courses.

"Next shows an overlay of the battle plan and disposition of units to drive the VC into the anvil at the end of this peninsula. That's how *we planned* it.

"Next. Now it gets a little sticky. The VC are very clever and resourceful. To paraphrase Baron Von Clausewitz, '*Engage the same enemy too long and he adapts to your tactics.*' They learn quickly. From our prior operations and probably a little inside information, they were ready, and our battalion was what they were after, not vice versa. They had their mortars sited and a plan to concentrate and break through Alpha Company in order to surround us.

"The next slide I call *Ouch*. Two mortars bracket my headquarters position. I lost my sergeant. major, radio man, medic, and I'm sitting in a wheelchair, but the fight doesn't stop. These are real time photos, some from ground level and some from the command helicopter. They are fascinating, instructive, inspiring, and sad. In this situation you are not trying to remember what happened. You are reacting to your training and the mission, and your men are reacting as you trained them. I thought I was going to die in my fox hole with no communication, but now I can see I actually crawled to Bravo Company to get a radio to control the action.

"Next. This is the mess that was going on in Alpha where Captain Scott was in command. He thought I was dead and was trying to communicate with the other companies, the Navy and the battalion commander, while his company was being attacked by an entire VC battalion. The VC had planned to overwhelm his company, then surround our other two companies while they were engaged by another VC battalion.

"Next. This slide shows rows of dead VC as a result of Captain Scott's experience and foresight to load up on Claymores when defending a fixed position. Some VC were actually on top of soldiers in the middle of Alpha. There is no way to overestimate the effect of those 700+ screaming steel balls from a Claymore on an attacking enemy.

"Next. This is another wave of attacking VC. Probably 40% of Alpha has been wounded, and Captain Scott and his 1st Sergeant have taken over a machine gun after its gunner and assistant were killed. By now both have been wounded, and that is the radio man crouched in the emplacement trying to keep Scott in touch with the other companies and the Navy.

"Next. There are about 100 dead VC in front of Scott's machine gun, and that one you see is falling on top of Scott with a grenade. Fortunately, Scott was able to shove the body on top of the grenade. So, the three of them only received some shrapnel in the legs.

"Next. Shows me crawling around behind Bravo and Charlie trying to keep up the fight. By now Scott was talking to me on the radio through his radio man while under attack. It is a little hard to hear with all that gunfire. You need to anticipate and react.

"Next shows the VC shifting the remainder of their first battalion to join the attack on Bravo when they couldn't break through Alpha. We had a problem in direct fire support from the Navy because of the raised terrain we were on and a low tide. Plus the Navy and our mortar barge were under rocket and RPG attack from the other side of the river and our reserve company had been drawn off to aid the ARVN. The VC had this well planned except for what they encountered with Alpha. They left over two hundred dead in front of and among Alpha, but they still had over two hundred to add to the battalion attacking Bravo.

"Next. Shows Scott out of his machine gun emplacement and urging his men to attack the VC flank, when he realized the attack had shifted from his position.

"Next. Shows Scott leading a charge of the remnants of Alpha into the VC flank in hand to hand fighting.

"Next. Shows me urging Charlie Company to press from the other flank.

"Next. Shows the Navy coming in, to fire on the rear elements of the VC and land Delta Company, our reserve company. The flanking attack by Alpha had completely disrupted the VC attack and they were unable to get organized to meet the Navy and Delta Company.

"Next shows Scott on the ground with the last VC he killed with a bayonet and the medic trying to get blood into him, while Lieutenant Colonel McCauley had jumped out of the helicopter to lead his battalion in the fight. Dr. Stern at Martin Army Hospital confirmed that by then Scott had twenty-seven wounds when he led that charge. About that time air support arrived and it was over. The whole thing had taken about an hour.

"We were lucky, but without the fire discipline and initiative they teach here, we were lost. In the lesson plan we are preparing we will give you a more complete picture of riverine warfare. Captain Scott do you have anything to add?"

"No, sir. I think I have relived that one hour enough for the time being."

General Jaworski stood up. "I have one more thing to add. Along with these real time photos, Lieutenant Colonel McCauley sent me a recommendation for a second Medal of Honor for Captain Scott, endorsed by Major Jameson and the brigade commander. There have been very, very few second awards and never have they been supported by actual photos of the whole action. Captain Scott's initiative, bravery and determination in those few minutes were the difference in this battle. For now, I need to get back to the Pentagon. Major Jameson, I look forward to a copy of the lesson plan." Looking out over the assembled officers, he said, "And I hope you gentlemen do also. We will be sending some of you into that environment."

"***Attention!***" barked the school Sergeant Major.

On the way out the Chief of Staff stopped to shake Old Tom's hand, leaned over to whisper, "Get me some real political heat on this one," and patted him on the back. Old Tom smiled that very knowing political smile.

He turned to Denise, "Take good care of him, Lieutenant. We are going to need him."

General Bergeron winked at her as he followed his boss out. Tommy's mother and Mrs. Bergeron had skipped this presentation, having been warned it would be very graphic, but Dr. Jacob Stern had stayed. Even he had to wince at the very real photographs of combat and rows of dead and dying.

By the end of the month Scott was out of his wheelchair, finished in residence the Advanced Course, and had received orders to report to General Bergeron at the Pentagon. For their work on developing and presenting the riverine warfare addition to the curriculum, Major Jameson and Captain Scott received Oak Leaf Clusters on their Commendation Medals and Master Sergeant Scott received his first one, along with orders to report to Officer Candidate School at Ft. Benning. Major Jameson received orders to report to the Infantry School to continue developing and teaching the riverine warfare section.

A side effect of all this was the reassignment of Army Nurse 1st Lieutenant Johanson to the Pentagon, where she shares a very nice three bedroom apartment with a fireplace on the Potomac River with a certain Captain Thomas MacD. Scott.

CHAPTER 21

THE PENTAGON

ARLINGTON COUNTY, VIRGINIA

The five sided building of 6,500,000 square feet with five floors and two basement levels was designed in 1941 and completed in stages by 1943. The pentagon shape had been required by the original shape of the land to be used and was constructed with a minimum amount of steel because of the war effort. The plan had been later shifted to a larger tract of land, but President Roosevelt liked the design, and it was kept. It houses the Department of Defense and all military services.

Day one in the Pentagon, Scott was assigned a small office adjacent to Gen. Bergeron. "Sir, the general wants you in his office," were the very firm words of the Sergeant Major assigned to Bergeron.

On entering and saluting, he noticed it was appropriately decorated with Army memorabilia and a framed Green Beret with the yellow and blue flash of the 8th Special Forces Group over the general's desk. A short, oriental-appearing Army colonel was sitting to the side.

"Tom, this is Colonel Wong from G-2."

The colonel reached out his hand, "It is an honor to meet you, Major."

Scott hesitated a moment, "Sorry, Sir. I am only a captain."

Colonel Wong's eyes never moved from Scott's, "As of this minute, you have the temporary rank of major, and here are your oak leaves and your orders, Major."

The general came around the desk, "Tom, you turned me down a couple of times for that second lieutenant commission. Now it's my turn for surprises."

The sergeant major removed Scott's captain bars and the general pinned the gold oak leaves on the epaulets of his green jacket.

"Congratulations, Major."

Scott was thinking, *Here comes the big chess board again.* He was right.

"Colonel Wong and I served in Korea together before he got smart after his CIB and Purple Heart. He switched to intelligence. Now we want to talk to you along those lines. You have more glory than you will ever know what to do with, and you are too smart to stick you back out in the lines, and you speak four languages."

Scott did not say anything. He just waited for the other shoe to drop.

Wong was thinking, *Very good. No reaction. He's just waiting.*

A knock on the door. The Sergeant Major stuck his head in, "Sir, Mr. Spalding is here."

"Send him in."

Jonathan Spalding walked into the room looking ten years older than the last time Scott had seen him. He smiled, "Good morning, General, Colonel," and turned to Scott, "Tommy, nice to see you again," and shook his hand.

Scott acknowledged him, but was thinking, *Surely, they don't want me in the CIA.*

The Sergeant Major knocked again, "Sir, he's here."

"Send him in without the guard."

Scott turned to see a man in a business suit.

"*Ola, Tomasito. Mucho gusto a verte,*" said North Vietnamese Army General François de Rousseau, looking very much like he belonged in the Pentagon.

The chess board was taking shape.

Scott could not help himself. He took de Rousseau's hand and turned it into an *abrazo*.

He looked at Bergeron, "Pardon me, Sir. This goes back two wars and a revolution."

"We know," said an expressionless Colonel Wong.

Scott stared back into the cold eyes of Colonel Wong and wondered how he could ever work for this cold fish.

As if reading his mind, Wong said, "You will not be working directly for me. You are assigned to General Bergeron, as am I. Mr. Spalding will be our liaison with the Agency."

Scott still said nothing.

Sensing some animosity developing, de Rousseau said in French, "It is not so bad, Thomas. I am not betraying my country, and Colonel Wong and I are actually related through my Chinese grandmother."

Finally, Scott addressed de Rousseau, "How is your son, General?"

"He is recovering, thanks to you."

"As you did for my father, General."

Another knock from the sergeant major, "Sir, the Chief of Staff is on his way down."

Two minutes later the door opened. "Attention!" was the sergeant major's announcement.

"As you were, gentlemen. It looks like everyone knows each other. Good. And I see we have a new major. Congratulations, Scott."

"Thank you, Sir."

General Jaworski looked around the room. "I'll be brief. I have met everyone here, and I am familiar with this operation. I have approved it, but I will not be involved. I don't expect it to cross my desk again until there are some positive results. You have all been carefully selected for this Top Secret 'Eyes Only' mission. Major Scott, just for your comfort, I can assure you that General de Rousseau has not been tortured or turned against his country, and you will be working toward a mutual goal. That is all."

The sergeant major called "Attention!" and the Chief of Staff left the room.

My God. Scott was thinking, *This chess board is really too big.*

"Well, gentlemen, you heard it from the boss. Let's get on with it. We need to explain to Scott what we have put him into," Bergeron said as he sat back down behind his desk.

Spalding took up the briefing, "Tommy, briefly, this mission is to get both sides talking to each other off the record and through back channels. Thanks to you, General de Rousseau is here and his son, Captain de Rousseau, is alive and has been discharged from the hospital and assigned to a prisoner of war camp in Can Tho. Your familiarity with this area and some of the Special Forces and ARVN officers there will be critical. First, we need to establish communication between the general and his son regarding our intent. Next we need to *arrange* his escape to further communications with the North." Spalding stopped and smiled at the disbelief on Scott's face.

The next day, before Scott could even figure out the floor plan of the mammoth building, he received a call from Bergeron to report to General Jaworski. *Now what?*, was all he could think.

He met General Jaworski coming out of his door. "Scott, we're going to see the Secretary of Defense. Don't worry. He just wants to meet you. Obviously, your second nomination has reached his desk."

The Secretary's assistant announced their arrival and escorted them in. Scott didn't know whether to salute or stand quietly. Jaworski solved that problem.

"Mr. Secretary, this is Major Scott."

The Secretary of Defense looked up over his glasses and walked around his desk with his hand extended. "Major, it is my honor to meet you. You may not have met the Chairman of the Joint Chiefs of Staff, General Stinson, but he and I have just signed our recommendation for your second Medal of Honor. Congratulations."

Scott had not noticed the Chairman sitting off to the side, but now he was shaking his hand and stammering, "Thank you, Sir."

The Chairman added, "I understand you already met the President. I'm sorry I wasn't there with General Jaworski. I also understand the Secretary has met your grandfather."

"Indeed I have. A fine gentleman," acknowledged the Secretary. "Well, we just wanted to meet you and offer our congratulations. We also want to keep you around for a bit. Thank you for coming, and for your service to your country."

It was obviously time to follow General Jaworski back out of the office.

The general turned to Scott with a big grin, "Well, Scott, how do you feel?"

"I'm not sure, Sir."

"That's OK. Get over it and get back to work."

"Yes, Sir."

He reported back to General Bergeron, who had a very big smile on his face. "Well, how was that for a surprise?"

"Overwhelming, Sir."

"Good. Get back to preparing your plan."

It was late April now and still cold enough to light a fire in the fireplace. Scott and Denise lay naked on a fake bear skin rug under a blanket in front of the fire. Scott had been trying to figure out how to tell her he had to go back to Vietnam, when she suddenly said, "You're going back again. Aren't you?"

Startled at her intuition, he simply said, "Yes, but no combat, and it's temporary."

"Oh, bullshit. Every street corner over there is combat. It's Bergeron again. I knew it."

He rubbed her smooth back and whispered, "I love you."

He could feel tears running down her cheek and onto his arm as she replied, "I love you too, and I can't stand the thought of losing you again."

She suddenly sat up, her fair skin and blond hair reflecting the flickering flames in the fireplace. "I'm going too. An Army nurse needs front line experience, not a desk job in the Pentagon."

He reached up and pulled her down into his arms and whispered, "Tomorrow."

The next morning General Bergeron received two requests for his assistance and influence. Both were requests for assignment to Viet Nam, from Denise, and Jacob Stern. Both of which he had relayed to the Chief of Staff, who raised his eyebrows in warning to the obvious request for influence.

"General Bergeron, under any other circumstances I would be upset, but we probably owe these two individuals something, and the Army does need medical help over there. You have my permission to make an *inquiry* with personnel in my name."

"Thank you, Sir."

By afternoon wheels were turning in the Personnel Division for two medical personnel to be assigned to units in Viet Nam.

CHAPTER 22

C- TEAM HEADQUARTERS, 5ᵗʰ SPECIAL FORCES GROUP

CAN THO, VIET NAM

Scott entered the office of his old C-Team. The new sergeant major showed him to the office of the commanding officer. The sign on the door read **Mario A. Thibodaux, Lt. Col.** with a Special Forces **De Oppressor Liber** emblem at the end.

"Goddamn, Scott. I was warned you were coming. What brings you back? I see you are not wearing a Green Beret. So, I assume this is not a social call…and wearing a gold oak leaf. My, my, I guess wallowing around with the pigs is one way to get ahead."

Scott smiled. "Hello, Mario. I was glad to see you stopped loafing in a hospital bed and got back on duty. I like that silver oak leaf on you. I'm surprised they sent you right back here."

"Well, they knew I like the swamps, and I took all the credit for your crawling around in the pig shit. Been pretty quiet up there ever since. Besides, they gave me a Silver Star, and I wanted the promotion they offered for my heroic deeds. What's up?"

"*Sneaky Pete* shit, Mario. I already cleared you at the Pentagon, because I need your help. The 5ᵗʰ Group was ordered to cooperate."

"Pentagon stuff, eh? This sounds threatening. My orders just say 'COOPERATE.'"

Scott smiled. "You have no idea."

Thibodaux rolled his eyes. "Oh shit. Every time the *real* Army tells us to do something we do end up in the shit. Well, *garçon*, you done saved dis Cajun's ass two times. So, I am happy to save yours." They both laughed.

"*Muchas gracias, Jefe.* Let me close this door, and I'll blow your mind."

Scott briefed him.

"Jesus Christ, Tom. Does the 5th or MACV or the ambassador have any idea about this?"

"Nope. Just you and me and Bergeron's little group…and the Chief…and the Chairman…and the Secretary… and the CIA. I need you to connect me with a 'trustworthy' guy in the ARVN at the POW camp or higher."

"Damn, let's go over to the club. We've improved it since you were here."

The painted eyes on the cutoff bow of the junk looked even more menacing and suspicious than the last time he looked into them, but the whiskey rack behind them was bigger.

"Inn Keeper, bring this ex-SF guy a rum and Coke," Thibodaux ordered the NCO behind the bar. "I know he loves the smell of rum mixed with the sweet smell of the delta."

He turned to Scott. "I heard about that mess up at Dong Tam. They always say you can't stay out of trouble, and Bergeron sent you right back into it. Is he still trying to get even?"

Scott laughed. "God, I hope not."

"I also heard a rumor that they put you in for a second Medal."

"So I heard. I don't even remember what happened that day, but they had photos of the action. What I do know is that I have twenty-seven new holes in my body… and morphine does work wonders. In any event, no more running around with bayonets. This requires your sneaky Cajun mind set, if you are up to it."

"You got dat right, *mon ami*. Let's talk about it before I pick the right guy. Are we goin' to pay him in real money or that phony CIA shit?"

"Ten grand, real. They will even put it in an account for him in the USA."

"Damn. I might do it myself." Both laughed.

"First, I need to get in there and deliver a message to him from his father, the general. At this point, he knows nothing."

"Well, you're the guy who captured him and saved his life. I think we can get in there on some pretense, but getting him out is somethin' else. Let me start with our U.S. Army Military Police advisor at the camp. They have a real mess over there with women VC, children, NVA, and regular VC."

Scott thought about that. "Let me talk to Bergeron. I'm sure we can get a polite request from the Pentagon to this captain's superiors before we talk to the ARVN."

By 1300 the next day the *polite* request had been conveyed and relayed to the camp commander and his U.S. advisor.

Scott and Thibodaux were met at the camp gate by Captain Heinz Orwig, U.S. Army Military Police. "Good morning, Colonel, Major. Welcome to our Boy Scout camp."

Scott smiled and thought, 'An MP with a sense of humor… and a little accent. Good.'

"Major Scott, I understand you captured Captain de Rousseau and his father, a general."

"Yes. Not very difficult. They were pretty shot up."

Orwig didn't press it. He knew the Medal of Honor story, and had been advised to *cooperate*.

He escorted them to the camp commander's office. Major Cao looked up and greeted Thibodaux in French, and Thibodaux introduced Scott in French.

Orwig had been warned that this may be a sensitive Pentagon matter. So, he excused himself, also in French. Scott was thinking, *I like this captain. He picks it up in a hurry.*

Some polite conversation followed and recognition of Scott's role up at the Cambodian border. Major Cao's eyes showed he knew something more was up than a polite visit to his camp.

Cao said, "Let us take a walk down to the vegetable gardens. That is where we have the captain working."

Scott was surprised at the amount of vegetables growing and could not help but wonder what they used for fertilizer. On second thought, he did not want to know.

"De Rousseau, come here," ordered the major. The captain dutifully came with his head bowed.

"This American major wishes to speak with you. If you do not recognize him, he is the one who captured you and saved your life.

Be grateful."

Scott and de Rousseau stared at each other. Both tried to re-member what the other looked like that night. Scott looked at the thin figure of a once handsome young man and smiled. "That was a difficult night for both of us. But I have met with your father and he sends you his love." Their conversation was in French. de Rousseau's eyes brightened at the mention of his father. Now he was remembering all the stories about the Scott family.

"Major Scott, you may walk around this area with him. I will signal the guards to allow it. Colonel Mario and I have some wom-en and drinks to talk about. Take your time." With that he made the grand gesture of showing Thibodaux back to his office via a short stroll around the perimeter.

Scott turned back to the young captain. "Jean François, if I may call you by your first name, I have a letter here from your fa-ther. Take your time and read it. I will have to destroy it when you finish." Scott turned away to avoid the man's tears. He was aware of the watchful eyes of the guards in the towers and the surprising submissiveness of the other prisoners in the vegetable garden. Ei-ther these prisoners were sufficiently glad to be able to work in the garden or they had been broken down enough that they were not a threat to escape or riot.

Scott turned back to Jean François, "You may read it a couple more times, but I must have it back. I do have a recent picture of your father that you may keep when you are finished."

Scott knew that there were certain expressions and wording in the letter from the father to the son which would verify the authenticity.

With trembling hands he returned the letter and accepted the photograph of his father in a business suit, which contained some words which only they understood. "My father says I should listen to you and do as you say."

"Yes. This is for the good of both our countries." Scott then re-lated the plan he had devised with Colonel Wong. "At this moment Lieutenant Colonel Thibodaux, who met your father the day you were captured, is talking to your camp commander on his terms and the method of your *escape*. It would appear that he has certain useful connections outside of this camp."

De Rousseau's eyes were becoming brighter with hope. Circumstances had led him to believe that he would not be eligible for a release with others being released or exchanged because of overcrowding in prisons. "Whatever you say, Major."

"Good. We will talk again." Scott turned and left him to his vegetable tending, but he could feel his eyes all the way back to the camp commandant's office. Scott and Thibodaux walked slowly back to the jeep. Scott raised his eyebrows. "Well?"

Thibodaux continued to look straight ahead. "The sonofabitch wants $20,000 and $2,000 for his helpers."

"Don't worry, Mario, its only CIA money, not Army."

Mario grinned, "Same old shit."

"I told you it was *Sneaky Pete* shit. *Laissez les bons temps rouler.*" They both laughed at Thibodaux's favorite Cajun expression.

Two days later Jonathan Spalding showed up in Thibodaux's office with Scott, and that evening Jean François de Rousseau slipped into a sampan to disappear into the delta.

CHAPTER 23

The Pentagon...Paris

Three days later Scott was back in the Pentagon trying to shake off jet lag. Denise was still waiting for orders to Vietnam, but very happy to see him back.

"Major Scott, the general wants to see you," announced the sergeant major, in his usual official manner through the opened door.

Bergeron looked up, "Tom, well done. We'll have to give Thibodaux a Commendation Medal for 'classified services rendered for the good of the service.'"

"Just more *Sneaky Pete* shit, Sir." Scott said.

Bergeron laughed, "I remember such things. We have contacted your friend, Lieutenant Colonel Benoit, in France and told him you would be coming to Paris. He is currently assigned to an intelligence unit and teaching at Saint-Cyr, their military academy. I don't think the wheels are turning in North Vietnam quite yet. They still need to verify some things. So, we have a little time to set things up. Can you use a little time in Paris?"

"*Absolument, mon General.*"

"One other thing. I understand Denise is being assigned to a hospital in Vietnam, but she doesn't have to report for forty-five days." Bergeron got a very sly grin on his face. "I understand you two met in Paris. Would you object to her being assigned as your assistant on TDY for that period of time? You do need an assistant don't you?"

"More than you know, General." They both broke out laughing.

"I don't want to spoil your fun, but Colonel Wong is already there talking to some of his friends in French intelligence."

Scott grinned, "I will try very hard not to let it spoil anything."

That evening at supper Scott wore a very serious expression and told Denise that he had to tell her something. She used her best narrowed eye stare to warn him that it better not be another abandonment.

Scott cleared his throat to prolong the suspense. "Denise, I have to leave again."

"Where, may I ask?" she said with her eyes still narrowed.

"Paris for thirty days." He let that soak in as her eyes widened. "But I will have an assistant."

"Who?" her eyes were narrowing again.

"You...Your orders are already being cut. You do type. Don't you?"

Open-mouthed, she didn't know what expression to give him. So, he put his wine glass down. came around the table and kissed her on the forehead and said, "No shit. Thanks to Bergeron."

She looked up, "You SOB. Bear skin rug time, *tout suite.*"

Two days later they were circling in the landing pattern of Orly Airport in Paris. As familiar landmarks passed below, Denise's hand tightened on his. "Oh, I feel it happening all over again."

After *abuelita's* death Old Tom could not bring himself to sell the Paris apartment furnished by her in real Louis XV decor. He just let friends and business associates use it. Now it was available, and the same maid, Marie, had kept it clean for many years. She was delighted to see Tommy and even remembered Denise. It was like a homecoming for both of them.

Scott smiled, "Well, shall we go to our favorite restaurant or go to sleep after that crossing?"

"Are you kidding? I'm going to enjoy every minute and spend all this TDY *per diem* money."

"Don't forget you are here as my assistant on Army business."

"Yes, *SIR*. What would you have me assist you with in this moment?"

"I'll give it about ten seconds of thought."

Later, supper on the *Avenue des Champs-Élysées, la plus belle avenue du monde,* was as good as they remembered, and dreams were very pleasant.

At 0700 Scott picked up the telephone with one eye open, barely remembering what language he was supposed to be speaking, "*Bonjour.*"

The unusually friendly voice of Colonel Wong came back, "*Bonjour, commandante.* Are you ready to go to work?"

"*Qui, colonel.*"

"*Bien,* meet me at the Café du Monde on the corner in thirty minutes."

"Yes, sir."

Denise turned over, "Who was that?'

"Colonel Wong. Go back to sleep. I'll be back before 0900."

The Café du Monde was a small open air café two blocks from the *Champs-Elysees* and quiet at that time in the morning. Apparently, the colonel knew his way around Paris and expected Scott to know also.

Scott had shaved and put on his casual civilian clothes. "*Bonjour, monsieur* Wong." He was careful not to use a military greeting.

Wong sat drinking his coffee and eating a beignet. "*Bonjour,* Mister Scott. Please, sit down and have some breakfast." Scott had to smile as he watched Wong sipping his coffee out of a saucer in the very French manner.

Scott wondered if the owner had copied the famous café in New Orleans by the same name. Those Cajun doughnuts sounded great and coffee was a necessity. He laughed to himself and wondered what Thibodaux was doing now.

Wong lit a cigarette, inhaled, and looked at the scenery along the street. "I love this beautiful city. A man of any background is welcome and can become lost from the world."

It was a subtle reminder that Wong's business was appearing and disappearing and knowing things others did not. He obviously had something to discuss.

Wong inhaled deeply and repeated. "I love this city. Maybe that is why I liked Saigon so much. *The Paris of the Orient. C'est magnifique.*" He paused for a moment. "But that will all be gone, and that brings us to you. You are the only person in the world we could use for this. You speak French like a native Parisian, father actually fought alongside Ho Chi Minh in WW II, have old family connections to a North Vietnamese general, whom you actually captured in battle, and you saved the life of his son."

"As I recall, Mr. Wong, he is your relative."

Wong sipped his coffee and again looked down the street. "Yes, the Chinese claim relations even if it was five generations ago. Perhaps it gives them some sense of security by that distant connection, or a false belief that they are dealing with an honest person. Whatever, it does give them an opening in the conversation." Scott remained silent. Wong smiled and looked back at Scott thinking, *This boy is clever. Very good.*

"In any event, Mr. Scott, with the help of my friends here in French Intelligence you will now become a French businessman trading in the African nation of Côte d'Ivoire. The purpose of this is to give you a French passport and background in order to enter North Vietnam. Once there you will arrange an exchange of prisoners for the general. Of course, Captain de Rousseau will meet you, and introduce you to *certain government officials.'* Scott still remained silent, waiting for the other shoe to drop.

Wong's eyes narrowed to those slits that Scott remembered from the first meeting. "*Tu me comprends?*"

Scott's eyes met his. "Yes, Mister Wong. I understand what you said. And Denise?"

"*Bien.* She will still be your assistant in the *true French sense of the word.* She will even travel with you to Africa to meet some *merchants.* We were counting on the fact that her French is reasonably good. She has been cleared, but her need to know will be limited. You both will select new French names for your new passports."

Sonofabitch. They built her into the equation all this time. Now they stuck me with handling her, were his first thoughts, but he just said, "Yes, SIR."

"Good. We will meet again day after tomorrow. Go enjoy the sights of Paris…again, and start speaking only in French…and start growing a beard."

Scott remembered he was told a month ago to let his hair grow to a length which could be combed and styled like a European businessman. Now it looked like they really wanted to disguise him, and cover up his *sabre scar.*

When he returned to the apartment, Denise was fixing coffee. He definitely needed more, without the chicory.

"*Ma cheri,* this trip is going to be more interesting than I imagined."

"Oh?"

"We are to change our names and from now on only speak in French, and I have to grow a beard. What name would you like on your French passport?'

Her eyebrows went up. "*Tres bien, mon cher.* This sounds like fun and very mysterious. You will look *magnifique* with a beard. My first name is French anyway and my mother's name was *Dufor* I think I will keep them, but what do we do with a Scotsman like you? "

"You know, I have ancestors named Rousseau. I shall be Jean Thomas Rousseau…and you will have to cut that gorgeous blond hair even shorter to look more like an *assistant.* But for now, let's go back to Napoleon's tomb where all this started, before we become different people."

A very big smile spread across her face after a short pout about the hair.

Breakfast with Colonel Wong at the Café du Monde meeting included Denise.Wong smiled, "*Bonjour.*" He seemed much more relaxed in Paris than in the Pentagon.

The French teacher in Denise could not resist asking, "*Monsieur* Wong, where did you learn your French, to be so fluent?"

His smile broadened. "Actually, I was born in Saigon of ethnic Chinese parents during the French colonial era. So I grew up speaking French, Cantonese and Vietnamese. I had to learn Mandarin later and get rid of the accent in my French. My father worked in the American consulate. So, I learned English, and before the French political situation in Vietnam became very difficult, we immigrated to California. I joined ROTC at UCLA, and here I am… and that's as much background as you will get."

Scott whistled his admiration, "*Mademoiselle,* I am impressed you got that much out of this gentleman."

She tilted her head sideways and raised her eyebrows. "So am I."

Wong laughed. "Now I have a surprise for you. I see your new wardrobe consultant arriving, but first tell me your new names."

Scott spoke for her. "She is keeping *Denise* and using her mother's maiden name *Dufor.*

Wong nodded. "*Bon.*"

"I am Jean Thomas Rousseau."

Wong's eyes narrowed, but Scott met his questioning look. "I have ancestors named Rousseau, and I feel comfortable with that name."

Wong thought for a moment. "OK." He turned to watch a tall, attractive brunette approaching their table. "And here is your consultant, Madame Benoit. Your employer will pay for whatever she recommends."

Madame Benoit held out her hand. "*Bonjour,* Monsieur Wong." She looked at Scott with some surprise. "Tommy Scott, is that you behind that scruff on your face?"

Scott laughed, "Hi, Madeline."

Wong was taken aback and his mind raced through backgrounds. He thought, 'Of course, her husband is a colonel in the French Army and served in Bolivia when Scott was there. Bergeron was right, this kid is full of surprises.' He kicked himself for missing that.

Denise was still at a loss for words by his familiarity with this attractive French woman.

Scott smiled at her. "Don't worry, Denise. I know this gorgeous woman's husband. He's a French Army Colonel."

She could only say, "Oh."

A warning look from Wong told them not to elaborate. He simply said. "Yes. The Colonel is currently assigned here in Paris with an intelligence unit." He calculated that the mention of *intelligence unit* should end any further conversation about the connection, and it did.

Denise also thought she better stick with the unexpected pleasure of *paid for shopping* with a real fashion consultant. Being the wife of an intelligence officer, Madame Benoit knew to stick to business.

The next week was a combination of fun for Denise (now Denise Dufor) shopping with Madame Benoit and learning with Scott (now Jean Thomas Rousseau) about foreign imports in French.

At the end of the week Colonel Wong had his usual breakfast with them at the Café du Monde and announced that they would be going to Côte d'Ivoire (The Ivory Coast) the next week to negotiate coffee and cocoa imports. It was located on the west coast of Africa, on the north coast of the Gulf of Guinea, bordered on the west by Liberia, the country settled by expatriated American slaves, and on the east by Ghana. Côte d'Ivoire was a former French colony named after one of its original exports, ivory from elephant tusk. At the moment it was a thriving independent African country leading the world in the export of cocoa, third in the world in coffee and leading Africa in exporting pineapples and palm oil. French technicians and businessmen were in high demand. In contrast to the rest of Africa, more foreigners had migrated in than out since independence in 1960. The current president, Houphouët-Boigny, was a popular leader emphasizing trade, and a former trade union leader and cocoa farmer. He had even been hosted by President Kennedy in 1962. Scott was further informed that he would be met there by certain "representatives."

At the airport in Abidjan, Scott (Rousseau) and his "assistant," Denise Dufor, were met by an official government car and taken to the President's Palace where they waited for a meeting. Scott, by himself, was escorted to a waiting room adjacent to the president's office where he waited another hour. When escorted into the president's office, he was met by a very pleasant President Houphouët-Boigny, with an Army colonel standing off to the side.

"*Bon jour, Monsieur Rousseau,* I only wanted to meet you to assure you that I am aware of your visit and have no objections. As a former Member of the French Parliament and minister, I am kept informed of anything unusual in my country. I sincerely hope you enjoy our country, and your business is successful, and our country makes a profit as well." He thought for a second and added, "Oh, I met your late president at a reception in Washington...and your grandfather there. Perhaps he would even be interested in exporting some of our cocoa at a very good price. Thank you for coming. It was a pleasure to meet you."

Scott tried to not show any surprise or concern. "Thank you, *Monsieur President*. It was my honor." With that he was politely escorted to the door.

The president turned to his colonel after Scott left. "A very interesting young man. Make sure nothing happens to him."

On the way back to where they had positioned Denise, his mind was racing, *What just happened? Obviously, he wanted me to know that he knew why I was here and who I was. Was it a threat, or was it an assurance? Did he really want to sell more cocoa? Did he really know my grandfather? It's going to take a while to get used to the African mentality.*

Denise looked up. "What was that about?"

"I'll tell you later. Right now I believe we have a ride to the hotel."

The Golden Hotel in downtown Abidjan was not the old French colonial style he had expected, like Saigon. It had a considerably more modern façade, but was adequate and had conveniently adjoining rooms. A note was waiting for him at the front desk requesting that he come to the bar at six in the evening.

A tall, slender European man was waiting at the bar and waived Scott to a table. "*Bonsoir, Monsieur Rousseau*. I understand you have met the President."

"*Oui.*" Scott waited to see what was next and who this player was.

"*Bon,* my name is Charles Charbonnet. I am stationed here in Côte d'Ivoire, and I have spoken to your Mr. Wong. I am to assist you in your commercial affairs here and make sure you make a profit. I trust your quarters are adequate."

"Very nice, thank you."

"*Tres bien,* I will have your cocoa invoices and manifest at 1900, when you and your assistant are invited to supper. *Non?*"

"*Merci, Monsieur Charbonnet.*"

"Now I would like to introduce you to another Monsieur de Rousseau who is also on a trade mission."

Charbonnet turned and made a slight wave of his hand to another table. Another well-dressed business man came to the table, smiling as he approached. *Sonofabitch, that was smooth,* Scott laughed to himself as he arose to greet the real purpose of his visit.

"I assume you gentlemen know each other. Please excuse me. I will see you at supper. Monsieur de Rousseau, I assume you will join us."

"*Avec plaisir.*" Jean François took his seat, still smiling.

"Jean François, you look a lot better than the last time I saw you."

"Many thanks to you. Now tell me how you are using that last name."

"Very simple. Some of my ancestors came to America around the time of the French Revolution and quickly dropped the "de" from the name. I always wanted to use it and my superiors did not object *too much*. I don't think my father ever knew it, and I didn't tell your father. We were probably related in France about 175 years ago. Your grandfathers went to Southeast Asia and mine went to America. *C'est la vie.*" They both laughed at that little twist of fate.

De Rousseau turned serious. "I have discussed this exchange and the intent behind it with both the President and the General. In truth, they are both curious to meet the son of their old friend, T.R. Scott, who has given our Army so much trouble. However, this does not guarantee much progress on overall relations at this stage. There are many other factions influencing decisions. I do not believe at this moment much progress can be made, but as Confucius said, *"Journey of a thousand miles begins with one step."*

"Indeed, and we both know that Ho's father was a Confucius scholar."

"*Touché, Monsieur Rousseau.* And how is my father?"

"I have letters and pictures here for you, your sister and your mother. Actually, they are unopened, because he gave them to me personally. Please do not tell my superiors." They both laughed.

"*Bien, Jean Thomas.* Since we are traders, I have black pepper. We are one of the world's largest exporters of black pepper and rice, but at the moment we need our rice for our soldiers."

"Ah, *Jean Franois*, today I just happen to have a bargain price for cocoa. Let us make a deal."

They agreed to make a deal and toasted it with Napoleon Brandy. "Until supper."

Back in the room Scott advised Denise who they were going to have supper with and cautioned her to act like his *assistant* and not the inquisitive French teacher. This would be a pleasant evening, but the whole mission revolved around the next few days or week.

"*Tu me comprends, ma cheri?*"

"*Oui, Oui, Monsieur Rousseau,*" she replied with her lower lip stuck out. They both laughed.

Fashionably, they all showed up late at 2000 hours (8 o'clock). Charbonnet was accompanied by his *secretaire, Michelle,* a striking blonde who made no attempt to look official. *Jean Franois* came alone, but Scott could clearly see a Vietnamese couple across the room trying to look inconspicuous. Their drab dress was very communist-official looking. She was certainly not a pretty girl in an *ao dai* that you would see on the streets of Saigon. Obviously, government supervision had been required. The African version of French cuisine was considerably bland, but the wine was excellent and the native *chanteuse* was very good entertainment. The conversation was about trade and the boom times in Cote d'Ivoire. Denise was informed that Michelle would show her the city and the shops tomorrow while *Jean Thomas* met with cocoa suppliers and *Jean Franois's trade delegation.*

At the *trade delegation* meeting, the *officials* were only introduced by their first names and obviously had only been informed of a possible prisoner exchange and nothing more, nor did they seem to know who he really was. A list of senior American prisoners was delivered as the exchange for General de Rousseau. Scott was advised that it would take a week to check the names and determine if there could be an exchange. Scott was aware that the current U.S. administration had been rebuffed several times on exchanges.

The meeting with the *trade delegation* was delayed another day, and Scott and Denise both went sightseeing for the day in the port city of Abidjan, one of the busiest cities in Africa. He also knew he was selected to do this, because he had the hole card and the connection no one had held before.

On returning to the hotel, an envelope was waiting at the desk. It had the very official looking seal of the President of the Republic of Côte d'Ivoire. Scott thought, 'At least it's not an arrest warrant or order to leave the country.' The desk clerk stood to the side, watching intently with no attempt to hide his curiosity as Scott opened the envelope.

"Hmmm, the President has invited me to lunch," he said, smiling at the clerk, whose eyes were now very wide.

As far as he knew, no one at the American Embassy was aware of his presence, and he hoped no one at the Presidential Palace had any reason to mention it. The French were obviously his source not the Americans, but this president seemed to do as he pleased. He called Charbonnet for a short meeting to make sure. He had been warned to stay away from the embassy because of possible press leaks which could spoil the whole purpose of selecting Cote d'Ivoire and a French passport. He was sure the language, his hair and beard were a pretty complete disguise, even if he had received some recognition in the American papers, but he could not be absolutely positive. He had the feeling that someone was watching him, but a white man in an African country was always the subject of curious native stares. He was even starting feel like a *secret agent.*

This should be an interesting experience, he thought, and he was anxious to give Denise the news… and some caution.

He and Denise were picked up the next day in a Presidential Citroen with a military escort and taken back to the Presidential Palace. Scott had noticed that the President actually rode in a heavily armored German Mercedes-Benz rather than the French Citroen. They were escorted to a private dining room and introduced to the President's wife. This meal was very French and the wine even better.

By the time lunch was finished the President had related his and the country's history and the logic behind the success of Côte d'Ivoire as opposed to most countries in Africa who were freed from the colonial powers. To him it was a simple matter of discipline and continuing with existing economic success instead of turning everything on its head in the name of independence and alienating the governments most able to help. Of course, his long service in France in the French government as a member of the National Assembly or Parliament, and a Minister under many presidents, including De Gaul, being a tribal chief himself, and one of the largest cocoa farmers, were all substantial aids.

"Now, Monsieur *Rousseau*, since you now know my story and I basically know your story, even that you and the lovely Mademoiselle *Dufor* met in Paris, I have some business to discuss."

Scott was thinking what an amazing individual this African president was and where was this really heading. Denise was still trying to adjust to being there and keeping her inquisitive nature under control.

The president waved to an attendant who brought in a telephone. "Thomas, I want you to call your grandfather, and I will offer him a discount off the world market on cocoa. I think the Hershey and Nestle people need a little competition to stir them up. They have been taking us for granted too long. It is now 8:30 in the morning in Miami. *Qui?*"

Scott sat thinking for a moment what a strange set of circumstances this was, but he simply took the presidential phone, said, "*Qui,*" and placed a call to his grandfather's private line.

A sturdy "Hello" came on the line.

"Good morning, Granpa. How is the breeze on the bay?"

"The sky is clear. The breeze is a steady 12 knots. Are you ready to go sailing?"

"Yes, sir. I truly wish I was on the boat with you, but I am a few thousand miles away having lunch with President Houphouët-Boigny in the Ivory Coast."

A laugh came through that could be heard across the table.

"Well, Tommy, I am never surprised at where you are. Tell the President "Hello." I do remember him. And I won't even ask why you are there."

"I can only tell you it is official."

The President reached for the phone. "Monsieur Scott, it has been a long time. I will use my not- so-perfect English instead of getting your grandson to translate for me. Congratulations on having such a fine grandson. We have enjoyed meeting him."

"Thank you, Mr. President. He always pops up in far-away places, but I am never surprised and always pleased. How may I be of service to you?"

"As I told your grandson, the big chocolate companies need a little competition here with our cocoa. I am going to give you a 20% discount off the world price in order shake them up a little. I know you are the person to do it."

A surprised whistle came through the phone. Without hesitation Old Tom said, "Mr. President, I would be delighted to take all you can give me. I haven't had the opportunity to pull Hershey's tail since I was growing sugar in Cuba. I have a ship up in Morocco that I can reroute to you. I'll make a few calls."

"*Merci beaucoup*, Mr. Scott. Here is your grandson."

"Well, granpa, I bet that was a surprise."

"You got me there. Looks like I'm going to put at least a million dollars in your Valor Fund and get some fun out if it, too. Marie told me you have Denise with you in Paris. Give her my love."

"Yes, sir. Hold on a second." He handed the phone to a surprised Denise.

"Hi, Mr. Scott. Imagine talking to you here."

"Hi, sweetheart. Hanging around with that guy can put you in the damnedest places."

"You can say that again."

"Call me when you get back to Paris. Love to you guys." And the phone went dead.

Scott smiled and said, "Mr. President, I'd say you picked the right man for this job."

"I know," said the President with a very satisfied grin.

On returning to the hotel, Denise said, "Wow. Was that part of the plan?"

"Nope. We will wait. Let's go to the bar. This has made me very thirsty."

"Amen to that."

"Denise, you are in the Army now. The proper response is '*Roger that*'." They both laughed.

The ubiquitous Monsieur Charbonnet was waiting at the bar. "Monsieur Rousseau, everything OK?"

"*Absolument.* He just wanted to talk business with my grandfather." He raised his eyebrows and looked Charbonnet in the eyes. "Quite amazing how much he knows about me."

He was met with a smile and a raised wine glass. "Quite so. *A votre sante,* and you also, *mademoiselle.* There is nothing against making a little profit in this business."

After two glasses of wine, Charbonnet melted back into the streets. Scott smiled at Denise. "I like this French style."

The next morning a call came from Wong advising him to stay another week and sit tight.

A second call came from the President's office inviting them on a short safari to see the famed elephants of Côte d'Ivoire, which gave the country its name, and a visit to the President's plantation to get a first-hand view of cocoa production. Scott could not help but laugh to himself. *I have seen coca production in Bolivia; now I am going to see cocoa production in Africa. I better keep the words straight.*

Smaller herds roamed the rainforest belt in the southern coastal region than the earlier days when ivory hunters made fortunes. The government had since made attempts to regulate the trade, but the sight of the magnificent elephants still gave them a thrill.

The visit to the plantation with its vast expanse of cacao (cocoa) trees was an interesting experience and very different from mountainside coca growing in Bolivia, but the most surprising fact was that the growers and the workers did not know the actual use of cacao beans or its end product. They simply harvested the fruit and processed the seeds and collected money. They were too concerned with trying to survive.

After four days they were flown back to Abidjan in a government helicopter. The transition from coastal rainforest to grass lands, to mountains, to the beginning of desert to the north was a fascinating introduction to sub-Saharan Africa. Scott was thinking he would never again look at a Hollywood movie about Africa the same way.

Back in the hotel Denise sighed, "That was a real experience."

Scott was only half listening while he looked at messages. Wong requested a call to know what was happening. It brought home to Scott that he personally was the only real contact with the North Vietnam on this mission, not Wong, not General de Rousseau, nor anyone in the CIA, Department of Defense, nor State Department. It was a poor secret that the current administration had already been rejected for prisoner exchanges, but he had the *ace in the hole and the people in the know.*

The President sent a message hoping they enjoyed the trip. The most important one was from Jean François requesting a meeting on buying black pepper, an obvious reference to making a deal.

At breakfast the next morning Scott was greeted by a smiling de Rousseau. "Well, *cousin,* as you Americans say, 'We got to first base.' I will meet you at the airport in Hanoi, if your president does not bomb it, in five days. Your visa for your French passport will be waiting in our consulate in Paris when you return. You will be staying at my father's house. We will have a plan by the time you arrive, and you will buy some of our fine black pepper. I have permission to trade a small amount for cocoa to make it look good. The balance will be in Swiss Francs."

Scott smiled, "I know just the person to arrange it."

His next call was to his grandfather, who arranged through his French subsidiary to buy and trade through nominees with the company named by de Rousseau in Paris. Scott would finalize the transaction in Hanoi ...along with other arrangements.

When he opened the room door with a big grin, Denise's face brightened, "We are going back to Paris?"

"Oui, oui, ma cherie. Tout suite."

By noon the next day they were circling the Paris airport aboard Air France.

Marie was happy to see both of them and messages were waiting from Wong and Old Tom. The next four days would be busy, but he could not tell her where he was going. Wong had made that very clear. She was not cleared that far into the plan, but she had a pretty good idea.

Wong had collected and destroyed Denise's French passport and returned her American passport. Goodbyes were said and Scott promised to see her back at the Virginia apartment before she left for her Vietnam assignment.

As Scott watched her plane take off, he thought to himself, *Well, old buddy. They say you just can't stay out of trouble. This caper certainly probat regulam* (proves the rule).

CHAPTER 24

HANOI

Circling above Hanoi, widespread bomb craters surrounding the city were clear evidence that a war was going on somewhere. He was hustled around immigration and customs by de Rousseau into an official government car, an old Citroen left over from the last of the French colonial days. The glory days of that era when Hanoi was the glamorous capital of the French Asian Empire had long since faded through lack of fresh paint and no need for garish neon signs. The drab appearance of socialist cities throughout the world was his first impression.

Scott's second impression, unlike Saigon, was the quietness of few cars on the streets, the lack of heavy carbon monoxide in the air, clean smells of street vendors' food, no sex movies or numerous loud bars and prostitutes. There were no screaming sirens of military cars or tanks rumbling through the streets. There was a certain calm, which gave him a slight feeling of guilt as to what the American invasion had wrought, but his *was not to reason why*. The all-knowing, all-powerful men in Washington decided such things or what they would do if or when they destroyed Hanoi and the port of Haiphong. He needed to concentrate on the task given to him.

They were passing the center of the city with its lake built by the French, referred to as *Petit Lac*, bordered by huge, shady trees and an ancient pagoda rising from the lake connected by a stone causeway. Small refreshment stalls surrounded the lake along with air-raid shelters covered with dirt. Most were planted with flowers and even vegetables. One end of the lake led to the old European part of the city with its broad, tree-lined avenues and now fading villas. The other end was the ancient Vietnamese section of the city with thirty-six streets laid out and named on a craft basis; leather workers, gold and silver smiths, jade, wood workers, etc. Although many of the trades no longer existed, the street names were still there. The sight of ivory workers' street brought a smile to his face thinking about the historic colonial connection with Côte d'Ivoire and the French ivory trade.

They passed the old French Governor General's villa, a little faded and only used as offices. Jean François pointed out that Ho Chi Minh and General Giap only lived in the old servants' quarters without any show of elegance. The de Rousseau family had been allowed to reclaim their old townhouse once the French had moved out. It also showed its age and lack of former luster. Other villas were in better condition, because they were occupied by foreign diplomats.

They were greeted on the front steps by de Rousseau's mother and teenage sister. Scott was startled for a moment; he was back in Saigon looking at a beautiful Eurasian young girl in an *ao dai* of soft pastel shades instead of white normally worn by young girls from *good families.* So out of place in the drabness, it was a step back into a quieter time in Vietnamese history. Their French was soft and lyrical with its colonial tones.

Apparently, they had not been told his real identity or purpose in order to protect them. He was simply a French merchant who lived in Paris and might even be a very distant relative. Jean François was able to keep questions to a minimum, but his sister's beautiful, almond eyes watched and probed. As far as they were told, the meeting the next morning was with the minister of trade. No mention of Ho Chi Minh and Vo Nguyen Giap.

The private meeting with the president and the general in the president's living quarters was scheduled quietly before the minister of trade's formal meeting. The old servants' quarters were equally faded, but were clean and much better than the living conditions suffered by Ho Chi Minh through many years of war against the French and the Japanese, then the French again.

Scott waited in the small anteroom while Jean François went into the president's office. He looked around the sparse room at the faded pictures on the wall until he came to one of a small guerilla group apparently in WW II. The door opened quietly behind him and a voice in English said, "Yes… That is your father in the back of the group."

Scott turned to look into the sad smile and intense eyes of the man who had shaped the history of French Indochina for almost half a century. He had wondered how he would feel when he finally met Ho Chi Minh. Now he felt his heart began to race and his knees becoming weak, but he managed to say, "*Bon jour, Monsieur President.*"

"*Bon jour, Monsieur Rousseau.* Please come in. "

He followed Ho into the office where another legend awaited with a smile, the former school teacher, Vo Nguyen Giap, commanding general of the armed forces, who extended his hand. "*Monsieur* Scott, what an extraordinary twist life to give us this glimpse into the past and the future. We are most pleased to meet you even under these circumstances. Jean Françoise has told us of your father's death. He was always a brave and passionate man. We are saddened, but sure he died for what he believed. That is an honorable death, and we shall remember it as such."

Ho looked up with the same sad smile. "Those are my sentiments also. Your American medics saved my life many years ago in those difficult times fighting the Japanese. I am now sad that we find ourselves on opposite sides, but glad you bring us the opening of a possibility to bring an honorable end to this suffering and the return of our dear comrade General de Rousseau. The colonels you wish in exchange are of no consequence to us. Indeed, we are confident that they have no idea what they are fighting for, nor the history and the destiny of the Vietnamese people."

Ho looked down at his unadorned desk for a moment in silence, then looked into Scott's eyes. His face looked older and the smile sadder. His scraggly white goatee even seemed older, but his eyes still flashed. "You must understand, as I am sure young Captain de Rousseau has told you, I am not the sole voice of this peoples' government. There are others who have suffered our travails as well. Their voices and passions are strong. It is only through the strong arguments of General Giap and myself, plus the fact that your prisoner is our old comrade François, that this exchange will take place. Any peace initiatives will be strongly resisted by Le Duan, who considers only a complete political and military victory to be acceptable for the people of Vietnam. As a strong member of our Politburo, his voice will be heard. As I am sure you can imagine, we pay close attention to your television and newspapers. This war is not popular, and it should not be. Supporting the corrupt politicians in the south is not worthy of the great American people. We are not puppets of the Chinese. We have fought and resisted them for a thousand years. Your government does not understand Asian history. We are not a domino in world communism. We are the people of Vietnam and time is on our side. But you did not come to receive a lecture from me. I have something for you."

Ho reached into the drawer of his desk and pulled out a picture similar to the one on the wall with a grinning T.R. Scott in the background. "Please give this to your grandfather with our thanks for his son's service. If we can arrange any talks, we will communicate through representatives in Paris."

Jean François raised his hand as if to request permission to speak.

General Giap raised his eyebrows, "Yes, Captain?"

"Sir, I just looked at the prisoner list you gave me, and I see a Thomas (NMI) Scott on the list. He was a 1st Lieutenant in a Special Forces unit that we captured in Laos. I would like to ask Mr. *Rousseau* if he knows this officer. I remember a Special Forces sergeant by that name, who saved my life when he carried me from the battlefield."

Scott felt that he must have turned white as a cold chill ran up his spine. He had not heard this, but felt sure it was his cousin.

Giap turned a questioning gaze at Scott.

Scott stammered, "I am sorry, sir. I am unaware of this, but I do have a cousin with that name who is a 1st Lieutenant in Special Forces, and he is the one who carried Captain de Rousseau off the field to the medical helicopter."

As if to momentarily divert attention, the general said, "By the way, Jean François, you have been promoted to major in the intelligence branch."

It was young de Rousseau's turn to be surprised. "Thank you, sir."

Giap continued, "Now, major, what do you intend to do about this situation as an intelligence officer, considering your own prior situation? He is not of sufficient rank to be considered in this sensitive prisoner exchange." The meeting had suddenly turned from political to personal.

Ho was watching and listening carefully. "Gentlemen, I don't think I want to know the answer to this, but you do have my support. This meeting has been a long overdue pleasure. I am sure you will solve the problem, and tell the Minister of Trade that I completely support this black pepper sale."

With that statement by the President everyone left the room, and Scott's mind was now preoccupied by an unanticipated complication.

The general turned to de Rousseau, "Major, report to my office after your meeting with the minister. I will give you all the authority you need to solve the situation. I will let your superiors know that you will continue as my special assistant."

"Thank you, sir." was his answer without knowing what he was thanking him for.

Scott was still numb and his mind racing now with images of Big Tom in a cramped, filthy cell being interrogated. He idly looked at the photo in his hand. On the back was written in English, "Best wishes to the Scott family" and signed by both the President and the General. He thought it would be a long time before anyone could ever see this except his grandfather.

The young minister of trade did not speak French, and Scott was just as glad to allow de Rousseau do the talking. A few documents and bank wire instructions were signed for the Swiss bank handling the payment of the extra funds. The French banks may have moved out of town but their over one hundred years of experience in French Indochina had not disappeared, just reshaped itself. Money always found a way to move. His grandfather's agent in Paris had already acquired the cocoa in Cote d'Ivoire through the French company. The cover story was going smooth. Now the tricky part of prisoner exchange had to be worked out, and what to do if this really was Big Tom in prison. Big Tom was not and could not be part of the equation. That was purely personal with de Rousseau and the two most powerful men in the country.

De Rousseau instructed his driver to take Scott back to the villa while he had a private meeting with the general.

"Jean François, the president and I are in sympathy with you on this Scott thing, but you will have to develop a plan. I will have him released to you for intelligence reasons. He apparently is a sensitive item because he was operating in Laos, not South Vietnam. Therefore, release to our intelligence service is a logical request. From that point on, I cannot help you. But the Red River is wide and only 120 km from the sea, as was the Mekong when you escaped to us." The general stopped for a moment to let that sink in. "Now it is your problem. You understand?"

"Thank you, general." de Rousseau picked up the folder with his orders and left. Next he had to verify the prisoners to be exchanged and whether this Thomas Scott was the same. If so, he had to find men loyal to himself. He needed to have a long conversation with *Rousseau.* He was starting to get a headache to go with the knot in his stomach.

Scott, aka Rousseau, meanwhile was sitting on the wide front porch with the young sister, Jacqueline, having a good time describing the sights and history of Paris. She had never been to Europe. The turbulent political times of her youth had kept her at home. Scott had found the perfect gift, a Paris fashion magazine he had purchased at the airport. It was intended for Denise, but he could buy another one. She was a very clever young lady but he managed to confine his conversation to history, schools and where he lived. Mama sat alongside them and smiled while she rocked in her chair.

The day was pleasant. A cool breeze blew through the shady trees left over from colonial days. Scott was interested to see military trucks on the nearly abandoned streets. They were clearly Soviet and Chinese. Some were obviously driven by Russian soldiers.

Hoa Lo prison was located near the old French Quarter and formerly named by the French as *Maison Centrale*. It was built in 1886 to hold Vietnamese prisoners, particularly political prisoners agitating for independence. Torture and execution were part of the norm. By 1954, near the end of French era, it had been enlarged numerous times and ended up overcrowded with 2,000 prisoners in filthy conditions. When the first American prisoners arrived ten years later it was put into use in the same miserable conditions and sarcastically nicknamed *The Hanoi Hilton.*

Today Major de Rousseau stood in front of the old prison commandant. He was a veteran of the war against the French, then the Japanese, then the French again. Now he was too old and crippled from wounds to fight the Americans, but he had served the cause well and they found a use for him. He looked up and smiled at the young son of the man he had fought with.

"Jean François, what can I do for a brand new major in the Peoples' Army?"

"Honored Commandant, I bring you greetings from the President and Commanding General to an old comrade-in-arms."

The commandant nodded and smiled at the recognition. "And...what else, my young friend"?

The major handed the papers with the names for acknowledging the trade.

The commandant grinned. "This is wonderful news, Jean François, your father, my old friend, will be returned in exchange for these three worthless Americans, who will never be able to fight again. If their plane crash injuries did not cripple them, those fool interrogators probably did while trying to get worthless confessions that no one would believe anyway. The French tortured me in this very prison with the same methods, and they killed General Giap's wife." Tears had begun to form in the old man's eyes. He had to pause and look down at the papers.

He cleared his throat and looked up. "I will make the arrangements for you to pick them up." He noticed the silence and expression on de Rousseau's face. He raised his eyebrows. "Is there more?"

"Honored Commandant, this is for your eyes and ears only."

The commandant rubbed his thick neck trying to imagine what could be next. "Yes?"

"Do you have an American 1st lieutenant Thomas Scott?" He handed another paper to the commandant. "This must be destroyed after you read it."

The surprise so evident on the old man's face caused him to revert to French. *"Sacre bleu, c'est possible?"*

"Oui, c'est possible, commandant." The note was directly from Giap explaining the family connection and soliciting his assistance if it was the same man.

De Rouseau went on to quietly explain Big Tom's role in saving his life and the real facts of his own *escape*.

The commandant stared out the dingy window down into the prison yard for a full minute at several prisoners being marched in a circle and another being carried and dumped into a small cell. He slowly turned back to de Rousseau. "I have lived too long in this world. It was simple when we fought the French, then the Japanese, then the French again. Now we fight each other and our old allies and friends, the Americans, who we torture like the French did to us. Our ancient enemies, the Chinese, are our backers against the Americans, both to keep us in their debt and to neutralize Russian influence. The Russians supply us to keep the Chinese off balance." He looked down at his desk again shaking his head and struck a match to burn the second note in his ash tray.

De Rousseau tentatively asked if it would be possible to identify 1st Lt. Scott here in his office tomorrow before making a decision.

"Of course, tomorrow I will explain to the interrogators that the intelligence service wishes to see this man. Then we will see. Thank you for coming, and give my old comrades my best wishes."

The knot in Jean François' stomach was starting to ease as he walked out of the prison gates and breathed some cleaner air.

Back at the townhouse he and Scott took a long walk along the quiet avenues while Jean François explained the situation. "First, we must get the American colonels out, then as a member of the intelligence service I will take Thomas out of the prison under guard, if it is truly him. If it works well, he will just disappear."

He looked up at the overhanging trees and sighed. "Many people disappear here. Is my father in Paris yet?"

Scott nodded his head. "Half my communication about cocoa and black pepper is coded to confirm that. He will be at the French consulate in Bombay, India, day after tomorrow awaiting my arrival. I will continue on to Paris. The colonels will be flown to the U.S. military hospital in Germany." Scott hesitated a moment, "Am I to go to the prison with you to identify Tom?"

Jean François sighed again. "Do you speak any Russian?"

"*Nyet.* How about French with a Russian accent?"

"That will be sufficient." They both smiled at the thought.

The next morning both showed up at the prison, with Scott identified as an advisor to the intelligence service. The Russian accent seemed convincing along with the commandant's verification.

Once in the commandant's office, the old man turned to take a long look at Scott, his eyes, his nose and mouth. Even with the beard and long hair it was obvious he was looking at the son of the American he knew many years ago. As he sat down heavily in his chair, he looked at de Rousseau. "Are there any more you did not tell me about?"

"I am sorry, commandant, but I needed to be sure and the general agreed."

Big Tom was brought into the commandant's office looking like a shadow of himself in filthy clothes. The commandant could clearly see the prisoner was of mixed race. Even with the similar features, he had to ask, "*C'est possible?*"

From the corner of the room Major Scott slightly nodded.

Big Tom had not noticed his cousin sitting there. He only vaguely saw a man with a beard and long hair. Now his cousin put his finger to his lips in a slight motion to indicate silence. Hope and confusion set in, but he kept silent.

De Rousseau spoke in a firm voice with his broken English, "I am Major Jean François de Rousseau of the intelligence service. We wish to question you."

Big Tom began to put the pieces and names together. His mind was clearing. He nodded in the submissive way and humbly said,

"Yes, major."

"Were you captured in Laos?"

Big Tom squared his shoulders and said, "My name is Thomas Scott, 1st Lt. United States Army, my serial number is…"

De Rousseau cut him off. "Did you ever serve with Special Forces on the Mekong River near Cambodia?"

Big Tom was getting the idea now that they were communicating to remind him who he was looking at. "My name is Thomas Scott…"

"Enough! I believe this is our man, commandant. We will come back for him later to do a thorough interrogation. You can throw him back into his cell."

The guards lifted Big Tom out of the chair and dragged him out of the room. He glanced at his cousin on the way out and received a very subtle wink. He had to laugh to himself. He knew what he was going back to, but things were a lot brighter. What was going to happen next?

Walking back to the staff car, Scott's mood was mixed. He was relieved to locate his cousin but sad to see his condition. To de Rousseau he asked, "Can you get his medical records?"

"Yes, but we have to get the others out today, cleaned up and on the plane tomorrow. Then you will have to leave him to me. You got me out. I will get him out. There must be no more conversation."

Scott knew he was right. His responsibility was to make the exchange and pray. A military guard detail was already on the way to pick up the three colonels to transport them to a holding facility in preparation for the flight in the morning. A decent meal would be served, and clean, if ill-fitting, clothes would be provided. They would still be unaware of what was going to happen until Scott and de Rousseau arrived in the morning. Today de Rousseau had many things to arrange before the day and night were over in regard to the unexpected appearance of Big Tom.

The last night at the de Rousseau house was pleasant and Scott promised to send Jacqueline some Swiss chocolate from Paris. They still regarded him as a French businessman trading in agricultural products.

The morning was rainy, and Scott thought to himself, "Good, everything will be less conspicuous with umbrellas obscuring faces and physical features."

The small nondescript building looked even more nondescript in the rain. Inside were the three closely guarded Americans finishing their breakfast with a very welcome cup of coffee. Apprehension showed through their haggard exteriors in spite of the sudden good treatment. One of them spoke reasonably good French from his time with NATO and provided the communication with de Rousseau, who explained that they were to be part of a prisoner exchange and Scott was a French Intelligence Officer expediting the exchange. Scott then introduced himself in French as Thomas Rousseau and cautioned them not to speak until they were on the plane. At that time they would be told details.

Hope appeared in their faces but they had been subjected to so much false hope and promise and physical deprivation that they dared not believe...yet. Scott very badly wanted to reassure them, to tell them who he was, but he could not. Basically, he was an enemy agent out of uniform in the capital of North Vietnam. One slip at this stage could blow up the trade and land him in the Hanoi Hilton...or worse. As Jean François had said, people disappear here all the time. Even though approved at the highest level, it was still secret, and the unscheduled Big Tom part was a complication yet to be solved.

An unmarked jet transport sat on the runway at the civilian airport, so far unbombed by the Americans. Only two armed guards sat in the back of the plane.

De Rousseau walked with Scott to the plane and extended his hand. "Thomas, thank you for all you have done. *Bon voyage et bonne chance.*"

"Jean François, thank you for this and what you are about to do. I hope we will meet again as friends when this is over."

"*Certainement, mon ami.* Just remember the Red River flows to the sea and down the coast to the DMZ."

Scott nodded and smiled as he went up the stairs into the

plane. He was thinking about the two thousand French Francs he had managed to get Jean François to accept as an incentive to his men to safely accomplish their mission. The last remark had given the method. He smiled some more thinking that this would not be the smooth sailing Big Tom had done on his grandfather's sailboat on Biscayne Bay.

The Americans were still in doubt as to what was happening and continued to glance at the guards in the rear. Scott held up his hand and said in French, "Patience and silence."

As the engines roared to maximum takeoff RPMs and the wheels slammed into the wheel wells, Scott smiled, reached into his bag and brought out a bottle of St. Remy Napoleon Brandy VSOP. He took a swallow to show it was good, he really needed it, and passed it to the surprised colonels. "*A votre santé*" were his only words.

The guards in the back were instantly on alert. Scott reached into his bag again and brought out a second bottle. He motioned to the guards and said in Vietnamese, "Bombay is a very long way, my friends. Please join us."

Broad toothy grins appeared as they came forward. For the rest of the flight it was a happy plane ride, because there were two more bottles.

When the plane taxied to a stop on a closed concourse, Scott could see four figures on the ground. One was obviously Col. Wong, with Gen. de Rousseau, and the other probably the Indian official, with a U.S. Embassy official to clear them through and around immigration.

As the plane door opened, Scott turned and welcomed home each colonel by name...for the first time in *English*. "Wait here. Colonel Wong will come to get you." Before their surprise could verbalize itself, he turned and went down the stairs where he was vigorously greeted by two men, whom he took off to the side. The warmth of the embrace was obvious.

"General, your family is well. Colonel, I left one complication behind." He then related the Big Tom story and requested the Navy be alerted that an escaped American prisoner may show up somewhere between the Red River and the DMZ along the shores of the Gulf of Tonkin.

Wong handed him his American passport and a ticket to Paris on Air France, watched him walk away and muttered, "Goddamn surprises."

Wong motioned the colonels to come down as de Rousseau boarded and shook their hands. The senior officer was the first on the ground, and watching Scott walk away, could only say, "Who was that masked man?"

Wong smiled as he watched Scott disappear into the terminal and said, "The Lone Ranger, of course,"

ACKNOWLEDGEMENTS

In addition to the many history books from Christopher Columbus to the Spanish American War and naval battle, to the Bay of Pigs, and to the Vietnam War, I want to acknowledge some individuals who lived it but not mentioned in my Introduction. **THANKS TO:**

Frank Tan, OSS, deceased; for his valuable insight into Ho Chi Minh and Vo Nguyen Giap as he experienced it with them in WW II.

Stuart D. Shaw, former Captain, US Army 1ˢᵗ Special Forces Group, Vietnam, deceased; for his service to his country, insights, comradeship and many adventures together.

Guillermo Lazaro Rodriguez, nephew of a Batista admiral, former Castro lieutenant, Brigade 2506 and my companion in many things in many countries; for his observations and advice.

John Crume, former Sergeant, US Army, a mysterious fellow paid by the Army but served the NSA in many things unknown… except in Paris; for his review, suggestions and insight.

R. Patrick Beatty , Commander USNR ret., deceased; for his advice, experience and life-long friendship.

James E. Harrell, M.D., former Captain US Army Medical Corps, and Vietnam veteran; for his observations, advice and friendship since grammar school.

Paul Kreuger, former SP/4 US Army, Aero Rifle Platoon, Air Cavalry Troop, 11ᵗʰ Armored Cavalry Regiment, Vietnam; for his observation, advice and friendship.

Manuel Almira, Executive Director, Port of Palm Beach, the great grandnephew of the first elected president of Cuba, Tomás Estrada Palma; for his advice and insight to Cuban history.

R.R. Brandl, a Shaman in his own right, my companion in the Amazon and into the spirit world; for his advice and observations,

Jim Saunders, English teacher, Sea Scout Skipper, sailing companion: for his help in editing.

AND to my many Cuban friends and classmates too numerous to list here, who shared so many adventures…some to talk about and some not,

AND to many friends and relatives on many days and nights sailing in the Bahamas and Caribbean,

AND even to the many loud sergeants at Ft. Benning's Airborne School and Ft. Sherman's Jungle Warfare School in the Canal Zone and the view of the Canal at night from a parachute.

AND last, but not least, to my son, Randall Scott Porch; for his support, and his design of the cover of this book, and for being my son.

CPSIA information can be obtained
at www.ICGtesting.com
Printed in the USA
BVHW04s0620020718
520618BV00009B/48/P